BULB

===========⚛===========

A NOVEL
Bradley Wind

1999 KIND Books 2019

For my wife, Charley.
I apologize to the Sus(z)ans for not dedicating it to you. You were mysterious and compelling and had me questioning what is operating in the universe, but Charley is all that, can iron out my elephant skin writing, and from the moment I met her has been the right to my left.

ONE

Someone put the wrong teeth in my mouth last night. The canines poked at the back of my lips as if they didn't fit. I wanted them either buried deep in the gums or all removed. I hate teeth.

Trash trucks moan like suburban whales while they back down my cul-de-sac. The truck eeping irritated me more than the sharp light. Wallpaper images of two windows beamed sunlight onto my head. BUD programmed the walls and sounds from archives of the room I had growing up for today's alarm. I needed extra help waking most mornings but especially ones like this.

"Shall I turn the alarm off?"

"Yes. Thanks, BUD."

A withering erection and prominent teeth dragged me back to the memory of my disturbing dream—another in the monster series.

"Would you care to dictate your dream, or will you be typing today?"

"In a minute."

Lying among the pillows for the rest of the afternoon would've been nice, but morning bladder ousted me. A glass-horn urinal emerged from the wall when the bathroom slid to a greater diameter. A glimpse of myself as the mirror flipped revealed the monster – although I guess there's nothing new about my dark circles and bedhead hair. The sight prompted me to dictate last night's werewolf dream while the concern for my mental well-being drained away with yesterday's juice.

Damn teeth! I could use a drink. The canines still felt glued to the inside of my mouth. In the mirror inspection, my little porcelain cleavers appeared normal. Gross, but normal. Most of the time, it only took the image of lips separating a fraction to think of an opened wound. Beyond the teeth, disgust stemmed from dripping saliva, hordes of bacteria, and raw flesh waves of the palate. It all made me question the stability of dentists.

The voice of my friend Laurel buzzed in my head. Study the dreams! Maybe the monster dream series could be about the accident. More likely, it was my brain's way of shuffling new memories into order. Not that I'd recently shape-shifted and attacked anyone, but the assaulted girls in the dream could be a symbol for my brothers or ex-fiancée Sara.

I returned to bed and lay down again. A holographic mailbox rotated above me.

"What's in the box?" I garbled through a yawn.

An envelope slid out. "It's from Susan Ross. Do you wish me to verify the sender?"

"Is it another salesperson?"

"She does not appear to be. Do you wish for more data on her?"

"Just display it, please."

A page slid from the envelope.

From Susan@rossskycity - Subj: Still looking for good book conversation?

Sunday, September 11th

Dear Ben,

Still reading?

I'm feeling almost too old to be doing this (27) but willing to give it a shot.

I was looking through a book club directory and saw you also enjoy tragedies and horror. I consume books. Voracious doesn't cut it. What's better than a tragic love story? I'm re-reading Anna Karenina by Tolstoy today on paper. I prefer the naked text of paper books where I don't have to be concerned with the linked marginalia, the potential or distraction of discovering what someone else thought as I'm reading. Those interruptions are maddening when I just want to experience an author's creation.

I'm worried about writing too much in case you're not into this anymore. I know your post is old. Okay, I live in that sky-stuck city, yes, among the clouds miles above Navy Pier in Chicago. A basic goddess of the air (ha!). My interests besides reading include...I hate this really, but it's probably important... I love cherry pie, bungee-room dancing, movies about the old west, unusual sexual practices (insect or animal), and visiting EY Beach - the one recently finished over the city of Aurora. Don't you love reading on the beach? Oh, and I love the sound of blue bells and snap dragons.

"He went down trying not to look long at her, as though she were the sun, but he saw her, as one sees the sun, without looking." - Tolstoy

That sun shining on you and me. That sun, churning out programmable light recording every aspect of life - available to you. But also, growing bunches of carrots and those little sweet peas and all of it recorded in the Grand Archive. After forty years of recording, where are the mysteries of today if not self-created? Nobody knows for certain who you are exactly. I don't. But I dare you not to go to my archives to see what I look like and what has happened in my life. I dare you to try to live purely. Let's live only with our words and let the mystery be.

- Susan Ross

What's this, a disguised dating service letter? "Is there anything unusual you can find about her? Any disturbing Archive records like hospitalization?" I asked.

"The Archives offer no history of mental illness, no instances of a blocked user," BUD said.

"Did she really find me on some book discussion site?"

"The sender is listed as having recently visited the site you posted on. Do you wish to view anything specific from her archive?"

I thought for a minute then recognized I needed this, needed a distraction and something to look forward to. "No, not now, I'll take her dare. Set a reminder for a few months to review some of them. I probably won't need the reminder, but with my brain, you never know. And send alerts any time Sara monitors the correspondence between Susan and me."

"A three-month reminder is set for December 11th, along with the new Sara alert. Today's Reminder: Call Laurel about your visit this afternoon."

Setting alerts... I could just hear Lenny's response if he knew any of my continued efforts. Two hours walking around Sara's neighborhood in the dark last night?! If you wanted to waste your time, why didn't you come over and clean my toenails? The thing is I can't help myself. I still love her or at least can't let go of that longing and loss ache in my chest. I don't think Lenny's ever been in love, let alone asked someone to marry him. I took the risk Sara would somehow stumble upon an archive and see my routines. Hoped is more like it; hoped she'd see I'm still willing to reunite, even with what she did. Or would I? Pathetic. After all of Laurel's efforts to help me move beyond I hadn't taken all the steps to do so.

"BUD, respond to Susan. Subject 'How's the air up there?'"

This felt dumb. I joined that site, thinking it hard to have decent conversations with friends about fiction - better to converse about the written through written form, but then no one ever responded to my post.

I shoved aside some of the books on my bed and thought for a while.

"Baked in black bread, I am wheat and weak from the plow of no decent dialog. Almost every man or woman I'm in contact with wants to talk everyday trash. I don't mind discussing movies — or unusual insect sex(really?). Refined Trash is acceptable, but books are what I'm mainly interested in. I won't bother with your archive until you request me to do so. I'm not really a fan. They exhaust me." The words scrolled on the wall screen.

What am I talking about? Bah, she'll think I want to be a poet. It's too early. I sat up and looked out the virtual window at the simulated sunny world of my youth.

"I'm, uh, 29 and live in Pennsylvania. I have a degree in neuronal painting. I wouldn't call myself well-known, but my work has been exhibited."

A door slammed, and loud shuffling sounded in the hallway coming towards my room.

"Let's see. I live with my seven-year-old conjoined twin brothers, Ed and Francis. They're connected facing each other at the chest by a flesh bridge. It sounds worse than it is. At least they're not craniopagus, which limits movement far more. Anyway, Dad worked at Lazaras and, I forget, but it was something about the Vestig production moving too quickly. They discard the rejects now, but back then, they didn't or at least Dad didn't want to discard his own. It's a lot of work caring for them. A lot. And a constant reminder of my father, being replicates and all that; same brown hair and eyes as he had - but they're six-foot-six and Dad was half a foot shorter, my height."

My door quickly opened before the twins wobbled in and moved through Susan's letter hologram, stopping too close to my face. Their breath kicked out a sour lunch-meaty scent.

"We're hungry," they said together.

"Hey, guys, you know where the cereal is."

"Oh, that's right!" Ed rocked their bodies.

They wobbled back out of the room towards the kitchen.

"I'll be there in a few minutes to help. Continue, BUD. My brothers ... yes, they're a lot of work, and it wouldn't be so bad if the scientists and government didn't bug us. I guess I shouldn't complain. Without the extra payments, I'd probably have to become one of the saints I help."

I heard something bang in the other room, but no shouts for help, so I continued. "Okay. What else would you want to know…? I volunteer at the Saint Center for Dr Mamon. He and Dad worked together at Lazaras. I guess that's why he invited me to help while I was recuperating from a car crash. Must have read about my father and wanted to give me a reason to get back to a real life. I heard about the saints all the time growing up from Dad. Mostly his complaining though, and now it feels a bit strange to say I paint to help the Saints, but I do I guess."

I glanced over at my overstuffed bookcase trying to think of what to say. "It's been a while since I joined that book-talk site. I also prefer paper books, but more because I'm not interested in reading The Book with how all books are linked when you're screening. The overlays, the references, the critique or praise. Sometimes it's fun depending on what I'm interested in, but mostly I want to read A book, like you, without the distractions — been reading more horror than anything else lately. Sure, I'd be happy to discuss books with you. Why not. I hope you aren't offended, but I'm not looking for a date. I met my ex-fiancée under similar circumstances to this and don't want that mistake repeated. Sometimes love, and trust can prevent one from considering the need for monitoring archives and, well, I suppose I should've monitored her more. So much for the Archives keeping people's morality in check. Anyway, let me know how Tolstoy progresses. End it there, BUD. I want to read that before you send it."

"Any special delivery options?"

"No, thanks."

The letter appeared in front of me long enough to re-read. I cringed a little, but added 'Sincerely, Ben Tinthawin' to the end, and sent it.

"A random shuffle, please." I grabbed a black t-shirt from the floor and tugged it on.

'Susie Q' announced before the music started playing in the apartment, and I suddenly felt a little ache in my head.

Idiot. I probably said too much. I often do. Loud noises from the kitchen got me out of bed again. I stood and felt a swarm of bees quickly arise behind my eyes.

White deer standing in the middle of the road.

Glass flying through the air.

More of the accident memory flashes. I pushed the visions away as my brain refocused on a crash resounding from the other room.

The song continued, and I realized why BUD chose it.

"Very funny."

"I thought you might appreciate the song in honor of your new girlfriend. It's a remake by Boynen. Originally written by Delmar Allen Hawkins and popularized by a band called Creedence Clearwater Revival."

"She's not my girlfriend. What, one letter constitutes a girlfriend?"

"You are occasionally voluble but rarely that verbose. You are needed in the kitchen." BUD increased the volume.

☲TWO☲

live in and manage what used to be a mall. My MAc (Mall Apartment community) was one of the last converted when the replicators crippled the already ailing mega shopping centers. Most of the old stores in malls were wide warehouse-sized rooms with high ceilings. I set up portable walls to section mine off. Some are made of topiary bush, dense, finely trimmed and tall; some are all tree trunks. They were an idea the twins had after visiting a local park.

In the kitchen, the same old caveman breakfast scene. Ed and Francis ate their morning junk while watching their beloved hovering screens. They sat on boulder chairs at our granite table. Milk and Treasure-puffed cereal speckled the tabletop. I stooped to pick up a dropped bowl.

"Hi, guys. Looks like you found the cereal."

"I found it!" Ed shouted.

"No, you didn't," Francis said.

They seemed surlier than usual, and as I started pouring myself some coffee their hands banged hard on the table causing Ed's bowl to spill over and the cereal popped into chests and diamonds and other treasure shapes as it scattered.

"Hey, that was mine. Gimme yours," Ed shouted.

"No!" Francis shouted back.

They rose up and began swinging around in circles, roaring. The milk on the floor splashed from their stomping and continued filtering into micro-sewage drains.

"All right calm down." I tried to avoid their pajama tornado. You have to get out of their way when they spin or chance heavy bruising. They aren't really malicious in any way. Some see them as the stuff of circus sideshows, but it's stale news to me. As quickly as their fight started, they slowed and stopped. Their screens floated back into position when they sat down again as if nothing had happened. I poured Ed another bowl and placed it in front of him.

"What do you guys have planned for the day?" I tested to see if they remembered our trip to Laurel's farm.

"I'm gonna watch that channel that's so good to see," Ed said, raising his baritone voice too loudly. He checked his screen. Francis didn't turn from his show to comment.

"Okay, but remember, we have the visit to the farm."

They looked at me wide-eyed. "Now, let's go," they said simultaneously, grabbed their bowls, and returned to their side of the apartment with screens trailing closely behind. The twins have a unique walking style. They're experts at walking in unison, backward or frontward, and manage to navigate nearly anywhere an individual could. I'd say it has a horse trot quality about it, but slightly more graceful.

I punched the breakfast button and found a message signal blinking on the countertop.

"Who are the messages from?"

"One from your mother and one from Lenny. Also, information on recent deposits to your account."

The glass door slid open on the replicator and delivered my omelet.

"Run the messages."

A strobing holo bust of Mom's head and shoulders popped up on top of the replicator. She'd had the youth treatments again. It was hard to view my mother when she looked younger than I did albeit with an abnormal youth-treatment sheen which many, but not I, appreciated. The image wavered, and her regular parrot voice spoke.

"Hi, Honey. I was watching some of my old ones. My god. I watched one where I was taking a bath, so darling, and it reminded me of the documentary I saw on exotic germs recently. That's germs, not gems! Did you know they're poised to take over our bodies! Right now they're everywhere. Gives me the shivers. I think you should look into having your genes reinforced with proper virus protection. I am. Love you." Her holo sank away.

Thanks, Mom. She has always been an extreme worrier, but since the accident and Dad's passing her focus has been more and more on the past and abstract oddities like exotic germs.

A blow-up of Lenny's nose grew where Mom's head faded out. It cruised along the surface of the replicator to the wall and grew giant above me so I could see inside a nostril with the hairy contents exposed. His nose shrunk in a split second and his massive mouth expanded to replace it. In a pinched-nose girlish voice, he said, "Time fer yer nose protection upgrade, Benjamin. Your nose-gold is growin' outta control. Please contact your excavator ASAP. Wait, forget that. I'll be right over to help." A massive finger grew out of his mouth and picked at me then shrunk to nothing once more.

Might have been a simple coincidence that they both left messages about body protection and that he used an odd voice similar to hers, but I wondered if it was one of those Synchronicity Activity Waves everyone talks about lately.

I placed my dishes in the sink, and a screen emerged above the faucet, listing recent banking transactions. The usual funds transferred into my account from Mom, Lazaras, and MAc tenants.

Natural parabiosis, the joining of two individuals during Vestig creation, wasn't typical. For that reason, the Lazaras engineers found Ed and Francis very important. I was glad because that also meant Lazaras forked over cash so I could afford to raise them. Not that I liked the engineers' constant intrusions, but without their okay, I couldn't continue to keep the twins with our immediate family. The government regulated that individuals couldn't own their 'bad' Vestigs related to concerns over potential abuse and enslavement. Those who oversaw Dad's production avoided a lawsuit by having Ed and Francis signed over to me instead of my parents. Mostly I don't mind, but it has the potential to encroach on my dating life. Potential is the keyword seeing as I don't have a dating life.

Dr Luc Mamon did the check-ups for Lazaras now. Even though he no longer runs it, Lazaras is the first company Mamon started so his ties there are helpful. He also mentioned looking into the possibility of the twins' separation. We've been told it wasn't likely because of "shared physiology" and they thought only one could survive the operation. If Mamon wanted to research further, that was okay by me.

I swiped an L into the countertop, and a beep-signaled Lenny accepted my call.

"Hey, what's with your fascination with my nostrils anyway?"

A small square screen emerged, and he came into view, holding a tiny brush dripping with hair paint. He swished a circle around his navel, and large tufts started growing "Oh, you know, friends should help friends out with that stuff. Yeh just caught me. I'm finishin' up and was about to head over." His voice slightly drawled with a casual Southern charm.

"How about tomorrow instead?"

"We're not all like you and can lounge around any day of the week. Some of us gotta make the green." Lenny waved the brush at his nose.

"But you're always lounging—" I started saying with serious annoyance when he cut me off.

"Yeah yeah, see yeh tomorrow."

The screen closed as the signal ended.

I didn't have to get the twins ready; they loved these trips. When I got to the front door, they were waiting. We passed the crowded food court on the way out and waved hello to our famous neighbors, the Panas. Stars of the MAc scene, they were always helping people out, always interested in what was happening. Ed and Francis really loved them. If the twins didn't enjoy our visits to Laurel's farm so much, I'd think of leaving them with the Panas who they love like family and often offer to babysit so I might go "find a nice girlfriend." It could be said that I'm closer to the Panas than I was my own family. I guess then it's not that surprising that when I saw them I couldn't help but wonder what they'd think of Susan. Smart, interesting, likes movies and books. Wish I hadn't agreed to leave her archives alone.

My friend Laurel was a great lover of living naturally, a romantic bushcrafter with a survivalist outlook that I found entertaining when she wasn't regaling me with why most of the world was getting it wrong. Still, leaving suburbia and spending time in rural areas, like Laurel's farm, did me good. When I lived here after the accident, Laurel did more for me than anyone else ever has. She has explained the guilt she carries for suggesting joining my parents, how I wouldn't have been in the accident if not for her, but I've never agreed or assigned any kind of blame since I might have gone with them anyway and even before that she'd always been a supportive friend. I owed her a great deal.

She and Lizard must've been a fun couple when he was alive. In the photos of them from many years ago, they look full of life and desperately in love. They filled their farm with all sorts of comical bits, like the mailbox at the top of the driveway. They'd added a raised middle-fingered hand signaling perpetual outgoing mail.

The twins flipped their middle fingers back at the mailbox and giggled as the tires hit the crunching gravel of the driveway leading to the farmhouse.

On the side of the barn, a smiling man stood waving his giant phallus. Painted with white paint by Lizard, it was fading now but always made for a funny maître d'.

I shouted hello, as we got out of the car, knowing Laurel would be working inside.

"I'm in here," she shouted back.

Clay pots, resting among the jutting straw and filled with herbs and spices, lined the dirty white walls of the barn. The heat from kilns kept the place nice and warm and heightened the rich olfactory fun that tickled my nose as I entered. Laurel made her money as an unusual "healthy living" counselor, but mostly spent her days packaging bulk spices and wholesaling them to dealers. The amazing blends she and her community of growers produced are a highly sought-after luxury item.

We entered and wove through to one of the smaller side rooms where tiny Laurel had her arms wrapped around a spinning clay pot. It was almost as big as she was.

"Laurel!" The twins crowded her while waiting for their usual heartfelt hugs and kisses.

"Here, hold this," she looked at me, pointing with her chin to take control of the spinning clay.

"What? I can't hold that thing."

"Yes, you can, I've seen how you ride, and if you can do that, you can damn well hold a simple spinning pot."

There was nothing simple about this pot. It was huge. I threaded myself under her arms and placed my hands on its sides. The wet orange clay rolled smoothly beneath my fingers. She scooted out from under me and stood looking at the pot, wiping off her hands on one of the "far too dirty to get her hands clean" rags.

"Tsk, that's a sad-looking one," she said, turning to the twins.

"Turn off those screens, you sweet muffins, and give Laurel some love. Mm, I could eat you two right now."

Laurel was small but dwarfed doubly so by the giants who bent over to receive a hug and thin-lipped kiss from her. She finished hugging them and sneakily pinched their crotches.

"Waaaaah, you should not do that," Francis whined, as he went to protect his groin in case she did it again.

"Always keep the kiwi covered, boys."

Ed turned his pain into a laugh quickly when he looked at Francis and saw his face squinched from the mild pain in his testicles.

"Laurel, you should not do that," Francis said.

"Aw, don't keep that up now, come on. Give ole Laurel a hug for real."

"I'll give you one, but you gotta, you gotta do something, you gotta make the dumplings," Ed said as he put his arms out for a hug.

"Do you think you could turn this thing off now?" The pot began to wobble. Laurel dropped to the ground from the boy's necks and turned to me with her hands on her hips.

"You can't finish that? It's practically done."

The clay wugged around, seconds from collapsing.

"Please turn it off."

"Come now, you're fine. What a baby." She pinched my arm hard, causing me to knock into the pot.

It finally gave and slid over onto me before falling to the floor. I looked as if I'd lifted myself from a mud puddle. The twins let out some low-pitched laughs.

"Great, thanks. Now, look at your beautiful pot." I flicked some clay from my hands at them.

"That one was nowhere near beautiful. Calm down and let's get you showered," Laurel said

She rubbed my back gently. "Boys, I'm sure you can find plenty to do till I ring the bell." We loved that she used an iron bell to announce meals.

"Yes, we can," Ed and Francis said, already looking behind pots for any creatures that might be lurking. Mice, spiders, kittens and snakes, all commonly found.

The leaf-speckled path to the back of her house was a short trip but long enough for me to remember I didn't like showering outside in the fall. Laurel pulled a handful of what looked like black pebbles from her pocket and held them up to my face. "Here, smell these."

I inhaled deeply, and they burned the way a hot pepper might but left a surprisingly sweet taste in my throat and mouth: peppery caramel and strong cinnamon.

"These seeds come from the Lushai Hills of eastern India. No damn replicator is going to make something so evocative."

I wasn't going to argue replicators work at the atomic level and could make an identical seed with ease. She was right in a way that knowing they were harvested there did make them more evocative, but the rest seemed like semantics not worth pursuing.

"What do you use them for?"

"Get yourself washed, and I'll show you later."

I sat down on the bench next to the stall to remove my shoes, and she went inside.

꠵THREE꠵

amon's spine cracked like kindling as he stretched against the back of his chair. Each popping vertebra signaled the need for sleep, but since returning from Venezuela, he could not rest. His work came first. No longer would he wait for the stronger ones, the triumphant ones, the merrier ones. He was going to transform, be the laughing lion himself. His legacy would be monumental.

Yawning pulled his chapped lips until the skin split. He smiled at the taste of blood and continued smiling to allow it to flow, the brutal flavor a reminder of the impending event with the Venezuelan tribesmen.

It'd been more than twenty-four hours since he'd eaten anything and his stomach gurgled, prompting him to wave his arm above his immense glass desk. A grid of random global archives blurred as an assistant's face materialized and sharpened into focus on the desk surface.

"Yes, Dr Mamon, how may I help you?" the assistant queried.

He looked at her and then let his gaze travel around the flower patterns of the stained glass that loomed above his cavernous office. Mamon considered her competency worth enduring the difficult glimpses of her goatish face. He desired the real, not the perfection of the virtual.

"Could you have a mizuna salad and some beef Jiaozi hand-made for me, please? I'm quite hungry."

"Certainly, sir. Possibly something to mend your lips?"

"No. Only the requested."

"Yes, sir."

"Leave it at the door."

"Yes, sir."

The desk reverted to the Archive grid. He opened his journal to a recently completed entry, and an itch called his fingers inside the white, cone-shaped fabric covering the top of his head. He scratched for an extended amount of time as it caused great pleasure and then read:

*** Most surprising discovery about the Guahibos tribe was neither their lack of ego, without the influence of the Archive, nor that they continued their violent traditions since Bonpland first wrote of them in the early 1800s - it was the extent of their Chlorophilia, their sexual relationship with plant life. The successful adolescents, those who've completed their second birth, have so far proven unhelpful.*

*- NOTE: Review more of the Unsuccessful — those who failed to see beyond the WALL ***

A directory titled SECOND BIRTH RITUAL — GUAHIBOS — PIPAL TREE remained highlighted at the corner of his desktop. He tapped it open, letting his fingers follow down the listings to activate the first item titled UNSUCCESSFUL. A holographic image expanded until it reached the vaulted ceiling. Paused, it exhibited a jungle scene with an unclothed teenage boy lying on a bed of flower petals at the base of an enormous tree.

(SECOND BIRTH RITUAL – GUAHIBOS - HITNU'S BIRTHDAY - UNSUCCESSFUL) scrolled across the top. The arc began:

Light blue powder-covered Hitnu's eyes and mounded over the back of his head as he lay next to the gargantuan tree trunk. A woman approached, wailing with grief as three men followed closely behind. Kneeling beside Hitnu's head, she gently touched his cheek and proceeded to blow powder from his eyes. Hitnu's serene face, now completely revealed, had a pallid, nearly dead quality, but he breathed slowly in a deep sleep. One of the attending men helped the woman stand and handed her a long wooden staff. She raised it and pounded the tree with great force. Within the trunk, a drumming rhythm began. The intensity of the woman's sobbing required the use of the tree for balance. She pushed away to stand on her own, scowling at the tree and, without hesitation, she leaned over and swiftly slapped Hitnu's face.

Hitnu's eyes opened as he gasped a great breath of air. The woman pulled him to a standing position. Blue powder drifted down in thin clouds from his head as they embraced until two of the men pulled them apart, pushing the woman to the ground. They led Hitnu around the tree, stopping before a wide gap in the trunk. Drumming increased as hands pulled Hitnu inside.

The arc transitioned from a view of the tree entrance to the trunk interior. Mamon tasted the blood in his mouth again as he forwarded through scarification rituals until the men directing the rite brought the boy to the endemic flowering plant Mamon sought but had not been given access to, during his recent visit.

Hitnu, clear-eyed and somber, stood bleeding from fresh cuts on the back of his head and shoulders. He faced a small mound of earth. At the top of the mound grew a plant with massive drooping flower buds. An oily substance dripped from each bud tip, and Hitnu slowly assessed the puddles before choosing the one with the most substantial volume and kneeling in front of it.

Hitnu applied the fluid to the tip of his penis as the percussion slowly amplified, stroking himself until engorged. He stood while those surrounding him began a rhythmic stomp and hushed chanting. The leader, wearing a sizeable yellow-petal headdress, stepped towards the mound and pounded his staff on the floor. Immediately the boy guided his penis into the bud tip.

Mamon paused the archive and circled the bud, zooming in at various angles to try to view the flower's interior. Frustrated, he could see nothing because of the harsh shadows and low lighting. Informed Light could only record archives wherever light reached. His failures with trying to enhance Informed Light not only to record anything it came in contact with but also be able to direct it were a great disappointment. A world where any darkness could be overcome would most likely never be. He zoomed back out and let the archive continue.

Hitnu thrust in and out, keeping a determined expression on his face as the pounding rhythm on the trunk increased. The circle of men waved broad green leaves and began to grunt in unison. Hitnu halted abruptly, flinching in pain and withdrew. The end of his penis, now speckled with light blue pollen, dripped blood from the ballooning head. The leader darted forward as Hitnu collapsed to the floor and rolled to his back. Painful groaning filled the space as the drumming halted. In a short time, Hitnu stopped moving, the tip of his penis lolled to the side, distorted and blackening. The leader placed his headdress over the boy's lifeless body. (=ARCHIVE END=)

Mamon stood and walked through the fading hologram of the body. He walked past his bookcases to one of the towering palm trees that curved along the wall at the side of the room, stroked the trunk and sighed. The stained glass in the ceiling caused a speckling on the bark, and he touched a portion tinted blue. He walked back, sat down again, and opened his journal to finish the notes.

** *Aime Bonpland's botanical journals correctly described the stamen piercing and related poison death. Blue powder on eyes and head now seem unlikely to be blue pollen from flower due to the potential for poisoning. Possibly the flower bud fluid is the missing element of Cohoba?*
-- Note: Review Bonpland's writing on ayahuasca and other indigenous drugs/related. Review staff progress on the propagation and flowering - Consider adding information about Eeden Monk's understanding of floral symbolism to next lecture tour. **

He selected a cell from the grid of images, and another screen expanded.

-=CURRENTLY RECORDING=- (VENEZUELA / ALTAGRACIA) scrolled across the top of the image.

A Guahibos dance ritual was in process; all tribe members, adults, and children moved in synchronized motions around the mother tree.

Impatient for the lengthy ritual to conclude, Mamon's fingers drummed on the surface of the desk. Another cell opened with a quick rap of his knuckle, and two arcs filled the room equally.

-=CURRENTLY RECORDING=- (SHANGHAI / JIN MAO BUILDING)

A crowd of Chinese businesspeople practiced tai chi on a roof, their naked bodies creating elegant shadows with light from the rising sun.

In Mamon's youth, this breast-and-buns business world might have produced wild outcries from certain public sectors denouncing its perverse nature, or at least questioning its potential to distract from matters of commerce, but no longer. Only a few generations later, continual personal exposure in the Archive allowed people to live with fewer body image issues, their egos, sense of self, now unchained.

He sat back in his flex-chair and pinched his fingers together toward the rooftop tai chi cell, shrinking it back into the desk grid and allowing the tribal dance to fill the room once more. Unhurriedly, he rotated his view of the Pipal tree. The astonishing beauty of its massive girth and thoughts of its extensive life, the many centuries it lived, were incredibly moving. He regretted what must be done to prevent others from discovering the flower and thus, potentially, configuring an antidote for his next grand exercise. He would not let this research spin out of his control in the way that Informed Light had. A great muffled thunder halted the tribe's dance. The doctor's eyes widened with anticipation. For the good of the many, he thought.

The ground beneath the Guahibos buckled briefly then erupted, firing the gargantuan tree and miles of surrounding land into the air before gravity helped the earth swallow the tree splinters and the entire tribe. A few minutes later, little remained but a dirt cloud and a vast cavernous hole.

He pulled a penlight from his shirt pocket and clicked it on. A yellow laser shot across the desk as he made an X over the top of the ended archive. The archive then minimized into a folder marked For Alteration on his desktop. He waved the laser around the room in a wide curve before turning it off and returning it to his pocket. All his preparations paid off so far, now to continue those he needed to arrange for Ben and his brothers' visit.

The desktop grid filled with bedroom images as Mamon navigated through recent entries in Ben's archive. He stopped at a few selected scenes from this morning: Ben's unshaven, sleeping face, hands grasping a light blue bed sheet, scattered open sketchbooks, and various angles of the cluttered floor. Ben's eyes flickered back and forth in a REM state. He rolled onto his back. Sunbeams began streaming into the room from window images on Ben's wall.

He closed the archive, and the desktop returned to the worldwide random grid. New thoughts needed documenting:

*** Treating Ben as a confidant has been ineffective. The accident must still grip his mind. His father's death? His sustained broken heart? He's too unfocused. A lighter touch may have been called for. I remain merely an old work acquaintance of his father's or more likely just the Center's director to him. A month with no contact has altered my view of our relationship. The selected saints' journals should work to occupy him while I attend to the Vestigs. Continue to use for Cohoba trials? ***

His head itched some more, and he considered unwinding his wrap to get at it better, but a light chime signaled dinner's arrival.

☰FOUR☰

Laurel was what most would categorize as a seer, something like a voodoo priestess combined with a homeopathic drug dealer, but maybe with less of the extra kooky fashion sense. She's pretty unassuming, a plain-Jane originally from Florida. Ours was a peculiar relationship, a blend of friendship, and unrequested therapy. Not that I minded, I loved how she refocused my views. She had eyes that could see the beauty in the debased. In fact, her eyes noticed many things others didn't. Every place cracks developed in her house; she'd fill with colorful tiles, pieces of discarded plates, ashtrays, or cups. Lines of embedded yellow glass shards meandered along the wall to the doorbell, a ridge of red pen caps stuck out from under the windowsill. The colorful additions weren't gaudy or overdone as could happen with a house decorated by someone less talented. This was her way with people also - filling gold in their cracks. Following a strict "wabi-sabi" line, she saw beauty in the imperfections, in the incomplete and the transient.

It was definitely the transient I desired as I pulled the water retrieval system chain and stepped into the stall - needed to get it done quickly. Wires carrying rainwater buckets ran along the rear of the house. Her water heating system worked best in summer. In the fall one tended to take very brief freezing showers out in the back. Her low-tech lifestyle grew a bit tiresome when I lived here. How could she have electricity and access to the Internet and Archives but no regular hot water for the shower?

I washed the clay off and listened to my teeth chatter along with the field of wind chimes hanging from the thin nodding metal poles that created a melodic border for her backyard.

"You get that bag of flesh washed up yet?" she asked, draping a towel over the top of the stall.

"All done." I shut the water off and used the towel.

She tossed some clothes at my crotch when I came out. I quickly put them on.

"A little small on you. I thought they'd fit better. Bah, his old rags are exhausting. Every time I go to put them in a box, it's another reminder of how long it's been."

"Maybe you just need to purge it quickly," I said and looked at some tangled wind chimes. "I hate to say it, but maybe selling this place is the answer. It's all so much work."

"How many times do we have to have this conversation? It's this farm that keeps me sane. I engage through being. It's you who confronts absurdity through rebellion. We both know that world out there is too busy obsessing over itself. I'd much rather live here protected by the fields and watch the cows make pie."

"No, you're right. That is excellent entertainment. Well worth the struggle."

"Damn right, now let's get to work."

It was unacceptable to talk about her issues, yet she nearly required it of me, but I guess our relationship has always been this way. Old grooves, ones we'd walked together even before my stay after the accident. Laurel called it the green room - obviously named - the walls were a pale soothing green. After my accident, she recognized the depression that had set in and at least a couple of nights a week we'd have chats in here. I loved this room, but it brought out a certain anxiety in me, an immediate feeling of being back in the time of all the ugliness. All of that became complicated by the pleasing views. The long window wall gave an amazing full outlook onto the farm fields draped in their seasonal colors. The camel and ginger-colored winter fields undulated to the horizon without a housing complex to mar its perfection. My stay was less than six months, but I felt somehow like I'd grown up on the farm. It felt like home. Mostly it was how Laurel connected me to the land. After the accident, once I'd finished recuperating in the bedroom upstairs, she put me straight to work during the day. I'd walked nearly every inch of it, dug the earth, planted seeds, love it and yet, I avoid her and coming here as often as I used to.

Laurel joined me carrying a tray.

"Here, it's my latest experiment. I call it calcified amygdala chai," she said, grinning mischievously while handing over a steaming cup. "Wait, don't drink it yet."

I looked inside. A couple of what I assumed were the dark seeds hovered above a mound of golden honey. Laurel took a little naked man-shaped pitcher, poured cream into each of our cups and stirred.

"Smells nice." I had a small sip. "Wow, it's great. What will this do?"

"Nothing special, only something to stimulate your senses and calm your nerves."

It tasted rich, a traditional chai flavor with a very sharp, spicy finish. It had my lips tingling.

"I thought maybe we'd explore something different today."

"No, Ben, no mind alteration today. It's been over a month so let's keep clear and start with what you've been up to?" She sipped.

"The usual I guess, hanging out with Lenny and the twins, reading books, watching movies."

"Anything worth reading these days?"

"Yesterday I finished one Lenny recommended. A bit heavy on the privacy protest theme, but it feeds that need for rebellion as you pointed out. Mostly it was about those from the DarkNow group and how quickly living without light negatively affected their health and you know, that we give off light internally, so there was no escape as they'd desired. The book had good stuff on the Faux Life Movement too. You'd probably like it more than me actually. It's called … hm, went out of my head, but the author's last name is Bruni. She covers more of the content in the FLM's comedy archives than the questions over how no one can figure out who they are," I sipped again and tried to recall the title but couldn't come up with it. "Mm, this is good."

"Thanks. I've been thinking about privacy lately also, but mostly in relation to personal dignity. You know, most people think of privacy as hiding something like those DarkNow people, hiding away so no one can track your actions, and there's something to that, but I think the dignity aspect is more about being allowed to have private thoughts during public interactions. That's where dignity lies. It has to be, right? How's the volunteering at his center been going?" she asked.

By "his center," she meant Mamon's. She blamed him for a great deal of society's ills even though most people sang his praises.

"Not bad," I said and took a deep breath trying to let go of the stress knot building in my back. "Maybe a little depressing."

"Do you feel it's helping you as well?" She took another sip.

"Yeah, maybe. I guess."

"Which is it?"

"I'd say it's been good to remind myself of other's struggles, but I can't say the saints' lives have made me feel better about my own in the way you hoped."

She paused. "I know you use their journals, but how about their archives. Do you use them for the paintings?"

"Their journals mostly. Those seem to be enough to get a feel of the individual and the images I want to compose for them, but it'd be great if I could transport myself back in time somehow to use my goggles. I'd be able to get recordings from my visual perspective the way old-fashioned filmmakers once did. One perspective, not every angle, any color overlays, any speed – leaving out the need for me to alter it. Just simple and the way I see it in real-time. The personalized views I get recording from the perspective of my goggles are much better, much easier, even if limited. You know... easier to create a meaningful... visual balance in the images than when I work with Archive items that aren't from my view, that I have to manipulate into my view. I guess it's hard to explain. The images I find in the Archives always feel too distant...or it's too much work directing angles to find something worthwhile to work with for the saint I'm painting an image for, and I lose the feel of what I'm trying to accomplish for them. I've said this already, haven't I?"

"No, not exactly, or I wouldn't have asked. I recall you expressing a difficulty with the paintings when you started, but I also know you've talked about the goggles being a way to create images from your perspective. That makes sense to me. The Archives are a universal view; the goggles help create a personal."

"Yes, that's it."

We both drank and sat for a time in silence. It wasn't unusual to spend a good portion of our sessions gazing out the window, but the session felt stiff in a way I didn't recall experiencing with her. I knew she felt it too. The setting sun colored the sky a slapped cheek and persimmon.

"How long's it been since you reviewed your accident archive?" She asked gently.

The knot tightened more. I started stretching and released a sigh unintentionally. "I still haven't."

"You haven't? Ben, the pain is growing in your back as we speak, isn't it?"

"It is, and you don't have to say it. What about personal dignity? What happened to how I should steer clear of all that pity and contempt for myself—take the reins and keep steady, right?" I stood to stretch it better. She let me for a while before she continued.

"I'd hoped you'd have taken the reins by now. With all of the body tension, all the nightmares you've reported—"

"There've been more lately. Just this morning." I glanced out over the fields. "Is it time for the trance stuff now?" I tried to hide the annoyance, but I'm sure my face expressed it.

Laurel's face softened. "I only use that when I'm trying to discover something I can't through dialog. You know that. You're really not interested in talking about this? We can stop if you'd like."

"No, it's okay, but I don't know."

"You don't know. You don't know what?" she asked calmly.

"I don't know when I'll be ready. Hey, I think I met a girl today."

"Is she possibly a boy?"

Ben smiled, "No, no definitely a girl. Her name is Susan. She sent me a message asking if I wanted to talk about books."

"She contacted you? That's unusual. I don't think you've seen anyone since Sara, have you?"

"I'm not seeing Susan. We just met. I don't even know what she looks like. I don't even know if I'll keep writing to her. I, uh, yeah we just met."

"Let me know when the hot stuff starts. I want to get back to what you're avoiding. Seeing as this must be at least the fifth time I've asked you about it, how about we review the accident right now?"

"Now?" my cheeks flushed.

"Yes, Ben. Right now."

Laurel put her teacup down, then directed us to face the opposing wall. "Wall panel. Ben Tinthawin accident archive," Laurel announced to her system. A bright orange rectangle emerged on the wall. My name blinked in white at the center.

Laurel sprang surprise exercises on me in sessions many times. It wasn't new, but this still took me off guard. I'd have preferred one of her revealing special trances. Those wrinkle-lined piercing eyes staring into me, directing my subconscious could cut straight to the heart of the issues. She had many ways of helping even if some didn't appear very helpful, like forcing me to watch the accident. I wish I found it more amusing how she hates the Archives but wants to review my accident again using it. Once was enough for me.

A view from the interior of my parents' house, the kitchen, faded up around us.

⊒FIVE⊒

"I wasn't spying on you! You can go alone with Ben if you keep this up," Dad yelled at my mother into the back of my head as if I were not standing right in front of him. I'd finished pilfering their kitchen for road trip fare. Anything handmade became instantly attractive, and the discovery of a bag of Amish pretzels nearly made me forget their arguing.

"Extra salty?" I offered some to Dad with a smile on my face.

Dad waved the bag away as his brows knit, grumbling about the necessity of watching her archives to time their departure appropriately. He often got nervous about traveling. Mom spent much of the morning primping in the bathroom while he packed and loaded the car. She currently sat cemented to the family room couch in protest of Dad's prodding to get moving. Her hearing somehow always improved whenever someone whispered. She started up the argument again. Hissing about if only he'd admit to being the one who wasted everyone else's time with his archive hounding and maybe she should watch every move he made. These were the same type of arguments I'd heard nearly all of my life.

I'd say, like my father, I rarely learned, even the hard way. My history with binging on cheesecake without first medicating for my difficulties with lactose came to mind.

Mm, cheesecake. Laurel wanted me to work on it, on not continuing to create a bad atmosphere for myself. She believed a requirement for getting over my being dumped should be to face sour dysfunctional relationships like my parents' - "to see what you weren't missing." So, I accepted her challenge and joined them on their trip.

We'd planned to leave after lunch but didn't get rolling until four. I tuned out their arguing over Dad's lack of work. He hadn't had a job he was happy with since he left Lazaras in what amounted to some kind of scandal. I've never bothered to learn the full details of, but I know whatever happened is related to having my brothers made. Mom hates when he spends too much time around the house as he tends to hound her and comment on whatever she's up to. I tuned them out sitting in the back seat using Splatter Farm, an old horror favorite. Fully cocooned in the movie an hour later, I only noticed we'd left Pennsylvania and drove along highways in the mountains of New York after some object hit the side of our car and startled me. I sat up to see if I could discover what it was, but nothing tumbled obviously. The wind blew fiercely outside the window, and their continued bickering matched it.

"They're staying with Ben's neighbors," Mom said.

"All I know is I'm not paying for babysitting. I pay enough already."

Dad glared at me as if somehow, I was to blame.

"Ben, how much do you pay? They really are too much work for Mr and Mrs Panas," Mom said.

The twins can be trouble, but she'd never know. Her addiction, gorging daily on personal archives, took up most of her time. Sadly, my parents held very little love for my brothers, and not only because they were conjoined. They saw Ed and Francis as a money drain and simple rejects and possibly retained a bit of guilt turned anger over passing them on me.

"You know they'd love to see Gram. The last time I spoke with her, she said she'd had a special bed built for them."

"And where would they sit? My car isn't equipped," Dad said, knowing his car had plenty of room.

Mom ignored me. She clipped her glass onto the dashboard, mixed some drug in, and drank it down. Her forced, warm smile told me there'd be no entertaining another conversation where I tried to convince her to spend time with Ed and Francis.

Late spring brought forth a verdant landscape marred with harsh shadows, now disappearing as converging clouds blocked the sun. The highway lamp sensors caused odd streetlight strobing that drew my attention from the movie. For the next ten minutes, I noticed Dad ignoring the dashboard-recommended exits.

"Pop, what's your dash saying? Don't you think we should get off and seek cover or something?"

"I can read. Bad weather conditions?" He flicked his hand at the dash and again towards the clouds, "Look at that. Plenty of blue. No lousy rain ever stopped traffic anyway."

There wasn't any blue sky left, only fluffy charcoal boulders threatening to drop. Five minutes later, still no rain but the wind blew fiercely, and we passed several fallen trees. Our headlights turned on. The car navigated easily through the debris, but you didn't see trees on the road every day, and I kept my mouth shut. We followed the curvy highway hills and discovered more trees lying on the other side of the median. Mom grew noticeably nervous.

"There must have been some of that freakweather going on here. There's a whole damn forest on the highway. Take the next exit, or I will."

"Bah, it's only threatening to rain. Why does everything have to be freakweather? A few branches won't kill us," Dad said.

This was more than a few branches. Something ahead looked like piles of dirt as if there had been a small rockslide off to the side. The streetlamp shone directly above it, and when we got closer, you could see it was two little dead deer. They faced each other heads to tails like some kind of strange yin-yang symbol.

"Oh, look at those poor baby deer," Mom said with her fingers pressed to the window. Their eyes, glazed and open, appeared almost alive.

"Look up there," Dad said, pointing off to our left.

A considerable deer herd speckled the hillside. Small points of glowing yellow eyes reflected the headlights. In the past, our family made deer spotting a competition. Dad liked to say this region was "infested" with them. I watched his face in the rearview mirror, a smile on his lips from his big score with the deer game, but it melted away as the rain started hitting the windshield. The fading grin was the second to last thing I saw before it happened. The fear in the profile of Mom's face was the last.

Mom shouted something unrecognizable as our headlights brought the deer standing in the road into bright view. The first deer looked like an albino, all white from the side -- head turned to us, eyes blank and SLAM!

And thwunk, another! Soft and solid at the same time, you barely felt the crunch of bone. Chwunn! Another.

A crowd of three together sandwiched as we banked off them into the ramp of the median that sent our car rolling. We ricocheted back over to the other side of the highway, up the steep embankment and rolled back to where the deer we'd hit lay ripped open. Glass, wind, and water filled the air. The chaos dampened to a halt making a glassy slush sound when we landed.

Rain began pelting my ear and neck. A line of bloody spittle stretched and quickly snapped as I pulled my face away from the armrest. Blood flooded my mouth. I tried the door, but it wouldn't open. I need out. I needed to spit but misjudged the broken window, and it splattered back against me, covering a huge swath of my pant leg sickly red. The sight of the blood must have made me realize what had happened. My tongue throbbed a deep rhythm. I'd bitten a piece off and touching the wound sent a blinding shock of pain along my spine. The whole scene felt unreal, dreamlike, monstrous.

I pushed myself into an upright position. One partially full airbag flipped up and down slapping against Mom's wet body, which stuck through the windshield and lay across the hood. She'd lost a shoe. Dad wasn't in the car. Where'd he go? I needed to get out, needed to help Mom. Her shoeless foot wasn't moving.

I leaned over the seat to try, but nothing worked on the communication system. Digital waste glowed along the edges of the dashboard.

"Mom!" I barked, inciting fireworks of pain from my tongue.

My hand instinctively went to my neck for the phone, but it was gone. Pretzels lay scattered everywhere but no phone. Did I put it on this morning?

Dad's side of the car crumpled inward so I pushed on the passenger-side door handle hoping the electric would work. No luck. The cracked sunroof angled off its track. A quick shove created enough space to crawl out. Somehow, the headlights remained on, and with help from streetlamps, all the carnage surrounding me worked my nerves into a frenzy. My stomach rose to the top of my throat when I found Dad.

I spat another mouthful of blood a safe distance and knelt by him and a mauled deer. His name tangled because of my tongue. "Dahd, Hey, Dahd." Blood puddled in the corner of his eye socket. I did what every movie had shown me one should do in such instances; I felt his neck. A weak beat thumped in the vein. No phone on him either.

My nerves flared again when I looked up at Mom's rain-slicked clothes. Blood flowed profusely from a jagged cut on her cheek. Jesus, Mom. I rolled her over on the hood, and her purse slid onto the road. The streetlight bleached all the color from her skin, harsh contrasts of the blood against her white cheek and neck. My hand couldn't stop the flow. I bent close to see the gash better. The rainwater washed some of the blood away, keeping her face a little less gory.

No headlights shone in the distance, no charging stations or housing complexes, no shopping centers — no sign of civilization in any direction. I shook out the contents of Mom's purse, remembering she always had a handheld with her. No luck. The middle of nowhere in the rain with no communication options. My head pounded blank and thick as the rain pelted me, causing chills to wave through my body.

I placed Mom's hand on her cheek, trying to hold the blood in, but the hand kept slipping down and revealing her teeth through the wound. I took off my shirt and wrapped her head with it, leaving her mouth uncovered so she could breathe. I thought she might swallow the blood, choke on it, and tilted her head to make sure that couldn't happen.

Okay. Okay, they were both still alive. Now what? I looked up into the streetlight. Yes, that's it. Surely, the Archive would've tipped off authorities and help would be on the way, but how could I know for sure when I had no way to confirm it?

I got down and rechecked Dad. No blood patches on his clothes, but little nicks bled all over his face. I couldn't sit still and watch them slowly bleed to death. The road sensors weren't blinking the crisis alert. I reached through the window and checked the power. If the headlights functioned, the car must still have some energy source working. I pushed the help beacon switch twice, and on the third try, the road sensors on the railing to the right and the median to the left began blinking. Relief! Someone would be notified. I lifted Mom onto the ground next to Dad.

Blood from the deer flowed away in a wide red streak. The fucking headlights blinded me. I felt like rocking. I was so cold. This must've been why people rocked back and forth in movies when they went nuts. Something to do with the way you feel your heartbeat. Mine felt like it was jumping up my throat.

Where were all the other cars? I grabbed Dad's hand and put it on Mom's. While getting up, I felt a snap as if I'd stepped on a deer leg. I looked down and saw Mom's handheld. I'd only broken the cover, but it wouldn't power on. I thought my nose was running, and without thinking, I wiped my face on my arm, streaking it briefly red with blood. The pressure from my swollen lips on my tongue made me jerk in pain. I kept looking at it and then threw it as hard as I could. I wanted to cry about the absurdity.

I couldn't leave Mom and Dad out in the rain. At the back of the car, the suitcases lay scattered along the road. Of course, no doors would release, but the trunk bent wide open. I grabbed some clothes from my bag, ran back, and spread a pair of jeans over her body. It didn't look like enough, so I went to get Mom's larger bag. A green and white striped dress worked to cover Mom, and a light pink one over Dad helped, but it was an absurd scene. One of Mom's small white socks had fallen onto the spilled entrails of the deer next to Dad.

I glanced about at the cutting rain, at the blinking highway sensor, at the blood flowing. No doubt help was on its way. No doubts. No doubts.

☰SIX☰

paused the archive, knowing what was coming and not wanting to continue. The view made me feel as if I was hovering just above the trunk of the car.

"Why didn't I think to grab the flashlight from Dad's car?"

Laurel gave me an impatient look. "Possibly with having seen both of your parents bloody and lying unconscious next to a mangled car, you were distracted. You seem to be avoiding the rape."

"Avoiding? I'm not avoiding it. Come on. I can't offer one observation?"

"No… you're right. I'm sorry. That was the last moment you saw him alive. It must still be difficult."

I looked away, fearing her concerned eyes might trigger tears. I have a photo of Dad on my dresser. In it, I'm laughing with him about a painting I'd done. I was eight at the time. The painting was projected on a wall next to him, a little larger than life-size with Dad written in big letters. A portrait of him with purple hair, a humongous nose and possibly an extra arm for a tail - doesn't look a thing like him. But, his laughing smile was filled with pride. He shared that smile with me many times over the years. I put the photo on my dresser the week we returned to the apartment because I thought that's what one does. Most of the time, when I'm getting clothes out, I try not to look at it. The supportive smile had become more of a burden.

I've thought about turning it down or putting the photo away, but the act seems disrespectful. I avoid it the same way I avoid his archives. The ache in my body over his loss felt very similar to the pain from the breakup with Sara. She remained alive, but it still felt like death. A five-year addiction culminating in a cold turkey heart attack. These archives, especially this one, kept all of those horrible memories vivid. There might be something left for me to gain from reviewing the final section of the accident, but I still could not see it.

We sat there in silence, until Laurel leaned over, put her arms around me for an extended hug, and let me go. I wanted to shrug her off.

"It's all the same as when I watched it the first time. Nothing new about his death or my feelings that we haven't discussed in detail. I still can't believe I left them. I've never lost that feeling I should've stayed."

"It's as you've said. There was nothing you could've done. You had no way of knowing how bad off he was and that the sensors already alerted support. You were too far from an EMS station."

"I know. I guess seeing it again also drums up the conflicted emotions I've had with his focus on extending his life. All those times, I worried about his health over the years—and how I love my brothers, but without his need to live longer, I wouldn't be...inconvenienced. I rarely saw him and my mother, still rarely see mom but... that feeling of had I stayed with them longer maybe I could've done something."

"Hold on, first, let's address your brothers at another time since I know at the base of that statement is slight resentment, but mostly love. As to your father, he worked at Lazaras so the temptation for a body replacement must've been tempting in a way that you or I can't comprehend." Laurel changed the angle. You could now see my face and body; then she froze the stream again. "Look at you. You were badly injured and probably had a concussion. You were doing the best you could. Yes, we've said this, but it's worth repeating that there was no way for them to communicate with you and certainly if you hadn't contacted the EMS, your mother would not be alive today."

I took a deep breath and shook it off. "I'm as good as I'll ever be about this stuff. I really think I'm okay with his death. It's just another absurd ending right. Why then? Why that way? So meaningless and we've talked enough about that, but it's the next part... No matter how hard I try, I still can't... I recall when we watched it last time and the unreal events in it. Right up to when I went running for help is still up here." I tapped my head. "But I don't remember those, those people, and nothing I can do, no movies, no books, nothing since has helped me recall those parts."

"That's why I've been encouraging you. There's nothing new about difficulty accessing ones' memories. In fact, we recall what happens to us in very weak detail. We have always relied on external sources, whether it's books or other people's memories. Certainly, the difference here is you appear to recall none of it, and that is also not unheard of but should have you asking why. Don't let the other cognitive tools you have at your command go to waste. We've been relying on video, audio, and handwritten sources for a very long time, far longer than the Archive. Repetition will evoke something honest, something true in you. A greater understanding. I have no doubts."

"You've said it… we've said all of this before in different forms. Can we please stop here?"

"Stop? But you just said you understo—

"I do understand, but I don't want to continue. Another time. Please don't be angry."

"I'm not angry. I want to help, but—one more thought and I won't mention it again until after you do on your own."

"You won't?"

"I'll do my best not to. The last thing I want to say is I know the great potential you won't review it. But, even if you find you can't, you might consider visiting the area the accident occurred. Go with Lenny to see the area where it all took place. I want you to give yourself a new memory of that space and those locations. It may help you feel differently. Okay? Just think about it. Why don't you spend some time alone while I get dinner?" Laurel stood and turned to walk out but stopped abruptly. "Also, you should keep corresponding with that girl who contacted you. I've mostly cleaned you up and made you presentable. I'd say you're ready. Please let me know if you'd like me to take the boys to give you some adult time alone."

"Okay, thanks."

She left the room, and I looked out at the empty fields and thought about traveling. I should take her up on her offer.

It was only when the dinner bell rang that I stopped watching the horizon. I joined everyone in the kitchen. There was no more talk of my archives for the rest of the evening and barely a note of concern during our goodbyes.

"How about we come over again tomorrow?" Ed suggested.

"I can always make time for you, Edward," Laurel said, taking his hand.

"How about me too and Ben?" Francis added.

"Of course, all of you. Anytime."

A glance at Laurel's face was all I needed to see the concern still filled her eyes. I smiled as reassuringly as I could as I got in the car.

☰SEVEN☰

I was in the middle of Zombii3 and halfway through a bowl of chips when my doorbell rang repeatedly. A screen popped up with Lenny waiting for entrance. "BUD, Let him in."

A few moments later, into my living room bumbled Lenny; cobalt t-shirt, no pants, no underpants, carroty socks, no shoes. Lenny found ways to enjoy every opportunity for fun and relaxation. He loved the nude life, loved not worrying about what he wore except possibly to entertain. He maintained a utilitarian sense of fashion where only winter breezes made pants necessary.

"Nice socks," I said.

He walked up close, looked down with his usual slightly dark-circled eyes, and frozen big white grin. "I like orange. Want ta goh far eh drive? I've made a discovery," he said with a bogus Irish accent. Lenny grew up in Dulac, Louisiana. I always thought somehow that his natural southern accent matched the proud gap he sported between his front teeth. He once told me the gap was a sign of higher intelligence. I've never doubted its veracity, but others might.

"Yeah but, maybe you could've contacted... I'm in the middle of—" I said with mild annoyance as Lenny's tall form towered over me, frozen with his toothy grin waiting for my reply. "Hold on," I said. I switched my movie off and called the twins. Loud footsteps in the hallway, they rounded the corner a little too rapidly and almost knocked Lenny down.

"You are here," Francis said to Lenny.

"Slow up, boneheads." Lenny rubbed his leg where the twins slammed him.

"Where're we going?" Ed said and jerked his eyes back to his screen.

"Riding?" Francis asked.

"Lenny and I are going out. How 'bout you guys visit with Mr and Mrs Panas?"

"Yes!" they said.

We dropped the boys at the Panas' place and stopped at a vendor for some Cubbie, hand-mixed bubble tea soda. Thunder crackled from dark clouds, greeting us as we left the MAc. On the front walkway, two young girls were throwing snaps at the ground. Their little white dog barked as each snap hit and made its namesake noise. Lenny walked by, staring intensely at the dog. He acted startled by a snap, pretended not to see the curb as he threw his soda forward onto the grass, then fake tripped and fell for them. He landed on the ground like a rubber band and flipped back to his feet. The girls giggled into little white gloves and skipped quickly away in the swelling breeze, pulling their frantically yipping dog behind them.

"Did you see that?" Lenny asked, plucking a few of the neon orange tapioca balls from the cup that no longer had soda left to go with them.

"All I saw was you wasting your drink." The wind hustled us toward Lenny's car.

"Ah, you know. Anything to get em laughin'. They should be heading indoors anyway, plus I wasn't that thirsty," Lenny said, chewing the tapioca. Lenny ranked at the top of the fun charts of any children he met, with most people really.

We usually turned off all guidance systems during our explorations, setting it to autopilot local random, but Lenny quickly programmed a destination and closed the screen. These drives were once about exploring those bombed out or burned down areas on the East Coast created during the first year of privacy riots - small cities or big towns like Allentown, Baltimore or those miles just outside of Boston, everyone roaring with anger at others knowing their every move. We had no desire to scavenge them as others did; well, occasionally there would be small items found which were too good to leave to rot, but mostly there was a certain fresh ghost town feel or a particular ribcage luxury we pursued.

"You wanna smoke?" Lenny flipped open a box of reeds.

"Sure."

"How's things?" Lenny asked as I lit his and he let the smoke hover around his nose. The energy from the hammering thunder lifted the hair on my skin.

"Eh, fine. Where're we headed?" I felt a bit annoyed that rain might make viewing the landscape challenging and slightly wished I'd stayed home to finish my movie.

"The find…I nearly forgot! I thought about showing you an arc, but it's better as a surprise. I'm tellin' you; it's gotta be something that'll grab the attention of the Faux Life folks. I mean as an addition to the Whig Party arcs and something attractive to those living off the grid."

"What'd you find?"

"All I'm goin' to say is great guest at a Whig Party."

"You found a Ben Franklin?"

"Damn, no, but I found an Abe," Lenny said with sincere disappointment.

We'd been searching for a Ben Franklin for years as he was a real rebel "fighting for independence" founding father American Whig party member, even if he wasn't a President. Mostly we knew he had a tremendous comical dumpiness that we'd love to find and interact with.

"I was roaming the recluse boards and noticed this guy ranting about no archives, no medicine, no genetically altered anything. He was making a big deal about no hair replacement and how his mother was a wig maker. A real chatty back-to-basics bird, another fan of the Faux Life Movement and he gave the up thumbs for a visit."

"Only you could get a recluse to okay a picnic. So where is he?"

Lenny's proud grin ate his cheeks, purposefully not answering my question. He took a deep drag.

"Wait until you see it. The damn thing looks like it might crawl off his head. It could be tough to get him to let us borrow it, though."

"That's great," I said with less enthusiasm than the situation called for.

"I know, I know. Hey, what's wrong? I know...might rain, right? Or are you worried he won't lend it? Could be even better if it were soaked, right?"

"No, nothing like that— not worried. I can't wait to see it. I'm just enjoying the mix." I appreciated his help, but even with the good news, I wasn't in the mood to talk. It could have been the music. The vibrations from the chirping whirr of the music felt good. I really only wanted to listen to what Lenny programmed.

Filtered wind from the exterior of the car, fuzzy tambourine, and wooden stick rhythms continued to play from the speakers. I sought the visual solace I occasionally found on our drives, but instead confronted giant suburban housing complexes bunched against the highways like cubic fungus. All painted in bland colors with stone or brick detailing, lawns dotted with immaculately groomed shrubbery and grass trimmed to manic perfection. I focused on the thin rainbow halos the clouds were exhibiting. I couldn't recall ever seeing rainbows work in that fashion. The sky vibrated oddly with them. My nerves started to feel a little frayed, and couldn't pin down why. I didn't mention the rainbows to Lenny. If he noticed the rainbows, he never said so.

"How's your tough-guy-tongue-lip coming?" I asked. Lenny had amassed significant and highly specialized archive clip collections. The last he shared with me was one where he'd fast forward through tough guy's archives until they would make a specific face. It's a face we've all probably seen but likely didn't choose to focus on.

"You need to see the one I found last week. This guy has the frizziest blonde fro and those glimmer pods sticking out of it." Lenny laughed. We'd spoken several times about how ridiculous the big idiotic glimmer pods looked on people. "His chest all puffed up to match his hair, shakes his head so the pods flop back and forth and then the tongue lip with actual bubble gum stretched through it. I nearly kept the fight in the clip. It was mostly a slap fight. Two big hair-painted bulls slapping each other. Chuckle revolution stuff. No stopping the laughter."

"I pulled up the collection on the screen and highlighted it for later. Wow, it's up to 147 clips."

"I'm pretty much done with it, I think."

Another of my favorite but less humorous collection of his had laugh-tears, people welling up while looking back on their children from a few years before. Originally, it also included people tearing up while screaming - angry people sometimes produced tears, but he'd mentioned it was easier to collect the parents, and he deleted the angry clips out. The last I heard about it he said even though the images were the height of emotional gratification he thought it too maudlin so gave it up. Maudlin is not a term I'd used to describe Lenny or most of his collections, but the pursuit seemed worthwhile to me.

Lenny's car eventually turned off onto an exit for Wilsonville. We saw a lake through trees in the distance. As the car slowed at a stop signal, I hit the forward-drive pause and flicked my butt into a trash gutter. I almost tossed out my remaining Cubbie when Lenny stopped me.

"Hey hey, what're you doin' there?"

"Sorry, I should've known after you wasted yours," I said. Lenny rarely turned down a snack - even half-eaten.

He took the cup and sucked up the bubbles. "Can I say something, and you won't bite my head off?"

"Anyone who asks that should be prepared to bleed."

"That's it, see, you need to feather. I'm sorry. I've been holding off but, you know, we used to laugh all the time." Lenny glanced over with a type of sincerity that made me want to strangle him.

"Feather? I'm laughing all the time. We're always laughing."

"No, I'm doing the normal, and you're grumblin' or keeping quiet or being bothered I'm calling you or interrupting your movie or wasting my drink. Who cares if I dump a drink to entertain some kids?"

I didn't answer right away. "Sorry. Maybe you're right. I guess I'm tired. I'm not getting great sleep. I had another one of my dreams a couple nights ago that keeps coming back to me."

"What were you this time?"

"A werewolf."

"You wanna share or is it all too much?"

"I can ... but I'm starting to think I should keep them to myself."

"Tell it like you did about bein' the lizard man, lotsa sloppy guts spillin'."

"I don't know this one is different. It makes me feel more ashamed than some of the others," I said.

"No judgment here, just let it roll."

"I guess. I guess it's not really me exactly anyway." I said and felt an internal darkness growing.

A tree ahead of us lost most of its leaves to a tough gust, and I began.

"I sat on a bed in my old bedroom from when I was young. It was dusk, I think, bright out the window, but the room was kind of dim. I felt frightened and sat, waiting for someone to approach. There were others in the room. I could hear the air suck in and out of their nostrils. A hand clapped sharply. The silhouette of a hair-covered man with a crooked spine moved in front of the window curtains. I couldn't see his face, but he kept repeating 'Press the spot to stop the pain! Press the spot to stop the pain!'

He seemed threatening, so I looked to escape, but he spoke it again, directly at me, 'Press the spot to stop the pain!' He waited for me to respond, but I didn't know what to say. Then he said, 'You have no choice. You must do as we do.'"

"Straight outta one of the old movies," Lenny said.

"My face started to shift and bubble. It felt like cicadas were buzzing in my eyebrows. I shook my head to stop it, and when I turned towards a mirror, I saw tadpoles swimming under this waxy film of my forehead. I tried to squeeze them out like a pimple, but they wouldn't budge."

"Pop that frog zit!" A thunder crack rang out when he said zit making Lenny laugh. Normally I'd have laughed too, but my nerves killed the humor.

"Yeah, I know, tadpole pimples, but they weren't, they wouldn't squeeze out. Instead, they moved with my face as it stretched towards the mirror. It hurt like hell. I mashed my fingers into my cheek where the buzzing was, and my flesh pushed out without pain like the guy said. Then too many teeth came from behind my lips. My arms and legs kinked weirdly, and I hunched over swelling to twice my normal size.

Everybody suddenly went jumping out the window, so I followed. We ran through backyards, and I kept smelling water like after a recent rain on warm pavement. But when the scent of some female got up my nostrils—"

"Lady hunter!"

"Okay, hold on." I closed my eyes, feeling even more disturbed and continued, "I arrived at a short hedge and saw two girls. I hid there, panting. A streetlight flicked on, and it made them bright and obvious. Their chubby, little bodies skipped in circles. They swished these wooden sticks with long plastic white fishtails tied to them. I looked around next to me and noticed the individual who'd given me directions about transforming. I could feel his urging to act. That's when the girls pointed their sticks at me and laughed. I'm not sure why they were doing it. It felt like I was being judged or tested, but I got angry and raced to them. My body altered to a half-human state as I grabbed one. I felt the shift of the kinks in my limbs just before I caught her. I ripped her pants off. Tiny pieces of her skin were in my nails. Jesus, it was incredibly real. It felt like I was starving, like when you're so hungry, and you don't even taste what you're eating. I don't mean I was eating her but... it was all... wrong and then she seemed bent funny and I looked at her spine where I noticed small glowing symbols branded along it leading up her neck. They were so bright, getting brighter as they neared her head. Bright like something would burst from her skull. I couldn't tell what the symbols meant, but I kept looking closer at them as I pounded against her and then a flicker from above me made me look up. The stars were switching on, and my eyes went towards the streetlight that kept getting brighter. That's when I snapped out of it. I became sick when I recognized what was happening and let go. She disappeared as the hair on my body sank back towards the skin, and my teeth felt huge in my mouth. That's where it ended, and I woke conscious of my canine teeth and had an angry boner."

"That was rotten. I felt like I was there. Just a nightmare, so don't worry about it but what a SAW."

Lenny loved stories of Synchronicity Activity Waves, we both did, but he sought them out for one of his collections, where I just had a casual fondness for them.

"A sync wave?"

"Yeah, you know - the two little girls with a wolf, and the two little girls with the dog I did the trip for."

"Right, but that was today, the dream was yesterday. I don't think it counts."

"Sure, it does. You're telling me now, so it works for me. Need to add the trip and tale to my collection."

"I don't know about that but, anyway, it was so real … awful… gross."

"Buck up and give me a pedosmile. It was just a dream," Lenny said and lit another reed.

"No, really, it was sickening. I didn't tell Laurel yesterday, but I probably should have. Maybe she'd have understood better why I'm not really interested in reviewing the accident archives again."

"I bet she'd want you to even more. Why do you fight her on this stuff?"

"Have you spoken to her?"

"No, not recently. You've told me about her asking you to review it before, and you always have an excuse not to. I've watched it. I mean, it's tough but—"

"Excuse? Really? Seems like it'd be self-abuse if I bothered with it. I think the dream is more about Sara because the girls were skipping at that parking lot over by Sara's house."

"I pictured it happening near that house you ended up at after the accident. Probably because of the weird girl rape at the house and the girl rape in your dream. So... you're still thinkin' about Sara?"

"Not really. She only comes into my head a couple times a day," I said half-joking.

"I know this cute shrink at work I could hook you up with," Lenny made a big boob gesture, cupping at his chest. "She'll improve your mood better than a Dulac dill pickle and get you over these Sara nightmares in no time." He turned up the music as sounds from the lake filtered in. We were driving towards the water's edge.

The car stopped at a dock, and Lenny scanned the area for other visitors. No signs of anyone so he pushed the bar, and we drove onto the water. Lenny left the tambourine music playing, switched out the wooden sticks and added some crowd cheering with the occasional announcer interjection that sounded like a transmission from a Mexican baseball game. That wasn't what he wanted I guess because he tuned to a classic spin station and turned up the exterior microphones that caught more of the water sloshing noises. We listened to the blend as we cruised out to the small tree-covered island.

"You're sure this is okay?" I asked.

He smiled and pushed the accelerator.

"Don't tell me he's a wig-wearing recluse who looks like Abraham Lincoln and lives underwater?"

"No. No, it's just up ahead." Lenny opened a screen and tapped on a blinking dot that showed Matool Island as our destination.

A few minutes later, we'd parked, and Lenny grabbed a box from the back of the car. The clouds continued to threaten, but still, no raindrops fell. We began hiking towards an oversized orb tent that was the only obvious housing. Oversized may be an understatement. I'd seen these tent houses built for a couple of people to camp in, but this one nearly reached the tallest pine on the island.

"I haven't told him about your infinity archive. He probably wouldn't care so don't bother using it to get the wig," Lenny said.

"I put together this recluse kit with special treats I thought he'd like."

Many people review their personal archives from the day before. Occasionally this leads to seeing yourself watching yourself. I'm sure someone has documented the first time this occurred, but I've never looked to see who created the first Infinity archive - someone watching himself watching himself every day at the same time -, but it has been a thing to do for a few years now. I initially thought I'd devote one to a commentary on how US Presidents went the way of UK Royalty, becoming mere figureheads, but instead, it's become an archive of Presidents who would never have been elected if they had to go through the genetic scrutiny the candidates do today.

"How'd you get him to okay the visit?"

"I simply told him we have been trying to attract the Faux Life people, and if they didn't approach us soon, we'd be interested in joining the ranks of recluses instead."

I'd never considered myself a performance artist. I still don't, but when I had the wig idea, I couldn't avoid bringing it to life. If I let it stand as purely conceptual, Lenny would've pinched it. Probably should've let him. His performances might have attracted the FLM by now. He's better at generating exciting rebellion — our semi-peaceful fight to keep meaning alive, to stay connected.

The Faux Life Movement spends their days living completely farcical lives, comedians who never leave the stage. Fighting the absurd with absurdity. This tiny clique of mystery men had control over the Archives like no one else and instead of staying off the map, chose to reinvent themselves daily. Everything light reached is recorded and stored in the Grand Archives, yet somehow the FLM had been recruiting new members without detection. Were the authorities in on it? Didn't these people have families, parents who could I.D. them? Why couldn't someone identify FLM members via backtracking through their archive histories? Why not open up an FLM archive, hit reverse on the main actor until you ended up in his past where you could tell where he came from and who he was? It didn't work. They'd purposefully alter their history to eventually look like they grew out of a discarded Band-Aid, dropped into existence from the hollow of an old woman's hairy armpit, or some equally surreal origin.

When Lenny and I heard they'd hired new members, our conversations immediately turned to how we might gain their attention. We figured if no one can find them, they must have to get in touch with new members directly and we hoped the Whig Party archives might excite them enough to contact us. They should've seen them already, though, and we both knew it.

Before we reached the tent door, a gangly man with an actual pitchfork came around the back of the house. When he saw us, he started galloping through the grass aggressively towards us. Lenny started backing away towards the car, but I stood there between the two of them too startled to act.

"What are you doing here? Get going! Move!"

Lenny dropped his gift box as he was wiggle-waving his arms, trying to signal me to join him.

"I'm sorry, but that's my friend Lenny. He contacted you on some board? You said you'd tell us how to live good lives as recluses or something?"

"That's Lenny? Why are his socks that bright?"

"I have no idea." This guy really looked like what Abraham Lincoln might have had he aged a couple hundred years - all sunken cheeks, big ears, and lanky sharp angles. His skewed not-gray-enough-for-his-age, dark brown wig looked unstable with the wind flipping it up at the edges.

"Hey! Get over here," he waved Lenny over with a fly-swatting motion.

Lenny nearly skipped back to us, holding a sheepish grin on his face. It dawned on me; his backing away was more of a show for our archive fans than his fearing a pitchfork attack.

"I could've killed your friend here now. You shouldn't sneak up on people like this," the man said.

"I'm sorry. I thought we agreed on today for a visit? I brought you the items you requested. Got em in this box with some other interesting items too."

"No, that was yesterday. Today I'm busy. There's stalls needing hay, and it's going to pour any minute." He pointed towards the back of the house with his pitchfork. A huge pronged streak of lightning filled the sky behind him.

"Could you spare a little time to show us how you manage things here? It looks impressive," Lenny said.

"No, I can't, and who is this? I never said you could bring a party to my house."

The prize looked to be slipping from our grasp. How would we ever locate someone this perfect again? Lenny looked at me, then at the man's wig, then back at the car.

"This is Abe. You've never seen a man who can jump as high as Abe. I thought you might like to meet him plus he put most of this gift together for you," Lenny said.

"What are you talking about? I've no time for your bright-sock baloney," the man eyed the box interested but switched back to his angry squint.

"Abe, show him how high you can jump." Lenny gave me a look and then gestured towards the wig.

"I don't think I could. I haven't been practicing much lately."

"Sure, you can. If you want that gold ring, you've got to go for it!" Lenny smiled big.

"This gentleman obviously has a lot of work to do, Lenny. Look at that pitchfork in his hands. Maybe we could come visit another day?"

"No, you cannot. Yesterday was the day I gave, and that was a onetime offer."

Lenny urged me on with his eyebrows.

"Sir, before I show you my skills, I'd like to thank you for sharing with us and know that we will return to you the favor you've given. In the meantime, please accept our gifts," I said.

Lenny handed over the box. He opened one flap, and a broad grin quickly filled his face but shifted back to anger with equal speed.

"I don't need to see you jump around." He fumbled the box, and it slipped from his arm. A couple of seed packets slid out. He bent down and quickly put them back in. "Please leave. Now."

I bent down and sprang up, giving a pathetic practice jump and a loud yelp to add extra showiness. The man looked understandably unimpressed but stood and kept watching me as Lenny eased his way closer. I bent lower this time, and when I jumped and yelped Lenny jumped and grabbed the wig. We turned and made a dash for the car. Neither of us looked back. We ran at top speed and got in the car much quicker than I imagined we could. I heard the man yelling as the car drove us quickly out onto the lake. When I finally looked back, I saw the man wasn't even looking our way. He was busy unpacking the box. Ridiculously juvenile of us. I could hardly believe it.

"You had to push me into that. He'll probably squeal," I said.

"Somebody like him? This'll be the most excitement he'll have had for years. And hey, he had a very long and difficult list of items in that box. I got all he requested plus I threw in a new handmade wig. Besides, we'll mail back his pube pile tomorrow with an apology."

"You really think he wants this back?" I held up our prize by two fingers.

"Pew, that thing reeks."

"Let's get this over," I said.

As we directed the car to an open field close to the lake, the rain started to fall lightly. We quickly got out. Lenny popped the trunk to get the costume he brought while I opened a screen on the side of the car. The wig barely fits and looked too large for me, but along with a three-piece suit, bowtie, fake beard, and big ears cemented on, it worked decently to get the vision across. I navigated to the last President I portrayed, John F. Kennedy, who's DNA exhibited Addison's disease. In the Kennedy archive, I stood next to Lenny outfitted with a white dress and a blonde wig holding the screen in which I was standing wearing a Grover Cleveland outfit. Lenny didn't bring a costume for himself today, so he backed away and let me stand solo and perform alone. I struck a serious Presidential pose gazing at me dressed as JFK and flipped the cards listing Colorblindness, Marfan syndrome, Presbyopia and strabismus and some of Lincoln's genetic disorders. I ended it with my pinky finger itching inside the fake right ear as Lenny timed the requisite sixty seconds and the rain started to soak us.

"That'll work," Lenny said with a wide grin.

The rain really started coming down harder. I grabbed a zip bag from the trunk and quickly stuck the stink wig inside but left the rest of the costume on as I climbed back in the car.

"How's the biosphere ship coming at OM2ME?" I asked on our way home.

Lenny worked for years at OM2ME in social engineering.

"The new ship's incredible. Wait until you see this thing lift off." Lenny lit the end of a pipe and blew a stem of white then waved it at me. "We still have a long list to complete, many months to go."

Before I inhaled, I said, "Some list I joined a while ago is still active, and this girl responded."

"List?" Lenny said with a breathy voice releasing his smoke.

"Book talk list, but you reminded me how I told her about the annoying scientists. Mamon used his clout to get Lazaras to let him observe the twins and report back. You'd think they'd have all they needed on them by now."

Lenny furrowed his brows and flicked his tongue up and down in an evil fashion. My smoked brain garbled his face, warping it like a snake until his head rolled back revealing rings of wavering light. He unfolded like an origami flower box and then collapsed back to his usual self, grinning at me.

"Hot sauce on a pepper. What's she look like? Redhead?"

Lenny loved redheads.

"She challenged me not to check her arcs, so I have no idea."

"A pretentious one then, or some kind of grizzled chicken, I'm guessing she's a pass."

"Maybe. I'll probably write her for a bit and see."

"Gruzzled chicken is best for the hopper," Lenny's face folded in reverse and I had to look away.

The rain ended as quickly as it started. Lenny opened his window when the wipers folded in, and the car drove us down a road with marshland on both sides. A cross breeze blew a dragonfly in. It jumped from place to place finally settling on the dash. Its wings pulsed then bloated with electricity, sending out brightly colored sparks as it flew to one of Lenny's sock-covered feet now resting on the dash and stopped again. Lenny started giggling at it and slowly waving it back and forth with his toes.

"A huge snake doctor! Just like the ones I grew up with. It's crazy powerful, look at the control the wings have," Lenny said. The dragonfly flew around the car and alighted on Lenny's arm, clenching onto some of his hairs. He began waving it around wildly and finally smashed the poor dragonfly against the seat.

"That fucker wanted to eat my arm. You never felt something so prickly in your life. Practically pulled my skin off."

I started laughing hard, and Lenny must've realized how crazy he sounded. He started laughing too and picked up the mangled fly to drop out the window. He saluted it in memorial, wiping away fake tears as it sucked away in the breeze.

"Did you bring anything to eat?" I asked.

"Only these, a favorite of ole Lincoln." Lenny grabbed a bag of oranges from behind his seat and dropped it on my lap. For a short while, the oranges banging into my thighs echoed in my memory as if they were bouncing up and down. I ripped one in half, getting pulpy skin in my fingernails and bright citrus scent that filled my head. I could feel the orange scent inside my eyes at the tops of my eyeballs. It was gorgeous, a timeless scent. I saw Lincoln bringing a slice to his lips and felt a great loving brotherhood as I handed over half of the orange to Lenny.

I spat a seed out the window and watched it sink, pop up, and then drop beyond view.

The roads curved, and the rain started up again.
We couldn't get enough; the peels flew as we ate the
whole bag of them on the way home.

⹃EIGHT⹂

The headlights poke my eyes until they grow used to the brightness. A gaunt hand with bloodshot fingernails waves me over. It's Diana, a longtime family friend. She's already talking when I approach.

"Get in, hon."

I do. We begin to move as I'm closing the door behind me. The car zips along a road I can't see. I crack the window and let in a dusty breeze while she continues to chatter. The dust burns my eyes.

"Well, I decided if I am going to raise my child properly, I'd better become one too. It was a shock of course when I found my youngest son with these" I keep rubbing my eyes, and as the dust clears, she smiles, revealing extended razor fangs and points at them. "But you understand all about it I'm sure. Right, hon?"

I smile back, nodding my head and faking that I understand anything she's said. Radio static drowns out her words. Odd symbols blink on the dashboard and distract me.

The car flies precariously around tree-lined mountain curves, and I'm relieved when we pull into a town checkered with lit windows. We stopped beneath a streetlamp at the top of a familiar ravine.

"Here you go," Diana says.

I fumble with the metal door handle. I need to get out. Without effort, it swings open and allows me to exit. The car smears away, dissolving with Diana's whispers.

I've been here recently. I look down to the bottom of the ravine but up the mountain on the other side is pulling at me. I must get there. Rocks and dogs follow along with me as I slide down on my ass. I cross a dry creek, and my feet barely touch when I charge up the other side. Gravity pulls at my cheeks, skin hugs my skull, and two sharp teeth push out of my gums. I speed up. Lightly grabbing and flicking myself upwards along the slope. The need to get there grows stronger. Others join me, and we fly through the showering dirt, running to the top. It's a cool starless night. I try to shake off the crud, but it's in every crevice. We stand as spectators among wisps of clouds. Others sit on the edge and look down at a sports arena. It seems far away, all bright on the inside with fields of giant flowers surrounding. A loud, slurping sound comes from someone sitting below me. I look in horror to see myself drinking at the sliced neck of a dog sagging over my legs. A pile of other drained dogs lay next to me. A woman I knew to be Susan stands up from the audience and walks up close to me as I'm drinking. She pets a dead dog and leans close to my ear. I can see and feel her lips against my lobe. She whispers, "Something stinks about this game, doesn't it?"

The stadium speakers echo up the mountain. The whistle blows, signaling the game to begin.

Trash truck alarm.

The book fell from my chest as I rolled over and found myself fully dressed.

"Good Morning, Ben. Messages from Susan and Dr Mamon are waiting."

In the bathroom, I poured some tooth cleanser into a glass. Orange juice tooth cleanser is much better in the morning than at night. The nano-particles go to work keeping my choppers in perfect order, thousands of minuscule robots all eating the gunk off. Shake the bots into activation mode, swish around your mouth and swallow. Mm, delicious. I remember them telling me as a kid that the bots were in the juice and I wouldn't drink it because I thought I'd be swallowing a million monsters. When forced, chewing on the juice to kill some seemed like a good idea. I wanted as few inside me as possible. Wonder if I'd have liked them more if I knew they help clean the sink before they expire. Tiny helpers, not monsters.

I recited the vampire dream to BUD and thought about reviewing the last half of the archive but decided to put it off a bit longer.

Hot water shower massage in the morning is a necessity for waking up completely. Just drop your boxers and step in.

"BUD, can you show me the letters now, please."

I soaped up as the first message scrolled along the shower tile.

From Susan@rossskycity Subj: Intimate details.
Saturday, October 30th

Dear Ben,

First, I must apologize for taking this long to reply to your letter.

Where do I start? I'll start at the top of your letter and work my way down. It's somewhat strange because, well, you'll see. Let us delve into a deep emotional abyss.

Intimate details:
What no one knows: (and I don't believe I'm telling you this.) Last month I was raped. At least I think of it as rape. I'm happy you're not reviewing my archive because it'd be a horror to watch. I constantly worry that a friend or family member will be checking up on me and see what happened. I suppose I'll now worry they'll be reading my correspondence and see this.

I hadn't felt like talking with anyone about the incident and haven't until I just found and re-read your response to my first book-talk message. Your response must've arrived right after my terrible event. Here I am, ready to expose all. It wasn't this shameful, horrific incident really. Well, that's probably because it's somewhat repressed. It was date rape. First and last time I EVER go out with a guy I meet at a club. I hate him. I hate myself. Okay, I have all these feelings going here, and they're not sorted yet. It wasn't like you'd think. I said no. He didn't listen. I do have a lot of anger, though. I made a feeble attempt to go to counseling, but that didn't work out. I've thought about pressing charges, because I don't think he should be allowed to do it again, but I know even with the archive it'd be hard to prove. I guess I'm just a coward because this is the easy way out, writing to you and not seeking real help. That's so pathetic, but it's the truth.

I'm not good at expressing my feelings.

You will probably know more about me than anyone else, and yet ironically, you won't know me at all. The world is a strange place.

Question:

What is your take on women? After your breakup with your ex-fiancée, do you think all women should be monitored closely? I'm guessing she cheated on you?

Another Question:

What happened in the car accident you had? I'd like details if you want to share.

Archive/Net people Question:

A friend of mine said that she feels people who spend their lives reviewing archives and living virtually on the Net are either lonely or have problems. I don't have much experience with virtual strangers. You're the only person I write to in this way. With everyone else, I use more immediate V.R.cHats, or obviously, in person. I don't know. What do you think?

Archive Question:

You said you don't like the Archives. Why is that?

Relationship Question:

I can relate to the relationship you had with your X. I had a four-year relationship with a guy I met at college. We were married briefly. He gave me a ring, and we were going to buy a house. We never lived together, though. I was supposed to move to Minnesota, but I didn't. I was upset, so I said I wouldn't move there, and we ended up divorcing. I don't want to be controlled. He was afraid to move to the Skycity. The city had only been aloft for about two years then, and people still thought it'd come crashing to the ground. Uninformed fools. Now it seems every guy I meet lives in another state.

Drug use comment:

I've never done any. Some of those new Other World pills tempt me, but it would have to be with the right person. On the outside people think I'm this conservative person. Appearances deceive.

Well, I've cried you a river I just hope you're an ocean.

-Susan

I hate that corny kind of letter ending phrase. Something does stink. I wait a month for a response from her, and this is what I get? How do you begin with date rape and end with a cute letter phrase?

"Response to Susan at Rossskycity. Subject is 'Soap on my Ankles'"
The words scrolled across the screen as water speckled the tile and warped some of the text.
"Susan, I'm not sure what to say to you. Here's my dilemma: I feel like I've heard this one before. Girl wants intimacy with new person she's met. She's heard a million times by the age of twenty in every tabloid form stories of mental abuse or date rape and uses such things to gain sympathy from a new person. I don't know if you're reacting to my letter and the way I wrote of telling intimate details or if you just want to get my attention. Sorry, but what you've written makes me wonder if you've watched my accident archive, breaking our agreement and I suppose I'm having a hard time believing anyone who's been raped would talk about it in a second letter without knowing the other person very well."
I stopped and re-read her letter.

"I guess we'll talk books next time. Send that with my signature, BUD."

I finished rinsing the shampoo and toweled off.

"Next letter." As I combed my hair, a message showed in the mirror.

From: Mamon@sc Subj: Your visit today?

Ben:

Two things. One, please consider attending my upcoming lecture in New York. I think the recent Eeden Monk discoveries would be of interest. Two, I wanted to remind you to bring your bag-of-wits with you when you come to help this afternoon. The Center has been a hotbed of upheaval and in need of some of your incredibly appreciated fine-tuning. Good news, I've been in communication with a team at Lazaras about further research on separation of your brothers. Will share details soon. As always, I am looking forward to seeing you all.

Mamon

A flush of pride filled me. Someone that famous writing me like I'm important, it felt great. I briefly wondered what the Eeden monks lecture would be about, highlighted the "my upcoming lecture" and "ADDED to your calendar reminders" briefly glowed above it.

The kitchen was a slop bucket again. Ed and Francis had been trying to make lunch for themselves. They'd replicated something that looked like noodles and tomato sauce and had both strewn across surfaces and plates around the kitchen. I typed in spaghetti with sauce on the replicator console and pulled out a plate fixed the way we usually eat it. "How about we eat this and save ourselves some time? We're going to the Center today remember?"

"Oh, yeah," they said.

They took a seat on the boulder and ate the warm sauce-covered pasta with their hands. Reminded me of the mess that the "book conversation" had turned into with Susan. I briefly questioned why I didn't mention her appearance in my vampire dream. It wasn't a romantic appearance, so why not tell her? She was warning me, right? Something stinks about this game, doesn't it?

⋮NINE⋮

Gigantic oak trees lined the driveway leading to the Center. The twins started giggling with excitement as we moved through the leafy tunnel of orange and yellow. Francis played suckerfish with the window. I can't get him to leave windows alone.

"Will you quit licking the window, Francis?"

Suction POP! Drool slithered down the glass where his mouth was.

"We're goin' to see the saints aren't we, Ben?"

"Yes, Francis, we're there now."

"Aaaacooorns," shouted Ed, pointing at the sunroof after one pelted it.

The building, a combination of church windows and science museum curves, had three light green vans parked at the entrance. I needed to get a full tour of it one day. Several people in matching green and white outfits pulled large boxes from the van. Each box had a flower petal cross and "FRAGILE" in red letters.

The twins, in their green pajama glory, ran, caught up to and passed the carton-carrying men. They stopped on the white marble steps at the front door, waving their arms to welcome, as if they owned the place.

The men looked to me for advice, and I shouted, "Don't make any sudden moves, and they won't bite."

Without expression, they turned and tried to walk past the twins. A man with thick bushy eyebrows got into one of those dances with them where you're trying to get by someone, but you each keep choosing the same path. The twins decided to go straight ahead, knocking him on his ass. His box and some of its contents came spilling out onto the ground.

"Hey, sorry about that. They get confused sometimes." I rushed to help him up as Ed and Francis stood there with embarrassed looks on their faces. Bushy Brows, ignoring me, quickly began to shuffle bags of shimmering blue powder back into the box. One of the last bag's corners must've ripped as Bushy lifted it to the box. The blue powder spilled on one of his hands. Immediately his skin began to expand as if boiling water. Small little popping noises sounded, and flesh-colored leaves came poking through fingertips. I stumbled back. It made me feel like I did when I was thirteen in gym class. This kid, Billy Haynes, wrestled Ted Buckingham. Ted rolled over and snapped Billy's arm, causing the bone to rip out of the skin, and we all stared with fright. Flesh leaves sprouting from fingers were worse. Bushy Brows held his arm branch to his eyes and began a tortured cat howl. Ed and Francis turned to hold me tightly, and I hugged them back.

"Don't worry guys, don't worry, it's just a game. No big deal."

Mamon suddenly emerged from the front door. He never greeted us before. Actually, I'd never seen him outside. His white cone-capped head and oddly regal look were quite astonishing to see.

"Take him and get that cleaned up."

The other two men stood still, not responding to Mamon's command, and watched the leafy arm.

"Now!" Mamon's voice knifed all ears in range and startled me.

They quickly put their boxes back in the van and carried Bushy Brow away. Mamon's narrowed eyes followed the men into the building, and then they widened along with his welcoming smile.

"Hello there, gentlemen. You're a little early, aren't you? No matter, don't worry about this. They have a special cream for that. I'm happy you could make it." He's an ice king in his white lab coat and witnessing his shifting personality up close like this made me feel uneasy. He always wore the odd white turban looking thing on his head. It's wrapped to look smooth and pointed with no noticeable wrinkles or folds. If he were from the Middle East, I might not question it, but he has no accent, and his coloring would suggest more of a Nordic descent.

He spoke about a need for redesigning the packaging, casually, as if incidents like that happened all the time, but Ed and Francis still clung to me.

"The twins were excited, so we came a little early." I tried to cover up my unease. "If they've caused too much trouble, we could come back later."

"No, no, it's fine, come right in. Come on now, boys. Truly, it's okay."

Still clinging close to me, the twins and I walked into the anteroom with its bright silver door inscribed with the Center's logo - a sun design with vein-like rays wandering from its center. Throughout the building, interior glass walls housed light blue crystal that is carved with tunnels like giant ant farms. They're home to dark metallic beetles. An occasional green blotch showed where you could watch the beetles' swarm. The building's low lighting helped enhance the blue glow the tunnels emit.

"Is that the same blue stuff he got on his hand?" I asked, pointing at the walls. Francis and Ed slipped from my side to get a closer look.

"Yes. Perceptive of you, Ben. The engineers here tried various methods to gather and process the algae, but nothing worked to create high-quality extract like the beetles." We walked closer to the wall. "The small size of the Lamprima adolphinae doesn't give you the right impression of the skill they have. They digest the arctic algae, that crystal you see them tunneling in." He outlined a path on the wall. "The excrement they generate is a product we use for things like a kind of fecal transplant to help the microbiomes of the saints. It keeps them extra healthy."

"I thought it just an attractive interior design idea," I said.

"Stop me if I've explained this before, but you're right, part of the original intent was to add to the splendor of our workplace. With the main structures of the Saint complex constructed of living plant matter, we felt compelled to bring other forms into the design that showed more of the gears in our company's engine. I'm sure the architects could have obscured the living quarters, but look at what we'd be hiding," Mamon said. He swept his arm around the room in a grand gesture and stopped where the twins now stood, close to one of the shimmering green spots. Francis's mouth stuck to the glass wall as Ed tapped. "Come here buggybuggybuggy," Ed said repeatedly. His tapping caused the smart surface of the walls to spit out information screens in consecutive waves.

"Francis, what'd I tell you last time we were here? Now someone is going to have to clean up your slop, and Ed quit tapping on the glass. You're bothering the beetles."

Drool spilled down the wall. "I like the greener parts."

"Don't worry about it. The boys are always welcome to explore. Francis, you're a smart boy, those are the most important parts of the beetle's housing. Those aqua-colored areas are the places they have gone to the bathroom." Mamon tapped the wall surface, and the information screen surrounding the aqua section disappeared.

Francis started wiping his tongue on his sleeve. "I don't like that."

"Don't fret, Francis, you can't get to the excrement through the glass wall," Mamon said.

Francis continued to wipe his tongue until I put my hand on his arm. I looked up at the edges of where the walls disappeared into the ceiling. "How do they remove the crystal? I don't see any way in," I said.

"Most of the wall housing can be extracted for processing. There are also special passages behind some of the permanent walls. It's not visible from this side. Why don't you take a seat in the waiting room and I'll see if I can arrange refreshments?"

I had the boys sit on the couch with me. As we sat down, scientists in white lab coats walked toward us, holding a glass jar. They were quite mesmerized by the contents. As they came closer, I saw inside sat a beetle on some glowing yellow substance. The few short phrases I overheard sounded like an Asian dialect. They stopped across the coffee table directly in front of us and continued their conversation.

"Hi there, looks like something interesting. What's in the jar?" I said, putting on my best authority voice, hoping to get their attention before the twins startled them.

No reply.

"Hi," I said louder.

The shortest labcoat tapped and the beetle crawled toward the tap point. They snickered with odd helium laughter.

"Do you speak English?" I asked thinking it likely they wore translators but were just ignoring me.

No reply. They tapped some more, and the beetle banged its head against the glass. They laughed again. Francis and Ed got up and went over to them.

"No tapping on the glass," Ed said as he snatched the jar, snapping the giggling scientists out of their trance. Ed hid it between his and Francis's body under the flesh bridge.

They started sternly speaking, trying to get at the jar while the twins spun around, making it impossible to reach.

"Uki naki buki wan wan a buki," Francis said, mimicking them in a fake angry voice and walked quickly away.

"Give them back the jar, guys," I said.

Around the table the parade began, six and a half foot twins in green pajamas with jar followed by the three five-foot white-coated jabbering scientists. You could see the scientists worried about the jar's safety, holding their hands toward the twins as they shuffled after. I got up and stopped them.

"Give it back now."

They unhappily complied.

"But they were poking at the glass," Francis said.

Ed scowled at them as the scientists moved swiftly out of the room with the jar.

"Sit back down, guys. Come on, Dr Mamon will be back with cookies in a minute."

As I said it, the door opened, and with long stern strides walked Mamon, a silver tray in hand.

"Here you go, treats for everyone."

He carried a tray of white powdered patties that looked lumpy and unappetizing. I took one, thanked Mamon, and found it cold to the touch. They didn't really look like food.

"They are fungus ice cream sandwiches," Mamon said as the twins suspiciously eyed the patties.

"You said he'd bring cookies." Francis took a bite, letting it fall out of his mouth. "This tastes bad."

Ed put his gently back on the tray.

"That's not polite. Thank Dr Mamon for bringing you a treat." I took a big bite of the cardboard with maybe a light maple syrup flavored ice cream sandwich and forced a smile to show how I liked it.

"Thaaanks, Dr Mamon," they said.

"I am sorry, boys. I was excited to learn about edible fungus and how it works together with the forest floors all around the world. My chef designed these for me after I spoke about the ways trees give fungus sugars. I like to think of these as desserts sweetened with trees. But I can see that probably does not satisfy, and I will get you something else while Ben is painting, okay?" Mamon turned to me and lost the smile he'd planted on his face for the twins. "I have been studying some recently gathered statistics. It looks as if there is a definite trend towards negative internal transformations with the saints. I need you to focus your energies on their comfort levels. Positive visions and all that. I know it has always been my request, but if the trends are correct, it appears more necessary than ever. We cannot have our saints going bad. I know you will not let me down. I have queued up two saints for you. Also, it is time for me to send my report to the Lazaras scientists. They have asked for more information. I thought I would jot some perfunctory notes about how the twins seem and then allow them to play while I ready my other tests. No time to discuss the separation research with you right now I'm afraid but do not worry, it is all in the works."

Going bad? That seemed an odd description for people and not fruit, but I was excited by his help with ending Lazaras's relationship with the twins and ignored my discomfort with his word choice.

"Thanks for all of this. I can't tell you how much we appreciate it. Hey, I'm not sure I have it in me for both paintings today. Would you mind if I returned to do the second tomorrow?"

"You may come every day of the week if you would like. Any help you can offer is greatly appreciated." Mamon lightly grasped Ed's shoulder and guided them forward. "Shall we start the games and find some treats you are sure to like, boys? Ben, you know the way to the saints' chambers."

I pointed in the direction I'd gone many times before.

"Will you need anything for your work?"

"No, thanks, all I need is right here." I patted the bag hanging from my shoulder.

"Come along then, boys."

"Be good. I'll see you in a little while," I said.

"No tapping!" Ed said with authority.

"No lickin' the wall!" Francis shouted at Mamon.

"That is right, my boys," Mamon said, putting his hand on Ed's shoulder again as the doors closed behind them.

⚎TEN⚎

The service manager glittered at the desk where I picked up the saint data packets. Sitting mostly naked in an oversized bright white long-haired chair with her feet propped up was Martina. I loved her Spanish accented voice nearly as much as the glowing makeup she used to emphasize her nipples and genitals.

"Hello, Martina," I said, hearing Lenny's voice in my head, urging me to get to know her.

She used her little finger to lower her screen. She glared at me with a don't waste my time air.

"I'd like records of work done since my last visit as well as the names of the saints I've been assigned to for today, please."

Her long nails tapped for information until she paused to let the screen gel harden so she could peel it from the desk and hand it to me. She didn't even bother to speak and returned to reading again. So rude, so sexy, she'd never go for me. I thanked her anyway and left.

The long corridor leading to the saints' chambers gave the impression of entering some Mediterranean cathedral - bright, soothing aqua light glowed from the beetle-housing walls. The hallway ceiling looked like a long flower petal made of red, pink, orange, and yellow stained glass. It was a petal that connected to the full flower of the ceiling in the main room. Upon entering the saints' chambers from the walkway, you could view the entire mammoth flower ceiling and the field of beds on the floor below. Blue glass escalators with dark vine railings led down like stadium walkways about every hundred feet around the room.

I felt tiny when standing in this aerial view, dwarfed by the immense bright room. Each time I entered, I got the same giddy feeling. The rows of beds and glass divider-walls were in concentric rings. Thousands of people in the beds surrounded the central glass vine column that grew to the ceiling.

Mamon told me an article published a year before he contacted me was how he found me and was surprised to learn that I was the son of his old colleague. ARTnews published a gloss piece about my work with nano brushes, heralding my combining art and psychiatry with the use of transfuse-images through the aid of peptide manipulation. Most people yawned after given that brief explanation, so I was rarely surprised when the media skipped by it and primarily focused on what the images depicted, but it made sense that Mamon would've found it of interest. With the stories of their fighting Dad shared, I was surprised Mamon called me. I'd heard Dad complain many times about how if the boys never happened, he'd be seeing the same successes as Mamon. Dad never came up with something like Informed Light or the replicating tech that Mamon had so a similar success was more fantasy than anything else. Dad just helped develop some of the technology after the fact, but I know he must've made serious contributions with the money he basically retired on.

Laurel was the one who said I should find some volunteer work to refocus on something beyond Sara and my problems. I'd just been sitting around, not doing much of anything except the occasional handyman item at the MAc and letting my painting skills grow stale when Mamon called the day after Laurel made the recommendation. I jumped at the chance he offered. I'd have been crazy not to.

I could see volunteering with my type of short-term offering, but I never quite understood why people signed on to donate their whole lives to the Center. The introduction of Infopil had already shown progress, allowing teachers to expand lesson plans and "deleting ignorance," but the problematic price was the donation of lives by those willing to undergo a lifelong sleep. Mamon and the Eeden monks found a property of REM sleep and its ability to help bind information to a digestible substance for human use. A pill that once ingested acted as memory. Surprisingly, a lot of people wanted to be part of the education revolution in this way. Mamon and his team began examining willing donors and offered qualified participants' families financial care for the life term of the saint. More people volunteered than expected, and soon they had ample supply for mass production.

Deleting ignorance in the world with a drug was the way to a utopia? Every media outlet spoke of it in that way, but even with my being a fan of what Mamon created with Informed Light, I had big doubts. We hate what we fear, we often fear what we don't understand, and stamping out hatred through education is a worthwhile goal, but I didn't believe it'd be possible to effectively disseminate it to the entire world or even a significant percentage. What do I know? Everyone is still onboard and promoting it, and I figure whatever I can do to help make the saints' service more comfortable or even enjoyable deserves my effort.

I needed a moment to get my gear organized after Martina gave me my assignments and always took a seat at the bedside of Joseph Myrton, one of the first saints I helped. I liked visiting with him, checking his progress, plus his space had a comfortable chair to sit in. Joe was one of the first saints to work here. He'd been in service for six years.

A picture of him and his wife rested on his bedside table. It's of them hugging in the middle of a crowd, confetti hovering in the air, a dreamy candid shot. Joe rested on top of the light blue gel bed, looking like he might still contain the joy he expressed in the picture. It could've been his high-on-his-head eyebrows that lent a certain smile quality.

Joe spent many years caring for his wheelchair-bound wife in her fifties. After she passed, he found he still had a need to be needed, but as he put it in his journal "a vacuum of free time opened up, and depression started to fill it." It could've been the parental quality, the way his face reminded me of my grandfather, that stirred up those questions you face when your actions could be considered wrong. He was the first to make me think about the ethical dilemma posed when reading other people's journals or diaries or private correspondence. If they've passed on, I suppose we feel as if we're morally safe, but for me, since the saints are in a drug-induced coma and still alive, something about it felt intrusive, even though they mostly left the journals for just such a purpose. I think especially in our current times of complete transparency, the realm of personal is relegated to either the purely internal or honor-bound realm of private handwritten journals. It could've been his wavering script but probably also that Joe's journals documented how he'd buried grief in travel and fishing. He'd read about becoming a saint, lending his energy and it offered a path to move beyond his loss. Joe wanted his energy put toward the education revolution, but more so toward others struggling, he wanted upbeat memory pills generated from him. I've confirmed they are following his wishes.

On the printed screen Martina handed me, the first of my assignments showed John D. Sellings. I checked the map next to the journal and followed the concentric paths to his bedside. Doctors and nurses speckled the room in their bright green uniforms. John's nurse, a short thick man with a wild mustache, nodded my way, wiped John's forehead and cheeks roughly, and placed his arm back at his side. He could've learned a few things about caring for others from Joe Myrton. The headgear covering the back of the saints' heads looked like a semi-transparent dollop of whipped cream with tubes running from it into the floor. Liquid with the appearance of mercury swirled through the tubes. It always disturbed me a little, as if a blender mixed their brains and the fluid poured out a brain cocktail. The nurse clicked something on the back of the dollop beneath John's head. It didn't seem to be to his liking, so he took it off and clicked it back in place with greater force, making a sound that reminded me of bones cracking. I started unpacking my gear on a rolling tray as the nurse packed his washing supplies in a tub. He looked about to leave but changed his mind and turned to me.

"What's with the weird supplies?" He waved somewhat brusquely at my arrangement. I imagined the large syringe was of most interest.

"Oh, hey. I'm Ben. I'm uh, a painter. Dr Mamon asked me to help. I create injectable paintings to keep the saints happy."

The nurse gave me an odd look, almost angry.

"Injectable paint? Can't be healthy."

"I don't actually use paint, but there is a certain liquid involved. My paintings work with their bodies, a sort of therapy. The images I create act more on a subconscious level. Sort of difficult to explain. If I were to inject one into you, it might surface like a daydream. Depends on the individual really but that's been my experience."

His face remained blank as if he didn't even hear or care what I said. "Okay. Don't leave that stuff behind. We keep these areas clean." Smoothing his mustache, he nodded at John and scuffled away.

He kept looking back at me until he left the area. I tried to ignore him as I finished my material setup and sat down next to John's bed. John's eyes rested low in their sockets, tortured, without eyelashes, and small scars dotted along the outer folds of the lids. He was 62, but from his fit build, I'd bet he'd been some sort of athlete. His right hand had small nubs where a few of the fingers were missing. I tapped opened his journal file, and a picture filled the screen of a much younger John looking stiff, proud, and tough in a military uniform. Other images of him in battle moved along the top. His service to the Center start date was only two months after Joseph. I tapped again feeling excited to get to what John had written.

☰ELEVEN☰

The Journal of John Sellings

I'm dictating to a woman named Martina.

She said she'd write it out for me. I want this handwritten. I want this personal.

I'm to leave this as part of the orders for my proper care, but I'm thinking of it as an admission, and a way for anyone interested to know I'm here for atonement, to do something, some way I can give back for all that I've taken.

I was a soldier for the Soni-Amix Corporation, but before that, I was a child who grew up on a farm in Washington State. Maybe I was always a soldier. I can't recall a time when I didn't think like one or at least there was very little in the way of transition from child to soldier on that settlement, that two-acre property created by Rhiver Scientific Inc. when corporations were dividing the states. What else do I say here? The orders aren't entirely clear beyond telling who I am. Before we began Martina suggested I talk about serving in the Green Wars since that was where I entered service, where I got my start. Let's see. The Green Wars, well, anyone visiting here, my brothers or whoever, should probably already know about Informed Light and how it affected everything after it was unleashed. I wonder how many remember the driverless transportation revolution before that and how it put hundreds of thousands out of work in less than ten years, factor that in and you can see how it pushed the limits of an already unbalanced society with ease when the Archives went live thirty-something years ago. Same air-can cheesedicks who didn't plan for out of work drivers, didn't plan for their bedroom doors to become full of peepholes.

But then the good news was those same corporations who put so many out of work got payback when they found themselves struggling to keep their data hoarding secret once the Informed Light started revealing everything. Really it was the same deal. Nobody thought about what the repercussions might be before they unleashed the light. Maybe they knew its effects would begin to connect everything, every goddamn sun in the universe, but they definitely didn't know how much it'd change things or how quickly. All those heartless corporations were resorting to violence for improved positioning in the marketplace, no hiding, no shame, and people were still buying what they sold. I teamed up with Soni-Amex. They were the winning corp in the early Green. Green with envy over what others owned. Green for the money we all knew the reign of terror was about. Green for the weaponized biotech infection popularized in those early battles. It was not Green in the classic save the planet narrative. The idea was to enforce control, and we did that. This was not a time of civil interactions. Fear over what everyone thought was the death of civilized society, the end of control and privacy, and propelled the world to that blood blistering pointless run for cover. I hold no romance for those early years. No one should. I can only say the years after were better, but not much. I'm purposefully not giving specifics to any of the horrors. They are easily accessible for anyone who enjoys self-torture.

That's probably enough about that or all I'm interested in any way.

I have two brothers. Andy is two years younger, and Matt is a year older.

No Informed Light when we were kids, so not every action was recorded. Run free without your parents knowing exactly what you were doing. Might be the last memories of what I'd consider simpler times. I'm sure my comments on them will trigger some archive alert. Maybe Andy or Matt will think of those days and remember I'm still alive.

Back then, we spent most of our time on movies and gaming. We especially liked war movies. Space wars. World wars. Robot wars. You name it. If it contained fighting or destruction, we watched it. The movies educated us, a way to get better at our games. Andy, Matt and I played combat using the virtual overlays to battle other kids on the farm and in town.

You know, Martina, no one wants this. Not worth going back. Those times were just proper training for my service to Soni-Amix.

They called it terrorism back then, but it was small acts of war. Modern tech too quickly displaced skilled labor, and those obsolete employees had an abundance of time on their hands, but even with the trials of Essential Income strategies, there was no going back. Between the factions of these anger-filled civilian militias and the rivaling companies, it was impossible to know every angle of the battles you were assigned to. We just followed the Soni-Amix management orders. You didn't know if you were benevolently policing their territories as they preached or aiding a special marketing plan as most imagined.

I guess I can just cut to it and tell you about my eyes and fingers. You can see who I am by watching my archives, right? Right.

My last days in service to Soni-Amix had me stationed in South Dakota. Several attacks caused S-A and two other corporations to send in troops to create an MDL, um, military-dominated location. It all had to do with the S-A owned buffer zone and possibly about sanctions that had been placed on Micronesia. I say that because I remember viewing a clip of this boney Asian man wearing a thrift store uniform in a small toe-grit town ironically called Scenic. I'll never forget him holding that rubber octopus over his head. Probably a high paid man in costume from Eastern Corp, who knows, but at first, it seemed like a media stunt.

Would you pull it up, Martina? ... Yes, sure it'd be depressing, but it's easier, and they probably want to know. ... Come on, let's take a break with this, and you describe it then I'll explain. [triple beep]

Okay, the guy shouted "Lidakika Lidakika!" as he was waving the octopus and then beneath the footage is written something like Lidakika is a mythic octopus who helped people cross a sea to Pohnpei - an island in Micronesia. I don't get that. He needed to work on his messaging. What? This crazy guy was looking to help the people settle Scenic with his stuffed octopus? More like settling a debt for something about those Micronesian sanctions. He certainly took himself and all the people there on a ride to a 4-mile wide island of uninhabitable black death. People were surrounding the guy with the octopus. Why that would draw a crowd, I have no idea, but this one short old man squeezed through the crowd. Must've been a speedy old guy because he managed to knock it out of the shouting man's hand. When the octopus hit the ground, it detonated. Four miles of nothing but scorched, blackened earth. There already wasn't much around Scenic except some drab landscape and a lot of cattle, but S-A had ties to that property, and I guess they thought it better to keep the death going. I didn't ask, I just followed orders and went.

We were running muscle around the southern side of Lake Oahe in central South Dakota, north of the detonation site. I'd been sleep deprived, coming from two weeks of combat in Southern Italy and not in the best shape, but this seemed like it'd be cake. After the first strike, whether the octopus really was planned and part of a corporate hit or not, there were more bombings of small cement and sand processing factories. More strikes were predicted. It was probably an attempt to gain control of the main trafficking route for S-A goods. S-A had most of the Northwest and North Central zones. The Eastern Corp tried to take over North Central through competitive business means but could've decided to get more aggressive.

I remember that morning my H-40 hovered along a row of pine trees at an Industrial park. There was a shared parking lot between a corporate complex, an industrial park, and a childcare center. I waited beyond the lot. It was half-filled with company vehicles, and beyond it, children buzzed about a playground.

Earlier in the morning, some delivery trucks tried to gain access through the front gate. An outdated diversionary ploy used by artless tactic directors one finds running these minor offenses. We had all six gates guarded with cloaked H-40s.

I switched to a low spectrum radiation screen and started scanning the area for any p5-particle nano-line that the Eastern Corp. troops were so good at stringing. These lines were often installed along routes of entrance or escape. I thought I discovered a patch of it a little beyond the childcare. I had to try and disinfect the lines. Most nano-line is made of a nearly indestructible chain of titanium atoms that is stretched between two points and can work like a cutting laser. Soni-Amix produced a spray that dissolved the line into dust. To cripple the line, you only had to spray a small segment, and the rest would fall, like cutting a string of pearls. Flying to do this was too dangerous. Better by hand.

I heard an explosion at the industrial plant. People ran about everywhere. I started my scanning equipment on the areas I'd detected the lines. Just as I found their location again, I noticed a group of children running towards them. I pushed myself to top sprint speed, unpacking the disinfectant cartridge as I went. It fumbled about in my hands, but I got the right end up and removed the trigger seal. My finger found the button. I held it out shooting test sprays as I went. One little boy was carrying a ball. It dropped from his hands, and he kicked it forward with his running steps. The ball popped about four meters ahead. I was yelling at them to stop, but all they noticed was a loud man in uniform holding his arms out, which made them fear me more and run harder. I knocked several kids to the ground; hurt I'm sure, but still alive. Three of the taller kids, two boys who could've easily passed as twins of Andy and Matt, were left. I grabbed one boy by the hair with my free hand and started spraying towards the lines with the other. Sickening wet clicking noises reached my ears, as the lines cut through the boy's small bones. Their bodies fell into heaps, like cards scattered on pavement. Their hands! Their little hands. I can't get any of it from my mind, but their severed hands won't leave me alone. A few of my fingers dropped with the boys as the spray, and my reaching hand arrived at the lines at the same time. I disabled it in the milliseconds it took for the rest of my body to pass through.

Green smoke from the building transformed into odd vegetation, broccoli clouds as I looked around for what? For help? There was nothing to do. I'd seen this scene many times, but this time the sky also seemed against me.

I watched the other children run towards the burning building where the warning lights twirled, and a panicked woman waved her arms at them. I sat down next to the slain children and looked at them. Something in me shut down. I'd seen plenty of adults butchered, plenty only a few days before while in Italy, in as many ways as one can imagine, but children... this was something I'd never been as close to experiencing, never like that. Never. I couldn't look away from their bodies.

My hand gushed blood from the severed fingers. I was on autopilot, maybe like I was a robot, but I didn't think about picking up the can, I know that. I grabbed it while looking at the dead kids and my missing fingers and sprayed my eyes 'til the canister shook empty. Everything blurred. The pain in my head so shocking I blacked out. I woke in a hospital in darkness. Calm pleasing darkness.

They asked if I wanted new eyes or surgery to repair the ones I'd mutilated. They could only be brought back to a fifty percent or less working state. It was replacement or nothing. I'd still be legally blind with surgery. I chose the third option, stay blind, no surgery. And then sometime later I heard about the Center, and here I am.

Okay, Martina, that's it. I'm done now.

☰TWELVE☰

Susan's working day never started before noon. She felt no great compulsion to generate as many reviews or articles as others who wrote for the same outlet and could dash them out quickly in any case. Before travel, before parties, even before basic hygiene, it was always the reading she wanted. She was more productive at work until she joined the FLM and they began paying her rent. Skycity was expensive, and she needed to earn enough to stay, but with the help, she could put a more significant dent in her piles of novels instead. For the first couple of months exploring the city's bookstores gave regular reasons to leave her couch, but it became easier to have them delivered. Eventually, she ignored the outside world the same way she ignored what was actually taking place on the checkerboard walls of archives filling her apartment. No longer did she tune into the protests or movements she volunteered for. She'd quit them all for fiction. Susan thought the best books always felt more real than if they actually happened. Sometimes, when she was lucky, she'd come across one that filled her with a particular atomic vitality, energizing every cell, every particle of her body in a way that made her confident the rest of the world could possibly collapse if it didn't read it. She'd go out into the streets, into the crowds and find a place to look down on the planet so she could feel the expanded world and wish them all to read it now. Unfortunately, her hope was fading that this would be one of those books.

She sat forward on the couch, folded an empty container, and placed it over an ansible sci-fi book she was attempting to read. It focused on instantaneous communication from people that moved through time in reverse and had a lot of conversation about food so nearly every time she read it, she'd interrupt the reading to replicate something from the book. The freeze-dried whale-fat chunks didn't quite fulfill her the way it had the protagonist, and she found herself paging back through the book to find other recommendations. Glacé nudibranch was found in the same passage about the whale chunks. She'd loved their name, Glacé nudibranch. Light, slippery and delicious, similar to oysters in the way they slid down your throat, yes, more, please. She retrieved a smaller replicated cup of them and returned to watching Ben's live archive. His seated position next to a saint hadn't changed for the past half hour, so she decided to take another look at a 360-rotating projection of her current body state.

Good, she looked good, sexy even. She licked a bit of the nudibranch glaze from her finger and thought it appeared even sexier as she spun in front of herself. She kept her fingers in her mouth and slowly removed them, wishing he could see it all. How could he not want to join her?

She smoothed the fabric covering her breast, accidentally getting some saliva on her shirt and decided to remove it. Her hair was all mussed. She took a brush and spent a long time watching herself separate the central part in the hair on her chest to make the design looked symmetrical again. The hair stripes she had painted for him lined up perfectly along her chest and shoulders. Although she now wished she'd gotten it in gradients of pink instead of blue, his favorite color, it's highly unlikely he'd ever see. Why did she bother? It was fun to be pampered, and that should be reason enough, but she wished somehow he'd check-in, look at her new designs, and notice what she'd done for him.

Filled with shame, that's how she felt. If you'd told her a few months ago she'd fall for Ben she'd have said you didn't know her at all. Yet here she was playing dress-up for someone who'd never even seen her. He was a painter, but would he be interested in this? His archives didn't reveal whether he liked a specific hairstyle. Yes, he took notice of adornments, but what did he think of hair. The percentages said he'd be compelled, but she couldn't be sure if it would be the same for him looking at it on her.

Susan could hardly believe Ben had been true to his word. The requirement the FLM had placed on her to wait a month before she contacted him again felt like an eternity. She checked daily, figuring he'd quickly lose patience waiting for her to write back and decide it was okay to look at her archives, but he hadn't. What would he think of all her what-if questions? What if he became interested in her? What if they somehow ended up together, in love and both working with the Faux Life Movement? His emotional open wounds could be healed, maybe with her help, but his other traits far outweighed those concerns: smart, talented, trusting even with his history. Stats on them showed a high rate of compatibility from her vantage.

How was she ever going to get away with this?

She swayed her hips back and forth for a little while, raising the cup to an imaginary Ben and placing her other hand between her legs. She looked up at him and thought of his hands exploring her body, of him standing above her. He'd probably love her snack, salty-sweet and truly beautiful as you brought them to your lips. She brought the cup back down and swallowed the last one. All gone. She stood and whirled the projection of herself a little faster, then stopped it with her back facing her. Her ass looked square. She thought of how hair might plump and round it. She'd revisit the salon next week.

The greater cause made it all worthwhile, but still, something felt wrong. Deception could eventually destroy anything real they'd build, especially with his history, but she couldn't back out now.

His rejection would be like thinking about episiotomies. In her mind, she saw the knife head between her legs, could nearly feel it slicing into her. Both words raked at her but especially rejection. Her response to his message would have to be appropriately contemptuous. She'd also have to pay stricter attention to how she phrased things. Stupid of her to start with the date rape. She should have somehow ended the message with it instead of that crying an ocean line, should have gently ushered him toward asking more questions, draw it out of her.

Susan returned to her couch and continued to watch Ben for a few minutes before she tapped the coffee table to retrieve the keyboard and begin her response.

☰THIRTEEN☰

There was very little left of tradition in my method of painting except possibly in the classic view of painting as liquid that is allowed to flow downwards, to flee to whatever form your canvas takes. I use goggles to create the virtual canvas and no need for a bristled brush for mark making. Instead of paint, the liquid I use is the pepsin in my equipment. It breaks down the proteins for peptide creation I combined the images with.

I imagined myself looking like a great orchestra conductor to others – or a kook – waving my hands in the air while I blend all the images I'm seeing through the goggles floating in the air before me. I prefer goggles because I can make the paintings as large as needed without worrying about running out of space. I imported pictures for John from my image wallet and John's journal files from Martina: compelling landscapes of places he'd visited, photos of his brothers, children battling aliens, all that came to mind while re-reading his journal. After a few hours of working the collage, the translation to chemical format didn't take long, but I had to wait a minute for it to calibrate.

At John's side rested a small flesh cube called a caroca that houses his fitness system. Covered in goose-pimpled skin, hairless and warm to the touch, a caroca is a lab-grown organ connected the exterior of the body by a thin umbilical-like cord made of the same material - something an adolescent prodigy biologist might spew out after a mad threesome of bestial chicken love and his revered game controller.

The cube is gross, especially the vestigial-type nubs of flesh that look like they could grow into a finger or toe. However, they accomplish nothing less than miracles. Gene maps and bodyware help the carocas keep the saints in perfect health. In the tutorial on how they work, I was instructed on launching the peptide bound image from it rather than another fleshy region like the buttocks or upper thigh. As I injected, the liquid in the syringe shouted to my bladder the way a running faucet will sometimes. Simultaneously, my ring started the skin tickle, indicating a message waiting. I packed my bag and started hiking to the restrooms.

When I walked in, I noticed a short man in a lab coat facing the mirrors along the far wall, his back turned to me with pants hanging at his ankles. His arm wigwagged in an odd aggressive motion, possibly sexual but I couldn't quite tell and didn't want to stare too long.

I chose the unoccupied urinal furthest from him. His blurred image reflected in the polished steel. I tried to go slow hoping he'd leave, but he was still there when I finished. I stupidly glanced at him in the mirror while washing my hands. He wasn't masturbating. He was petting himself or more like grooming. I felt a little sick when I saw he had tufts of leaves growing down there. Similar leaves to the ones I'd witnessed growing from the moving van man accident but much smaller. By their look, I suppose waxing his broccoli would've been more appropriate.

He caught me looking at him. His face scrunched up and turned towards me, leaving everything exposed but lifting his shirt higher and patted his stomach.

"Too many tacos for lunch," he said with flat humor.

"Uh-huh," I said as I shook the water from my hands and walked to the dryer by the door. I heard him moving toward me but didn't look at him. The door behind me opened and swung shut as he exited the bathroom. My ring finger tickled again. My mail icon glowed. I waved my ring over the journal tablet and "Susan@rossskycity Subj: Lack of Intimacy filled the top then the message started beneath.

Saturday, October 30th

Ben –

I am certainly not fond of starting my days construing messages from uncaring creeps if that's who you really are. I don't want your fucking intimacy. I'm not the one who mentioned intimacy anyway. You are. Do you know the Blake 'A truth that's told with bad intent beats all the lies one can invent'? If not, you should. I share a distressing story with you, and you dismiss it as a fabrication to garner your attention. Maybe you're too scarred from your other female relationships? Maybe you could've simply lied to me and taken a chance on making me feel of value until you knew the truth for sure. I know I said let's leave the Archive out of this and I hope you'll still be able to. What I'm most interested in is discussing books and life. I think if you try to analyze yourself too much like those that watch their archives every day, it's pathetic. Move on. There's better things to do than to harp on some issue. No matter what it is.

You are right. I don't know you. How could you possibly understand anyway? If you don't want to trust me, I don't care. We don't have to talk about personal issues. Obviously, you have a problem with critical analysis of yourself and invoke this upon others. Ever read Spenser's Faerie Queen? Archimago?

Okay, let's forget it and try to move on.

What're your favorite types of seafood? I love candied nudibranch, don't you?

Oh, right, and what are you reading?

That's what you signed up for right? Someone to discuss books with? Fine.

Have you ever heard of the writer Cece Fox? I'm not big into Sci-fi, but my friend Edward loved it, a massive following or something, and gave it to me after a conversation he started up about Tachyon particles. He wanted me to read her seminal book because it's the first to predict what aliens are and their relation to Tachyon particles. Edward said we found all those worlds where light reached, and life existed but none that could communicate on our level, so they don't count or something. I don't know, I felt obligated to read it, but I haven't really been enjoying it. It isn't horrible, I guess. It's called The Wrong Way, and I do think it a shame she didn't live to learn of her great prediction. I suppose light still takes years to go out and come back to Earth to transmit the information, so it's not surprising she didn't learn much about any of the discoveries. Maybe if she did, she wouldn't have dreamed up what she did. I think scientists should try to bind information to Tachyon particles now since Tachyon particles move faster than the speed of light.

Anyway, that's the big joke Edward had to share -- about us being "Tardyons." Re-tardyons, get it? Terrible. Oh, I should explain that Tachyons move faster than light but in reverse time to us, and aliens are reverse time beings. Maybe you know all this with your greater understanding of science matters? Is mine too simplified? Am I making sense? Yes? No? If you're interested or have read anything by her, please let me know.

Sincerely,

- Susan

P.S. I don't know if you'll be writing to me again, even if you don't - Have a happy Halloween.

I'd almost forgotten tomorrow was Halloween. This was a perfect day to remind me of it. Saw a person growing leaves out of his arm, helped a saint who has had a life of war and horror and got flashed by some freak broccoli crotch. It's probably a bad idea to continue the correspondence with Susan, but I punched the reply button.

"Response to Susan at Rossskycity. Subject is, come on now. Body of message begin. Listen, I think I spent a decent amount of time in my last letter explaining why I would wonder if you were lying about the date rape. And you already know of my difficulties with women who deceive. I'm sure you're an honest person, and I'm sorry if I offended you... still, you should understand how it could read from my end.

No, I haven't read Spenser's Faerie Queen, but it sounds like Archimago is not a character you like. Should I be offended? You're right. Let's move on.

What an odd day I've had, talk about stories of aliens.

I'll explain more later."

A push of the send button and off it went. I really did feel bad. The message program faded, and my saint listings emerged again.

Next up, Amelia Figg? With all I'd confronted today, I was happy I'd asked Mamon to finish up tomorrow. I signaled to the boys and Mamon I was on my way to the car and that I'd meet them there. I sat inside, staring at the sky through the roof. I kept thinking of broccoli shaped clouds and felt claustrophobic - a tremendous feeling of wanting out. It was a huge relief when I saw the boys walking my way. Without their distraction, I believe I'd have had one of my panic attacks.

☰FOURTEEN☰

"That is the farm. Why're we near Laurel's farm? I thought we were going home." Ed said as one of her fields came into view.

The pain from the knot in my back grew with each passing second.

"Didn't I tell you this is where we were going?"

"No," Francis said. "You said we were going back to the Center tomorrow. You did not say we were going to Laurel's today."

"Sorry guys, I've been distracted. I need to see Laurel about my back."

"Your voice sounds funny. Yes, this is okay. We stopped here after the Center last time," Ed said.

I hadn't considered it before, but Ed was right. We often stopped at Laurel's after the Center.

Laurel came walking out of the barn as we pulled up. I rolled our windows down.

"Look who's here. I'm so happy to see you boys," she leaned in the window, kissed Francis on the cheek, and tweaked Ed's ear.

"Hey, I wanted the kiss not the pull on my ear."

"Get out here and give me one then."

They quickly exited the car and picked up Laurel between them, taking turns kissing her cheek.

"Who's hungry?" Laurel asked as they put her on the ground.

"I am," they said together.

I slowly got out of the car, trying to find a way to protect my back from worsening the pain as I did.

"You don't look well," Laurel said and touched my arm lightly.

"I've got a knot the size of an orange in my back."

"Boys, go play while I get the dumplings ready and Ben-the-bent here fixed up. I'll ring the bell for you."

Laurel took me directly to her massage table and went to work on my back.

"This is more like a grapefruit. What's got you so wound?"

I spoke to her through the donut hole of the head pillow my face rested in.

"Day hasn't been an easy one."

"No?"

"Started with another monster dream this morning, vampire this time."

"Well, a bad dream didn't cause this. What else did you do today? No, wait. Don't answer yet. Let me finish first."

She hit pressure points and kneaded me until the knot came apart. We moved from the massage room into the kitchen where she prepared tea.

"So, what else?"

"A little trouble with that Susan I mentioned, but also could be the journal I read by one of the saints. None of them has been easy, but this one blinded himself. I mean he ruined his own eyes. There were several disturbing visions at the Center today actually."

"That knot only flares up in relation to stress connected to your accident archive."

"No, it doesn't. I've gotten that knot plenty of times when I'm not thinking about the accident."

"You've gotten knots in your back but not in that location or that size."

"Maybe..." I stretched my arm to see if I could keep my back from seizing again. I could feel the tension returning already.

"Can we watch it now and see how you do over the next couple of weeks. Maybe you'll be worse off, but I'm betting it alleviates more in you than you expect."

"You know... you know... okay." She'd worn me down.

"Excellent. Let's go in here."

She led us into the green room. It all felt tremendously rushed. I wanted to stop her and ask for more time to consider, more time to discuss it, but she'd pulled up the archive to where I'd left my parents and started running along the highway so quickly you'd think she'd planned it.

(BEN TINTHAWIN - NEW YORK STATE / HIGHWAY / ACCIDENT-)

The perspective of the archive was the aerial slightly behind the subject, me. I stumbled ahead to see what I could see and rested on the median for a minute. My frustration looked obvious. I probably wondered how much time I had and where was everybody. Pants and sneakers weren't enough for the cold I guess because I ran back and grabbed a rain-soaked shirt from next to Dad's body, put my arms through and buttoned it only at my waist and neck. Was that the last time I saw him alive? No way to know if he was at that moment. I looked at my parents once more and started running. The view changed in the archive.

A first-person perspective - I ran along the highway, breathing heavily with my hands covering my freezing ears. At the bottom of a slope to my right lights shown through windows. I slid on my ass most of the way down an embankment heading towards a house.

I ran through scrub brush with prickers scratching at my arms and stomach. It must've hurt because I held my arms up to avoid them. I tripped over tree roots and rocks and suddenly splashed through a wide stream. It came up to my knees. I'd forgotten about the stream from the first time I watched this, and it surprised me all over again. I was wet from the rain but not soaked through, as I was when I got out. All the extra water weight in my pants must've been heavy. I climbed up the bank and stopped to catch my breath.

The single-floor ranch style house loomed a few yards ahead at the top of the slope. I pulled myself forward using the tree trunks for balance until I reached a fire barrel at the edge of their backyard. My hands rubbed vigorously in the smoke glowing from the flames below. A security spotlight from the top corner of the house switched on. I hope the warmth made it worthwhile because it must've stunk horribly with all the fish offal and carcasses around the barrel.

A shift again to the aerial view: Two dogs in a chain-link fence yanked their heads up and down until I thought they'd snap off while they barked at me. In a little window, a person peered for a moment and moved to a sliding glass door. The silhouette revealed a short body leaning towards the glass as it looked out from the sallow yellow glow inside. It ran away and returned with another someone about the same size. I got to the edge of the patio, and the door slid open. The spotlight shone directly on me, and I had my arm up, trying to block it. A man shouted, "What're you doin? Those dogs are trained to kill, you know!"

"I'm sorry, there's been a crash." I looked like some kind of lunatic with my soaked and bloodied clothes.

"Don't move. Stay right there. Watch him, Marta," he said then whispered something to Marta and dashed off.

"Mark will be right back, just stay where you are, or I'll set the dogs on you. Mark is coming right back okay," a scared female voice said.

"I'm nod going to hud you. My pahwens are hud on the highway."

"I can't understand whatever it is you're jumble talking, hold on." She looked inside, and Mark returned with something in his hand.

"I bit mah tongue," I said, pointing at my mouth.

"You what? Come closer but put your arms out and move slowly," Mark said.

I put my arms ahead of me as if I was flying over to them.

"You don need thad. I'm not here to hurd you."

"I'll be the judge of that," Mark said.

A light switched flipped, and everything became bright under the porch overhang. Mark waved a knife up at me. Marta's hand moved back from the light switch, and they both looked at me and flinched.

"Ew. What's happened to your face?" Mark's voice changed, and you could tell he no longer considered me a threat. "You look like shit, boy."

Marta bent closer, looked up at my face and down my body, shaking her head. The dark circles of her eyes seemed strained by her pulled-back hair. "He looks awful. My gawd, Mark, look at his eyes, all filled up with blood. Don't let him in my house with those," she said, pointing to my feet and glancing sternly at the mud on the patio and backing away inside the house.

"My name is Ben. We hid some deer on the highway. I need a phone."

"An accident, okay, hold on, come on in son, but take 'em off," Mark said.

He waited as I removed my shoes. We did a little dance of who would go first. He couldn't seem to decide which would be the better option but then had me lead.

The archive shifted to a view from inside. We stood in a kitchen. Dirty pans, coated utensils, and bowls filled with different food remnants covered the counters. The sink overflowed with fish and more knives. I don't know why, but I went over and shut off the running water.

"What're you doing there, son? That's not for you to be doing. Keep your hands at your sides."

"Sorry, the wader was running." The absurdity of the situation hit me again as I listened to my voice. I sounded like a cartoon character. Why didn't I see the danger at this point? Why didn't I force them to call the cops? Any average person would've run to the phone once they heard of an accident.

"That water needs to be," he said, opening a drawer and sweeping some of the knives from the counter into it.

Marta waddled back to the kitchen with a washcloth. They were very short and looked like brother and sister - almost the same height, and plainly stuffed a lot of food in with each meal.

"Here, Mark." She gave him a cloth.

"You might want to wipe your face up some. It looks like a train ran into it."

I took it and wiped around the edges of my mouth.

"Just so you know, polite people use front doors around here," Mark said, pulling on his chin whiskers.

"We hid some deer on the highway... thah way," I said, pointing to the backyard. "My pahwens need help. I need a phone!" I mimed a car crashing and stuck my tongue out in an exaggerated deadman face, and from the flinch, must've caused myself considerable pain.

"I'm sorry, Ben. It's Ben, right? Come in, come in. Mark put that knife down, can't you see he's been hurt. Do you want some juice? We have orange and prune."

She looked at Mark and gave him an odd wink. Mark didn't put the knife down.

"Yeah, uh, you want some juice then," Mark said, catching on to whatever Marta was winking about.

"I'm not thirsdy. Could you jus call the police for me?"

"Why don't you come in and catch your breath first, hon? We can call them in a minute."

They led me into the next room where two Downs Syndrome young men sat in folding chairs at a card table. The musty gray curtains of the windows were drawn and hung on bent rods. On folding tables around the room lay fish in various stages of being stuffed and mounted.

The far wall had a small fireplace barely lit and above it hung about a dozen mounted examples of finished specimens. The men sitting at the table looked at me, looked at a filthy dipping section of a couch, and quickly turned their faces to the tabletop.

"This here's Freddie, and that's Ernie. They're a little shy, but they bring in their share of the rent with their expertise as you can see," Marta said, putting her hand on Freddie's shoulder and pointing around the room.

Freddie looked up at her and pleaded, "It wasn't me who did it. Suzy did."

"Who did what?" Mark raised his voice in a threatening tone.

"Who did that," Freddie mumbled. He looked at the dipping section of the couch but gestured my way.

"No, Freddie, Ben here's come to us for help. He's been in an accident."

"He hasn't been with Suzy?" Ernie asked, looking at me now, his mouth forming a wide smile.

"No, he hasn't and shut your trap. You were told he's been in an accident now haven't you." Mark marched over and slapped the back of Ernie's head hard.

"I'm sorry. They usually are much more polite, must be your face. You want me to get you anything else for it?" Marta offered. "Here, why don't we get you out of that wet stuff? Mark, go get him some of yours." Marta pulled the soaked shirt up over my head and took my pants down. I looked like I was three, and my mother was undressing me.

"Can I have the phone now plee...I need to sid down. I feel... dizzy."

"Clear him some room on the couch. Have a seat, Ben. We'll get you fixed up," Mark said.

Marta moved ahead of me and pulled some boxes to the floor, making a small space away from the broken side.

"I thing I jus need a liddle rest. Is there a phone? A phone!" As I went to sit down, my legs looked like old parsnips, rotten and wobbly. I dropped back against the couch. The boxes toppled to the ground, and I ended up on all fours near Ernie's legs. I stayed there, blinking and looking dazed. Ernie patted my head. Each time he touched me, it looked as if I'd fall over.

"Jesus, Em, you think you could've found a little more room for him. Come on, Ben. Let's get you to your feet. Don't worry none about that mess," Mark said.

I tried to stand, and my legs looked worse. I fell into Mark's arms. Marta came over and grabbed my arm and wrapped her other around my waist, hiking up my boxers. The two of them were so short I could have rested my elbows on their shoulders.

"Are you okay? Can you hear me? I think he's dying, Mark. Hon, we'll call the police in a minute, okay?"

Mark grabbed my chin, and my eyes were still cracked open. "Look, he's fine. He's just a little mussed. Let's put him in the back room."

"Can't you walk, Ben?" Marta asked.

"Just clear out, Em. I'll carry him."

Mark dragged me into the kitchen and down a low-lit hallway past an open bathroom with fluorescent light pouring out. He leaned me against a door as he took out a key. When he finished unlocking it, he pulled me against his chest and pushed the door open.

"Em, this is your deal, you take care of matters when it's finished."

"He won't even know. Suzy needs someone to be around, the boys won't go to her, and lord knows you've stopped," Marta said.

There was a little light coming in from the spotlight in the backyard.

"You know why I stopped. Quit acting like it wasn't your idea."

Then Mark lifted me a little and shoved me in. I hit the wooden floor and must've passed out because I didn't move for a while. They locked the door.

The dogs barking in the backyard must've helped wake me. I rolled to my side and looked in bad shape. The leaves that circled the window created a shaggy square of light on the floor a short distance from where I lay. The only thing besides the cracks in the boards that the lighted squares shone upon were clumps of foul looking dirt, possibly more fish offal. Something near the square moved, and once again, and when she slumped into view, her massive naked form was revealed. Light lit the long shaggy hair that ran over her shoulders, bare and flabby.

"Marda, please help me."

She grunted or growled a kind of pained anger.

"Marda, is thad you? Mark? My eyes aren working right."

She lumbered towards me, sluggish and animal-like. The boots she wore shuffle-clumped along the floor. They had to have fed her buckets of food. She grunted again, and I tried to lift myself with my arms, but I must've been too weak. Her unwholesome face leaned close to mine, and she smelled my neck.

"Hey, get away," I weakly protested.

She pulled me by my ankles and dragged me into the light. Her cheeks, swollen with fat, dripped down towards me like those of a bulldog with a disturbed longing in her recessed eyes and wilting brow. Her rolls folded and climbed all the way to her chin. My arm bent out to the side, and she pulled it closer to my body. She must've had a horrible odor or something in the room did because I started holding my nostrils shut. I pushed her with a small ineffective push. She appeared more handicapped than the two at the table. I went to shove her again, and my hand mashed into her chest. She grabbed my elbow and moved over to sit beside my head. It looked like she might sit on my neck until she settled into place, her hips pressed closely, smothering my ear. She pushed hard on my shoulder, crushing me against one of the piles on the floor. The sausage fingers from her hand passed over my eyes to touch some of my hair.

I lay watching her, looking weak, miserable, and trapped. She wiped my face and touched my swollen lips. She continued to groan. I looked as if I could have been falling asleep because I closed my eyes and started breathing slow and heavy. I was feigning sleep. She pet my hair for a few moments more then moved down by my legs, and her hand landed on my navel. She smoothed my stomach hair, and her hand went to my crotch. I snored a little, just a little but it sounded forced, and you could see me peeking up at her. She leaned over and rested her head on my leg. She moved her hand up to my stomach again, and it seemed like maybe all she was doing was getting comfortable for sleep, but instead, she grabbed my boxer elastic and began to work them down. I moved my arms into place, and when she pulled my boxers again, I pushed myself up. She shifted up on her knees.

"Don do thad okay? Plea jus leave me alone."

She gave me a hard shove, and my arms caved. I must've blacked out because I didn't move while she capitalized on my wasted state. Black-skin fish tank snails have small red mouths on the bottom of their bodies that you can watch as they move on the side of a tank. Little pointy teeth scoop out of their fleshy red mouth and back in, scraping at the algae on the glass for food. It's a sickening vision that has always stuck with me and observing Suzy rock on top of me with her mouth wide open reminded me of it.

Laurel gripped my hand as we watched the scene. I was lucky I wasn't awake for what took place. An awkward torturous primal act of desire. When I woke, my boxers lay at my ankles. She was still on top of me. It looked like she'd crush me beneath her. I reached down to her leg and pinched it, making her scream and back off me. Her knee hit my stomach as she stood up. I was free of her for a few moments and looked incredibly relieved.

There were many ways to worsen captivity. The stolen sense of freedom after owning it for a moment was one. Low in her chest, the howl began, and upon release, I thought the increased volume could only bring help or curiosity from Marta and Mark, but before anyone arrived, the first stomp hit the side of my face. It ripped some skin, and my cheek and ear looked barely attached. Her boot slammed my jaw, and a final full-on boot beside my eye was the last before she left me alone and trudged back to a mattress in the corner.

We sat there for a moment after the prompt for the next part of the archive came up.

"Do you want to watch any of the items about how Mark and Marta took you back to the highway or your trip to the hospital with your folks?"

"No, that's enough."

We sat there, not saying anything until Laurel hugged me gently and let me go.

"It's all the same as when we watched it before. Right up to when I went running for help is still up here," I said, tapping my head. "But all those events afterward aren't there. I see them when I watch them. I rationalize it's me in the archive, that the events in it are real, but it's not up here," I said, pointing to my head.

"That's why reviewing is important, I know it's terribly difficult to watch, but there is a reason. Please promise me you will again. Watch it until you understand, until something clicks. But, let's try thinking of it all differently." She shuffled the teacups onto a tray and tidied up a bit as she spoke. "I want you to think about Sara leaving you, and all that you struggled with from your heartbreak. Then think about what your mind must've been dealing with having gone through a frightening crash and seeing your parents in that state. You know, there must be many beings out there suffering in the dark. Hungry and unfulfilled. We should find pity for a poor creature like Suzy. As a symbolic figure in your history, especially for the events in your life that preceded her entry onto your stage, she's perfect. She is each suffering individual who seeks to transcend existence, but when they couldn't, became twisted instead. She is that bloated lump of love, modified by pain, trapped after it has been rejected. She is a horrific vision for you, I'm sure, and you might be feeling the responses someone who has experienced that would. Fear, anger, confusion, shame. They're all perfectly understandable. Since I first watched it with you, and every time we've come together, I've hoped something in you would recognize her symbolism for yourself."

"You're right. I'm angry when I watch it. I'm angry at that beast and those people for forcing her on me, but I'm only angry because I see it there, not because I feel it here. Feels more like watching a movie where you get upset at the characters. I'm sure I should just accept it, but my only true emotions are for my Mom's well-being and the deep sadness I feel over my Father's death. It's no different for me this time. Okay, yes, I get the symbolism you suggest, and it works. Bloated lost love. Sara...I clearly recall you saying sometimes we have to do something unforgivable to move beyond where we are. That was what Sara was up to with cheating. She needed to move beyond me for whatever reasons. But come on, look, if it's not here," I tapped hard on my forehead. "If I keep looking around for something that doesn't exist, and I watch this, and nothing feels right, what can I do about that? And even if I can forgive people, which I have, I've forgiven Sara. I still say fuck her. It's right. It's true. Eventually, the anger may not be here," I tapped my head again, "and it feels much less today than it did a few months ago."

Laurel looked at the floor, considering my words.

"That sounds like progress anyway and a good place to end for today, I think. Maybe you should spend some time alone with it while I get dinner ready for you and the boys. Can I get you anything? More tea?"

"I'm fine, thanks."

"How about the boys stay with me for the week? I've got a lot of lifting they could help with, and I'd enjoy the company."

"That'd be great, but Mamon's been helping me with that research about separating them, and we're heading back to the center."

Laurel gave me a strange glance, and then added, "I'll leave my offer open if you want to drop them by someday soon." She left the room while I looked out at the empty fields trying to focus on all she said.

I tried to shake the lingering anger at my inability to recall. All there, documented in the archive, but nothing to pull out, nothing to find in me. It leaves me feeling numb, and as if I've wasted more time on it. My focus drifted to the lines of harvested crops, to the lines of the horizon, to the sky.

⊟FIFTEEN⊟

I think confused by my disappointment was the correct way to describe how I felt about not hearing back from Susan. I figured I'd at least get a response before bed and further surprised I'd found nothing in my message system this morning or on my way to the center.

Thoughts about dating monopolized me and then morphed into a ridiculous chant as I made my way to my next assignment. A man has his needs, a man has his need, and it kept undulating in my head until I reach Amelia. Her gothic beauty startled me. Mainly because her skin was a striking white marble, making her looks a bit corpsy but still incredibly compelling. As if that weren't enough, her right arm and both legs were missing, and yet I felt something extra for her beyond the others I'd worked with and only from my first glance.

Amelia couldn't have been any older than twenty-five or twenty-six. I studied the variations of pastel colors of her skin, the grace of her sweeping wing eyelashes and the delicate slope of her eyebrows. Long straight black hair stuck out of the headgear. On her neck rested a brown mole that two tiny hairs grew from. It was the only beauty mark showing on her body. Smooth pink scars marked the ends of her stumps along the embedded outlets for prosthetic nerve connectors. I knew these journals were mainly for friends and family that visited the center. I know occasionally they also used them for marketing to attract new recruits, so it was odd that instead of a photo of her, the first image in her journal was a dried bunch of clover with a little white flower that had been flattened and scanned.

The Journal of Amelia Figg

Instead of plugging in my legs to walk on my own, I had my caretaker Alberta bring me to this field today. Being dependent upon automated prosthetics is trying at times, but, I suppose in many ways, it's a blessing. Don't get me wrong, you're free of a wheelchair, but also reliant upon technology and there's little more embarrassing or frustrating than being in the middle of a crowded city crosswalk, thinking move hand, bend leg and the connectors are failing, making you a human roadblock. But forgive me, telling you this is not exactly what I'm here to do.

Without the generosity of people like Alberta, I'm not sure where I'd be. I don't have much to say to her, though beyond the great appreciation and love I've expressed on the trip here. She knows all of my life, and what makes me happy and entirely agrees with my decision to work for the Saint Center. I hope this allows her to live a life with more focus on herself. The proceeds from my time with the center are to go to her, and she deserves them. I have no family left. She has given so much. She's helped me travel to places I'd never have gone. Not that I've done much traveling and I guess compared to some I've traveled very little in the physical world, but Alberta made what I have possible. I wanted to do more, but I shouldn't complain.

I've seen many unbelievable places even if they don't exist out here. They are probably why I've spent the hours I have in my v-enviro; no worries about my body there. I know, you all think of MoPo as the big pop v-world many have written about, but it should be clear it's an FLM masterpiece or at least I think so. I'm a believer. No one has proven the FLM created it, but we all believe they do. I'd live there if it were possible, but then I wouldn't really be helping anyone, and I guess that's what I'm after. Too many have given of themselves to my care, and now I need to pay it back.

It's very lush and green here. The air is warm, as is the ground I sit upon. I left my chair so that I could feel the ground, the lovely tickling blades of grass. Over a little way from me is a marvelous old gnarled tree. I'm not sure what kind it is, but it's a tree-like I imagine Mamon spoke of in his speech, which led me to join the Center. I've no one to write this required journal for, beyond possibly Alberta and as I said she already knows all about me so instead I'll tack on the transcription to the end of this. I've just re-read it and can't imagine anyone not being inspired by him. Reading that would be best for a full view of why I'm committing my life to the sleeping world of the Saint Center. It's much better than struggling on my own. It allows me to help and possibly explore another world, but mostly, I just want to help.

Take special note of the part of Mamon's speech about the useless tree. None of our lives is without meaning. We all have something to contribute. – Amelia

⹂SIXTEEN⹂

Doctor Luc R Mamon
Annenberg Center, University of Pennsylvania
"A Primer: The Eeden Monks' Story"

Dr Luc Mamon: Welcome everyone.

The crowd roars. Several women shout, "We love you!"

One woman shouts from the front row, "Will you marry me?"

DLM: Will I marry you? No no, I'm only sixty-six. Now if everyone would settle down, I'd like to get right to what I've prepared. I'm pleased to have such a tremendous turnout. Thank you for coming. Before I get started, I'd like to see a show of hands. How many of you are believers in a specific God? [A few moments pass as most of the audience raises their hands.] More than I would've expected. I'm glad to see such open-mindedness from those of you with faith, or better still I should ask for as much unbiased listening as you can offer. It will benefit you. Let me shower it upon you immediately.

[The auditorium dims as a small spotlight focuses on Mamon. He begins molding something in his hands. An orb of fuzzy light buzzes and expands in his fingers until he throws it at the crowd. It explodes. A glob of electricity flies to audience members hovers at their faces, and finally, transforms into the glowing head of a Neanderthal man. Each person sees something of his or her facial aspects in the face of the vision. Every floating head stares briefly, blinks and disintegrates in flakey dust.]

[The crowd starts to murmur. Mamon raises his hands for quiet and elevates his voice in a commanding fashion. Above Mamon, a bloody man appears at an entrance to a cave. He dumps a beast for other cave inhabitants to view and rests his hands on the wall of the cave with pride and exhaustion. Red marks now decorate the wall. The man stares at the blood prints for a minute and adds a head to what looked like a body with four legs and a tail.]

The first sign is made! The first word that makes it from daydream to waking, the first theophany for man is created by that handprint, that symbol. The gods have been communicating with us directly for our entire human existence. The gods have been communicating with everything for the entire Universe's existence. Does this shock you? I can read on many of your faces that you aren't moved. What am I here to sell you, you're wondering.

As with our ancestors, the questions of what the future holds cannot truly even be asked. We barely have scraped the surface of what we can be and will be. Imagine asking a caveman what he thinks the future will hold or what he'd like in the future, and he might say I want a better club, or fire never to go out. You wouldn't hear him ask for a hologram or easy access to any place light touches. When you want to know the future, you can't ask the question because you can't think of the possibilities, but we've been interacting with those that might help us answer these questions and more. The more is what excites me the most.

The wisdom I've gained through the Eeden monks and by my own culling has brought me to a new understanding of the universe and the way gods interact with it.

The new proof is in!

[Mamon pounds on the podium.]

The gods are alive!

[Behind Mamon many forms and symbols swirl and glow in the dark then fade.]

We've been equipped to understand or decipher the gods' words. Any one of us can directly communicate with them to learn all they share. The questions in your mind might be, or should be, how? How does he know this? And how quickly can I speak with them? Don't you wonder what they have to say?

I'm sure a few of you have read the excerpts from the journals of Eeden Monks and have come here to see what more I can offer, or how you can experience it for yourself. Please be patient. I will address that. For those who don't know of them, the Eeden Monks are men who sequestered themselves to focus on lucid dreaming, to study their recent lucid dreams. I'll get into this more in a moment, but originally before their discovery became the prominent focus, I was more interested in the chemistry, the science that keeps the monks in coma-like REM sleep, mainly because it put them into a perfect state for energy production.

Please forgive me but if you do not know, my research is going into its fifth decade, and if you know anything about my accomplishments, it's probably about how I created our beloved Archive, and how it brought the great egalitarian culture we all enjoy. Without it, the spread of superintelligence could not have been curtailed. You would have A.I. overlords right now. It may seem extreme to acknowledge, and I won't belabor it, but I believe pointing it out is essential.

So why acknowledge it at all? I would like you to have a certain appreciation of the esteem I have garnered so that you will also respect me when I deliver these truths and will listen carefully about what the monks have pointed me toward. I suppose if you do not know about my history, then my telling it won't matter, but later you may decide to research my standing, find a new respect and listen to future speeches.

[Cellular images, genetic code, subatomic forms float glimmering in the air about Mamon's head.]

Early in my career, I started focusing on patterns that occur in many forms of life. From the similarly constructed stories of different world mythologies to the forms repeated and connected in all of nature, I examined and am examining all I confront. It is in the patterns of life that the final keys of the Lexicon will be revealed.

[Images appear above Mamon of veins in leaves that blend into veins in hands that blend into veins of the Earth's rivers.]

When the Monks first contacted me, I was skeptical. They did not talk of the gods as one traditionally hears. Eeden monks are more scientists than priests. They are studying the gods with one goal in mind. Real Truth. For years they have induced dream comas upon themselves, they use lucid dreaming techniques to translate what they at first only guessed but soon knew to be the symbols or words of the gods.

[The crowd starts whispering. A shout from the back of the auditorium triggers waves of a chant that reached a fever pitch, "Sleep is for Sheep! Sleep is for Sheep!" Guards pull the main instigators from the room, and all quiet down as Mamon signals everyone to calm.]

I understand some of your distaste for our work. I too felt as incredulous and angry. I was infuriated when I read of the Monks' conceit. How did they know it was a god they were coming to understand? Mine was a jealous anger. They had found the bridge first.

Here were men offering the vision, the potential for true communion with the gods, beyond any skeptic's doubts. Offering weapons to fight the ignorance, to fight the smothering nihilism - weapons far more powerful than those of the old gods. Rationality should have stamped out old deities long before they had the chance to cause so much death and sorrow in the world.

Religion was born of the senses. Our brains are constructed in such a way that made ideas of God and faith unavoidable. Yes, I'm saying your brain is hardwired for God. Religion continues to exist because of snail-paced evolution. Our minds need Gods to fill in the abstracts. As the great writer and monk François Rabelais said, Nature abhors a vacuum. We comprehend the complexities of life like no other time, but religious ignorance still reigns.

[Grumbling begins throughout the crowd again. A woman walks to the edge of the stage and tosses a book at Mamon's feet. Mamon gathers it, and the woman quickly leaves the auditorium.]

A Bible! No surprise here. [Mamon waves the book in the air.] People don't want to part with their support structures. Well, she did, I guess. [a portion of the audience laughs] I understand why people don't want to give them up, but please, you must listen to me. Changes are coming. Preparation is needed.

[He gently places the book on his podium]

I'd like to address pain and suffering for no life exists without it. God is good. The great master of all is good. This is a basic tenet of any advocate. God is good. Let's look at such a statement. Under the dominion of an omnipotent God, whose goodness is infinite, the Earth has always been and remains drenched with the tears of the miserable, the bewildered, and the lost.

[Ghosted figures of Soldiers begin shooting and killing other soldiers on the opposite ends of the auditorium. Skeletal beggars in rags move through the crowd. Malnourished women surrounded by dying children appear in the air above. Troops of incarcerated people in gray uniforms march behind Mamon's podium. The holographic visions fade.]

How can he consent to let them suffer if he is a benevolent god? If he knows all, why reprove his chosen ones, from whom he has nothing to fear? If his power can't be rattled, why make himself uneasy at the insubstantial conspiracies they would create against him? If God is omnipotent, why not obtain for them at once permanent happiness? No trials of their allegiance, no waiting for the afterworld, for the next life, give them bliss now.

Apologists will fill you with suggestions that the judgments of his or her God are impenetrable, not to be understood entirely by his chosen ones. That the judgments should be followed in faith, and all one must do is listen to the perplexing contradictory words of the prophets through which he has revealed the truth. What a toying God, a tyrant, playing with his slaves. Can't you hear him? He'd say, 'No, I can't give the truth to each of you, but I can give it to a few. You can battle throughout the centuries about the meaning of the words. Yes, I shall give such limited substance known as the word, those objects, both written and auditory, that don't cover the full experience of reality. For I am Good!'

[Mamon raises his arms to the sky and looks up.]

Give me, oh mighty gods, the plain and forthright experience of You.

[Mamon looks back to the audience.]

Not likely my friends, I'm sorry to say that hasn't been the case, at least not in the way that any of your religions have imagined thus far. Free will is a gift we are told. A gift from the god that says, 'You can do as you please. I will not be your puppet master.' I say free will is a form of torture, not some holy charity.

[Mamon paces away from the podium and promptly returns.]

I need you to listen. Can't you hear the people crying, 'I don't know which way to go, God! I have infinite choices. What is right? Oh, this feels good. Yes, more, please, more. What? I should not do that because it feels good?' Torture! [Mamon pounds on his podium.]

[Images of religious rituals flicker by. Images of crucifixion and of sacrifices flash.]

Let's try another vein.

I began by saying life is suffering. Let me now reverse that and offer what dominates life is joy and beauty. Suffering comes first on the path, with birth, with the ephemeral nature of everything, but it doesn't have to rule. What if avoiding that which you yearn for, was not indeed the path to god or understanding? Still, you chose to spend your time without taking part in all that life offers? What a great tragedy to have missed out. God may be all about us, in everything, and tuning into it may be a proper act, but not in such a way as you tune out of all the sensual activities of life as humans. That kind of god offers you death bridges. An ascetic life lived in sacrifice to a great void or rebirth.

Now you may be asking, isn't that what the Eeden monks do? Haven't they tuned out of life and into dreams? Aren't they ducking the joys and pleasures of life for their god? Why should I believe in their words?

[Holograms of sleeping Eeden monks lay in beds floating above Mamon. Formulae and masks, letters and forms from nature bubble up, animated to look as if they were floating out of the monks' heads.]
They are explorers in the most significant historical tradition: travelers of the mind, or a better way of stating it, travelers of the Universal Mind.

The Eeden monks have been fulfilling pleasures in the manner so many dreams can give, and bringing back for us plunder unlike any ever taken. They retrieve for us the never seen before words of Gods with tangible directions on how each one of us can experience the words for ourselves, how we have heard these words in our dreams throughout life's history, and how we can now stop all those unnecessary trips to disenchanting places. They shout at us. Tune in! Tune in!

Many of the answers to your questions begin with lucid dreaming. Some of you may have experienced this for yourself. You were in REM sleep, or dream sleep, when suddenly you realized you were not awake and the world you were in was magical, far distant from your waking life - a place where almost anything was possible. Often dreams take on a form the way light will leave spots in front of your eyes when you look into a light bulb or the sun. You will have a burn image from some episode in your life, and your mind will hold tight to those burnt patterns. That's why we have recurring dreams. Or why happenings from our day will show up in a dream at night. The energy or light of the object or interaction was so powerful it seared your mind. But don't take me literally. They don't burn your cerebral cortex. I speak of Archetypal symbols. Archetypal symbols are energy forms that fill the universe. Most people wake in moments of recognition of dream activity. Some stay on to play for a while; the Eeden monks live there. It is their laboratory, their schoolroom. The language they study in Dream is Archetype.

[More symbols float by over Mamon's head.]

Physicists study the smallest subatomic particles by taking note of the traces they leave. Carl Jung, one of the great psychologists of the twentieth century, knew the symbols he studied were archetypal because they left the same traces over time and space in many different unconnected cultures.

[Symbols continue to emerge and dissolve in the air above Mamon.]

A superior intelligence is alive in our dreams: a wisdom and cleverness that guides us with these multicultural time-transcending tangible symbols. Illuminating insights are conveyed, danger is warned, the future is predicted, and we are slowly steered in the direction of a wise attitude towards life.

When I began to sift through all that was retrieved by the monks I thought how inane, how ridiculous to think we could ever comprehend, ever compile the symbols in such a fashion as to Understand. Who was I? Nothing. Then I recalled the words of a lyricist. A man from long, long ago, and known by the name Chuang intuitively grasped some of the ways of these dream gods. He sang great songs of worth helping me see I could accomplish this task. One of the most encouraging tales went something like this.

[A landscape rises behind Mamon, and the story becomes illustrated with animated characters as he speaks.]

Atop a green plateau, there stood an old gnarled tree. One hot and bright day a young man came along carrying a sack on his way home from the market where he sold apples. He stopped and rested on a short wall a little beyond the shadow of the gnarled tree. Soon an old man hobbled along the same path returning home from the market as well. He stopped by the young man who was shaking his head in disgust.

'Is there something upsetting you, sir?' the old man asked.

'Why yes,' the young man said, 'it's that ridiculous tree.'

'What are you referring to?' the old man said.

'It is useless. Look at it, all bent and knotted, its branches hanging low. It bears no fruit like my good apple trees, just takes up all that space. Someone should cut it down.'

A few children ran past and scampered up the lower limbs of the tree.

The old man followed them, smiled, and watched them play. He beckoned the young man to come over, but the man stayed behind the wall.

'Do you not see that here in the shade it is cooler? This must be a better place to rest than that wall, don't you think. And look here at these children with their smiles and their laughter, aren't they a pleasant sight after such a long day of work?'

The old man pointed to a branch high in the tree that contained a wispy nest.

'Do you see that nest up there? Do you not see what a perfect spot the birds have chosen?'

The young man bowed his head.

'Everything has its beauty, everything has its use, just not everyone is capable of seeing it,' the old man said, and he sat beside the tree's trunk and rested.

[The screen fades, and the spotlights increase on Mamon.]

What could be of more importance than bringing an understanding of why we are to the world? What could be of more worth than the lessening of ignorance that has permeated our world for far too long?

I am here to bring to you great news, to help you see past the Wall, to end any feelings of uselessness. The gods are alive. They are still obscured, but they are now at least accessible. Your religions have been helpful in that they have prepared you to accept the straightforward words of the true gods. I have built a Center. Its purpose is to house those who would donate the energy of their brains. That energy will be used to produce a substance that will increase knowledge, in hopes that the knowledge will be transformed into wisdom and that that wisdom will comprehend and speak the language of the gods so that life may once and for all have a real and known determination.

Each and everyone one of you is a valued being, capable of helping with this venture.

I am looking for volunteers to join me, those that have the strength and wherewithal to facilitate this grand cause. Yes, as you have heard, it means the giving of your life but only for a life of enriching dream, so that all dreams may come true.

It also has a reward beyond the truth you will help bring. Once you commit, your families will be completely taken care of, never having to worry about finances.

Your body will also be well taken care of, and it is a potential that one day, your service will no longer be needed. You will be awakening to a world of no ignorance, a world where wisdom is the norm, and hopefully, a world of beauty and refinement beyond our greatest fantasies.

That is my final goal.

Thank you for listening to me today. Even if you do not wish to donate your time, I beg you to continue learning, researching more into what I have discussed.

Thank you again for joining me.

[Mamon bows, the light fades on him, and the glowing symbols surrounding him die away.]

⹋SEVENTEEN⹋

I put the journal down and looked at the long aisles of gel beds. I felt ready, full, wanting to join in as I imagined Amelia wanted. I could see how all those sleeping saints around me must have felt after they'd met Mamon. I stared at her again, thinking about what she'd look like with all her limbs. Of all those, I'd painted for she was the first I wished written a bit more. I had enough from her Archives, but the inspiration I felt was more related to Mamon than Amelia.

Oddly, the first image to come into my brain as I put on my painting goggles was a wide-open baby skull. The first portraits I painted while staying with Laurel after the accident were of in utero CRISPR babies. Silly but those early days of recovery had me thinking of myself as starting fresh, and the idea to paint baby portraits became fetal portraits became painting genetically altered fetus portraits using images of their code to build up layers to construct a final portrait. During the research, I stumbled upon a collection of pictures of children with not yet fused fontanels. Fontanels are the gaps between the bones of the skull before they fuse. These were young children about two or three years old, and the images haunted me for nearly a month. This wasn't the first time since then that the memories of their open skulls have come back to me. I've recognized and discussed with Laurel that it's likely about my brothers. An odd concern for how they came to be maybe. Still, I hated it when visions like this stuck in my mind. I tried to shake them and sifted through pictures that might benefit Amelia. Saints needed comfort and inspiration, just like Mamon gave, and I sought images that would deliver that. Rolling green landscapes with gnarled apple trees in bloom. I pushed back through the multitude of landscapes that didn't quite fit and pulled forward to release similar images, variations.

Amelia's archive held me mesmerized far longer than usual. I kept selecting small items to view from her timeline until I finally started a video montage exhibiting thirty minutes of 3-second glimpses from her life, starting with infancy up until she joined the center. Many early clips of her struggling with new prosthetic tech, but also a good deal of her time in the v-enviro MoPo world where she seemed incredibly happy. I finished Amelia's painting by adding images of her and Alberta together, of Amelia sitting on a blanket by the sea in MoPo, and washes of color: large doses of prairie green, fire yellow, whale blue, and citrus orange.

I downloaded the painting for infusion and laid my hand on Amelia's caroca to stretch the skin taut and make sure I found an entry guide before I gave the injection. It was warm, and I wondered if she were awake, would she have felt it as if my hand were on her shoulder or knee. It felt a little creepy. I took my hand away and signaled the twins I was ready to go. I waited a few minutes with Amelia but no reply, so I figured I'd go to them. I stopped off at Martina's counter on my way. She barely nodded when I returned the tablet. In the main lobby, I started toward where I'd seen Mamon take the twins, hoping it would lead me quickly to them, but instead found another long corridor lined with open doors out of which wafted a heavy greenhouse scent.

Each windowed room I passed contained bizarre, almost alien-looking plants, not that I could claim to have any knowledge of plants beyond maybe a couple of everyday flowers. I stopped at one door when I noticed something like a dance party. A huge industrial lamp swayed from the ceiling over top of what I'd call a flock of Geese. Geese with their beaks pecking toward the swaying lamp. The plants tilted their leaves in unison like ruffled feathers, and wherever the light went, they followed.

As I approached the end of the hall, I could hear Mamon's muffled voice talking. I thought he might be practicing for one of his public appearances, but when I arrived, I found him speaking to a group of scientists. They gathered around the twins who sat under a large yellow light with their heads partially shaved.

"Notice when Dr Sajon shines the laser into the Cohoba reactive portion there is no major difference in response from the vestigial fontanel or any unusual dicot activity."

My heart jumped as I heard fontanel spoken.

I couldn't tell if they were finished, but together they turned to me as if I was somehow the finale of the presentation.

A calmness in them was shown which suggested I hadn't interrupted, but still, I said,

"Sorry to interrupt, I was looking for Ed and Francis."

Two of the men took brushes and painted hair onto the shaved portion of Ed and Francis's heads. The boys started laughing but not as if the brush tickled. Their laughter was delayed, seemingly related to something else.

The scientists gathered plants resting on the table next to the boys. A few whispered to each other and eyed me up as they collected their materials. They exited out a side door as Mamon spoke somewhat sternly to them in an Asian dialect and joined me at the doorway. "You've finished your work early today. How did everything go? There weren't any problems, I hope. I know the patient I listed for Martina to supply you with was in desperate need of your masterful skills," Mamon said, putting his arm around me and guiding me away from where the boys continued to laugh about something, still not noticing my arrival.

From my new angle, I could see they were staring at a screen flashing with geometric symbols. Their hovering screens had gone blank, no wonder they didn't receive my page.

"It went fine, but I hope I didn't interrupt anything important."

"Not a problem. We leave our facilities accessible to all visitors. Interruptions happen occasionally but are rarely a bother. We were almost finished here, anyway. Sometimes these scientists can be a jumpy bunch. Too much alone time with plants. I made some good progress with your brothers today."

I understood leaving the center open to all visitors to some degree, but it seemed nearly ridiculous to think of how the place could be overrun with just anyone. I didn't question it.

"They look like they're having a good time. I have to say it's been a weird couple of days with the twins bumping into that guy and his arm yesterday, and I'd agree your scientists are spending too much time with the plants. I think some are starting to mate with the shrubbery or something. I didn't get a chance to tell you yesterday, but I saw one growing leaves out of his groin. He flashed me in the bathroom."

"How unusual," Dr. Mamon laughed, then looking at me, "I can see it's not a joke. Yes, very odd. I'm sorry you had to witness that. I will check the Archive's record of it and have him reprimanded. But you must be mistaken about his growth. He probably pasted the plants onto himself for some Halloween prank."

"I don't know— it looked pretty convincing to me," I said with a nervous laugh. "I had no idea this place was such a greenhouse. Why all the plant propagation?"

"Some are used within the complex for structural purposes, but mainly it's for the memory drug production, and some to aid the saints, for health purposes. You should let me give you a detailed tour of the wonders of modern biotechnology in this building sometime."

"I've been meaning to ask for one, thanks."

"Have I explained how we're standing inside a partially alive structure? This complex has been combined with various organic forms. Look down. All of the floors are varieties of dense fungus. Imagine a future where your home could be grown instead of built and work with surrounding environments to produce a natural balance in the world. The objective I'm interested in accomplishing is not just the enhancement of the mind but betterment for all life in the Biota." Mamon looked over at the twins who were still busy laughing. "As you can see, they're having a great time with a game I worked up for them."

"Seems like it. What's the game?"

"I created it as a distraction so that I could examine their active brains. You'd have to play it to understand, but mainly it's a puzzle game. The boys are extremely good at reading symbols. It's a property found in most twins, but they are especially good at it. If you follow along, the flashing symbols will tell you a story, usually something with a humorous character to it. Everyone loves to laugh, right?"

"I know they do. Thanks for making it for them."

"My pleasure. Shall we see if they're ready to go?"

"Sure, but I have a quick question—"

As I was about to ask what he'd found out about their separation, he abruptly said.

"I've only just begun my examinations related to the challenges. It'll take a good deal of research before I can give you definitive answers of how and when" he smiled and added. "if that was what you were wondering."

"It was. If you could just let me know as soon as you have a better idea, I'd appreciate it."

"Of course, this is the plan."

The twins were so mesmerized by the game they didn't notice me. Mamon punched something on a control module, and the game symbols slowed, fading to black. The twins' screens popped back to normal, and they moaned with disappointment.

"I want to hear the rest of that," Francis said, shoving away his screen.

"It was getting really good right then where it ended," Ed whined.

"Sorry guys, all done for the day. We'll come back again."

"I'll have more of this game when you come next time," Mamon added.

"Yesss," Ed said and wiggled his hands up and down quickly near Francis's face.

"Cut it out," Francis shouted at Ed and slapped Ed's hands away.

"Hey, you don't do that," Ed shouted back, and they began another of their twisting spin fights, knocking over the table in front of them.

"Alright. We're leaving, come on now," I told them sternly and tried to bring their hulking bodies to a halt using my arms with little effect.

"Is that the way bright boys like you behave?" Mamon said firmly. The twins stopped, looked at him, and said no in unison.

"I'll show you all out if you like." Mamon gestured towards the door.

"Thanks. Sorry about this." I said, answering more out of habit when I really was feeling a little uneasy at how quick they were to react to his command.

"Don't worry about it. They're just fond of their games. Aren't you, boys?"

We were near the exit when Mamon grasped Ed's screen and adjusted it. Some static on the screen blinked and blinked back to a station's preview mode.

"There you go. That should be clear now," Mamon said and left his hand to linger a little too long on Ed's shoulder until Ed grew annoyed and twisted away.

The strange fontanel coincidence came to mind again but was replaced by the thought of his amazing speech. I was right in front of that person. The boys grew antsy and started walking toward the doors.

"I'll contact you next week, Dr Mamon. Thanks again."

"No, thank you, Ben. Please take care of yourself. You know the Center is always bettered by your presence.

⩴EIGHTEEN⩴

The grass blades tower like skyscrapers around me. Staggered troops moved in unison, wiggling like waves above at the grass tips. They watch. The worm army, a fat bird's buffet, swims through the air determined to get me. Heat from the dirt rises to my feet. The warmth fills and expands into me until my eyes are a foot above the grass line. I grow higher, hotter as a light blue toddler boy runs through the grass and - poof - like a disturbed flock of pigeons into the air go the worms when his legs kick through them. They twist into weird shapes around his head and disappear. He's being chased by the wind. The boy's running slows, and I continue to sprout. He meets me and freezes. I'm at my full height. My heat slackens, and a chill flows toward me. His prognosis isn't good. I take him in my arms as the wind picks up. His mother is missing, the yard empty except for the horrid cutting gusts. Plastic swings lurch on rusted chains, bending in the same direction as the limbs of the trees in the forest behind them.

Around the side of the house, Pedro and Anna materialize. "Pedro, here's your child. Your boy is okay. Don't worry, Anna. He's going to be okay. He was only alone for a little while. He was frozen, but he's fine." I babble at them, hoping to clear myself of some uncertain crime.

Wind streams through the layers of my thin skin and dry muscle. It threatens to disassemble me like a stack of unbound paper. Another gust and my fingertip muscles flip away, exposing the bone beneath.

I watch as all three of them spin up into the air. The trunks of the trees behind them glow with a strange fluorescence. Anna and Pedro wave farewell as flaps of my neck clap against the blackened remains of my esophagus. Yards above me, Anna tosses the light blue boy out, his tiny form contrasting brightly against the storm clouds. He sucks back into a tornado, whips around and around until he splits in two, continuing to fragment until I can't tell if anything is left whole or if he's completely shredded.

Worms leak out of my pant legs, running from my rotting body. The tornadoes sweep up grass as I cover my head to block the roaring. My ear pulls away, and I find a desiccated leaf in my hand. Wind sucks it twisting into the vortex.

I shrink as the tornado builds and pulls everything, including petals of skin from my body... In... Up... Away...

***

Fake tornadoes whipped around the bedroom wallpaper that I'd programmed the alarm as a reminder.

"BUD, another dream for my monster collection. Last night's should be labeled, uh, maybe zombie or the undead? I don't know, guess you can title it." I finished dictating and then laid in bed, urging my body to get going. My nose looked gigantic in the reflection on the silver capsule that contained my riding suit. I took it from my bedside table and began rolling it between my fingers. I popped the capsule apart, and the liquid slipped onto my wrist. Black and white, the armor gave a chilly massage as it slithered about my body. I used to pretend I was a superhero powering-up as I'd watch them cover me.

"Hey guys, get up, we're going riding today remember!" I shouted at the wall.

"I'm sleeping," Francis said.

"Get up. I'm getting up," Ed said.

I could envision Ed ready to go with a wanting-to-sleep Francis anchoring him to the bed.

"Get up Francis, you're in for one of your favorite kind of days," I shouted through the wall again.

"What's my favorite kind of day?"

"You remember, we're going riding today," I said.

"The tornados?"

"Yes, the tornados now get up, Francis," Ed shouted.

"Ben, I believe there is an inebriated tenor at your door, quite possibly it's your friend, Lenny," BUD said.

"Put him on screen for me."

Lenny appeared on a portion of the wall, a full shot of him singing and swaying with his bright tye-dyed patterned riding armor on.

"... She'll be comin' round the mountain when she comes ... she'll be comin' round the mountain, she'll be comin' round the mountain, she'll be comin' round the mountain when she comesss," Lenny sang. He started whistling the same song and did a couple jumping jacks.

"BUD put me on the intercom." A tiny chime told me Lenny could hear me.

"Try ringing the bell next time," I said.

He finished whistling. "Bells are fer butlers, and the end is nigh! Let's roll!" He pantomimed as if he'd jumped on a horse's back and started riding in circles shaking his head around wildly and smacking the horse's ass. He ended by colliding with the railing at the edge of the walkway.

Minutes later, we were ready, stuffing muffins in our mouths for breakfast and walking out the door. We found Lenny sitting on the railing, dangling his feet over the edge, waving to the people standing around the coin fountain below, probably frightening them. He pretended he would jump into the fountain, the crowd below gasped, but instead, he rolled back towards us and flipped to his feet. The twins applauded.

"Thank you. Thank you." Lenny bowed.

A few people gave Lenny dirty looks as we walked past to the parking lot, obviously not impressed with his antics.

It's a two-hour trip to the riding location in central Pennsylvania. Lenny had his facemask pulled up, making his hair stick out. He told the twins about how great the space station was coming along and how we'd all be living in space soon. While they chatted, I checked my messages and found another letter from Susan. She'd been writing a lot lately, and the book discussions had me reading more so I could intelligently contribute.

From: Susan@rossskycity.
Subject: I've decided to forgive you.

Thursday, November 30th

Dear Ben,

Forgive my formality, but I feel I should begin by saying how much I've enjoyed our correspondence this past month, merely discussing books since Halloween. I like the way your mind works and think you've got a little something more than rocks up there.

I'm about to change our purely literary conversational path. I know we decided in the beginning not to examine each other's archives and beyond the pre-Halloween difficulties I've tried to keep our correspondence focused on literature.

When I changed my mind about not writing to you after Halloween, it was because I believe you didn't mean to hurt me with your disbelief in my date rape. I might not have believed me if I was in your place. It was early in our writing relationship, and I think I know why you lashed out, but now I trust you. Trust you mainly because, yes, I've broken our No-Archives contract. Please forgive me! That's why I'm detouring onto a personal avenue. I hope you're not upset. It seemed wrong to do, but I believe if you care about someone, viewing their archives without their permission is not wrong.

I know, I know ... I'm justifying it. Sorry! I stuck to mostly viewing ones checked by you as good for the general public. I do think you're quite handsome, in case you're wondering. I'll list for you all of what I watched: the first two were your birth and part of your first day of grade school (what a shy little boy you were). I also chose your first kiss at the abandoned house with Sara (adorable!), the moment you fell in love with Sara, and a day at a pond on some farm with your brothers where you're teaching them how to fish (I love your brothers! You have so many farm archives. Are you sure you don't want to become a farmer?), plus one other episode.

Now, I must say the final life episode I watched I feel nervous telling you about. Your response to my date rape is far more understandable. I'd really rather have heard in your words your experience of the accident with your parents. I watched it up until I saw you were okay. It was horrible. I'm sorry I watched it, not because I think you wouldn't want me to but because it seems like such a traumatic event in your life. I know you're not a fan of the Archives and that some people choose not to review certain significant events like that. Much has been theorized about this, but I agree with the ideas of leaving specific memories to only experience.

In your letters to me, I've noticed that while you're good at the literary discussions, you're not as good at the sharing of yourself. I mean, I know you've joked with me, and I know you like me. You do like me, don't you? Ha! Maybe I only write that knowing what I do about you — knowing that there is much more to you. I'd like to apologize if I've offended by watching without your permission. I won't speak about them until you've given the okay, but please forgive me for saying I'm glad I've viewed them and feel much closer to you now than ever before.

Much Love and many apologies if I've upset you,

- Susan

My heart raced along with the Appalachian mountain chain, darting past my window on the horizon. Blurred leafless tree limbs washed by too and the morning sun strobed through them into my eyes. She looked at my archives. She must be thinking of me, romantically. I started to get a headache from the light flickering at me, and that woozy feeling melted from the tips of my ears down and continued behind my eyes.

Bleeding gash on Mom's face.

Scattered wet clothes on the road.

I shook the visions and focused on the cartoon Ono music Lenny blended with Japanese opera that twittered from the car speakers. The red and yellow waves rolled on the music console showing the music's peaks and valleys. Ono sang, "A thousand suns shine shine shine. Melt on down down down. Eat a tuna! No, eat two tuna! fish fish fish" The twins punched each other in the back seat to the beat of fish fish fish, laughing and trying harder to hurt each other.

I couldn't wait to know more and quickly pulled up Susan's archive with a freeze-framed image of her. There she was. I could finally see what she looked like. She seemed a little off, brittle looking but maybe pretty like one of those models. Yes, definitely pretty but awkward. Not someone I'd normally gravitate towards.

"You brought the saddles, right?" Lenny asked.

"Don't I always bring the saddles?" I said with unnecessary annoyance as I looked back at Susan's image and closed out the screen.

"Well, you could've forgotten. You've had your noggin straight in the bog lately."

"What? I have not."

"So who's the message from?" Lenny asked in an I-know-you-too-well-fashion.

"Ah, it's another letter from Susan."

"You still writin' with her? Must be some romance."

"It's not," I said a little too quickly. "We're still talking books mostly. Except, she did just write about checking out my archives."

"She's checkin' out your body."

"She said she didn't. She said she looked at some life-shaping events."

"You sure she didn't look at some of your splatshots. Sounds like she's lookin' for love to me."

"Splatshots?"

"Come on... we all have our arcs of it. So, what'd hers look like?" Lenny let go of the steering bar and squeezed invisible breasts.

"I haven't watched any archives, but I've seen an image of her," I said, smiling at his invisible-nipple squeezing fingers, "I'm not interested like that really."

"Come on, not even a little?"

"All right, a little. Actually, if I've been interested in anyone, it's this saint Amelia I helped recently. Only a couple of problems, I suppose. Her journal didn't give many details about her and then there's the fact she doesn't have any legs or an arm and well, she's a saint."

"Let me see if I have this right. You're interested in this Amelia, who you've met once, don't have much info on her, and no chance you'll ever be with her, never spoke with her, never heard her voice even but the woman you've been writin' to for the past coupla months who is checkin' out your private arcs and who is probably the only woman you're involved with these days, besides maybe Laurel, you're not interested in and don't believe you're in a relationship already?"

"Okay, it's a relationship but not the sexual kind. We're only talking about books. We write maybe a couple of times a week."

"Whatever you say, but I think you're moments from putting on the VR-zip suits and goin' wild."

Ed started getting louder from the backseat.

"You're not supposed to hit my face!"

"You got the suit on," Francis yelled back.

I was always surprised that they still get a kick out of the no-pain punching. Every time we go riding, they ended up punching each other practically nonstop until they've caught a ride.

If you've ever rubbed the surface of a sapling that the bark's been peeled from, the texture of the suit is the same. Not wearing one is an excellent way to get large chunks ripped out of your body from the debris that's often found whipping about inside the cyclones. A few of the early riders who were testing the saddle didn't have the suits for protection. They looked as if they'd been in some kind of shark attack when they grounded. Now everyone wears the bodysuits with the balancing saddles when they ride.

I looked in the rearview and caught the twins exchanging hard-handed face slaps.

"No hitting in the face unless you have the hoods on, guys," I shouted, knowing their faces must've been stinging.

"We know."

"Doesn't sound like it. Keep it below the neck."

"Okay," they said and continued their body slugs and laughter.

A mostly cleared section of land appeared and stretched on to the horizon. The occasional bent skeleton of a defunct electric tower, trailer remnants, and car shells inhabited the region like an unearthed truck stop boneyard. Houses and other buildings' concrete foundations created scattered tile patterns along the dirt-covered roads of the abandoned suburb. It all felt haunting in a way that excited me. If you've ever discovered and entered a derelict house left by its owners with contents not completely removed, you know the feeling. Curved tracks of torn earth cut wildly across the land as if someone took a giant tractor and started plowing without a care. Cracked tree trunks, telephone poles snapped with no lines and bent billboards came in and out of view between the mad silver wind tops, spinning along the surface of the Earth and dominating this region. This was one of the many freakweather sites.

Packs of miniature tornadoes began to appear like ocean tides in central Pennsylvania. For the first several years, before the cyclones found their rhythm, the people who populated this region continued to rebuild after each of the decimations. Eventually, they wised up and didn't return, but some early pioneers came back for sport.

I first visited during winter to see the sculptures I'd heard about. In winter, the cyclones don't grow to full size because the moisture they trap leaves fragile ice cone sculptures killing the cone's momentum. The sculptures created are phenomenal, and if they last, it's only for a short time before winds knock them over.

The body armor and balancing technology that OM2ME developed was adapted for Cyclone riding. Anyone who has ridden one and been thrown will tell you that the suits may protect you from flying debris but don't prevent all pain and landing can twist you in ways that hurt more internally. After my first day of riding, or I should say flinging, my body looked like a spotted leopard from all the bruises I'd acquired, but no broken bones or severe injury. It was worth it. It always is.

We arrived at the cavernous Stage carport, and I retrieved the saddles from the trunk. The Stage, a vast flat horseshoe-shaped area at the base of the rounded mountainsides, was where most riders launched and the best location to watch the action. The twins began their excited squawking and went running from the carport into the main complex. Rows of translucent blue oval chairs hovered like Calder mobiles, cascading back and forth along the aisles. The mile-high window pane dotted with circle-shaped screens gave you multiple choices to view all angles of riders. The chairs moved automatically to face the action and swing so one could feel more part of it all. It's a great option, but many choose to stand on the floor close to the windows instead. The twins screeched down the steps to press up against the pane, frightening some other unaware observers along the way. They cleared a large space for an up-front view. Their heads just missed the legs dangling from chairs positioned close to them as they giggled and jumped up and down like a seesaw. Lenny and I strapped on our saddles, a wide thick belt that wrapped around the waist and emitted a gravity-balancing wave.

"Here guys, put these on," I said as we joined them.

They quieted down, wrapped on their belts and masks, and moved toward the entrance of the launch deck. The scent of popcorn wafted everywhere. I was somewhat surprised the twins weren't bugging me for some, but the windows held more interest for everyone at the moment.

At first, I felt nervous, allowing the twins to ride. There's no controlling their excitement in such an environment, but their insistence worried me more and when they acted as if they might jump onto a cone without the suits or the balancing belts I knew I had to get them set up for safety. Didn't matter who was up next they went charging. Nobody stopped them; they have celebrity status. Even if it frustrates the interrupted party, it's accepted. They've made it into a few of the trade magazines and are referred to as The Birdboys. A conversational buzz began on the deck when the twins were spotted, and a runway cleared for them, but they weren't quite ready.

Dust swirled in small circles, the first sign of a rising cone. Most of the time, they swept up and dropped down, not accumulating enough speed to get funnels flowing. Riders stood at the edge of the launch area in the high wind and watched the circles build and die.

Little could compare to the deck experience. Until you donned your mask, wind stole into your mouth and pulled breath from your lungs. When no grips were available, to stay standing, you had to push against the continually shifting gusts.

Several riders came inside, and as they did, the twins squeezed past. They must've noticed something unusual about one of the wavering dust circles because they went dashing to the front of the launching deck. Their arms stretched out wide, dancing and flapping like the double-winged bird they get their nickname from. They did a rapid little side-to-side hop, eyeing up the cone's motion as it grew in seconds to a fantastic thirty-foot monster. It was like bullfighters before a gargantuan bull, and with a fierce charge, the cone swept in close to the twins, and they leaped as if meant for the sky. Whipping around the lower portion of the funnel, using their belts to help slowly glide upward, they had it tamed quickly and began their fun. They squeezed the cone like a pet, giving the great beast a hug. The funnel drew inward at the middle and thick clouds swirled below and above them. Their legs stuck almost straight out from the center like wiggling squid through the air. Bringing knees in quickly, they shot up to the top of the cone looking like they'd squirt into outer space but slowed and did some swinging around the top for a while. I wondered if they could communicate as they went - communicate in a way that I've seen them do without talking, making me wonder if there isn't some kind of telepathy going on between them.

Bending the top of the cone, they began the high speed "rodeo" ride I know is their favorite. Each held on with one arm as their other arms flailed behind, winging around for extra balance and control. They whizzed out towards the electric towers like hummingbirds, flower to flower. Fraying aimless cones, moving with no riders aboard, appeared to wince and dodge aside as the twins blasted by. In and out of the crippled steel structures, the twins wove and came frighteningly close to the shredded metal edges that would be sure to slice off an armor-coated arm or a leg with ease. Most wouldn't dare to. I wouldn't and didn't like watching them around that area.

Faces filled with roaring cheers and broad smiles dominate the crowd, all eyes on the Birdboys. I glanced over and caught a young couple kissing. The girl's hand hanging over her boyfriend's neck held tightly to a paper cone filled with popcorn. A couple of times, the popcorn cone barely missed being knocked free of her hand by a chair waving midair in front of it. Probably not a Synchronistic Activity Wave, who knows, but it caught my mind in an odd visual transition as I moved from the vision of it nearly being knocked back to the twins so flying away from the jagged towers.

A few new twisters formed. Riders popped onto their surface one by one and sailed out to join the twins on the playing field. I noticed Lenny at the edge, readying himself as a small cone quickly grew. He jogged to one side then back to the other and leaped like a three-legged grasshopper onto the bottom of it. His feet bashed on the ground a couple of times, but he swam up to the middle and gained control. Whoosh! He flew to the top and humped over awkwardly, trying to get composed. The cone started to sputter as if it might dissolve, but Lenny dropped into the center and disappeared. Lenny loved merry-go-round style. You almost never saw him except for the beginning and end of his rides. He's a glutton for punishment. From inside, it's like looking through frosted glass. You could make out the division of earth and sky but little else. That kind of riding always made me nauseous. He popped out and tried to build the size of the cone before slipping back in again.

The twins caught sight of Lenny and went zooming to him. They made broad circles around wherever his cone moved. Their arms waved and fluttered at him, but Lenny saw little beyond the swirling cone interior. I could imagine their laughter now.

I found myself cheering with the crowd at the twins' antics. They were playing with Lenny's ride, directing it. You could often catch riders using each other's cones for different tricks, but I'd never seen one cone manipulate another in the way the twins batted Lenny's around like a cat 'n' mouse game. Lenny emerged from the center of his cone to see what was going on. He noticed the twins, waved them on, telling them to leave him alone, but they thought it was good fun, waved hello back, and continued to circle. Lenny shook both arms and lost control hurtling out of the twister and under the twins, disappearing in a mass of wind and dirt cloud. Nothing for a few moments, then an arm appeared, then a leg. He whipped around like a rag doll. His head and shoulders emerged into view from the cone as he was battered and all at once he was spit out, landing knees first and onto his chest into a large mound of plowed earth. That had to hurt.

I saw promise in a building cone as I turned my head from Lenny's crash. You didn't have much time to think about this stuff. I moved swiftly through some riders who must not have seen what I saw, pulling my hood and mask on as I ran, and leaped into the air. The wave of moving sky shrieked at my chest as the tornado built to an ideal height at precisely the right moment my body reached it. I took a big chance, but it paid off. The gravity belt strapped me to the cone, and I wrapped my arms around and began to direct the air, so I'd move up to a good viewing point. My head stuttered with a loose vibration until I tensed my neck muscles. A sense of empowerment came over me as if I could do this without the tornado to hold me up. Connected to the Earth and sky, I coasted out with the cone, letting her direct herself and got a view from the air of Lenny running from the skirt of the twins' twister. Apparently, they thought kicking Lenny around was a game. I moved my legs out, feeling the great roaring energy flow, turned and went buzzing after the twins before they did some serious harm. They saw me coming and shot away, looking for me to chase them. Lenny stopped and waved to me in weary appreciation.

I caught up, and the beginning of a race ensued. Many didn't bother trying to race. You felt lucky enough to catch a ride most days, but occasionally riders did, and almost every time the boys and I had a ride at the same time, we gave it a run. We traveled as a pair, heading out miles from the Stage. The ground rolled and roared and the same urge I've occasionally gotten while looking at the edge of a large sharp knife overcame me. Part of me wanted to peel back my gloves, lean down, and touch the ground. My hand would be sanded off in seconds and going that low with a cone this big would fling me worse than Lenny must've experienced, but I couldn't control these thoughts arising. I'd never do it anyway.

I let the cone build as we moved to the crooked pine grove for a starting zone. After a one-two-three wave of my arm, we jetted toward the forest on the horizon. A bush twirled at the base of my cone giving the twins an advantage, and they moved easily into the lead. A bush may seem like nothing, but it can pose a real problem, and if sucked upwards it could be like getting hit with a rubber bullet at close range. The bush had to be freed, or my cone could crap out. She started to weaken, so I went towards a small grouping of boulders. As I passed over, the bush dislodged, but my cone wavered.

Up ahead the land shimmered, a sure sign of water. I noticed the muddy pond in time to maneuver away. The twins didn't and worked across the shortest route. It's a wide pond and must've formed since the last visit. I lost time circling around but kept a close watch on the twins' progress as they navigated the water. Riding a cyclone on water is called a snailshag. It felt great against your body, like a massage, but the weight of the water tremendously slowed momentum and made the cone challenging to manage. The twins seemed to have it under control, and even if they lost their cone, they could tread water, and I doubted the pond was very deep. With great force, they trudged, reaching the outer banks after I passed them. I looked back as their cone shook the water like a dog, a power shower all over the land around it.

The woods' passage loomed, followed by the Great Drop and area we considered the finish line. I loved the woods, although it's the area you're most likely to be bashed off with all the fallen trunks and pits left after trees had been ripped from the ground. The path through is much easier now, it had widened over time, and no doubt would not exist for much longer. I looked to see where the twins were, and just as I did, I failed to notice two pits. I should've been watching where I was going. The air shifted beneath me as I rode up and down through them and jagged branches swiped precariously in my direction. The cone began a spluttering spin as I twisted away from the branches, making it difficult to stay in one place. I looped into a clear area and started getting nauseous. The twins caught up, and their passing gave my cone a little extra energy and helped me back on track, as I rounded the side where the woods clear a bright concentric bullseye of rainbows filled the sky. I'd seen plenty of rainbows before, and some freakweather areas had been documented with substantial double or triple rainbows, but I'd never seen anything like this. A great joy filled me as I flew closer towards it.

I rode through the rest of the woods and flew to the enormous drop staring at the rainbow, but that was when my cone died. A stretch of rocky soil came soaring into view. I did the practiced twist, dropping with excessive speed to land in a way that my butt got most of the impact. The dirt settled on my legs and feet as the wind slackened, and everything became comparatively still. A small breeze laughed in my ears. My body did a "post-elevator" wave, and I noticed the twins losing their ride too. Nothing to do but let it dissolve. They dropped to the ground about twenty yards away as their ride whipped from beneath them. Their backs were to me, and they faced the rainbow when I caught up with them. I called, but they didn't answer and instead kept sitting staring at the rainbow. I walked around a wide ditch, climbed down a little further and came to see them from the side. They raised their hands to their heads, covering their ears, and their mouths were open with a look like they might be laughing, but as I came closer, an odd humming or singing was coming from them. It stopped abruptly as I called them again and they turned to me like nothing was going on.

"Come on, come on, let's go," Ed shouted.

"We stayed on longest. We win," Francis said.

"Okay, you win. Now sit tight and wait for the pickup."

I climbed to the bottom of the incline and reached them, noticing the transport vehicle heading our way.

Back at the Stage, Lenny waited with an angry grin on his face.

The twins went running up the steps, pulling off their hoods as they climbed, anxious to give Lenny a hug.

"You were under our cone," Ed said with exuberant mirth.

Lenny put out his arms as if he wanted a hug too but sent them flying to the ground with a nasty trip. Their weight and size made the crowd turn to see what had happened.

"How'd you like landin' on the hard ground?" Lenny said and glanced guiltily at me. I knew he couldn't hurt them and that he knew he couldn't, but I could see his real anger.

The twins laughed even louder, which made Lenny fume. Two short men who were probably fans rushed over to help the twins up. One dusted Ed's head as he lifted them.

"Hey, cut it, my head ain't hurtin'," Ed said, pushing the guy's hand from his head.

"Aw, Lenny, you're Mr Trickster," Francis said and put out his arms with Ed for a hug. Lenny didn't budge for a moment, then gave up, and let them hug him. They pulled him between them, flipped Lenny down onto his stomach, and sat on him. Ed rode facing backward, Francis forwards.

The crowd whooped with excitement.

"Guess this makes me the hotdog, fun buns. Now, get off me." Lenny begrudgingly smiled as he struggled to free himself.

The crowd shifted their focus from Lenny back to the sky. The bullseye rainbow looked larger and had a slight pulsing quality. Then it shimmered and faded away.

"I can't see how it was physically possible," Lenny said. "Where is the sun angling from? I guess there could be some rain in a weird pocket, but I've never seen anything like it."

"Intense. You should've seen the boys' reaction to it. I'll show you." I started to navigate but stopped feeling the boys watching me. "I'll show you later, I need to review the archives of it," I said.

Lenny gave me a strange look, not quite understanding.

"Come on, come on. Bun-bun," Ed said, urging us to leave.

"Forget it. I'll explain later," I said.

⊟NINETEEN⊟

On the way home, everyone felt exhausted. With the boys sleeping in the back, I explained what I'd observed, but Lenny didn't think it much to worry about and only commented on how they're always a little odd in their ways. I shrugged it off too. He was probably right. He mixed some deep-sea beat station with a bit of fir forest wind and the twins slept. Regular cracks in the highway added an extra layer of rhythm to the music. A bloated rotting woodchuck lay on the roadside and flicked by. The yellow navigation lines made my eyes bounce as they pulsated towards me. A vision of Dad lying on the highway morphed into a morose rhythm. Found Dad dead in the driveway. Found Dad dead in the driveway. Found Dad dead in the driveway. The music dissolved the chant as the ache from my head and body became more prominent.

What would Laurel say about my morbid subconscious? I should remember these things to share with her. I knew it but avoided the thought of therapy by brainstorming paintings I might do. The sober landscape of central Pennsylvania's suburb coated hills, housing tracks, gray trees and leftovers of non-government run farms were all visuals I'd considered for use or used many times. The clouds seemed to ascend as we left the vicinity of the Stage. Up there, up above the layer of smothering pigeon cloud was where she lived on a regular basis. Seemed like an odd choice, not to live walking the surface of the Earth. No matter how populated it gets, I think I'll always want to be able to kick some grass.

"You really think she's into me?"

"What're you talkin' about?" Lenny asked.

"You think Susan may want me more than just for book discussion?"

"What girl checks you like that if she isn't thinkin' about romance? You'll be flying to see her on that hoverin' hovel in no time."

"Hovering hovel? Weren't you all excited about Skycity when it first assembled? Wasn't that the reason you got into the tech-sociology stuff your junior year?"

"Don't be so sensitive, when you going to realize there's no proper parameters to get a hard-on or a heart-on."

"Nice modbop," I said without humor.

"Stop dissectin' every ting til it's got no meanin' left far yah. Feeeeel it, mon," said with a straight-faced Jamaican accent.

"I guess, but long distance? Probably not. I need to see what she viewed from my life. She mentioned some archives that'd be fun to see again," I said and pulled out my pocket console.

"Hey, you want to head to that new hang dancing lodge?"

"Why not. Yeah, soon, this weekend even," I said.

I thought of Susan as Lenny turned up the music.

We drove on and I navigated to some of the ones she watched. Her choices seemed generic. I suppose I did tag some as fit for anyone but if I were interested in my archives I'd much rather look at random days of adolescence than the day I was born. I'd seen it with Mom and Dad on practically every birthday growing up. There's nothing like repetitive conversation to kill the romance of a memory. The archives of my youth weren't of interest either. I skipped to the ones with Sara. I re-read the message from Susan quickly to see what else she reviewed. In my archive's "dating" section, Sara had a folder all her own. This ought to be good and depressing.

Susan said she watched the moment Sara and I first fell in love. I'd no idea when that was. Many times, I'd thought it odd how the Archives cataloged our memories, characterizing events you couldn't yourself. Sara could've marked the event and it then updated in my archive listings, but somehow that didn't fit her personality. She wasn't much for organizing or details. I scrolled through the folder and there it was, "Moment first fell in Love." I clicked it open. We were sitting by a lake on the wooden dock, the sun was setting, and Canadian geese floated by in a huge V landing in the water close. It seemed too common romance movie-ish. I tapped the sound zone on the screen to make sure it'd project the sound for just my area of the car. Then I zoomed in on Sara and me and turned up the volume.

"... Peach, I guess peach," she took her hands from her eyes.

"How'd you know I'd bring that flavor? You must be psychic."

"You always bring peach yogurt," she said knowing I knew I always bring peach.

"I do? You love peach, don't you?" I said knowing she does.

"Sure, here." She peeled the lid and handed me the small tub.

"You know in Chinese art the peach is a symbol for women. Turn it one way and you have a nice butt, turn it another and there's a nipple, cut it open," I pantomimed opening and looking inside a peach and smiled.

"You tell me that every time we eat peach anything, Ben."

She eats the rest herself, puts her hand on my hand and gives a little squeeze.

Yep, that was it. That was the moment. I think. It very well could be in any case. I wondered what algorithm could clue the Archive into our mental state. There had to be many moments like that which would say, "He loves her." My chest started to tighten with that pain of loss, so I moved on.

I returned to Susan's message again. "A day at pond on farm with your brothers where you are teaching them how to fish." I switched to an aerial view of the farm from that day. A near-paradise in my mind: the hilly plowed landscape with apple orchard. I can almost understand why she never leaves the property. I think this archive was from around the same time Laurel first explained about how her husband had left her and later died.

"When was the last time we went out to visit Laurel's farm together?" I asked Lenny.

"A little while after you stopped livin' there. We needed ta git sum fresh air if I remember co-rrectly," Lenny said with a thicker than usual southern accent.

We pulled into a streetlight lit parking space at the Mall Apartment complex.

"Saturday good for the hang-dance club?" Lenny asked.

"I thought we'd visit with Laurel this weekend?"

"How 'bout the followin' for Laurel?"

"Fine by me, I need to call her and okay it. I've been stopping by unannounced too much lately."

"Alright. See you guys later."

"Bye," the twins said perking up from their nap.

"Hope your body ain't too sore from today," I added as Lenny lowered his window.

"Ah, don't worry about it. I'll get em back next time. You guys better watch out."

Lenny squealed his tires as he pulled away, waving his watch-out finger out the window.

"Yeah right!" Francis shouted at the car.

"You better watch out," Ed shouted as well.

***

I wasn't ready for bed or to start reading yet.

"BUD, open a screen, I'll write Susan back," I said, swinging the keyboard up from beneath my bedside table. A digital light gray square appeared on the wallpaper in front of me.

"Would you rather dictate it?"

"No."

The cursor blinked for me to begin.

To: Susan@rossskycity. Subject: Cyclone ride/Archive review

Thursday, November 30th

Just got back from riding. Have you tuned into any of the footage of the pro rides I recommended? We had fun. The twins did well, except for messing with Lenny's cone. He was a little bruised but fine.

On the drive home I looked at some of the ones you viewed. I don't know if I'd have recommended them, but I'm not upset about it. I'd never thought of the exact moment Sara and I fell in love before. A perfect reason why I don't like the Archives.

Do you have any recommendations for what I should view from yours? Any moments you wouldn't want me to see? You owe me now you know. I took a look at an image of you. I'm not sure what I expected but I was surprised, in a good way.

Okay then, I'm off to do some reading before bed. I'm giving that Dostoyevsky a try. Not sure if there is any subtext to your recommendation? I found out The Raw Youth is also known as The Adolescent and that many thought of it as a failure. I'm pretty sure this is related to my comment about thinking the Russian word for ass жóпa sort of visually looks like what it stands for.

Ben

"Send that for me BUD and attach a picture of the twins whipping Lenny around from today, thanks."
"Your message has been sent."
The picture of Lenny's face with a confused expression upon it, popping out from beneath their cone and the twins laughing flashed up on the wall screen.
"That's great, BUD. Thanks."
I'd swallowed a mouthful of toothwash, wiped a warm wet cloth across my face, and as I hung the cloth up a request to live chat came on the mirror from Susan. I looked at my reflection and thought I looked haggard. Panic hit me, and I didn't know what to respond because I

didn't want to offend her and was excited at the thought of a session, but now was not the time for it. I quickly sent a message of apology and that I was going to sleep but would catch up with her another time. I folded into bed, barely able to sleep. My mind only stopped racing as I focused back on Dostoyevsky but the first phrase on page 206 was "…common among the best people, for we all suffer from the incontinence of our hearts."

☰TWENTY☰

"Put it back!" I drew an excited breath as the morning light filled my eyes.

BUD's voice filled the room. "Can I help you with anything, Ben?"

"No, BUD, just another bad one." I rolled onto my back and dictated what I could recall of having my dead dream wife slowly peel away the skin from my skull with the bandages in me as a Mummy dream.

"Would you like me to queue up some classic horror films for you to view later? The monster motif seems to be gaining momentum."

"No, I'm sure it's only a phase. Remember how I used to have all those flying dreams. This is probably like that," I said feeling a little mentally exhausted from the night. Not an easy way to start the day.

"78 separate documented flying dreams. You have a message waiting from Lenny."

"What's he want?"

The wall filled with Lenny's face.

"Hey, I just talked with Sheryl. I forgot we made plans for Saturday night, would you mind if she came along? No oranges but she said she's got some fresh melon this time!" He opened his mouth wide and took a big fake bite. "Call me back!"

"BUD, contact Lenny."

A chime told me Lenny accepted my call. His face, eating an egg salad sandwich and with a nice sized yellow glob on his cheek, filled the wall.

"You might want to wipe your face."

He smiled wide, showing more yellow egg on his teeth.

"What's all this about bringing Sheryl tomorrow night? Thought we were shopping, so to speak."

"Yeah, you can shop solo. Show em your pig bits. Do you mind?"

"S'all right," I said, yawning and not really caring about meeting someone anyway. I'm sure I could manage better without Lenny's help in any case.

"You just getting' up? It's lunchtime."

"I was up late reading. Oh, and I haven't spoken with Laurel yet about the following weekend."

"You think she'd mind if I brought Sheryl along then too?" Lenny walked around wiggling his hips and waving the white bread with lettuce flapping to the rhythm of the music.

"I'm sure she wouldn't care. There are always extra beds at her place, but what's going on? You getting married to Sheryl now?"

"Nah, just a lot of French kissing." His egg coated tongue swiped at the sandwich.

"Eugh. See you around eight tomorrow. And don't wear that cologne you wore last time, all the women cleared out of our zone like we'd stepped in something."

"Hey hey, Sheryl and the ladies love my scents."

"Right... see you at eight."

"I'll bring the melons."

The wall panel faded.

"Ben, this is your usual reminder about your visit to the Saint Center this afternoon. Would you like a lunch prepared for you, Francis and Ed?" BUD said.

"One will probably be provided. Tell the twins to get ready so we're not late," I said.

***

Driving up to the Center placed me in that bubble of odd nerves, my insides pushing out. It's the enormity of the place. The trees were bare this time of year and gave the Center an even greater baroque look. So many surfaces adorned with beautiful growing design. The texture of the fungus tile forest floor at the entrance was bright and caused my eyes to vibrate oddly like an optical illusion might. I stood there for a moment dazzled by it when Mamon suddenly opened the silver doors, smiled coolly at the twins and welcomed us in. None of us were quite prepared and I sort of turned toward the Twins instead of immediately greeting him. An unusual urge to flee filled me that I couldn't quite pin down. It was awkward, but it wasn't only me. The twins froze a little when they saw him.

"I am very happy to see you all again." He patted the twin's heads, one spider fingered hand on each head. "Let me take your coats." Mamon handed them to an assistant. "I have a request for a few of the saints that will need your help today. I have left specifics with Martina. Can I get you anything before you begin Ben? Some lunch maybe?"

I was distracted by the aqua glow of the walls where a mass of the beetles was pushing up onto the surface layer at the top of the wall.

"Some lunch would be great. We ran out of time before we left," I said.

Mamon led us to a small cafeteria where men in lab coats ate in silence. As we sat down most turned, looked at us briefly, and continued eating.

"Can I have some egg salad?" Ed asked.

I wondered if they'd been watching my conversation with Lenny earlier.

"Yeah, I want some eggs in a salad, and some bread with mustard," Francis said.

"Certainly boys, you can have whatever you like. Is there something you would prefer Ben?"

"Best make it egg salad sandwiches all around, thanks."

Mamon tapped his communicator and in a few minutes, a small blonde man served the sandwiches. He gave us water in wine glasses with vine shaped stems. Mamon had a plate of what looked like dirt-covered celery. He picked at it as he talked with us and I wanted to ask him what it was.

"How would you like to play that game we tried out last time you came?" Mamon asked the twins.

Something in me wanted to say no, they should stay with me, that I no longer wanted his help, but his speech flooded back, and I couldn't pursue that thought with any conviction.

"I love that game," Ed said, spitting yellow egg bits onto Francis's shirt as he talked.

"Don't talk with your mouth full," Francis said with his mouth full, wiping the Ed-spit into a big streak on his shirt.

"I've got it all arranged for you to play again while Ben helps me out with our beloved saints. This should be a fun afternoon." Mamon looked at me and grinned.

Two nurses walked by talking about some stats from a chart they were monitoring but saw me and immediately stopped talking.

"Can I ask you, have the saints I've recently worked with seen improvement?"

"You're doing splendidly Ben, don't worry. The last report I reviewed showed you and the others who help have increased the saints' output of energy by about eleven percent. That's a significant increase, and I hope you realize how much we appreciate it."

"Okay. I'm glad I could help out," I said but felt a little like he'd delivered a politician's answer to some degree. Possibly if he mentioned their wellbeing instead of their energy output would've been better, but all of it didn't feel sincere.

The twins sat waiting, already finished. Not wanting to hold everyone up, I left my unfinished sandwich and suggested I get to work.

I hiked to the saints' arena and found my way to Martina's desk. She saw me coming and turned her screen off. She peeled a screen for me, tapped at the surface and placed it at the front of her desk.

"Hello there, Martina," I said. Her body adorned with a shimmering cellophane dress revealed powder orange glowing breasts and matching painted hair rings.

"You're expected to complete all of these today," she said shoving the screen a little closer to me.

I tapped the surface to see the list of saints. John the soldier and Amelia were among them.

"You sure these are right? I worked with two of them already."

"Yes." She leaned forward towards me, and a rush of her perfume filled my nose. The scent caused a warmth to fill the top of my spine. She grabbed the screen from my hand and looked at the list.

"Make sure this one is done." She highlighted the one at the top.

I took it back and read the saint's name, Beattie Calez. She tilted her head down to return to her reading causing her hair to lurch forward menacingly.

"Always a pleasure," I said, making kissing lips at her without her seeing.

As I walked into her space, brooding keyboard music played. Someone spent time adding makeup to her deep brown skin. The makeup looked a little out of place on her naked body. No other saints I knew of had it or music playing for that matter. Her lips were perfectly glossed. Images bubbled up in my mind. She was a swan, long and elegant. Her folded arms smooth with small pinched elbows that darkened a little. She seemed to have a confidence I didn't recall in the other saints, a certain assured composure. As with Amelia, I found myself interested in what might happen if I met Beattie under different circumstances.

Something about Beattie said she was awake inside her catatonic shell. Many other saints seemed robotic, almost dead but not Beattie. Peach fuzz smoothed her cheekbones at the edge towards the ear. Her nose was small and flat with little nostrils that slightly flared as she breathed. Someone had styled in looping curls, colored nails, and neatly trimmed and shaved her pubic hair. I clicked to the first page of her journal. She'd drawn groups of little circles, like a dollop of caviar, or bubbles at the top of a glass of champagne. One tiny bubble was filled in with, "That's me" written at the top.

On the second page, she drew several concentric circles as if she'd cut a tree trunk in half, dipped it in ink and pressed it into the page at different places. Next to this one, she'd written: "That's me, sparkling in the night behind the black." I put my goggles on and recorded the image, then kept just the concentric lines of the drawing itself so I could see the rest of the room through them and around me. I wanted the lines as the bones of the painting. I saved it for after and cleared the view, returning to the journal.

On the third page, the writing began.

⚏TWENTY-ONE⚏

The Journal of Beattie Calez

Choctaw is where I was born, in the Appalachian Mountains of Virginia. What do you want to read, I had a hard life, that I came to this Center to escape my hard life? Well, don't go taking the shine off your eyes because that's not my story, and mostly it's not true anyway. I've lived what I would call a very average life, albeit one of high hues, feathers, and show-stopping shoes.

Only thing that truly makes my life unusual was Pinky and that Mom and my younger brother Billy passed on when I was all of fourteen years old. I've missed Mom and Billy every day since. I never knew my father. He left Mom after he found out she was pregnant. I'll begin about the time they, meaning Mom and Billy, leave my history and Pinky entered it.

The day before they died, June third, I was at my favorite rock where the sun hits you best in the Summer, the wind kisses you most in Spring and Fall, and where you can watch for miles as the land below goes all white in the winter. It's one of those places where a person gets draped in cloud dresses and can get close to what's important, you know, feel like you're on top of the world. More than any other time of the year I spent my summer days there reading. The rock's surface was always warm in June and if you left your biscuit on a napkin by a fourth or fifth chapter it'd taste like you pulled it from the oven. I remember I'd already laid out the cut flowers and placed some butter I'd left in the freezer overnight on the side of the bread. I'd wrap it up real tight in paper towels so that once the sun had readied the bread the butter was at the perfect temperature for spreading. I loved that rock. I hope all the spring bulbs I planted are still blooming around it and I bet my name is still there, but maybe it's worn away by now...by the time you're reading this. You! Who are you?

I stopped reading her journal because a buzzing started on the back of my ears. I tried scratching and massaging to see if it'd stop but it didn't. It was an unnerving sensation. I grabbed both of my ears and applied pressure which caused it to increase in my skull until halos of rainbow suddenly emanated from Beattie's head and morphed into a cloud of dark pink static that flipped like confetti and briefly obscured her face. There was little doubt of what I'd seen but I didn't have the time to think differently or explore what it might be because as I took my hands from beside my ears it disappeared. I tapped my goggles to begin recording ridiculously thinking I might and tried squeezing my ears again to see if I could replicate the vision, but nothing worked. It wouldn't happen again. I placed the journal down and stood up to look around. Only the usual activity of nurses helping other saints could be seen, the usual blue glowing beds and light from the stained-glass roof. I considered for a moment that the halo may have been some kind of reflection from the multi-colored roof, but the dark pink static could not be explained away. I sat back down thinking about what to do, maybe ask one of the nurses. I glanced at Beattie's journal and saw the words "...that make your body vibrate" which might only have attracted me more if they said make your ears vibrate. I started reading.

... that day had one of those storms that make your body vibrate when it thunders. I knew I only had a short time until I had to leave my rock and head home, but it was so exciting with the lightning and all. If you ever watched a thunderstorm approaching from the side of a mountain, you'd understand. I remember I heard a thunder crack to my right, so loud you swore it would knock you down. It was ugly, and the falling tree was what caught my attention first. A mama bear wandered too close to the edge of the mountainside with her cubs when the tree started to fall. I had the distance and could see clearly that the tree wouldn't have even come close to hitting her or her two cubs, but she was the same as Moms all over the world. She saw danger and reacted to protect. Out of fear, she ran herself and the closest cub with her over, which must've seemed safer than getting swatted by the tree. I watched them tumble head over clawed toe all the way to the bottom, scraping at the air, fur limbs twisting fiercely. I knew by the time they were halfway down they weren't going to survive. If you ever want to experience a heart-wrenching scene, watch a cub watching its mama plummet to her death. The cub was so sad and adorable. I started crying with her. She sat at the edge looking down and making little rough squawks calling for her mama to come back, not sure if she should jump after her. They were the most tiring squawks you could imagine.

I hiked quickly down to where she was. The wind roared at us, but I went slowly to not spook her. I put one biscuit on a patch of grass. The butter was sweet-smelling and with the wind sending the scent straight to her black nose, it didn't take long for her to come over and gobble it up. She trotted after me all the way back to the house. I left her in the barn with my biscuit and my heart as she sniffed the air with that same searching look in her eyes she had at the cliff's edge. I ran through the back door to tell Mom I'd be in the barn until the storm cleared, but she wasn't home. When I came back, I found Pinky sitting with her tongue flappin' away at the butter spread all over her nose and mouth. As soon as I saw that big pink tongue shining brightly against her dark fur, I knew what her name would be.

A hallmark day for Pinky and me seeing as Mom and Billy died that afternoon too. While I was out, they left to deliver a shipment and were run off the side of the road. The archive showed the tractor-trailer not being able to avoid them as it was rounding Gentry's bend. Guess it doesn't matter much which way it happened, still left me with a farm to tend and myself to take care of, let alone a very quickly growing Pinky.

The repetition of the word Pinky had me uneasy - that odd pink static cloud. I skipped to the last page to see how much more she'd written. There I found a drawing of a bear with a bow around its neck sitting across from a girl in a big multi-layered dress. Little pink stars, and spirals densely decorated the air about them. An arrow pointed at both and read, "I am she who raises the claw, she who bears the honey. I am she who grins with electric teeth of heaven's bright in great wind and turbulence. I am she who stands with fists to say, 'You of breast and milk, you are the provider with pistol and your many mirrored world can be filled with the glory and the glamour. Strike!'"

The dense stars had me standing, and once again the thought of fontanels came into my mind. Wide open skulls dark pink and disturbing. I stood up and felt a great urge to get the boys and go. I left Beattie's journal at her bedside and started moving through the aisles of naked sleeping saints with patches of hair and bodies of skin but no sign of rainbow reflections coming from anywhere.

☰TWENTY-TWO☰

I started imagining my brothers falling off a mountainside and then my parent's accident and that led to me thinking how I have no control over my thoughts - how these things just come into my mind and why didn't I have more control. Fontanels and falling brothers and dead deer swirled in my head.

I knew the general vicinity of where they would be and decided to look for a shortcut to where I'd found the twins with Mamon before. I followed a couple of scientists to the exit close to me which seemed like it might run parallel to the hallway I'd walked down last time. It was a labcoat colony here. They buzzed from room to room. None seemed to take note of me. A few people pushing plants in glass containers on a metal cart were a couple of yards ahead and turned left down where I imagined I'd be able to connect with the other hallway.

When I arrived at where they turned left, it opened into another large room, a processing zone of sorts. Mammoth oblong cars traveled through a tunnel, stopped, split, and glass walls of the beetle housing swung out. They came apart like opening a giant book, emptied and were filled again with fresh aqua blue crystal. Small men in green suits transferred caged animals off one conveyor belt and onto another. Each cage passed through a showering mechanism completely soaking the frantic animals, who appeared fine once they arrived on the other side.

I found no exits as I continued down to an empty hallway. Long ribbed opaque walls became transparent glass, showing a tropical wonderland beyond. The land appeared in motion, undulating sections like an earthquake or a landslide in action. Colorful flowers floated and stirred. It looked like one of the virtual worlds I'd visited, but I didn't have a suit on, no helmet or contacts inserted. This was real. I found a door to an observation room, which allowed me a greater place to experience the landscape and sudden grotesque panoramic view. It was somewhat like bending to smell sweet flowers and finding they're made of garbage. These weren't floating flowers. They were animals with leaves and vines growing through them, some sort of plant-animals. One jumped and leaned on the window. When I made out what it was panting at me, my head ached. It undoubtedly was a dog, or once was a dog. It looked like a cross between a German shepherd and tangle of vines. It panted at me with cloudy excited eyes asking to be let out. Maybe it was only in some plant-animal haze. Tiny leaves wove in through the large vine on the arch of its nose. Thin cream flowers with red veins shot out from where its ears should be. Thick woody vines and grassy leaves replaced fur-covered skin. How did it stay together? It looked so fragile. I put my hand up to the window where his paws were. He moved and licked at my hand with a dark pink tongue, smearing the glass with black slime.

It felt like watching an animal with its skin flayed off and left lucid to experience the torture. The dogbush jumped down, ran around among what could be limbs or torsos, littering the ground. Some things were moving but I couldn't make out most of what they were. Then the dogbush ran back and jumped at the window. THUD! It fell to the ground and a small part of its hip fell off. It got up and ran back with the rest of the plant animals, rollicking without an understanding of its loss. The thud started a light flashing at the end of the hallway.

I crooked out and through a few doorways and found a stairwell that I started down. The stairs looped down and around in a wide spiral with no doors. I finally came to the end and leaped out of the stairway with too much momentum landing painfully on my knees.

Why was I running? I wasn't doing anything wrong. I was lost. No doors had locks in this place. My brain trotted along with my heart. It could have merely been research I didn't understand. I could've asked the center employees where I was, told them I was trying to find my brothers and needed directions. Okay. I'd find an employee and tell them I was lost. They'd understand. Gaudi's winding cathedral was less tangled than this place.

I stood, went to the double doors, and knocked. Strange acoustics increased the volume of my knuckles on the wood. No answer so I entered. Bright yellow light came on from the edge of the walls illuminating thousands of photographs in a tall domed room. The thermostat in the room must have been set too high. It felt warmer than the rest of the center, like a sauna but possibly necessary for the plants. Two soaring palm trees arched over a glass desk in the middle of the room. They reached toward light emanating through a circle of multicolored glass at the ceiling. The walls fluttered with paper like a mangled art gallery.

The fluttering pulled me close to see what the pictures had to tell. Most of them flapped from one secured corner. They were of people involved with every sort of activity imaginable, like a printed Archive room. No common theme that I could detect except most had people interacting or posing outdoors or with trees or plants. I found a group pinned close together that showed people without some of their limbs, standing or seated in positions that gave the appearance of putting their lost appendage, their stumps, on display and thought of Amelia Figg.

Behind the glass desk hulked three rows of impressive overflowing bookcases. The tables in front of the desk were strewn with large drawings of plants, hardbound books opened, and notes written up and down the margins. I read a few titles of the books. There was a stack with the Eeden monks' logo on the spines. The rest were exotic, expensive-looking collector's items. It all felt a bit like finding your parents sex toys while digging through their closet.

I turned to the desk and found books piled on its edge. They were labeled "Journal: Dr LM Vol. III", "Journal: IV", "Journal: VII", etc. I picked a stack of the journals up finding them surprisingly lightweight and carefully fanned through their pages knowing later I could freeze-frame and read what I wanted. I stopped to read a section because I saw something about SAWs.

... (Notes for lecture on Synchronicity Activity Waves *have visualization appear in front of each audience member in shades of red*.) Notice the balloon hovering in front of you. Watch as it's pinched in the center and now looks like a doughnut or as is known in scientific circles: a torus. This is our universe sitting before you. Notice the white dot on the edge of the torus. See it begin to revolve about and through. Its path travels into the center and back out the other side. In, around and out it goes repeatedly. This is the simplified motion of our galaxy in the universe propelled by dark matter. Now let's talk about Bohm, [add visual of Bohm behind/above me] one of the great physicists of scientific history, who spoke on the nature of physical reality. His example of that nature is as follows: [add visual for each audience member] Take a cylinder jar and place it inside another. Fill the space between the two jars with glycerin and add a drop of ink. Now watch as the ink drop stretches out into thin strands as the inner jar is rotated. If you keep spinning the inner jar, eventually that drop of ink will look like it disappears. But not so fast. If you reverse the rotation, we see how the drop of ink reforms back to its original drop. Now let's think of this white dot revolving around a torus-like that drop of ink [visual shifts from cylinder/ink to torus/white dot]. In our universe, as we expand out from the center of the torus, our life/the white dot or drop of ink, moves faster. Our focus and the signs of the connectedness of the universe become more and more blurred. We see more chaos in everything, entropy increases. Rounding the edge of the torus and heading back to the center, everything becomes more cohesive. The ink drop unravels back into view.

This action is occurring now, for the first time in human history. We're heading back towards the center of the torus. The Synchronicity Activity Waves are purely a result of time/space coming back into alignment. We all have been experiencing a heightened sense of déjà vu.

At the bottom of the lecture notes was added:

Alignment = Use Geodesic strings that bind the universe to tighten/control. Easier to combine Mindlight.

Activity blinking on the desktop drew my attention. I pushed the journals back and looked down to see what was streaming. Thousands of squares of images flickered. While most sections changed from one scene to another, the largest section, about a quarter of the grid, remained steady on two people - my brothers. I saw a current feed of them walking in a hallway with Mamon now. The other squares flipped through various items in their archives. Nothing lewd but why watch their archives? It could have been prepping for today, for his reporting to Lazaras. It could just be to help them, but still, I felt nervous at the sight.

I tried to think differently. People must know about all of his actions, must be tracking everything he does, right? He's famous with huge legions of fans. If he were up to no good we'd all know in minute detail, but somehow, maybe not. I adjusted my goggles to prep them for a refined speed recording and flipped quickly through as many journals as I could for easy future freeze-framing and as I returned the last to the desk, I noticed a small two-buttoned control square blinking on the desktop. Overwhelmingly compelled, stupidly, without much thought, I tapped the first button thinking it'd show me more of what he'd been reviewing. Instead, a loud humming noise filled the room and a slit along the top of the desk widened. Bright light poured from the desk, originating from the floor. Light like I'd never experienced. The humming increased as the gap widened, and my half of the desk and floor slid backward. The intense light severely hurt my eyes, and I forced them shut as I darkened the goggles to block more. I kept tapping the desktop where I thought the button would be and the noise and motion stopped but I'd never get out if I didn't find a way to turn the light off. I wildly tapped some more, and with great relief, the desk slid back into place.

I darted to the door and back up the stairway, heading the way I came. I tried new corridors and noticed the upward sloping roofline with the stained-glass ceiling. Happily, at the end, I saw into the saints' chamber. Martina was still reading when I reached her desk.

"Hello, Martina." She peered up at me as I tried to appear casual, "I, uh, was heading back to meet up with the twins."

"Do what you like." She ended by making sarcastic kissing lips at me and heat rose up my neck into my face.

I sat down for a minute before I saw Mamon walking my way with the twins and several scientists.

"All finished then, Ben?" Mamon asked with a voice that gave no lead on whether he knew of my activities or not.

"Just finished up. How were the twins? You guys didn't give Dr Mamon any trouble, did you?"

"We played the best game ever again," Ed said grinning.

"They don't make games like that anymore," Francis shared, appearing proud of his observation.

"That's right Francis, and you two are the best players. They were very good."

"Dr Mamon told us we can come play again soon," Ed said.

"But Dr Mamon said we can't take the game home because it's an only-for-here kind of game, not an everyday game like he said it might be," Francis added.

"Well, what I meant was you can certainly play it anytime you come to visit. I want them to have something to look forward to." He said it with great kindness, and I could see the boys were incredibly happy. "Listen, I have a new request. What are you doing Sunday? Any plans that can't be rearranged?"

I found myself responding without suspicion, "Nothing special, my friend Lenny and I were talking about going out Saturday night, but other than that I'm free."

"If you'd be available to leave Sunday morning for Skycity I've some new saint prospects I'd like you to review for me. I've been thinking you and some of the other scientists might benefit by getting to know the saints before they join us. You know, see how they operate in the waking world. Couldn't you create the visual peptide manipulators more suited for the saint if you met and interacted with them while they were awake?"

"Didn't you say my work was helping?" I snapped at him a little.

"In fact, it was your question that led me to think of what might benefit the saints more, pre-interviews by those who care for them when they sleep could be one way. Your expenses for the trip would be paid for of course. Have you ever been to Skycity?"

Thoughts of seeing Susan in person tripped me up and without much thought, I answered, "No but, but uh, I have a friend that lives there. So, I guess that's a yes if the trip won't take too long."

"A day at most and I'd be happy to arrange care for the boys while you are gone. I'm sure they'd have a good deal of fun and I could possibly even further the separation research?"

"Yay, we'll get to play the game all day long," Francis said.

I felt pressure to respond. "I guess if it's only for a day that'd be fine," I said. "I wouldn't want them to be a burden to anyone. You know, I may be able to arrange for a friend to take them overnight? You boys would like to stay with the Panas wouldn't you?" I feared the Panas wouldn't be able to but felt stuck.

"It's no bother to me. Happy to have them. A late morning start sound agreeable to you?"

"Yeah, sure." I had no time to think.

"It's settled then. I'm grateful for your generous work and devotion here, Ben. Do you need me to show you the way out or will you be okay on your own?" Mamon asked.

"I think you'd better take us. This place is... big. I wouldn't want to get lost."

⚌TWENTY-THREE⚌

I found my car was on its way to Laurel's farm again like it knew what I needed. As we headed down the driveway, I realized I could've taken her up on watching the boys for my trip to Skycity. I knew she wasn't expecting me until next week, but with what I'd seen today I was sure she'd understand another spontaneous visit.

"We're going to visit with Laurel again. It's a treat for being good at the Center today."

"Laurel, yay!   She's gonna make us something delicious," Ed said.

"She might, I don't know if we'll stay for dinner," I said.

"She always has us for dinner. If she don't she'll be upset," Francis said.

"Don't bug her about it, be polite. So, what did you get up to with Dr Mamon today?"

"We told you already, the game, remember," Ed said.

"That's right. How about anything else?"

"He didn't bug us, just left us with the game. I can't wait for it again," Ed said while Francis poked excitedly at the window because he saw Laurel's farm.

I could see the lights on in the house when we arrived.

"Now, be calm with Laurel," I said as we walked to the front door, worrying that this really was pushing my welcome to its limits.

"Laurel loves our surprises!" Ed said.

Francis and Ed fought to push the eye that you poke to ring the doorbell.

She came to the door staring out at us with a quizzical look on her face.

"Look who's here again already, my favorite boys of all time!" She said opening the door with two bags of spices she must've been getting ready to ship. Two cats ran out towards the barn.

"Laurel, can you believe it? We're here like a surprise again," Francis said.

"Yes, you are," she said quickly putting the bags down and hugging the boys. "Come on in now and let me get you something to eat, everyone surely knows it's dinnertime, and you must be hungry."

"I'm sorry, really, but I needed to talk. I'll explain in a bit," I said.

"I'm sure you will," she said, giving me a somewhat stern look.

We walked into the house and joined Laurel in the kitchen where she put her spice bags in boxes and started cutting kernels from a plate of corn cobs that had been grilled.

"You won't believe what I saw today, Laurel, it's nuts," I started.

"Come on, everything with you is nuts." She mimicked my voice, "The wind blew four different colored leaves in front of me at the same time. Damn, that's nuts." She put her hands inside her shirt and poked out her pointer fingers for nipples, "That woman has breasts the size of coconuts nuts nuts." She cackled as she grabbed a brown egg and cracked it into a bowl.

The twins thought it all hilarious.

"Boys, would you please go play until I've finished making dinner?" Laurel said lightly.

"Aww, but we want you to make your nipples stick out again," Ed said.

"They'll be no more of that, plus you have to help me feed the cats," she said as she pulled a sack of dry cat food from a drawer.

"Yeah, cause it is time for dinner for them too," Ed said. They raced out the front door towards the barn.

"No, but this really was nuts," I said. "A stick dog. Have you ever seen a living dog composed of twigs and leaves?"

"What are you ... oh, sure, okay, yes. I have in my dream last night." Laurel threw her hands up in the air. "Haven't we seen about every kind of crazy vision in some form or another like that? The world is filled with surreal visions. I'm surprised you'd even notice it with every virtual world, every movie filled with that business. I've seen two perfectly happy boys the size of oak trees walk around connected at the chest. A stick dog, why not?"

"Sorry, I really caught you off guard tonight didn't I?" Ben mumbled.

"Where'd you see this dog? And what kind of drugs were you and Lenny experimenting with before you did?"

"No drugs, I was at the Center, and my ears started vibrating, and I saw this odd rainbow halo and pink confetti over this one saint's head. Which I know sounds kooky, but it happened just before I read the part where she wrote about thunder causing her head to vibrate. No really, this sounds crazy I get it, but then I took this hallway to find the twins who were with Mamon—"

"That crutch kicker. I told you about mentioning his name around me. There's a lack of love in that man."

"You've never even met him. I'm talking about watching factory operations of odd glowing liquids, animals on conveyor belts and some kind of experiments breeding plants with animals."

"I'm not condoning it in the slightest, but so what if he's doing that? Surely it should produce moral dissent, but come on, scientists have been torturing animals for centuries, so we can live long and so-called healthier lives. What's new and disturbing about that?"

"That's what I thought, but have you really seen a dog made of twigs and leaves?"

"No, but I—"

"No, you haven't, and that wasn't all. I ran when I saw it, and I don't know how they'd feel about me seeing their plant animals, I mean, everything is available in the Archives, right, but it seemed wrong, and with the other vision, I doubt they'd be happy. I ran and ended up in Mamon's library. It looked like a thousand magazines barfed all over the walls and then on his desk were archives of the twins, and then as a nice final touch I push a button I probably shouldn't have, and his desk begins to split, and the room fills with super bright light and luckily I got the damn thing shut and got out of there. No one seemed to know. Now maybe all that, examined separately, would seem of little consequence, but if you saw it and add in men growing leaves out of their hands and crotches, you'd be shaken too."

"I'm not sure what it is you're arguing for? That he's a mad scientist to be frightened of? Or that he's a friendly lovechild looking to make the world a better place with his wacko science projects—"

"It's hard to explain it all, a lot happened but I can't stop this feeling like my mind is out of control. My thoughts just keep going back to things like the boys falling off a cliff."

"I think you're going to be fine. Okay, let's stop this. I have an idea. Listen, I want you to do something with me for a moment." She finished wrapping the dumplings, put the tray of them in the boiling water and turned towards me, "I want you to close your eyes and breathe. Breathe in and out slowly till I say stop."

"What? I don't need to calm down like that. You're over-exaggerating how upset I am. I mean, I'm upset, but I don't need to calm down. I am calm," I said, and a throbbing started behind my eyes.

"Ben, we both need to. Relax your jaw and breathe please." She washed off her hands, took out a bowl of beans from her refrigerator and quietly began to snap off the ends, slowly breathing herself.

A few minutes of deep inhalation passed accompanied by the sound of beans snapping.

"I feel better now," I said with composure.

She looked closely at my face and squinted.

"Let's give this a try again." She wiped her hands and sat across from me. "Close your eyes and breathe for me." I immediately did. "Good, that's great. Now, open them and look at my face. Look into my pupils."

The first time Laurel tried this with me, I didn't know what she was trying to do. I still question it. I know it worked before. I know Laurel could do such unexplainable things, but it all felt goofy or hokey.

"Good, now slowly close your eyes again and please speak to me the first words that come into your mind." Her pupils pulsed at me and the skin feathered out on her head, wavering up and down as my eyelids gradually shut. I went somewhere in my mind, somewhere where people seem inverted.

We sat in silence for a few minutes as images of fire emanating from my ears soothed me. Then Susan's face popped into my mind.

"Now ease back, open your eyes and see me once more."

I opened my eyes to Laurel's stone face working on something in her head. I sat back and looked out the kitchen window.

"I had images of my ears comfortably being on fire and then saw Susan. I may get to meet her soon actually. What do you think?"

"I'm glad to hear about your growing interest." She looked away from me and dug some wax from her ear with her pinky. "Maybe the stick dog bothered you merely because you aren't resolving other issues, but also, maybe you're right to be concerned about that kicker's activities. Please, keep your eyes wide. Why don't you go ring the bell for the boys?"

The twins joined us, and we had another of Laurel's feasts. We sat stuffed and burped contentedly, while the table was cleared of emptied bowls and smeared flatware.

"Laurel, can we stay here with you forever?" Ed asked as Laurel served warm pecan brownies with vanilla ice cream. The steam entered our noses and lied to our stomachs that we had room for more.

"Of course, you can stay with me forever. I need a couple of strong hands like you and Francis to keep the cow stalls cleared. You wouldn't mind waking up at four AM tomorrow and scraping them clean for me, would you?"

She said this as I shoveled a nice chunk of dripping brownie into my mouth.

"Cows can kick their own stuff out, and we'll let you make us food all the time." Francis smiled.

"You've got all the great ideas my little-sugared turtle, but I'm afraid your brother would get awfully lonely if you two came and lived with me."

"That's right, how could I stand living without you guys and your beautiful singing voices," I said jokingly.

"What do you mean? We don't sing," Ed said, acting belligerent from knowing he wasn't going to be allowed to stay.

"I do too," Francis said poking Ed.

"Yeah, oh yeah, but I sing better than you do," Ed said.

"No, you don't. Laurel who sings better, him or me?"

"That would be a tough choice. Why don't you sing me a song and then I'll decide?"

"What should we sing?" Ed asked.

"I know, I know, how 'bout the song that we learned in the game?" Francis said almost singing his words.

"I don't remember it too much," Ed said.

"We'll use the screen, of course, we will," Francis said.

"You learned a song at the Center today?" I asked.

"Sure, it was part of the game. Dr Mamon said we should always remember it if we wanted to play the game better," Francis said.

"I thought Dr Mamon said you couldn't take the game with you."

"Yeah, but this isn't the game, it's the song," Francis said.

Laurel looked at me quizzically.

"Give it a shot then," Laurel said.

"Okay but turn out the lights. I sing better in the dark," Ed said shyly, probably still worried about remembering the song.

Laurel dimmed the kitchen lights. The twins did the vocal command for their screens that were recharging in the corner of the kitchen. They floated from the wall and hovered into place beside the twins' heads. Each gazed into their respective screens, said one of the tuning commands and the screens flashed into life, illuminating their faces and the room. Symbols clicked by in a steady stream, and the twins began to sway hypnotically, staring at them. Their low baritone voices began humming. It was more of a moan than a hum, the drone of a praying monk or of a dog about to bark. The light from the screens intensified. Laurel and I sat transfixed as symbols faded from one to the next. The twins' mouths moved as if they were working lyrics, but no words came. It was like some underwater Tuvan throat-singer, some other world karaoke and just as I recalled that I'd heard this song before the tones shifted with the symbols' speed and rhythm. Their eyes held wide, and the room transformed into an atmosphere of a mosque or a church. Space in Laurel's little kitchen seemed to expand. My lids became heavy as I tried to watch the symbols the twins were connected to. I looked at Laurel. Her head lolled to the side, asleep or mesmerized. The light increased as my lids slid shut.

"Who was better, huh?" Ed croaked into my opening eyes.

I felt like I was waking from a night's sleep.

"Honey, you know I think you have a great voice and I think Francis has a great way with his singing," Laurel said, confusing and complimenting them both.

Laurel stood cleaning the dishes.

"Did I miss something?" I said.

"Yes, you missed a second helping of my famous brownies, but with that post-dinner napping you have going there I'm guessing you don't need more anyway. Talk about rude, right as my boys were showing their singing talents. Let's go out and take in some of that cool fall air and glorious nightlife before you all hit the road."

"We can catch lightning bugs like that other time!" Ed shouted.

"I'm afraid it's too late for lightning bugs, sweetheart, but let's go see what we can find."

Still in a stupor, I followed them out to sit among the wind chimes and watch the stars. The twins were captivated like always by the sky. It held their attention in the same way the screens could. The blue glow from the screens lit up the sides of the boy's faces as we walked.

"Will you shut those things off, you won't be able to see the stars half as well with them monstrosities shining in your eyes," Laurel said.

The twins gave the verbal command, and the screens shut off. They took a seat on the metal bench. Laurel sat in their laps using their bridge for a backrest. She put her pinch fingers out and pretended to pluck stars from the sky for each one, sticking them in their mouths, up their noses, and in their ears. The twins laughed with delight, and it wasn't long before we were all getting chilly and had to leave.

At the car, after the twins had given Laurel their goodbyes and climbed in, Laurel pulled me aside.

"If you're worried and want to bring the boys around when you go to volunteer at the Center I'd be happy to have them, okay. Don't wait to contact me if anything strange is happening. They seem a bit off to me today."

"Maybe it's from your cooking." I smiled at her.

"Ben, you must listen. You know I have the gut to sense these things."

"Don't worry. I'm sure they'll come back and help you muck out the stalls another day."

"Forget it, it's your ears that need mucking out," She said, sticking out her arms for a hug. "Now go get some rest and call me if you need me to rescue you from some banana dog."

"Okay, I will," I said, and she squeezed me tight.

☰TWENTY-FOUR☰

A square with Lenny's name in it flashed on the wall. "Answer that for me would you, BUD."

A vibrating holo of Lenny standing on a couch in his apartment suddenly expanded from the floor to fill my bedroom. "You ready?"

"I just got back from dropping off the twins at the Panas - don't have to get them till tomorrow. What's with the pants?" I asked.

"You'll need to be brighter if you want eyes on you. At least get some color into that shirt."

I bent back my collar to reveal its tag and turned the saturation up on my shirt from a nice muted blue to an electric vibrant one. "Where's Sheryl?"

"Now that's what they'll be looking for. Power blue for you! Sheryl said she's done with me. I'm a free bird. Coat your braut in case you roll duo with a roaster. I'll be over to pick you up in a few shakes." He pumped his hips at my head as he and his couch dissolved into the floor.

A little hyper tonight. With the prospect of sex, no doubt he'd coat himself before he knew for sure. The only guy I ever heard of trying a ménage à trois. He called me the next day after they'd left his apartment and said, "My foot-long hotdog needs two sets of buns to wrap it. Extra mustard please." I doubted his activities were related to his looks. In any kind of mass appeal sense, I'd say he was not good looking, but put him in a party with a dozen women in attendance and more than half of them would have flirted with him before the night ended. He must blow some kind of hardcore pheromone through that gap in his teeth. About an hour later, he knocked at my door with an outfit so bright yellow I went looking for my clubglasses.

"Whoa, sunny boy, you're blinding me. Turn it down," I said.

Lenny jumped up into the air and wiggled like a worm. "No way. Wait till you see me hang dancing tonight. I'll have every woman diving in after me. How's your modbop?"

"It's up, and I'm joe, no bigbag," I said knowing I hadn't kept up with it the way Lenny had.

"Ah Mr RoughBurger, sounding like a newborn. As long as you don't trip talk when we're there. Your autopilot or mine?"

"Thought you said you were heading over to pick me up? But maybe we should take separate cars, if that love gel you have dripping out of your pants is any indication, it's going to be me hailing a ride."

Lenny hiked one of his legs up in the air and waggled his pointer finger back and forth, dancing in a circle as if he was a sprinkler system showering the surroundings.

"Sprin-kle your tin-kle in every sunshine bowl." Lenny crooned the lyrics from a popular advertisement as we left the apartment.

We took his car, and he'd queued up a song blend of chest-warming base on the car's sound system: animal-mating calls, a flute melody line, and an old mumble-voiced man.

"I was readin' today on the OM2ME info site about how Mamon Inc.'s forcin' a takeover of OM2ME. Something about majority stewardship given to the Saint Center for the lighting technology they developed has enabled Mamon Inc. to obtain full control. Do you smell what I smell?" Lenny sniffed around.

"Smell what?" I said.

"Mamon's pile. His group takes over OM2ME right after they launched the new biosphere amplifier. Do you know how long I've been working on this? Right when the coherence beams are about to hit the atmosphere, and parts of our work could really shine. Drives me crazy. Your company now controls mine," Lenny said.

"In that case, as your boss, I order you not to embarrass me tonight. I'd like to have a good time where we don't make a big scene, but I have to say I'm not surprised about the merger, especially if those coherence beams are a big deal as I imagine. It's not like they come around every ten years or something. Once in a millennium, right?"

"Right, longer actually, but you know he's as crooked as my bratwurst," Lenny said.

I couldn't help but feel a little guilty about not immediately filling him in on all the oddities, on not siding with Lenny somehow, but this was our way. "Mamon's got more good work going on than you know about. You just haven't taken time to research it." The city lights glimmered in through the windows and we glimmered back with our shirts beaming out the windows. Lenny flipped a reed into his mouth and lit it. Our windows lowered a crack.

"Who's got time for this kind of go-research-it business? With all the battles, all these plagues of marketing how can you point your finger at anyone? Mandelbrot loops of data to confound. Who do you protest against? Watchdog groups for watchdogs. Everything documented but no time to review it. All these continual mergers. Who do we bring down when we don't know who owns and controls what? I'm a flat tire from Mamon spikes," Lenny said exhaling smoke as he spoke.

"Come on, he's fighting to bring an end to that kind of cynicism," I said.

"With all the people he's in bed with and all the business-controlled wars going on, you have to wonder how much soap he's using."

"He's a pro-class innovator. Certain revolutions exact costs not everyone will agree with, I mean, you see, he's a, he's really a good guy that's all - all for now, for tonight," I said too much like a command.

Lenny lowered his voice some, showing he wasn't looking to fight. "Sure, I got you. Just keep your nose open. You're in a good position to smell it if anything wrong floats."

"You, Laurel and definitely not me, we're not geniuses like he is. I have to stick to the idea I'm involved with something that is capital G good."

The air from the cracked windows gave a soundtrack to the tense silence that followed.

I felt bad about the tension. Tonight was supposed to be a way to relax. I tried to steer us back towards something positive. "I'm going to visit Susan tomorrow."

Lenny took a long drag and then after an extended moment responded. "To the Skycity? It's about time." He started humming the sprinkle your tinkle advertisement jingle. "We're set to visit Laurel next week, aren't we?"

"I don't know... I had an unscheduled visit yesterday. Sorry. I know you wanted to go. We could probably still go next week."

"I doubt she'll want company two weekends in a row. What made you stop?"

"Please avoid the I told you sos after I say this, but I was wandering around the Center after I'd finished my work yesterday and saw some odd stuff. I was thinking after Laurel's last night that the processing plant might not be something to worry about. It could be part of the biotech that keeps the living architecture of the complex healthy, but the dogbush is still troubling."

"You lost me. Is that some kind of twisted ModBop? You were working, and you saw a dogwood tree in a processing plant, and this bothered you?"

I lit a reed. "No, sorry. I ran into some kind of indoor jungle at the Center that looked like it was swirling around, or uh, it looked like it was all in motion. Then this dog made of twigs and leaves jumped at the window. I found it all by accident. Then I ended up in Mamon's library or office somehow, and it was like an old magazine factory blew up in it. Pictures everywhere. A real crazy scene. On his desk were a bunch of feeds of the twins and I pushed this button and the room started to split apart and fill with light till I shut it off and got out of there."

"What? Were you smokin' something without me?"

"No, wasn't like that."

"A dogbush and a photo collage. Not exactly the stuff of our favorite horror movies ... Hey, look at those lights."

Lenny squealed to a stop in the parking lot of Club Parched, a line like a strand of Christmas lights wrapped around the front leading to the entrance. Most of them turned to see who made the racket. Lenny waved at the closest women, beeped the horn as he rolled down his window, and they gave him a dirty look.

He looked at me with excitement and sped around to the side lot. A few cars glided away on long spindly fingerlifts overhead. Spotlights followed them to their perches. We hopped out before ours was scooped and craned.

Lenny shoved a mint box at me after eating one.

"Howdya do. Howdya do," Lenny said to several women as I followed him towards the front of the line. "Ha! Hey, didn't know you'd be here." He patted a guy lit purple I didn't recognize. "The runway is now clear for landing," he said as he squeezed by them to the entrance. I barely kept up and tried to avoid the angry eyes of the others.

A colossal open mouth with a tongue flapping out for a welcome mat formed the club's doorway. 'Club Parched' wavered across the upper lip and steam billowed as it exited into the cold night. Mushy waterdrop shaped steps lined the path along the tongue to the stairs. A longnecked attractive woman with heavily glossed lips staffed the entrance scanner.

"Look here please," the woman said. Her arms were ringed with bright red hair.

Lenny moved in close, too close. He took her hand and touched her arm hair lightly. "You are not allowed to touch the hanging dancers," she said obviously okay with his touching her.

"You are a most beautiful creature. If the rest of the night is as magical, this will be one to review over and over."

He nodded to me to approach. She let her arm linger apparently looking for him to touch it again until I moved in to scan and hurry the line along.

A jelly-stepped escalator carried me through intense blue lighting, fast-moving humid air, and dense white cloud. It was a blend of sea and sky. The muffled sounds of the music above hit me as the clouds parted at the top.

"Only the first is free," a vibrant short and curvy red-tinted woman said and handed me my filled-to-the-rim glass.

"You're not allowed to touch the dancers," an ebullient man said as he shuffled us into an area out of the way of the other arriving guests.

Lenny guzzled it and began to laugh into the glass even before he'd finished. The water flecked his cheeks and sent out sparkled rays where the light met the water that rolled down his glowing shirt.

"Nothin' better, nothin' better. Ha! Hooooo! What're you waitin' for?" Lenny asked.

The bubbly liquid filled me, and I laughed until tears streaked my cheeks. The club pleasantly hummed while I stood there adjusting to the scene.

Before me, a giant oval room tiered upwards towards the hang dancing on-ramp pipe. There was only one transparent pipe standing prominently above the middle of the clear dance floor, but nearly every surface had a reflection or simulation of the drips giving the club an air of lava lamp. Bird and fish-headed human statues lined the perimeter of the room. Four spiral staircases led to the top where people stood about on the various platforms dancing while waiting for their turns to enter the pipe and join the dance. Bright red, green, yellow, and blue the platforms glowed and faded to the rhythms. Quivering white bolts of electricity zipped back and forth between the spaces of the railings and platforms, zigzagging all the way up the stairs to the tempo of the music. A line of people waited at the top near the pipe entrance. One at a time they stepped forward, becoming enveloped by the purple ooze as they lowered into the drip form and hung from the floor below. Their brightly lit clothing began to pulse from inside the goo as they languidly glided along the bottom of the floor and started a quivering style dance.

Lenny pulled at me. "Come on, come on. Let's hit it. Look at all the oozy dolls hanging," and he went bolting up the wide spiral staircase. I stood there feeling the great giddy laughter before it registered I should move to join him. How could he tell they were ladies? You could barely identify gender of the hang dancers. We wove through color-flashing figures, mirth, and more teeth, long pink shaking tongues soaked with laughing water. Lenny went straight to the top. Some basilisk eyes asked where we thought we were going; didn't we know there was a line. Lenny paid no heed. If he thought like I did, he was willing to wait for the tube but not for the view from the top. Higher and higher, it wasn't a short hike.

A woman sang in staccato bursts accompanying the deep metallic kettle drumming. People lined the railing at the edge of the platform. Couples acted immune to the presence of others - no doubt inspired by the vision below and mashed their lips together in a monstrous playful display. I squeezed past two of these couples to see the transparent drip floor below. The floor undulated where beneath figures flowed together in a ripple ballet. You could see them far more clearly from above than beside them on the bottom floor. The dancers seemed like blind people, their eyes wide but not seeing what moved around them. They waved their hips and lifted their arms as if choreographed.

The sensual riot marched in combinations of gunshot rhythm, coital scents, glimmering hang dancers, and tinted bodies with free-floating genitalia. Lenny gently elbowed the couple to my right and pressed along the railing to get closer to me. A grin so wide his head looked like it might snap in half. He flapped an elbow wing pointing out one of the male couple's groin.

"Haven't seen this many public bones since high school. Hey, I've been talkin' to Cherry over there," he shouted as if he wasn't a foot from my ear, "and she'll let us cut. Said she'd tell the others we're related to the owners." A bald woman, half-brown half-crimson skinned with long violet hair flowing off the edges of her ears monitored the dance floor for available space.

I looked over to find her smiling as she conducted another into the ooze current. I didn't say anything but followed Lenny's lead. He whispered something to her, kissed her on the cheek, and drank the rest of his laughing water. Smiling at him, she took his empty glass, shoved his sunglasses into his pocket, and he jumped into the flood of goo in a vertical belly flop kind of fashion. His bright yellow outfit and the purple of the ooze vibrated in my eyes then sluuuurrrp, he was gone. She looked at his drinking glass with minor frustration. I took it and placed it on a passing waiter's tray.

"Thank you for getting us in," I said near her ear.

"No skin to me. Dognose wouldn't trolley, no choice," she said with a thick Brit accent.

"Thanks anyway."

She looked over the edge and back at me. A smile filled her face as she removed my sunglasses, put them in my pocket, and waved me into the tube. The thick liquid streamed onto me, warm, so warm sliding down my shirt. My shoulders and back felt like they'd gone to sleep, all pins and needles. Panic hit me as it started coating my head. "How do you breathe?" I asked as the purple ooze swallowed me. Immediate joy followed with a complete release from myself, from any kind of negative self-consciousness. As I laughed, the fluid washed into me like fresh air, and I breathed easily. At first, I couldn't see anything that made sense. Wavering colored low light, a blurring dimmed kaleidoscope roiled about me. The top and back of my head had the quality of expanding and contracting as I eased into the rhythms.

Little sparks formed two static-edged circles in front of my eyes. Through them, I began to see a blurred dim landscape. The circles expanded, becoming one and a tunnel vision surrounded me until it was all I saw and I was in it, surrounded and moving quickly through. The sense of joy died away. I couldn't register my arms or legs. My body had become a worm or a stick of gelatin that began pulsing, moving through the female mountain. As I wavered through, she stroked and protected my body, connecting herself to me. I could sense her boundaries the way you could a car as you drove. I'm a small section of a massive mountain, massive force. I was being controlled and I started looking for her bare flabby legs with those black boots above me about to strike my head, but other worm forms joined me.

They brought the joy again and liquid metal blobs bounced at my eyes along to the music. Another form flowed up close. The blobs moved away. It didn't matter what direction I went; the new form matched my motions exactly. Encouraging vibrations attacked every part of me, and I sent them out in return until we came undone into each other and then a large blast and we were separated again. Released into play zones for recess from school. Free-falling from a plane. Warm cheek close to your face in the summer sun. I moved parallel to another and matched their movements. Together, as we traveled, the pleasure increased the mountain's caress. Another joining dance, another blast of separation.

Pulsing from the top and back of my head started as the thought that somehow electronic meant moved-away-from-nature before now. Music, when connected to the electric, quickened the rate of the Rhythm, the Pulse. I began to lose sense of words, and my focus turned into an electric pattern, crackling madly. A burst of rainbow discs appeared and filled my vision. Pulsing bullseyes of rainbow were all I could see. My head, at this point, felt swollen near to bursting but without pain. Suddenly in quick succession, I saw that house from after my accident. It spun in space and dissolved. Then the couple, Mark and Marta stood like robots, spun and dissolved into sand light. The same with the beast Suzie but her light dissolved into another view. This view was as if lying on my back rolling along as if I rested on a gurney. I could briefly see a gray cloudy sky but then was lifted through a doorway into a room. Lights shining down, many men surrounding me but the only face I recognized was Dr Mamon's. His hands reached toward my face. This last vision did not spin or dissolve. The rainbow discs returned obscuring it all, and I became aware of the pressure in my skull once more. A great pleasure moved through me as if experiencing a full body orgasm and the ooze thinned, split and began evaporating, dropping me gently to the floor. Grasping hands held me up while others wiped me down and led me to an adjoining room. I had to pee urgently.

"Drainage ditch to the left," a green-suited man said.

I could still feel a pounding rhythm from the top of my skull. White and purple light glowed ahead, and I followed the diffused figure-lumps of others relieving themselves along a wall. I looked for an open space. As my eyes cleared completely I was holding myself up by a railing that kept myself and others from wading into a purple pool to which my purple stream was contributing. I zipped and turned to the mirror. Lenny grinned back at me, his hands rubbed over and over again under the running water.

"Hey, big blue! Can you believe it? Can you belieeeve it," he said, placing his hands in the dryer.

"What? That my piss was purple?" I said laughing.

"You just experienced heaven, and that's your response?" Lenny said with overly furrowed brows.

I gave a big joking fake smile and finished washing up. I've played virtual full-suit games, and that was a lot like them, but never had I experienced something that pushed me so intensely into a transcendent state. Lenny trotted out of the bathroom, leading us through the crowd again.

We took an empty booth, and the occupied glow filled the tabletop in front of us. Our chair backs shifted hue to compliment the colors of our clothes.

A server strolled up with glasses for the fountain of laughing water that flowed at the center of the table.

"Do you need any help with configuring your menu?" she asked, pointing to the table's surface.

I checked the setup of the screen, and Lenny responded without really looking at it, "That's all alphabet and applesauce."

She seemed confused, but said, "buzz if you need," and left.

"I'm reborn! My system is fresh," Lenny said, easing back in his seat and looking content.

There was a great deal to take in, a lot surrounding and on the table monitors. I started flipping and exploring the displays.

"Many options." I pointed to a listing of singles-looking-to-connect on the table surface. The menu in front of us had ways to navigate to people in the club looking for "sex" "conversation" "friendship." They had a compatibility filter running to match you. Lenny selected several on his menu. The screen switched and expanded to show them giggling in their separate booths with friends. The screen expanded further, sharing directions to their location. Lenny started craning his neck as if looking for something in the crowd. He stood up as if he heard something.

"Hear that? All callin' for my love. Where do all these beauties come from?"

Heavy current rhythms washed over us. We quickly filled our glasses from the fountain and downed more. The laughter hit while Lenny pushed me out of the booth.

"Waaa-hey! Forget those boothies. We're going to get connecting in person," he said.

"Aren't you hungry?" I asked somewhat out of breath and not ready to get up again yet. He didn't hear and dragged me into the throng. We wandered through people and mazy corridors, weaving here and there with no particular destination until he drifted beyond me and I knew I'd have to catch up with him later. I didn't care really. A server came by carrying a multi-pronged display of snacks. I plucked one off, ate it, and wove to the edge of the stage.

There were others like me not in the goo, laughing and dancing with the drips. The laughter inside me erupted like belching, I had no control and didn't care, if I fell over, if I passed out, whatever came, whatever visions I'd keep moving, keep dancing and did even as sweat began rolling down my sides. The seismic joy shouldn't stop. Music and singing swirled about me, and a familiar voice began merging with the song. At the stage, a group of people created maelstrom music that flooded the club, taking it all to a higher level. Lenny danced with them, and his voice rippled through the air. He waved his arms like an old pro as if he performed like this regularly. He hit the air to a melted guitar beat. All the spotlights focused on him, shifting his form, transforming his figure. The band laughed and urged him on. They curved the music to grow and roll with his tones until his voice worked perfectly with it. Loud drumming eventually overcame it all. They looped his vocals into infinity as he kept pumping his fists and tin plucked chords took over.

"Hey," I shouted. He saw me and did his love gel dance pretending to sprinkle the crowd in front of him.

I moved in closer to where he was, but the current of others buffered me away, and I ended up near a table of people. A woman with green splattered breasts pulled me down to sit next to her. The sound in the space of their group had been muted so that the rest of the club noise could barely be heard.

"Hi, hi. I'm Jae. Now tell me, wasn't it all better when you were wee and nested with your oldies, when they made the decisions for you? Bubby says nay," she said and poked the guy seated next to her.

I felt like I'd surfaced from some underwater exploration into a cave of chatter-happies. I looked around the table at the other two women who were both laugh-talking at me. I smiled and didn't know what to say as I couldn't follow what was being said.

"Hi, uh, I'm Ben."

Jae tapped on the table at the other two to hush them, "This is Tee, and this is Bee."

They immediately began laughing and talking again. Bubby jumped up and shouted very loudly at me, "I am me! Look at me!"

"You did that for giggles in the a.m.," Jae said, flicking his arm.

She started laughing, and Bubby laughed at her laughing, and a ping-ponging began.

"No, you biddiebird, I did it to make today completely guh-reat. I shout it for shock during my twenty-four-fast forward." Bubby said and lifted her splattered breasts playfully.

"You're the biddiebird!" Jai said, lifting her own breasts repeatedly and on they went laughing again.

"No, you're the biddiebird! Life is better now! It's better now!" Bubby shouted at Jae, and they tried to muffle their laughter.

I stood and nodded at Tee and Bee who reached for my arms as if they wanted me to stay but kept laughing.

The music swarmed around again along with the crowd that buffeted me toward a figure teetering on the edge of the stage about to jump onto one of the hanging dancers. I got into a position where I could see it was who I thought. Lenny stood at a dangerous height. It was unclear whether or not he had a choice at the moment I caught sight of him. He leaped onto one of the drips, and in that instant, I recalled the warnings not to touch them. A great flash filled the room that emanated from the drips, and Lenny, unable to grasp hold, tried to slow his descent but slid quickly to the floor with great sparks flying and landed with a hard thud. My body suddenly felt weak again, differently drugged, nothing like the laughing water and the same top of the head pulsing began stronger than the times before.

Raindrops flickering in front of headlights.

Dad lying next to a deer carcass.

From between eyelashes of my mostly closed eyes, Mamon in a tight room with others. His hands moving toward my face.

Like multiple times before, the accident memories pecked at me, but that last memory was like meeting a separated-at-birth twin of mine, familiar as if I could've been there as if it could've been happening now - powerfully vivid. I tried to get back to it, for the first time instead of pushing them away I tried to recall the memory but couldn't. I could think of what Mamon in that room with his hands coming toward me, but there was no before, no after to walk through. It made little sense. All my flashes were always only of the accident, but this, but Mamon... Possibly my brain was muddled from the water and dancing. A fear filled me, a panic pushed at my legs. I wanted out of here. The crowd was still recovering from the shock wave. Confusion in most faces and most of the crowd appeared frozen until Lenny popped up laughing which relieved everyone, but all waited to see what might happen. The dancers hanging on stage continued along with the music apparently clueless. Lenny started waving his arms excitedly in front of a speaker at the bottom of the stage and everyone joined in the dance once more like nothing happened. Two attractive women danced up to Lenny and he twirled each one. I moved into the group. Lenny spun the shorter of the two my way. She stopped perfectly facing me and laughed breathlessly.

"Hi, what's your name?" She asked.

"Ben," I said.

"I'm Sara."

That slapped me, as names of past loves sometimes will.

"Hi," I said trying to conceal my awkward shock. I spun her to keep the dance going and moved to get near Lenny. "Hey, are you okay? We should probably leave don't you think?"

"What? The nights just begun," Lenny said downing more water and gave his glass to me to drink as his laughter manically burst from him.

"I know, but, you may have broken something. I have to get up early for my trip."

"You're kiddin' right. Oh, you're kidding."

"No, sorry, but I'm not..."

The dancefloor was packed, and Sara's hands were suddenly at my sides. Instant nausea filled my stomach and throat. I turned to see her pretty face speckled with pink and green lights smiling at me and I didn't want to throw up in her face. I smiled back and turned to dance not looking directly at her. I looked at my watch. We'd been there more than a few hours. It was closing in on 3 am.

"Sorry." I smiled goodbye to Sara and I started walking towards the exit.

Lenny talked with Sara and the other girl gave them a kiss and ran to catch up with me. I turned down the hue on my shirt.

"Should've coated myself more," I said flapping my elbows out to get some air into my armpits.

"Hey Hermes, hold on." He stopped and looked back. Sara and the other girl jogged up.

"Are you sure it's okay?" Sara said as she took down her long black hair from the wrap that she had it in.

"Am I sure what ... uh, yeah okay," I replied not knowing what I'd agreed to but noticed her beautiful face even more than I could while squashed up by the speakers.

We walked down through the Club Parched lips entrance. With my sweat, I felt like I came out of a sauna but the cold outside quickly caused chills. The energy outside was completely different. The lack of sight and sound weighed on me.

"Oh me oh my oh," Lenny sang following the girls out.

"Was it your first time too?" asked the girl whose name I still didn't know.

"Yeah," I said.

"Where to next?" Lenny asked full of energy wrapping his arm around his date.

"I kind of have to get to bed. I'm going to Skycity tomorrow." I apologized and tried to stop any plans from generating.

"How exciting, I've always wanted to go to there," Sara said taking my arm.

We walked towards the lifts, Lenny had his eyes scanned by the attendant and they craned his car down.

"Rebecca, where do you ladies live?" Lenny asked.

"Should we tell Silvia we got a ride?" Sara said.

"I waved at her when we left. I think she knows."

Rebecca leaned her head on Lenny's chest, moved up to his ear to whisper something, then down to his mouth and squished about sloppily. Their teeth greeted each other for a while longer as Sara and I got in the car. I didn't know if I was going to make it home as quickly as I would have liked but when I felt Sara's hands on my side I knew she was preparing for a longer evening. Once all were in, everyone turned down the glow of their clothes.

The open night seemed to galvanize them, and we were on our way. We drove to a river path Lenny, and I frequented. Sara cuddled up close, but I couldn't stop thinking about my trip and the bubblegum chewing sound she was making. I was eager to get away from the chewing when we got to the river.

It wasn't too hard to find our way in the dark and it gave Rebecca good reason to cling close to Lenny. Once we entered the path, the trees blocked most of the light from the sky, but it was easily navigated. Occasionally, the moonbeams freckled the dirt by our shoes. Lenny tried to get me to tell one of my monster dreams, but when I wouldn't, he did most of the talking about creatures of the night using his charm-filled southern accent. I wanted him to shut up.

Sounds of nature amplified in the dark as the flickering river accompanied Lenny's monster talk. The trees thinned, and I started looking across to tree trunks along the opposite bank. They had an odd glow.

"The moon must be reflecting off the water onto those trees, look how they're lit," I said.

"What are you talking about? I can't see anything but moonlight on the water," Rebecca said, possibly upset I'd interrupted Lenny's flirtatious joking.

"I see them, how pretty," Sara responded as if she were only humoring me.

"You two must have taken the same pill. I don't see anything. Wait, maybe I do see something. That could be where high goo-blins live." Lenny brushed past Rebecca's shoulder as he pointed.

"Hey, quit it," Rebecca said with fake anger, and he coyly put his arm around her.

"Must be I'm tired and my eyes are playing tricks," I said.

"I'm not tired." Sara tightened her grip on my arm, "but if you want to go, I'd understand."

"Let's walk to the end up here," I added.

A clearing opened where you could reach the river's edge. I looked over to the other side and the trunks glowed intensely.

"Now tell me those trees aren't glowing," I said, pointing at them.

Everyone stared for a second in silence. An animal ruffled in the trees behind us.

"I get it. You're trying to scare us. Is that it?" Sara said.

"What? Now you can't see them?" Rebecca asked sarcastically, calling Sara on her earlier statement.

"I thought I could before, but now I can't, okay?"

"Forget it. Lenny isn't there a picnic table around here?" I asked.

"Yeah, yeah there is. Come on Rebecca let me show you the great view." Lenny tugged her away, and Sara pulled me down to sit on a large flat rock by the water. I listened to the river and felt great relief when I saw her throw the gum in the water. I thought of it sinking quickly, becoming engulfed by the silt on the floor.

You could hear Rebecca chide Lenny some distance behind us, but the humming song of the river held firm as the most prominent voice. I closed my eyes for a few seconds and blinked to see if the trunks still glowed, wondering if I could clear the sight. No such luck.

"You really can't see the trunks glowing?" I asked.

"Will you stop it? There's nothing over there. I'm not scared by that kind of stuff."

"I'm not trying to scare you. I really do see glowing trunks. Maybe my eyes were affected by the hang dancing."

Sara gave a short-irritated sigh. "That hang dancing was wonderful. I didn't know what was up or down and did you look at your pee?" Sara said, swinging her hair to cover her neckline.

"I don't believe I've ever peed purple before," I said.

We sat in self-conscious silence for a long time. The river song made my head heavier with each passing minute. I gave Lenny what I thought enough time and ended our silence with, "I don't want you to think I'm making excuses because I'm not, but I think I need to get to bed. Not sure if it was all the laughing water or the atmosphere or what but my eyes are playing tricks and the longer I sit here, the harder it is to stay awake." She stood and started walking toward Lenny and Rebecca without a word.

Lenny helped the trip home with his music concoction of fire crackling noise and old man humming folk songs with a light steam kettle orchestra softly added in. By the time we dropped them off at Rebecca's place, I think Sara understood. She tapped my shoulder to wake me.

"Thanks, if you want you could contact me some time," she whispered and quickly got out of the car. As I yawned, I breathed in the air still redolent with her perfume.

Lenny had a nice long tongue kiss and pinched Rebecca's ass as she slipped out the door. She poked at the window, and he lowered it.

"Come here," Rebecca said.

Lenny leaned towards the window and Rebecca pinched his cheek.

"One for me, one for you. See you later, Lips," she said.

I got out and moved to the front seat.

"Lips? What is that?" I asked.

"Eh, you know how it is."

I didn't but didn't pursue it. He selected some muffled harmonica songs for the remaining trip and dropped me at the entrance to the MAc.

"Have fun up there tomorroo." He made a flapping bird of his hand.

"I'll give you a call and let you know how it went."

"Tell Dr M he should pay for you and a friend next time. I want to check that place out."

"I'll see what I can do."

⹉TWENTY-FIVE⹉

I wriggle down close and run my hands along the crumbling warmth. A little quiver shakes my palm and another at my knees. You've got to grow to be understood. That's her directive. Few others hear her promulgations, but if you listen, you'll know the reassurance the earth offers. I get to my feet still feeling her mothering beneath my soles and inhale the solid green grass blade landscape. Then dynamite hits my system and I sprout.

That's the way with security, you feel the potential of calm eternity, but that confusing bugger entropy breaks in, forcing motion. I fight the growth, but there isn't much to do to stop it. The grass goes from towering above me to cowering beneath me. I've been here before. Feels like déjà vu. Feels just like déjà vu. Gloaming gray all around, the forest-wall silhouette stretches across the horizon in front of me. I stride toward it and off slips my right arm, flopping to the ground like a stillborn calf. Not fazed, I pick up my pace but off goes my left hand followed by my left arm. I need to reach the wall.

"Why should you pass?" the trunks chant at me, voices vibrating more with each step closer.

"I've no other reason but that my eyes can see."

"Okay. What do you see?" It sounds like skeptical judges through a megaphone.

A blind man would've detected the radiance from their trunks.

"If the sea were the sky, in the ocean the birds fly, the angel sits upon the waves," I say.

"You're not in heaven here. There are no fish to be found."

My right foot flops backward away from my ankle, and I begin to hobble.

"Who's looking for heaven? I see your bright trunks, but your leaves are darkened."

"Okay. What do you hear?" they ask.

I hobble on hoping soon I'll get there, but my other foot flops off. I peg closer.

"I hear snail nostalgia, paths of the agony of returning home."

Both legs flop off at once. I roll but only in a loop for I can't find a way to go straight forward. My body halves and my head scuffles to a stop facing the trunks.

"What are you talking about, Ben? Save the flowery speech for your next girlfriend. It's time to start dealing with the straight signs, but first, you need a little work. Look at this bleak setting. Is this necessary? For you, it often seems to be."

The sky brightens from gray to blue. Long black vines curl and stretch down from the leafy tree heads to gather my scattered body parts and withdraw them into the leaves. Only my head is left. Then off the glowing trunks peel new feet, new hands and limbs, all new parts like strange fruit and once again the black vines stretch out to me.

Little hairs slither from the vines and weave the parts together. A thick strand rolls down, picks me up, and places me on the body husk. The hairs tickle as they weave through my neck. My eyeballs roll around to watch the whipping black tree strands as they wind themselves into one fat drooping cord and brassy metallic liquid pours out onto the ground from its phallic tip. Two orbs rise from the mercury pond and begin to rotate. I have no motion, no life outside of my head. A crackle of energy, a mad laughing in my ears, jagged bolts sear my pores. The orbs lower into the pool and flatten to a mirror, tilting forward. My reflection is bruised and angry. These parts don't look like they belong together. A glance shows my genitals, a rotten pear.

"There's no wall for you to pass, nothing imposed by us."

One by one, they pull their feet from the earth revealing arms and heads from behind the black leaves. Seven in all. The grass folds over in reverence and the tree-men fall in line, walking a single path. How can they approach me? Their light so warm and pleasing, my body so dead alive. I feel sick as the mirror floods to the earth, and in awe, as they encircle me. Their familiar faces vibrate like bee wings in flight.

"Guuurrrraaaaaarrr!" I yell at them, their vision engaging that place in me where fear is the reaction to brilliant beauty.

"You must stop it from happening. There is a key time for everything. You'll need this—" Each raises their arms in my direction and symbols flash from their palms toward my eyes. A curious story floods into me, "That is the string you must be ready to recognize. Review your Center."

I feel my nervous stomach rolling, about to give. The top of my head aches as well.

"Now who's using flowery speech?" I grumble having a hard time looking at them because of the disturbance in my gut.

Blackish vines burst from my navel with small red blossoms growing along them. They weave around the circle of seven and build a web lattice lifting me toward the sky. I enter an inverted lake, see a glimpse of a thin woman floating and smiling at me but yo-yo away from her, splashing down out of the water, returning to the glowing figures below. Their ring has another me sleeping at its center. I'm going too fast. My wet seams become untied and slip apart. "... Read your Center ... read your Center ... read your Center ...," they chant as I fall crumbling.

⚏TWENTY-SIX⚏

"Ben... Ben, do you need me to sound an alarm, or are you awake?" BUD asked.

"I'm getting there," I said still half asleep.

"You've received a message from the Center. They'll be sending a car to take you to the shuttle port."

"What about the twins?" I asked.

"I've sent a message to Mrs Panas already. She'll have them ready for the car. Reminder: Watch a few life-shaping events of Susan. Would you like to view them now?"

I hadn't known about my trip to visit Skycity when I scheduled the reminder for Susan's archive review. It almost felt planned. I shook the covers off. My stomach muscles ached from all the laughing last night.

"Show me an abbreviated version, please."

A square screen faded up on the wall. —fade— Title: ABANDONED BY FATHER - Susan at about age three, crying, and holding onto her mother's leg as a man squeals the tires of a car out of a driveway. Her mother stroking her hair and crying too —fade— Title: FAVORITE CHILDHOOD TOY: Susan plays with a zephyr rocket, dilapidated from many hours of use —fade— Title: KELLY BELL FIGHT: Susan kicks Kelly who falls and grabs her leg in pain. Susan looks shocked while sitting in an office as Kelly drifts past on a stretcher, leg wrapped —fade— Title: FIRST MENSTRUATION - Susan as a young teen, nervously sitting on a bus at school as they drive by a desert scene and the teacher is speaking. The kids get out of the bus, but Susan stays on. She waits for all to leave, leans forward, and blood shows on her fingertips. It's come through her underwear onto the back of her pants —fade— Title: WEDDING – Susan laughing and stamping on a glass at her wedding and winking at her husband —fade— Title: DIVORCE - Susan pounding on a tabletop as she yells at her husband across a lawyer's desk —fade— Title: SAINT PROTEST - Susan at a rally holding a sign that reads, "Sleep is for Sheep!"—fade—

I'd have to look into her files more closely later. I didn't know she was against people donating their lives for the energy. Odd that she'd never mentioned it.

She was lanky, skinnier than I remembered, bony looking for most of her life. Her face appeared longer than the earlier image I'd seen. These were life-shaping archives? They were generic.

Marriage, divorce, a fight with a girl when she was young, her first period? Something seemed off in a way I couldn't pin down. That face, it had a hawkish quality, yes pretty but bland in a similar way to her archives.

"BUD, will you back up the footage, zoom and freeze on her face for a minute."

Susan's face filled the wall.

"Shrink that to a five-inch and print," I said.

The image on the wall shrank, and a corner of paper peeled off, but stopped, staying attached until I pulled it the rest of the way. The void on the wall filled until the square could no longer be recognized.

"Send a message from me to Susan. Subject is better be ready. Body of message begin. As if you need reminding, I'll be there by early evening. You can meet me at the hotel.

I'll let you know which one when I find out. End it there, BUD. Make sure this gets to her before lunch."

I showered and was eating a fried egg sandwich when BUD informed me the twins were waiting at the Panas.

"Good morning, Benjamin. How was your night out?" Mrs Panas said, bathrobe still on and her hair covered in a little scarf.

"Yeah, how was your night out?" Ed asked.

"A lot of fun, I'll tell you all about it another time," I said. "I hope you got to bed at a decent time and didn't keep Mrs Panas up."

"They were angels as usual," she said.

"I should've asked sooner and hate to ask this right now, but would you mind watching the twins for the rest of the weekend?"

"No way, I'm going to the Center. Dr Mamon can fix our screens," Ed said batting at the blank screen.

"We're going to play more of the game, all day long. It's a done deal," Francis said.

"Watch it guys. Mrs Panas will think you didn't have a good time with her."

"We didn't have a good time with her, no, we didn't," Ed said, jutting his lower lip out.

"We had a great time." Francis and Ed bent over to pull her between them and hugged her.

"Too hard, too hard." She breathed in some air as her feet touched down and kissed their hands. "You're welcome to stay if you like, boys."

"We love Mr Panas too," Francis added, ignoring her invite. "I'm getting his bluebirds on my wrists when I get older too."

"I'm playing the trombone like he can when I get older," Ed said.

"We'll see about all of that. Are you sure you wouldn't like to stay for the rest of the weekend?" I asked.

"No way, you promised the game," Ed said. I hadn't promised but wasn't about to argue it in front of Mrs Panas.

"Alright, alright... Thanks anyway Mrs P."

"Anytime," she said.

We waved goodbye as we glided down the escalator.

"Okay, guys, now remember your best behaviors. I'll contact you early to let you know what time I'll pick you up tomorrow."

"We have to stay? You didn't tell that," Francis said.

"You can still stay here if you like. We can turn around," I said.

"You can take a long time if the game is still as fun as it was," Ed said, shutting down the possibility of not going.

We exited to the sidewalk, and the arranged car hadn't yet arrived. Francis's hovering screen, still not working correctly, swung to the back of his head when they squatted to pick up a mostly dried worm off the sidewalk. A strange sight this time of year, can't remember ever seeing an earthworm before spring or after early fall. I once read you could freeze an earthworm and it could still live. Maybe this one wasn't dried out. Maybe it was only frozen.

"We could save this one. All it needs is a little water." Ed spat on the worm and Francis wiggled it up and down trying to get it to move. It hung limp and for a moment, looked as if it might live but soon proved to be only gravity taking its course. Francis threw it into the grass.

"Go ahead on home now," Francis said, sounding a little like the way Mrs Panas might've.

We watched for a few seconds as it sat, not moving.

The twins stopped when the limos pulled up.

"Okay now, be good and say thanks for everything Dr Mamon does for you. No fighting. You don't want to wreck something and make Dr Mamon mad. He might not let you play the game."

"That game is gonna be great!" Ed said.

"Don't forget to pick us up, okay?" Francis said.

"Of course, I'll be there, and maybe I'll get you something from the Skycity, but not if I hear you weren't polite," I said.

They hugged me and got in the limo. As the car drove off, they popped their heads out of the sunroof. It's too cold for that, but they didn't see me waving to get back inside. Low hanging limbs hung along a tree-lined road, and I imagined them being knocked from the moving car. As that thought came to me they ducked their heads in, and the limo turned off, taking them beyond my view.

I watched the stiff worm still lying on the top of the winter grass as my limo pulled away from the curb. Reviving dead worms, Francis and Ed were always looking to help the unusually needy. The worms had me thinking of my Frankenstein dream. I hadn't documented it.

"Memo Frankenstein bedtime," I said aloud to set a reminder to dictate it before bed.

I still wished they were staying at the Panas. So few people were not frightened by them. Last summer, when I took the twins to the zoo, they ended up being more of an attraction than the animals. I could tell by their comments they felt a particular affinity. "I don't think they like the cages, do they?" they asked. "Those monkeys hate fake trees. I know it." "That gorilla is mad at us." We got to the zoo's aquarium and found the killer whale, Jiffy. They loved the subterranean walls that allowed us to stand closer to Jiffy until he suddenly went crazy. He repeatedly bashed his head against the thick glass of the tank like he was trying to get out to us. There was reflective material in the tank that kept him from seeing out. That didn't make sense when I found it out later. Did he think he was bashing into another whale? The twin's fear and concern intensified with each bash. You could feel the vibration created from smashing into the tank wall. Everyone felt nervous about it and wanted to help. The twins started banging back, trying to break through. Their great strength had me worried they might damage the tank. "We'll help you!" It only served to move the whale from where it was and continue to bang another portion of the tank. They stopped when a little boy started crying, and they realized they'd been causing a scene.

"The monsters are going to let the whale out," the little boy cried.

There was fear in the crowd around us. I could see the twins filled with concern. I couldn't snap them out of it and took them home immediately — not a good day.

Another cup of coffee would be helpful, along with some pain prevention. I could feel a headache building. I pulled on my goggles to begin organizing some painting images, but a freeze-frame of the journals on Mamon's desk showed. I tilted to clear the screen, then tapped the side. A directory of Archive categories appeared, and instead of navigating to my painting section, I tapped the goggle edge and said, "Events surrounding accident." The listings began with entries related to breaking off my engagement with Sara from over a year ago. It felt more recent.

The first on the list was titled: TWO A.M DREAM AND PHONE CALL - I woke that night from an intensely real dream. The screen exhibited a close-up of my sweaty forehead. I told BUD to call Sara. A bedside lamp lit my face, lined with pillow wrinkles, and the clock beside my head reads 2:22 a.m. Sara's fourteen-year-old sister appears on the small communication screen. Sara lived at home with her family. "Is Sara there?" "No, she's not home yet. She might've gone out with friends after like she does." "Okay, thanks. Sorry if I woke you." "You didn't I'm on another channel..."

Sara had made new friends at a job she'd started a few months before. She'd regularly go out with them after work. I never thought she might be cheating. Trust is like that. She knew I wasn't fond of the Archives and took advantage. No alerts set. No watching her during the day when we weren't together. The next day I told her about the dream that I needed her to say to me it was silly, and kissing someone else was only my imagination. She swore what I'd dreamt wasn't right, but she didn't add, "Go ahead, check my archive." Subconsciously that was probably my first clue.

The title of the next: SARA'S SUMMER LOVE - CAR EMBRACE appeared, and I tried to skip by quickly, but it glared at me. I'd watched the footage of her undressing in his car many times. I'd tortured myself reviewing it when I first found out.

Too much of the 'Events surrounding the accident' were cataloged with her cheating. Might as well put in my entire life history since all events are connected.

I hung out at my parent's house a lot after. I might not have made the trip that weekend if not for the breakup.

I nearly pressed the play button to watch CAR EMBRACE again when another screen opened on the back of the limo seat. I quickly cleared the goggles display as if I'd been caught about to do something embarrassing.

A chauffeur representation appeared, "It's not far from here, shall I order you anything for your flight? Let them know of any special needs?"

"Uh, no, I think I'm set." What was I nervous about? I put the goggles away.

We pulled up to an entrance.

"Gate thirty, sir, your flight is to depart as scheduled."

My nose hairs bristled from the cold as I got out, should've worn a warmer jacket. I had ten minutes to catch my shuttle.

I hustled to get inside. The interior of the Skycity transport station gave off a harsh scent of overblown ego. The planet's first quadrillionaire, Henry Ballard, decided he'd make one of his boyhood fantasies come true by funding the new city. There was no need for it, the stations orbiting our planet had plenty of space for more people at the time, but Ballard spent massive amounts to promote its necessity, "Built to alleviate the burdens of maximum population." There were hilarious banners with Ballard posing in weird regal-looking garb everywhere at the station. Lenny ironically decorated a wall of his apartment with one poster of Ballard bare-chested. Information spires, with small profiles of his face engraved, lined the walkways. I consulted one to find my station.

I'd seen commercials for trips to Skycity and the famous transport that took you there, and my heart raced a little with the coming thrill as I boarded the shuttle. Inside it felt much roomier than the exterior suggested. Around the perimeter was one long clear window with feathery lines that faded in and out.

A split in the building's dome above us widened, and we cut through it. The angles we moved at had me feeling as if I was in a simulator because I didn't perceive a shift in gravity. We flew nearly straight up, my back was to the ground at one point, and I felt like I still sat level.

Three months of steady letter writing, it would be strange to talk with Susan in person. For the first time, I'd thought about how she looked a lot like Sara. Well, more like Sara with an elongated face, but still they could be sisters in a way. I poked at the screen, navigating to the Archives again. There was a compulsive urge to continue reviewing the cheating episodes, but instead, I typed a search to find events that would show Susan's date rape instead. I needed to see if she'd lied. Only a few listings came up of arguments she'd had during dates or with ex-boyfriends and during her divorce, but nothing about a date rape. She seemed like a timid fighter, in most of the arguments she acquiesced, practically pulling into herself, or let the guy finish and walked away, but nothing violent. I wanted her to be stronger, to be someone who did fight, and it seemed wrong, but I wanted to find the rape archive. I refined my search to bring back any kind of physical aggression done to Susan by men and found only one listing of a man who accidentally tripped her on a walkway.

I navigated to a different section of her archive and found a CAUSES/VOLUNTEERING section. It listed the groups she'd been active in. As I read down the short list, I noticed they all had something to do with protesting the saints and Mamon's new energy form. Mostly activity with a group called Stop the Saints. I couldn't believe she was against the Center and never said anything. She'd known from the start I worked there. She knew the purpose of this trip was to interview new recruits for Mamon. I selected an archive of the last protest she attended about four months ago.

Stop the Saints scrolled across the top of the archive. A large crowd gathered around a spokesperson on an elevated platform, in what must have been a portion of the Skycity. Susan stood near the back of the group. I watched as she cheered on the gaunt, bearded orator but rolled ahead to hear the summation. The orator droned on with platitudes about inhuman monsters who could put a price on humans willing to kill themselves so that others may live so-called better lives. He took on the protest-patterned voice and kept calling the crowd "my friends" and adding in "Wake up!" every now and then.

"How is humanity served by education through death?" "These Eeden Monks, professing to understand the words of god. How long have we heard this from every other new religion that pops up?" "Mamon wraps himself in a cloak of nobility and moral righteousness to enable his research to continue, with no proven results except that of individuals losing their lives." "Mamon has to be breeding select humans for his pills. Eugenics rears its ugly head every other decade. It's time to make them understand! It's time to make them pay!"

As I listened, skipping through to the last bit of rhetoric, I noticed a figure with a head-wrap approaching Susan, startling her. She seemed to recognize him immediately. I encircled their heads on the screen and zoomed in, then focused the sound to their region. It was Mamon, although his face was altered with a beard and odd nose.

"... Before you cause a riot by revealing my presence, please hear what I have to say. I have told you, you fit the requirements and will be properly compensated. Plus, it will give you a chance to learn about the system from the inside, instead of receiving heated words of misinformation," Mamon said with the speech blaring in the background.

"I could easily turn this crowd against you. No one's fooled by that disguise. Why are you bothering me here? Look around... and anyway, I told you I wasn't interested. Not everyone has a price. Some of us believe in what we're doing."

"I believe in what I am doing. Do you think I would be here now if I did not? How else could I prove how seriously I want you to take my offer? We need to get started now. Recent discoveries have given me less time to accomplish what I must for all to go as planned. Come with me, listen to all that I have to offer, learn the truth, and then decide."

"There's a speaker coming up I want to hear. Why do we have to go anywhere anyway? Can't I just be given information to review?"

"You'd do better to witness what I have to show you in person. It's nothing to fear. Believe me, it'll be well worth your effort and so will the compensation."

"Fine, I'll join you, if only to find out what this really is and not for the financial rewards, but I'm turning on my alert monitoring system. This will be a recommended archive to the authorities should anything happen to me."

"I'd be happy to have you do so, my entire work and what I will be showing you will be public knowledge soon enough. Now please, if you will, my car is right over here." His arm folded around her shoulder, and they walked away from the crowd. I zoomed out and watched as they got into a dark blue car and drove off.

Why wouldn't she tell me about her protest activity or her relationship with Mamon? I did another search on "Interactions with Dr Mamon" and nothing turned up. Why if she had her meetings with him tagged for the authorities would it not show up in my search? There should at least be one in the listings for individuals Susan had spoken within her lifetime. We all had those. Nothing. I typed Susan Ross/Saint Center and pushed it into the include variations area, but it only brought different centers or music halls Susan attended. There was one with a reference to my messages mentioning my work with the Center, but none of them had anything directly to do with Mamon.

Now I was even more anxious with meeting her. With my overnight stay, I'd have plenty of time to get answers. As I thought that, my screen went purple and flashed "Attention" with the Saint Center logo beneath it. A list scrolled names and images of potential saints I'd meet at Gings— "a retro diner for every taste." Only two men appeared with registered next to their names — a list of hotels I could choose from followed. Seeing as I'd been donating my time to Mamon I didn't feel guilty choosing the classiest looking hotel on the list, "The Pinnacle." I found Susan's address and compared its location to my chosen hotel. It looked like it was on the other side of the city from her, but I noticed the port we'd be landing at was close to her. I tapped the teleconference section and pulled up Susan's information, and it began to ring.

"Hi." A 3D version of Susan's upper body and head emerged from the screen

"Hello. That's not all for me, is it?" I asked.

"What's not all for you?" Susan said.

"You look...all made up... and... And I certainly don't merit that do I?"

"Merit that do I. Listen to you. Are you nervous I'm thinking tonight will be a date? You may think you know me, but you don't. I dress like this all the time. Didn't you check out my archives yet?" She bent to smooth her green skirt, and the screen expanded to display her action.

"Funny you should mention that. I have some questions for you. You've been holding out on me."

"Who me? I don't know what you're talking about," She fluttered her eyelashes, "but we'll have plenty of time to unveil secrets. Seriously, I have much I've wanted to talk about."

"I've got to meet with the recruits at Gings. Do you want to meet me there around eight after I'm done?"

"I thought we were meeting at your hotel? I'd like to see you before dinner."

"I chose the Pinnacle, isn't that pretty far for you?"

"The Pinnacle? That shouldn't be a problem. I'm too impatient to wait until eight. Looks like a nice carriage you're on here."

"Yeah, I know. These clouds make me feel like I could walk to you. Anybody ever walk off the city into them?" I asked, making my fingers walk and fall over an imaginary edge.

"Probably the same percentage of suicide as with you surface dwellers, but I've never seen one. Are you avoiding my question?"

"No, uh, you can meet me in the lobby of the hotel." I flipped to the flight info screen and saw we'd dock in forty-three minutes. "I should be at the hotel in about an hour. I'll be the one looking for someone," I noticed a curious glance from one of the suits sitting up front. I waved at him, and he turned back around.

"Bye-bye to you too," Susan said, responding to my wave.

"No, I was waving to this guy looking back at me."

"Okay, well I've got to get going anyway. I'll see you in the lobby. Enjoy the clouds." Susan's transmission faded.

She was bonier than most of her archives showed. How did she keep up that cheerful fake attitude?

We traversed a wall of cloud and on the other side loomed the Skycity. Several other shuttles emerged from cloud hills. We lined up and circled the city, heading towards a slice in one of the buildings. The shuttle glided softly between a few glowing circles on the floor - landing as comfortable as our take off. The gray suits stayed in their seats even when the doors opened. They didn't move but remained transfixed on their screens. I grabbed my stuff and got off.

☰TWENTY-SEVEN☰

My ring started to tickle, and a man with a driver hat approached and waved me over to a car. It was strange to be driven by someone instead of just having a car take me wherever I wanted. I'm sure Mamon saw it as a fancy personalized gesture.

"Where are you staying, sir?" he said, taking my pack and putting it in the trunk.

"The Pinnacle please," I said.

We moved with other traffic along a large transparent tunnel, through which I could view parts of the city. Finely manicured trees and shrubs lined the road.

"Keep lookin' to the right and down for a great view of the Earth," The driver said.

There weren't any areas open to the sky. I felt like we'd been driving in some kind of giant terrarium. We turned down a new tube, the angle was severe, but I didn't feel a shift in gravity. The Earth loomed to the right. Pictures handicapped reality sometimes but not this; nothing could make this any less impressive. It must've been all of North America mildly dotted with bright clouds and directly below must've been Chicago or possibly Milwaukee, hard to say as they both are on the edge of the lake.

When I'd visited other cities, much of their character derived from being built over many centuries. The Skycity felt cartoony because of its all-at-once construction but the Earth views made that less important.

"Do you know why they'd name this place Skycity? Seems like something a child would make up," I asked

"You got it in one. Ballard's kid named the place. He was about six, and none too bright I'm guessing, but you know how parents are, their kids say something and its genius."

"Money can't buy brilliant kids I guess," I said not really believing his kid was stupid for coming up with the unfortunate name.

We drove through sections of the city as the driver gave names of places and what I could expect to find there. I kept focusing on the smaller pedestrian paths moving along every road we traveled. People were all about us moving on conveyors. We turned up a great wide road with parking for a variety of shops and restaurants that lined both sides, and the Pinnacle loomed at the end.

"This is our stop," he said, pulling up to what looked like a solid wall with no entrance.

A wall opened, exposing a line of parked cars. Our platform moved us inside and parked us next in line.

He removed my bag from the trunk and opened my door.

"Thanks for accompanying me." I tilted my tablet toward him and transmitted a tip. He smiled and got back in the car without speaking.

I walked with my bag against a heavy breeze coming from the only path available, which I figured led to check-in. A woman's white hair waved ahead of me. The small puffy white dog in her arms kept snapping at the wind and barking incessantly. I moved with them through an archway where the wind ended, and we found Reception.

The woman showed the dog around the room, chattering soothingly into its ears about how lovely everything was. I slipped by her to a check-in desk

"Can you tell me where I might find a friend I told to meet me in the lobby of the hotel?"

"Good Afternoon, Ben. What type of room would you like?"

"In a minute, I'm not ready to check in yet. I'm supposed to meet a friend in the lobby." The little puffy dog barked at me as its owner joined us at the counter. I put my hand out for it to sniff and it snapped at my fingers.

"We have ones that don't face out if you prefer?" she said, keeping her smile pasted on.

"I know I explained the last time I stayed, Mitz hates that windwash. I need that turned off. Room for Suzanne Ghant," the white-haired woman said.

"Hello, Ms Ghant. I'm almost finished here." The receptionist turned to me.

"Any room with a good view, please. Now can you tell me where the lobby is?" I looked at the woman with as much 'will you shut that dog up' as I could, and she placed the dog on the floor.

"Welcome, Ben, the lobby is through that doorway there. You're all set."

I grabbed my bag again and walked into the lobby designed in bloated mod chic. Plump upholstered chairs, oversized sofas made for a twelve-foot man, rubbery floor covering, and looping morphing chandeliers hung from the ceiling. A woman in a shiny metallic black trench coat rummaged through her purse, and I recognized her immediately. Susan stood by a front window overlooking the parkway with a gorgeous epic cloudscape in the distance. Her hair pinned in a tight bun with combs helped with her Egon Schiele portrait vibe, gaunt thin-skinned with awkward prim flair. I watched her for a little while, the veins on her hands, fiddling with an unlit reed between her bony fingers. She didn't seem comfortable in the clothes, a little swamped in the jacket and wobbly in the shoes. As I started to walk to her, she turned towards me. Nervous grins filled our faces. She met me halfway.

"Hey there." I put my bag down.

"Hi," she said with a tense squeaky voice.

We gave an extended hug as if we'd known each other intimately. I'm not sure if it was related to feeling her bones through her clothes or because I wasn't comfortable with the extended hug, but romantic interest immediately drained away. She smoothed out her coat after we let go.

"Uh… there you are… in person," I said, sounding ridiculous.

"There you are too. This is strange." She smiled and tucked a long lock of hair tightly back in place.

"It is. We know so much about each other, but this is just different."

"You're right." She looked away and cautiously back at me. We stood there scratching the ground like pigeons. "Do you want to get something to drink or something? I know a good juice bar near here."

"I just got here. Maybe I should drop my stuff in my room first?"

"How stupid of me."

"Oh no, no big deal … uh … you want to come up with me or wait here?"

"If you want me to, I'll come up, or I don't mind waiting ... either way ..."

"Come on up, it'll only take a minute to get ready." It felt dopey.

"Okay."

The elevator tubes were housed in a pear-shaped room. We waited for one as it moved along its clear and frost striped tube down to us. She coyly leaned close to me as we stood there and hooked her arm around mine when the doors closed behind us. I thought about slipping mine away but decided to let her bony elbow dig into my side instead. Luckily, the three hundred floors took only a few seconds before the doors slid open, revealing the door to my room. The door swung open at my touch.

"Welcome, Ben." Lights and music turned on in the room.

"I used to love this song," she said swaying as she walked to the back of the room and hit a button for the windows to clear.

I dropped my bag and joined her at the window. "That is something else. Feels like it's digital, not real, you know?"

She looked down at the smart table, tapped and dragged the menu and visitor guide side by side.

Beyond the city edge, a partial view of the Earth could be seen through the clouds.

"I should've looked at your archives closer. You didn't tell me you were rich," Susan said, taking off her shoes, placing them beside the night table and dropping back on the bed. "My god. Feel this bed. Are you sure we can't stay here all weekend?"

I paused, not wanting to sit down next to her. She noticed my hesitation.

"Come on, you really are skitterish, aren't you? I promise I won't undress you. Yet. We can leave as soon as you check this out."

I gave her my best give me a break look, jokingly puffed up my chest a little and sat down next to her. The bed molded to my body, hugging it a little. I laid back, and she nudged me with her toes.

"Wow, I need to get one of these for home. I'll have to write the government for an increase in the twin's support check," I said hoping she'd notice the fact I wasn't rich.

I sat up, and Susan began picking at her fingernail. I kept thinking if I looked at her in different light she might look better to me, but even with the physical similarities to Sara, I couldn't stop noticing all the angles caused by her bones or the vein along her forehead or the dirt she hadn't yet wiped that she'd dug out from the fingernail.

"How did you like the trip here? Was the shuttle very crowded? I've heard they can feel crowded." She asked, rolling over to her side and propping her head upon her hand with the unwiped dirt.

"It wasn't very crowded at all," I offered thinking she could see during the call we had it wasn't and immediately thought of my not finding any rape archive for her and the meeting she had with Mamon at the protest.

She scratched at some dry skin on the side of her nostril, waiting for me to say more.

"I'd like to talk with you about something serious I watched on the way here."

She didn't respond, no quizzical looks, no movement from staring at the bed quilt and it caused some awkward silence. I hadn't planned on how I would ask whether she lied about knowing Mamon because I couldn't recall one specifically, but she did keep their relationship from me. I wanted to know the full story and didn't know what route would lead me there. Susan rolled onto her back and rubbed her eyes as if they were bothering her.

I started to ask about Mamon, but Susan cut me off, "I felt really bad after I watched that stuff you know. I didn't realize the accident would be... graphic and personal. I only watched it until I saw you were okay, but I'm so sorry about your father." She looked at me with a bit too much sincerity.

It looked like bad acting, but I didn't know her well enough so instead of switching to her relationship with Mamon I answered, "You weren't too bothered by my, well by the end where I was sort of raped?" I asked.

Her face quickly shifted to irritation. "What rape? I was talking about your accident, not my rape. Do we really need to hash this out again?"

My face flushed, and I immediately regretted bringing anything up. I started to clarify, "No, at the end of my accident archive. The large woman you saw taking advantage—"

"That's a bad joke, Ben, especially with my history."

"Susan, I'm talking about my rape. That horrible ending to the accident. I thought you said you watched it until I was okay?

"I did. The car stopped, and you got out. You were okay but," She paused for a painfully long time and then continued. "Are you telling me you were raped? A man ... raped?"

"Thanks, yes, a man can be raped, and especially with the state I was in. There's plenty of statistics on it, plenty of other men ... I think maybe I'll shower, and you should take some time to review the last part of my accident. Then maybe you'll understand why I had trouble with your second email."

"You're worrying me, Ben," she said.

"Don't be worried. I'm not some crazy person. Here." I aimed my watch at the window and tested. It registered smart, so I outlined a square. It clouded over, and the transparent square went black. "I'll skip to the end, so you don't have to deal with the wreck again."

"Do I want to watch this? This is the strangest first date," Susan said as I closed the door to the bathroom. First date? So she was thinking that.

A half-hour later, I'd finished, and she stood by the window smoking.

"I wish we'd talked sooner about this. We've had a lot in common all along." She acted confused as if she didn't know how to proceed. "If you need anything ..."

She came up to me with her arms out, looking to hug me. I clumsily avoided it by clicking the screen on the window off. "Or if you want to talk about it now or Sara or anything that'd be okay too," she said, taking a seat.

Sara? Why would she bring her up?

"Oh, gosh, I'm sorry. I don't know why I just mentioned her," Susan said.

The room started to feel small, and I walked to the far portion of the window, trying to think of how to proceed. I decided Sara was more comfortable than talking about the rape.

"On the way here, I looked at some of the Sara cheating items. I guess we all have stuff we'd rather not remember. There really should be a way to put a block on them. I bet some people know how, sometimes I wonder about it when I can't find something easily," I said.

Susan glanced oddly at me but stood up and failed at her attempt to appear nonchalant. She walked to the little kitchen area and brightly said, "There are people. The FLM are one. Haven't you seen their archives? … You want something to drink?" Susan asked, clicking away at buttons. "I'm having a cocktail." She pulled a glass from the shelf and stuck it under the spout where pink liquid began to fill it.

"Some water, please. I think we talked about how much Lenny and I have wanted to meet up with the FLM."

"So, you tortured yourself with episodes of Sara? That's probably a bad idea, but it must be hard not to." She finished filling my glass and waved it at me to join her at the window. "Take a look at the color of the Earth down there."

I looked out at the fading purple land and the neon orange clouds hovering above the ground as light glinted off a few shuttles in the distance. "I didn't try to torture myself. It was just related to the accident archive. Oh, wait, not sure how long it'll take to get there. I have an appointment to meet with the new saints in," checking my watch, "about an hour."

"Smooth, I know my conversation hasn't been exactly scintillating … you want me to leave is that it?" She pulled reeds from her purse and lit another.

"Now who's getting defensive? No, in fact, why don't you join me for the dinner. I'm sure Dr Mamon won't mind if I have a guest."

"I'd love to help out," she said with a laugh and a sly grin.

"I take it you were planning on it already?"

"Sort of. Hoping is more like it. What would I do? Ask questions to help?" She added, badly playing dumb now.

"I need to get to know them, so I can create proper images for enhancing their stay." I ended the fake conversation. I had no plan, but I really couldn't take this skip-hopping around.

"Listen, I have to stop here for a minute because otherwise the whole time I'm talking with you tonight, I'll be questioning what you say."

Susan shifted in her seat, blew out a stream of smoke and made her face blank.

"What's with you?" she said, keeping her face clear of emotion.

If she were going to continue, I'd put the truth of it in front of her face. I got up, tapped the window, and navigated to the archive I'd been to earlier, fast-forwarding to the end of the protest with Mamon. I watched Susan continue to feign ignorance as if she didn't know what she was watching. She looked over at me with a slight smile and raised brows in a question.

"I'm not trying to be rude, really. I was checking out your archives like you suggested and I found this." I enlarged the section of her getting into Mamon's car and turned to watch what kind of response she'd give.

☰TWENTY-EIGHT☰

Susan's face turned nervous white, but it didn't last long. She sat up straight, and her plastic mask slipped away.

"People think they're so focused, so careful. Obviously, they're not." Her features hardened, and she stamped out the reed before walking to the bed. "Come sit with me again, will you?"

"What?"

She sat down and laid back.

"Just for a minute. I'll explain later." I sat down, and she pulled me beside her and climbed on top of my body.

"Is this your idea of sex?"

"No. Put your arms around me for two minutes, will you."

"Uh, I don't know what you've been thinking ... but if..." Her bony hips were pushing into my thighs, and I could smell the sour-sweet smell of drink on her breath.

"Just keep quiet for a minute." She instructed.

We stayed there. Time crawled slowly, our stomachs moved into each other as we breathed. She smelled desert dry and flower musky. Then as if it was all perfectly normal, she rolled us over and sat up. She looked out the window with preoccupied glaze and pulled a pen-sized instrument from her pocket. She adjusted it, and a small electric click and hum sounded. It sent a broad yellow laser line out. She waved the laser along the walls surrounding the room, which made everything glow a little. Just then, the lights came on in the room, startling Susan.

"It, it must be getting dark enough in here that they turned on automatically... There goes the ambiance, I guess," she said, turning to me, still without the plastic qualities. "I know you think this is all very odd, but can we save this conversation for after dinner?" She pointed the laser at the screen I'd created on the window that had stopped on the car Susan and Mamon had gotten into. She narrowed the laser beam's diameter and placed an x over the image. It went blank, leaving the x glowing on the screen. Then she navigated to a different screen I didn't recognize and checked several boxes. The hum of the laser pointer ended as she clicked it off and placed it on the table.

"Before this technology, if a child went missing, it would take a very long time to... I mean potentially never finding these children... the statistics on the amber alerts are horrible, were horrible. Do you know about this stuff? All those tortured and isolated children? I mean once you start hearing about that, how can you possibly protest Mamon's work? He knew what it would do to the world, to the universe really, but he wouldn't stop it, he unleashed the light, so others couldn't find a way to use it solely for their purposes. He democratized it. Do you see?" Susan said.

I didn't know how to respond.

"Well, those archives shouldn't be a problem now. Can't believe they missed them. Must have them do a better job combing my archives. There's much to tell, Ben. I've got to check a few other sources, but we'll fill in the blanks post-dinner. We need to stay on schedule."

"I don't mind waiting for answers, as long as they're not going to be something like 'But I didn't know how else to trap you in a relationship. I'm a secret stalker looking for love and I knew you'd be into my odd sexual practices.'"

"Hey, I think you're attractive, really, but I'm… not looking for… that from you… and even if I was and I jumped on top of you, I'd do a lot more than just lay there like a log. Sorry, I know this is all confusing. I'm confused myself, but I'll explain later, okay?" she started adjusting the hair on her cleavage in the mirror and then I noticed a shift in the way she held herself as she spoke, that casual fake quality came over her. "If you'd like, we can take the walkway instead of hailing a car or the tube."

"Is it a long walk to Gings? It's quarter to seven now," I said.

"We'll be fine if we take the express."

The city glowed strangely now that night had come, everything lit with an ambient radiance. The sidewalks moved in four aisles, each group flowing at a different speed from "Very slow" to "You better be young and fit to ride this one." The railings were equipped with handholds for balance. Susan stepped on behind me, said, "Gings," and pulled the handle next to me. My section of the sidewalk brightened, lowered, and started moving. At the next corner, I turned without having to step off and onto another walkway. I looked to see Susan a long way behind. She was looking down at her shoes and laughing. Maybe she thought it cute to let me ride alone. The next time I looked back, the crowds on the walkway filled in, blocking her from my sight, and when it cleared, I couldn't see her. I hoped the sidewalk would indeed take me to the restaurant.

It wasn't long before a polished steel diner with Gings in neon came into view. I waited outside on the platform for a few minutes but didn't see Susan. I checked my watch, found it a little past seven so went in.

"Hi. What's your name?" a hostess in a cranked-hue chartreuse grass skirt asked.

"Last name is Tinthawin. There should be a reservation made by someone from the Saint Center. I'd like to add another to the reservation. My friend will be along soon."

She clicked her tablet. "Yes, Ben. Two from your party are already waiting at the table. I'll have them add another setting for your friend. Follow me, please."

The deconstructed spilled-neon design of the restaurant could be found in many hotspots these days. Overdone retro cut up and collaged together. I moved through a bouncy harmonizing gallery of song and dance, servers performing for their tables. As we arrived at mine, I found two men looking my way, a hearty older gentleman with a white beard, and a middle-aged bookish guy with fat glasses that wrapped around his head.

"Here you go, sir." She pulled my chair out for me. "Your waitress will be Sue. She's already performed tonight's specials for the others, but they're listed on the menu." She tapped on my menu's screen and swiftly left.

"Did I miss anything?" I asked, offering my hand to each. "Hi, my name's Ben."

"Not unless you enjoy getting food options sung at you. I'm Jim," the older gentleman said and stood as we shook hands.

"Nice to meet you. I'm Mark and I thought she was cute but not a solid performer, but then I wouldn't go to dinner seeking great thespians. Was our meeting not set for six thirty?" He adjusted his glasses, checking his info screen, and sat back.

"Uh, I just got off the shuttle a bit ago and was told seven."

"No problem, no problem. We've been having a nice conversation. Haven't we, Mark? We were discussing how Mark here spent several years serving as a lighting technician for the American Theatre Company in Chicago and never received corrective eye surgery because no one in his family has."

"Well, I use them for augmentation also." Mark adjusted the tilt of his glasses again. "I mean most folks have contacts to help direct, I guess. ATC, I worked there for six years. Have you ever been to Chicago?" Mark asked, trying to shake off his annoyance with having been made to wait.

"Yes," I said, breathing out as I settled into the scene. "I did a quick day tour when I was in high school. Mostly just saw the tourist traps like Navy Pier."

Our server twirled to our table in a doughnut-shaped short skirt and clear plastic with chrome-snaps top. She flipped her stylus and clacked it against her order board.

"Hi, I'm Sue. Are all the members of your party here now?" she asked with a big glossy smile.

"Do either of you know if any others are supposed to meet us?" I said.

A few other seats sat vacant at our table.

"You mean you don't know?" Jim asked.

"I'm sorry," I said apologizing to the server, Jim, and Mark. "This is a new program. I should've gotten more information. I'm expecting at least one other—"

"You'll need more time then, okay," and she danced off on her toes.

"I've got a friend who should be joining us any minute now. I don't know what happened." I craned my neck to look for her at the entrance.

"Did she come with you?" Mark asked.

"I thought she was with me, but then she wasn't."

"You lost your date? Is that what you're telling us? I prefer clarity. I prefer focus. Would you be losing our bodies at the Center like this?" Mark asked.

"She was right behind me on the walkway, and then when I turned around, she was gone."

"Maybe she ditched you on purpose," Mark said.

"Are you getting cold feet here, Mark?" Jim asked, smoothing out his beard.

"Cold feet? About what?"

"Your comments make you sound like you have cold feet," Jim said.

"Do I know you? I was just joking with Ben here. If you knew me, you'd know my joking. I'm excited about joining the other saints." Mark took a long curly breadstick from the vase at the center of the table.

"I guess I could get started instead of waiting for the others to show? I'll begin by telling you what I do at the Center. I'm a volunteer who helps with—"

Sue stopped by our table again.

"I'm sorry to interrupt, but could you come with me for a minute, please," she said, putting her hand lightly on my shoulder.

"What for?"

"I'll tell you when we get there."

Her face read sincere and excited.

"Sorry," I said, looking at Mark and Jim. "I'll be right back, I guess."

I wove in and out of tables quickly following her towards the bathrooms.

"I received these instructions with a really great tip if I followed them properly. See here," she pointed at her order screen where a 'message awaiting transmission' flashed and accompanying it was a tip I'd bet she'd have a hard time making in a week.

"I almost never receive correspondence at work I swear. Don't tell my manager, okay? Sign here."

I took her stylus and signed the screen. She tapped it and asked me where I'd like her to transmit my message. I held out my watch and wondered why the message wasn't sent to me directly from whoever wrote it.

"Could you please read that in the bathroom? That was my last order."

I nodded, quickly entered and locked the bathroom door. It looked retro dingy with yellow light, cracked tile floor, and peeling walls.

My watch scrolled the text:

Meet me at 27 Park Ridge. The walkway will take you. Go behind the main building. You will find a small door = looks like it's for trash removal. Go through and put on one of the suits you find hanging. Store your clothes in one of the bins. At the end of the hallway is a stairwell. Follow it up two flights. A greeter will be there, pass him as if you belong. I'll be in the first room on the right.

Leave NOW. - S

⩵TWENTY-NINE⩵

Having two options, to stay and fulfill my obligation to the Center or to follow the directions of what could be some kind of serial killer, I chose the latter. I left the bathroom and walked through the crowd to where my waitress was. She looked busy taking an order, and I glanced over at the table where Jim and Mark glared at me with anger.

"Tell them to go ahead and eat. I'll be back in time for dessert. Okay?"

"For that tip, I'll sing all the way through dinner if they want. And don't worry, I'll make sure the two extra chairs remain pulled from the table as she requested." Sue slid over to kiss me on the cheek.

"Okay," I said, not fully understanding, but wanting to get on my way.

On the concourse, I said "27 Park Ridge", and tugged on the handrail. I cruised along several steep walkways through circles of light that lined the clear tubes. The tube had been lit so one could still view the night sky beyond. I crossed along a bridge between two large sections of the city and felt like I flew through outer space when I saw the lights of the city below and the stars above me.

A mostly naked couple stepped on to the walkway several yards ahead. The girl had curly hair growing from her waist and swayed to an unheard beat, gently bumping into her companion. She distracted me until the street names and numbers started blinking on the rail "Park Ridge" … 24 … 25 … 26 … and at 27, my section of the walkway stalled for a moment. There were three connected buildings. I walked around to the back of the largest one.

They didn't bother with much lighting behind the building, but I still found the trash chute where she said it would be. I climbed on discarded cubes and climbed up. I pushed out at the top and saw a row of caution-orange suits hanging on a rack next to large bins of shredded plastic.

Matching orange glasses stuck out of the suit pocket, so I put them on too. I noticed myself reflected in the window of the door that led to the stairway as I walked towards it. I looked like a superhero; the suits were brighter than many at Club Parched. At the top of the stairs sat a man at a desk to whom I nodded as if I belonged then walked past.

I picked up speed and entered the first door on the right at the end of the hall, finding a lift, not a room. I got in, but there were no buttons to make it go. The door closed on its own, and the lift flooded with a bright yellow light and moved sideways rather than up as I expected. Flashes of more brilliant white light through the door crack indicated movement, and I immediately wanted out.

I stood to the side of the elevator when I felt it change direction, heading upwards, but slowing. It stopped, and the doors slipped away. No one roamed the hallway. I re-read her instructions and started quickly walking until I got to the first door on my right. Susan opened it before my knuckles could connect.

She looked me over. "I'm happy you're here … I'd say orange is your color, but you won't be needing these." She lifted the glasses from my face.

Several men sat behind ergonomic small black desks with square screens filling the surrounding walls. Images of people, objects, and animals were flying about, cut out of one panel and pasted into another. One image showed a tubby woman in overalls walking down a street lined with houses. A pointer selected it and it freeze-framed. She's highlighted and promptly disappeared, only to pop up on the adjacent panel where she continued walking down a hallway in a house now. The lighting changed on her, a shadow altered. They drew large yellow x's on some scenes, similar to what Susan had done back in the hotel room.

I felt disoriented, nearly drugged.

"I'm sure you're dying for an explanation." She led me over to a desk behind those working, and we sat down. "Are you thirsty, hungry?" She spoke with a grating motherly tone.

"All I want is an explanation," I said with agitation.

"That's why you're here. I—"

"You lie to me about a date rape. You lie to me about knowing Mamon. You lie on top of me and tell me not to move, and then you ditch me … I'm wearing stupid clothes and crawling up chutes— "

She waved at someone and he came over. She told him to set up some kind of demo, lined up two chairs, and we sat down.

"I really wanted to tell you. I didn't want you to hate me…forget it… look around, what do you see?"

"I don't care what I see. Start from the beginning and finish with why I'm here."

Susan looked hurt, not quite offended, and she obviously didn't like the demanding tone.

"I know you know about the Eeden monks and their research, right? How familiar are you with the Faux Life Movement?" she asked.

"Fairly familiar. I know I told you about how Lenny and I have been trying to get their attention. Didn't you look at any of my Whig Party archives?"

"Yes, and similarly the FLM make fictional archives that they mix with their correct histories."

"They live fake lives."

"No, they replace some of their real archives with fake archives."

"I thought that's illegal. Isn't there some kind of block for that?" I asked.

"There was, still is for everyone else, but the original FLM found a way around it. All the FLM do is replace their real activity with instances of odd faux life fun so they can work for the Eeden monks and Dr Mamon."

"Then the whole system is corrupt."

"Well, yes, but no not really. See that's why I was finally won over by Dr. Mamon. Without light being recordable, the technology to falsify experience, all that computer-generated news made-up by big business or governments, without some way to have a reality check - cultures were struggling. You know, you know very well with your presidential art, think of the way all those competing falsified video documents made politics, or um, not just politics... maybe even how it made all of modern life almost impossible to manage. You couldn't believe anything that wasn't live right in front of you, right? The instability...you could say Dr Mamon saved us all, right?"

"I get that, but the Archive is possibly far worse if there's a way to game it. Before, everyone had an idea about the deception. Bogus news caused unrest, but at least people were aware. I don't know. Maybe I need to think about it more. This certainly isn't the equivalent of some little white lie."

"For most of the world, the Archive is merely a personalized memory book. Life is generally or mostly just leaves unfurling or microbes multiplying right? For matters of crime and politics and world history, I suppose the Archive is as unreliable as magazines or, or I guess all of historic documentation, but at least with this system, there is the potential for more corroboration of facts."

"So the FLM live real lives, but plant fake archives? Their archives aren't in real-time?"

"Real-time, no, don't worry about that. Let me go back a little further. Do you know about Dr Mamon's research and how he helped with the introduction of Informed Light?"

"Not much. I've read some, but not committed it to memory."

"Before the Center, it started with the Eeden Monks. You know they're scientists, right? Informed Light came from their research into brainwaves and new ways of recording and translating it. The monks wanted to record dreams to help catalog the symbols they'd been discovering with lucid dreaming. Dr Mamon was helping to perfect the technology when he figured out the process for inscribing light with information. Our bodies emit light; the information moves through us, and he felt it is everybody's to own. As I explained before, he wanted to democratize it in the way it deserved, to set it free so others couldn't use it for evil purposes. He started the Archive but didn't want others to access the Eeden research. He worried about government interference. Most people still don't take the Lexicon seriously. He knew they would eventually and wanted a way to hide the discovery, so he could control the information and make sure it wasn't utilized inappropriately."

"He created the Faux Life Movement and it's allowed him to cover up the monks' work enough to keep people in the dark about it," I added.

"That's it. Also, it created a scapegoat for any discrepancies found in the Archives. If an oddity was found, they could blame it on the socio-political art of the FLM. Many members of the FLM are Eeden monks who work behind the scenes, but there are also those that Dr Mamon is able to trust and retain to help the cause, actors basically."

"You're a member of the FLM too?"

"I'd say I'm with the good FLM. As with any cause like this, you'll have factions. Some of the FLM weren't fully informed about the research Dr Mamon conducted with the Eeden monks. Some were kept in the dark. Had they been better informed they might not have thought to use the Archive alteration for covering up criminal activity. They might have seen the higher purpose of Dr Mamon's work. We still don't know if the other group is in bed with any corporations or governments. We doubt it, figuring that if they were with another government, that government would probably have shown their hand and tried to coerce Dr Mamon into revealing all his research. Look around."

I looked and thought about what I'd witnessed already. These men were altering or creating archive replacements.

"These are Eeden monks of the FLM?" I asked.

"Not monks, but they're part of the FLM."

"And this is where you alter the Archives?"

"It's one of a few locations."

I shifted in my seat, wanting to trip her up, tell me something she shouldn't, but my brain whirled. "Tell me why the lies about the date rape and not telling me you knew Mamon."

"Dr Mamon set me to work documenting the progress of the movement. When I read the Eeden monks' 'words from the gods' I found them ... so profound. Anyone who reads them must know Dr Mamon can only be working in an enlightened fashion to help us see beyond the Wall as he says, to bring the world to a true Utopia."

"Utopia? I'm surprised after what I've read in your letters that you'd believe that deeply. Then again, what is true about you?"

"Utopia might be a strong word to those who haven't studied the monks' findings," she said placing her hand on my knee and smiling, "I'm not an expert, but you'll understand one day and then you can come back and apologize. How much of the available Eeden monks research have you read?"

Her condescension drove me nuts. "Only that they've been working on the Lexicon. What I've seen isn't solid proof they've found anything at all. The jury's still out, right?" The thought that I recorded Mamon's journals flashed into my head.

"Don't feel bad, it's a lot to take in. No matter if it ends up a Utopia or not, you've done important work for the saints. Plus, your reaction was the one I'd hoped for and was assigned to create."

"What?"

"Dr Mamon assigned me your case. I feel terrible saying this, but we spent that first month after you agreed to write me, figuring a way to get you to stick around so I could monitor you. He wanted me to create a relationship where we shared secrets, where if you learned somehow about the rest of Dr Mamon's activities, you'd tell me. He wanted you interested in the Center just enough to keep coming but not enough to get you active in the real research. I was directed to make up the date rape because we thought it would gain your sympathy. I admit to being slightly confused why Dr Mamon never told me about the rape ending of your accident archive. I'm sure I would've found more ways to handle you had I been told about that."

"Thanks, real nice."

"That was what I was assigned to do, and I really thought I was helping you. They said my rape would make me seem weaker, in need of your help, less capable. I'm sorry. Really."

"Why don't you have a fake rape archive then? I looked, there isn't one."

"They wanted to make one, but my family might've found it. I knew if you tried to find the archive, I'd have to tell you the truth about it and by then I hoped we'd have something else to cement our friendship. Most of our relationship has been real not lies." She opened her eyes wide, attempting a look of compelling sincerity that came off as more of her plastic.

I felt sick. Disembodied arms writhed through a screen on the wall and were pasted on a limbless body in another. I walked over to one of the screens, and my legs had a strange weak feeling. All of the manipulation was making me dizzy. What could one believe about the world without solid documentation? What was real now? Susan came over to me and put her hand on my shoulder. I shrugged it off.

"It's all been lies. Even now, how can I believe what you say?"

"You've got to believe me." Susan gently rested her hand on my shoulder again and left it there. "If only there was time to let you read the monks' journals. You'd know I'm telling you all this now, so you can join us in an honest fashion. It's always been the plan for you to be one of the informed, but now is not the time to reveal everything."

"Why not? Why couldn't I have been told earlier? Why couldn't I have been asked to join like you were, pulled aside and given access to everything?" I wanted to walk out, to get some distance from the dazzling screens and Susan's hands so I could figure it out.

"Ben, think about it. You're an artist. People around the world have seen your work. It's difficult to remove people from the Archives, very, very difficult to cover and alter without it being traced. There's a great deal of planning that goes into all of this," she pointed to the screens.

"Sounds like bullshit. You could probably create a program on a single computer that would handle fictionalizing the lives of the entire human population."

"Not like this, you know as well as I do computers are limited without human intervention. Even with certain levels of A.I., they have to be told what to look for, and the details and connections in the Archives need an emotional understanding that computers don't have."

"I don't know enough about how it works, that's true, but I've seen other things that don't fit into this picture."

"Such as?"

"Such as what's with all the plant and animal experimentation happening at the Center?"

"That's a separate issue. Dr Mamon and I discussed your bathroom incident. I don't know about the details exactly but all you've seen are components of his environmental research. It probably spooked you even more because you saw that man's arm sprout."

I stopped for a minute and watched the screens on the wall some more. I understood what she was saying but still felt uneasy.

"Okay, let me go over this again. You're telling me all I've seen are parts of the Center's energy production, that what I've believed about Mamon from the start is correct - about him working towards a good cause, but he's been manipulating me so that I'll only be somewhat informed and can continue to help the saints without having to be part of the FLM. You and he have gone to a lot of trouble to keep me ignorant until he decides to reveal everything to the public and has altered your archives in case I or anyone else would find something we shouldn't."

"Yes. That's why at the hotel I became unnerved when you showed the archive with Dr Mamon. All those were to be removed or altered, a great example of how even computers with human help aren't foolproof. I had you lying on the bed with me to make it easier for the FLM to alter our archive to show us getting romantic on the bed and not see us discussing my connection with Dr Mamon. Here, take a look, it has already been altered."

She tapped the panel on the desk in front of us and brought up the archive in the hotel room. We're on the bed only she isn't just lying on top of me now. I'm licking around her ears, and when in real life we get up, it instead shows us taking off our clothes and rabbiting our groins together.

"I think they had fun making this one," I said with irritation.

"It's much easier if you give them something to work with than if they have to erase and make it all up. Let's look at what they've done for the restaurant."

She tapped and Gings appeared on the screen. Now it shows Susan and me sitting with the other men at the table.

"I had the waitress leave two of the chairs pulled out so that they could place us in them easier."

I felt like I was viewing a movie where I had a really good body double, all my usual movements, and even my stupid sounding laugh is mimicked. I watched us chew and look like we listened intently to Jim and Mark and wondered who in the world would be reviewing this. Could there be people that interested in my life they would follow my archive this closely?

"Now wait, what about future conversations they may have about how I missed the interview with them? And come on, what if I don't like it that my archive has a history of me fooling around with someone I don't think I would've? This is my personal history," I said.

Susan looked at me with an arched brow, "They'll leave search flags in place to fix future conversation discrepancies but… you don't find me attractive is that it? Why've you been writing me all these months then?"

"I've never even seen you until recently. Come on, I've been honest about not wanting anything, haven't I?" I said.

"Yes, but you've also done a lot of flirting. Not that I'm really looking for something either, but it's not pleasant to hear, I guess."

I glanced at her small ears encrusted with tiny glittering decoration and her bony chin. "I look at you and see a — healthy woman, but you aren't my type. Maybe after Sara, I've developed an overly cautious attitude. I'm sure I have, and you've given me some serious reasons to be cautious, right?"

"I'm healthy looking? Healthy? That's a first... Don't work yourself up. However, you've got it figured out, I'm fine." Susan looked away, obviously hurt.

I tried changing the subject. "How am I supposed to handle missing out on the interviews with the future recruits? That was my whole purpose of coming, right?"

"Dr Mamon hasn't gotten back to us. I've tried to get in touch with him since I left you on the walkway, but there has been no response. I'm sure he'd want it handled this way. You could just watch the archive of them talking at Gings and use that for getting to know them, right?"

"That's all faked isn't it? Wouldn't be helpful."

She looked at her watch and cut me off. "We've got to get back to the restaurant soon, so the FLM isn't wasting any more time than they already have on us. Maybe you can contact them, and we could meet for dessert?"

"They can't still be at the restaurant, and would you be interested in talking with me now if you were them?"

"We have to go anyway. They'll make it look like we stayed after the others left." She filled some worker in on our plans, grabbed her small handbag, and gestured for me to join her.

Back in the elevator, we waited in the yellow light, and I found it strange how Susan could shut me out this easily. She held herself differently, staring straight ahead. I couldn't get a good read on her. Was she upset about my rejection? The door to the elevator clacked open, but not to the same hall I came through earlier.

We moved through a maze of corridors and worked our way to where I'd stashed my clothes. I changed as fast as I could. The chute I entered through was now our exit. We left the building's perimeter, back to the walkway, without running into anyone.

It was as if someone increased the hues of reality. Colors looked brighter somehow, everything felt more open, space pushed outward and I sort of wanted to start jogging. I felt so alive, but people, people seemed entombed and more mechanical than before. Everyone looked a shade darker, trapped in plastic and on their way to nowhere special. I wanted to do something. This wasn't going to be recorded. I'm living outside of history. I started to sing loudly, "OOOO-ohhhh, say can you SEEEEEE by the dawn's early LIIIGHT."

"What are you doing? Shut up." Susan spun around and glared at me.

"... WHAT SO PROOOUDLY WE HAIL BY THE TWIILIIIIGHTS LAST GLEAMING..."

"Have you gone crazy?" Susan grabbed my shirt and looked around in minor panic, so I stopped.

"What's it matter? This is going to be deleted. That means we can do anything we want and it's not part of history, right? I want to let go, go nuts, I don't know what," I turned around and thought about punching someone. I couldn't figure out what to do, but I wanted to ... wanted to do something I couldn't before.

"We still don't want to draw attention. It's more work if others interact with us, and your singing like a tortured monkey is sure to attract some crazy people."

"This is why they do what they do ... you people of the FLM. Of course, you want to keep it secret. I used to think we were free to do anything because everyone was watching everyone, and no one could get away with anything, but that has nothing on this. It feels so ... great, I feel like somebody out of the past, like I've time traveled. I've got to talk to Mamon, see how I can join—"

"Don't worry. I'm sure after today you'll be asked to," Susan gave a worried look, "or forced to."

I felt the knots in my back immediately tighten. "That's true, what if I don't want to be part of the FLM. What would Mamon do?"

Susan touched my wrist gently and said with a mild concern in her voice, "I don't know. I think this is a first. How could you say no to it, though, after experiencing what this feels like? I know you'll especially want to join when you're given the monks' findings to read."

I pulled my arm from her touch. "If I was forced, I'd be confined more than I am now. At least now I'm never alone, there's always someone there watching, even if there isn't, it feels like it. That's a comfort. If I were removed from the Archive's eye, who knows what could be done to me. I could be killed, and no one would know."

"Slow down. You're taking this too far. Besides, you could still be killed whether you joined or not. We all could be killed at any time, but you have nothing to worry about from Dr Mamon's side. Remember the FLM has split; there are others with the technology, and they don't have the same benevolent motives as we do. There is no going back, no stopping the light. There are great benefits," She paused for a brief second, and I saw a flash of doubt in her eyes, "there just are."

Susan turned around and drew close to my face, then kissed me on the mouth. I started to pull back, but she moved with me until I joined in. We briefly continued until the walkway took a sharp turn and unlocked us. She averted her gaze from mine.

"You have pillowy lips," she said in a whispered voice looking up at me.

"Uh, thanks," I didn't hate the kiss as much as I did her cutesy comment, but even the kiss felt robotic, somehow not myself during it.

"I figured you might not mind, seeing as it will be erased and no one will ever see it." She placed her hand on mine.

I glanced around, people were close by on different walkways, but none seemed to care if they even noticed. It felt hard to pin down, as if I were a homeless man with people milling about me and not caring or looking my way, or, or thinking you picked up a glass of clear soda, but when you take a drink you find its flavorless water almost as if I didn't somehow belong to my body.

"No one will see it, that's true." She looked about to kiss me again, but the walkway shuffled us apart. "I guess a kiss is nothing compared to what they would see if they checked the archive on me and you in the hotel room," I said and Susan pulled back.

"I don't understand you, why do you want to hurt me when I'm this nice to you?"

"What?"

"I'm going to ask again. Would it be so bad if people saw us in the hotel room?" She seemed sincerely interested.

"Let's not get back into this, okay. The kiss was nice, my only one out of recorded history. I'll cherish it always. Is that what you want to hear?"

"Forget it." She turned around and rode without speaking until we got to the entrance of Gings. I stumbled a bit as I got off. Susan took my arm and squeezed it then briefly held my gaze with an Are-you-Ready look.

⊟THIRTY⊟

Susan exited the walkway and I followed. After checking her palm board, she motioned for me to turn around. Her body stopped moving, giving her best mannequin impersonation. Her nipples stretched her shirt and had me questioning if she'd had them enhanced.

"Stand still for a minute, would you." She said, pulling me next to her. "They'll need to join the fake us with the real us. Remember it'll all be going on record again."

A group of people walked out of the restaurant, and as they passed, Susan began to walk with them. I stayed frozen, not knowing if I should move too.

"Come on, what're you doing?" She said, looking back at me from the group, now coated in the old mask again. I felt smaller as the world shrank back around me.

"Jim and Mark seem like good candidates, don't they?" I asked as I got back on the walkway behind Susan.

She gave me a little knowing wink.

"They were nice, but only you'd know about their potential. Um, where'd you like to go now?"

"Is the lake far?" I asked.

"That's an excellent idea. If you only have a day in Skycity, the lake is a must-see."

"Skylake," she said and gave a tug to her railing handle. I did the same.

"I'd say you have your work cut out for you. I'd hate to have been them in there," Susan said.

"Why's that?"

"All your game show host questioning, Jim and Mark were real sports."

I wondered how she could talk now about what we'd discussed at dinner. Would that tip someone off if I didn't ask game show host questions? I wanted to ask her but couldn't.

"My turn, what's your favorite archive series, or do you tune into anyone in particular on a regular basis? I'll give you my answer first, okay? I watch this lovely Ethiopian couple go to bed every night. It's soft. It's so natural, just makes me feel like things are right somehow," she said.

"Are you serious?"

"Yes, come on."

"I don't have favorite archives. I don't tune in much remember."

"Sure you do, everybody does."

"I don't."

"Okay, fine, if you could be any animal, what would you be?" she continued.

"This is dumb. I didn't ask them questions like that. I never would."

"I don't know what you are talking about. I was sitting right next to you and I heard you." She looked at me with a little glaze to her eyes.

Do I play along and talk in a way I wouldn't? I'd already had to live with a sex archive I didn't want. Would I end up torturing myself with it like I had the ones of Sara cheating? Would all my conversations with her from here on out have to be thought of as fiction?

"There's a difference between asking people about themselves to have them reveal their character and asking questions to entertain an audience. Maybe you heard what I was asking them in a way that I didn't mean it to sound." I figured if I was vague enough I could get away with it. "There's a difference between: do you like tall or short men, and what happened on the last date you enjoyed? The first question might give you a little insight, the second reveals more of the psyche and is of greater help to my work."

"You've never even asked me about the guy I've been seeing, you know," Susan shot back and seemed truly hurt.

"You're seeing someone? No, I didn't know—"

"I know you don't know, and I also know you never asked me about it."

"Why would I ask you about a guy you're dating when I didn't even know he existed?"

"Just because you can walk away from someone who's cheated on you and never look back doesn't mean we're all that strong."

"What?"

"I kept dating him even after I knew he'd cheated on me, even after he'd admitted to it. There's a difference for women and men. We're seen as sluts or whores if we sleep around, but somehow in some women's minds, it makes their man more of a challenge if he has other women interested. He has a spiked virility. You know you shouldn't go back, but since others have found him attractive, you want to have him too. You probably can't understand."

"You're right on that last bit. You lost me at the beginning. You've been dating some guy that's cheated on you?"

"Yes, and I know you can relate."

"I guess I can. I never went back to Sara like you said, but it was less about her cheating and more about no longer being able to believe her. I'd have to second-guess everything she said from there on out."

"I bet you could get over that if you wanted to. We all want to fight for love."

"Maybe you could. I couldn't. I could forgive everything she put me through except for the lies about the guy. I started to see her more as a run-over dog. You want to look at it, its grotesque magnetism. You can still picture what you once loved, but now you only see its bloated fear and vulnerabilities." My head began to ache at the thought of a wounded dog.

Deer carcasses on the highway.

Tiny bleeding cuts on Dad's hands.

"Now we're even because I don't know what you're talking about. All I know is you haven't asked me one time if I was okay."

I heard what she said, but my eyes were still looking at Dad's hands in my mind. I hurried to shake it off and answer.

"You never mentioned..." I paused because I didn't know what the hell I should do here. "Are you okay? Do you want to tell me the whole story?"

"I don't want to talk about it." She turned her back to me.

We sailed along the city's border, all monumental curves and sandwiched glass and metal.

"Have you... seen him lately?" I asked.

"I told you I don't want to talk about it."

I looked at her plastic features, her face looked angry, but I couldn't quite believe she was. My only option was to act like what she expressed was something real.

"Is there really some guy you've been dating?" I said, trying to flavor it with the questioning of what was real and what was for show.

Her body noticeably bristled, and she continued looking forward, not answering. I tried to think of something to change the subject, not wanting it to turn any uglier.

"How's your mother doing?" popped out of my mouth. Dumb choice.

No response.

With all my conflicted emotions, I decided to simply shut up. We rode on for about another fifteen minutes without a word until the lake came into view.

The silence broke as we said, "Look at that," at the same time. Hers a directive, mine a statement of astonishment.

I couldn't believe the enormity of it. The dirt and gravel walkway along the coastline was dotted with tree-shaped lamps. In the far distance, you could see light reflecting off the giant arching dome that housed the lake area. There's no mistaking this was human-made, but it struck a chord of awe in me. We stopped at a metal park bench. One light lit the area. "You come walking here a lot, right?"

She didn't answer.

"Listen, if you want to end the day here it's okay by me."

She started crying.

"What's this about?" Crying people make me nervous and a little mad for some reason. Crying faces, especially ones I can't sympathize with end up annoying me. She continued, and I clumsily put my hand on her shoulder.

She breathed some and squeaked out, "You."

"Me?" Her crying was a ridiculous whimpering snivel, and it wasn't letting up. "Come on, let's have a seat," I sat down, avoiding a little bar that divided the bench. "I'm sorry I didn't believe you about that guy."

"How do you know I lied?" she said, continuing to stand.

"I don't, but you never mentioned dating anyone..."

She continued to cry and a little snot formed at the corners of her nostrils.

"This isn't how I expected it to go," she said, snuffling and wiping her face on her shirt.

I felt the *I have feelings for you* kind of talk coming on and I'd already been struggling with the if you don't have something nice to say rule.

"It's been ... a revealing day, really noteworthy. Good, I'm mean really good. There's no reason for all this crying is there?"

That only made her start up again.

"Listen... let's start again. Let's forget all this and just enjoy the rest of our time together," I said.

She began to compose herself. "You're right. This is confusing for me too, you know. I just thought ... I thought..."

"Let's not deal with this now. You're going to think I'm nuts, seeing as we already ate, but I'm still hungry. Are you?" I hadn't eaten anything since the shuttle food, and my stomach was tightening.

She looked over and laughed a little, seeing I was still playing along.

"I could eat something," she said. She went to sit next to me but didn't notice the metal bar that protruded slightly and divided the center of the bench. She sat down hard on it and quickly jumped up. She put her thin hands over her face, obviously mortified.

"Ooow, are you okay," I felt embarrassed for her. Her ass bone must have been killing her. I almost went to rub it like you would a child when they get hurt, dust it off, but I pulled my hand back.

"Fine, I'm fine, let's go, okay?" she didn't remove her hands from her face until I stood.

If this was acting on her part, she was a pro. She started walking in a fashion that showed she was in pain.

"There's a food court down that way. It's towards your hotel."

"Sounds good." Anything would have at that point.

The food court served a world-culture themed cuisine. A little disappointing, it was all replicated stuff. When I go out to eat, it's nice to find handmade options. I gave up on reviewing the choices and bought a burger, she a small bowl of oily vegetables and noodles. She gingerly eased into her seat.

After a few moments of poking at her food and finding a comfortable position she started in, "Isn't your chemotrophic painting a form of nanotechnology? What is your favorite application of nanotechnology?"

"Really? You don't seem like you'd really be interested in nanotechnology."

"I've been reading up on it, and hey, I'm the one who's read all the science fiction books remember? Besides, when I look at this rep food, all I think is nanotech."

"Okay, let's see ..." I took on a professorial tone. "when I was in college, they were just developing the nano-brush technology I use for image creation. As you probably know since you've done all that reading, Molecular Nanotechnology is a technology that manipulates matter on the atomic level. Rearrange atoms in coal and you have diamonds. Combine atoms from carbon, water, and air, and you have a potato. I guess I'd have to say my paintbrushes are my favorite application. There's a certain type of connection I feel even though much of what I do is taken and altered by the software for the individuals I share the images with."

"Wow, sounds complicated to me. Okay now, we've talked a lot about books, but you've never answered this one. What's your favorite novel and why?"

Her face shined at me as plastic as the tabletop, excited by her own game. I don't think she even heard what I said. I had to get out of this. I played along for a little while, trying to stuff my face so I didn't have to answer.

"Who would you be if you could be anyone else in history? How many girlfriends have you had, and which was your favorite? What's the worst day of your life?"

I felt my mouth slightly gape in Oh-come-on fashion as I began to wonder if she even gave that a second thought in regards to what she actually knows about my history. You'd think the game would grow old with her, but the more I listened, the more I wondered if this wasn't the real her, and the person I saw back at the hotel and in the FLM building was only a small part of her personality. I looked down from Susan to my half-eaten burger. The pink juices of the beef soaked into and squeezed out of the bun along with the mayo-ketchup-mustard combination. Her voice echoed in my head. A glumpy bit of chopped onion plopped onto one of my fries as I took a bite, and in it, I found inspiration. I wiped my forehead and cheek with a napkin as I chewed, hoping this would work. I closed my eyes for a minute while she droned, rested my face in my hands, and stayed there for a few moments. Then wearily I raised my head and interrupted her answering one of her own questions.

"I'm sorry. I've got to find a bathroom." I quickly stood and hustled to where I'd seen one as we were looking at the food selections. The bathroom door closed behind me. I took the middle stall. How long would a half-eaten burger take to vomit? A few minutes of sitting with my pants pulled up and reading the faux graffiti on the stall door passed the time. "If it's brown flush it down, yellow leave it mellow." "Wouldn't you give your soul for a flower about now?" "Don't read this." A Keith Haring styled black marker drawing of a massive dog biting the ass of a naked running woman was at the bottom of the left wall. It's the last thing I noticed before I got up and went to the sink. I ran cold water over my hands, splashed it up on my face, and stared at myself in the mirror. "What's the worst date you've ever been on?" Her voice inserted itself into my internal dialog. I slugged out to the table with my face still a little wet, going for the clammy look.

"Sorry about that," I said.

"Are you okay? You look a little sick."

"I just was," I said, making my voice a little too froggy. I made a face at the remnants of the burger and pushed it to the center of the table. "I hate to do this, but I think I should go back to my hotel and lie down."

"Sure, do you want to finish eating or leave now?"

Didn't you see me push my wasted burger to the middle of the table?

"I think it was the burger that made me sick." I stood while she slowly sucked in a last oily noodle and dumped her napkin on the table.

Back on the walkway, she started up, "We should report that restaurant. Do you remember the first time you got sick in school? I was in the first grade and I threw up orange juice in the middle of the class. I was really embarrassed. Did you ever get sick in school?"

I worried she'd get the idea later to watch me throw up and know that I'd been faking it with her.

"Do you mind if we don't talk? I feel like shit."

"Sure, I'll walk you back to the hotel, okay? We don't have to talk. God, being sick when you're on vacation is lousy. Not that this is really a vacation for you, but it is in a way."

From the restaurant to the hotel seemed like an eternity. She ignored my request and continued with how great her mother was when she got sick, and that she wondered how people dealt with long-term illnesses, and then on to hospitals and the latest genetic therapy cures and on and on. I almost wished I'd left her on the bench by the lake. We turned a corner and were finally at the hotel.

"If you like I could come up and rub your back till you fall asleep. Mom always did that for me when I had an upset stomach."

"That's really nice, but I think I'd rather be alone ... you know in case I should get sick again."

"I'm the same way. I hate to have people see me throw up. This is a terrible ending to our first time together. I don't mean to offend you by that. You couldn't help getting sick I know."

"Hey thanks for everything, I'm sure we'll be in touch soon."

"Maybe you could come back again. I'm sure Dr Mamon will be pleased with your work here when he sees you." She grinned at me again with the good-job teeth glowing and nervously pulled a reed out of her purse. "Okay, come here and give me a hug." She pulled up close, and I turned my head away from hers and felt her xylophone ribs against my stomach as she hugged me tightly.

"Thanks for everything tonight," I said again.

She lit her reed, "Anytime, okay, bye now." She waved with the smoke quavering and got on the walkway looking back at me.

"Hey, wait a minute." Susan jumped off the sidewalk, almost tripping, she ran over to me, dropping her reed on the way. She looked around, avoiding my eyes. "I wanted to tell you one more thing."

"What's that?" I asked trying to keep the sick look on my face.

She leaned over to get close to me and fell into my shoulder, banging her mouth.

"Jesus, what are you doing?" I said, holding her up and feeling worried for her. She turned bright red.

"I wanted to tell you something," her bony hands covering her face again. She pulled them away from her eyes, keeping them over her mouth. She looked at me seriously and leaned over to my ear again, cautiously this time.

"I love you." She kissed my cheek and waited for my response.

"You love me? We don't even, we barely... I don't know what to say."

"Don't say anything. I just can't go on with this, and no one has contacted to let me know what I should do. I mean, what am I supposed to do? I'm feeling like I should just go with what feels right and what feels right is being honest. Let's go up to your room again."

"I'm still not feeling well— "

"I know you're not sick, Ben, I watched while you sat in the bathroom, but I don't care that you lied. Look, I mean, I want to be alone with you. I have something else I need to... Your room would just be so much better than the sidewalk." She looked nearly pained as she was saying this.

I felt invisible others watching, a continued desire to manipulate me, but also, she had a certain sincerity that confused me - not quite sure what she was after but if there was even more I felt it best to get it all out now.

꞊THIRTY-ONE꞊

We entered the hotel, walking through another hallway that shot us from all directions with a mild blast of cleansing air. On the way to the elevators, we passed a gift shop, and I remembered I told the twins I'd bring them something back. I hesitated, wondering if I should. It seemed ridiculous to stop now with Susan. I could tomorrow on my way out. I paused at the shop entrance.

"I need to stop in here, okay?"

She gave me a curious look, "We should really get to your room."

I ignored her and quickly found two little terrariums in the shape of Skycity with little air plants growing in them. 'Grow Your Own Skycity! Insects not included.' It reminded me of the Saint Center too. They'd love them.

Back in the room, she directed me to sit down and drew another screen on the window as I dropped my gift bag. She navigated to an Archive section that seemed to take special swipes to direct and flip through.

"You might want to get yourself a drink. This will probably come as another big shock."

I was still standing and decided to sit down as I could see she was quite serious.

"Look the thing is, we can't control how things turn out no matter what we want. The world has other plans for us, right?" she said.

I gave her a frustrated look.

"I want to give this to you now, Ben. Think of it as a gift, please. Okay, there's a whole subsection of the Archive. This is the entrance." She pointed at the screen. "They created it to keep our true histories intact so that after the revelations are delivered, we can join this true record with the rest of the Archives. I should've told you earlier especially when you were upset over the fake arch of us having sex, but I was hurt… Don't worry, here, just let me show you."

Susan navigated to an archive where she's just lying on me, no sex between us, exactly what happened. "I wanted to show you this even though I don't understand what is happening and even though I think it's disturbing. But I need to prove that my love can eventually be shown with all the real history between us. That other fake history won't have to exist forever."

She didn't wait for my response and instead navigated to a section with my name and the accident. She started the archive after the crash but set it to fast-forward through the start: my exiting the car, checking my parents, and then walking away from the scene for help. All of which I remembered, but then it showed me collapsing on the road. Even with the fast-forwarding, I could tell I lay there for an extended time, not moving. Then it switched to an aerial view, showed vehicles flying in and setting up the area. They installed pylons with bright yellow lights around our bodies. The highway had blocking sensors arranged miles before and after, routing traffic around. Trailers arrived and navigated the wreckage on the highway to get to our accident site. They spent a long time inspecting Dad but finally took each of us into a separate vehicle. I was lifted on a stretcher inside one of the trailers where Mamon and other scientists gathered around my head.

"Alright, stay focused, he's dead, all our work with him is ended. The genetics are basically the same with Ben, so we'll have to start with his now," Mamon said as he waited for one of the scientists to mix blue gel and some other liquid in a glass pan next to my ear. Mamon wiped my hair and face clean and coated me with the blue concoction. The instruments they attached to the back of my skull caused panels to blink. Mamon seemed satisfied with the readings. He nodded in agreement about something to one of the scientists. They continued to add wires and Mamon injected a long needle with a lighter blue substance into my eye, possibly further into my brain.

"Is the replacement complete?" Mamon asked, looking at the screen next to him.

"It's almost set to deploy, sir." I could see the fake archive me frozen on the screen. "We'll add the same face contusions and a few stitches to match the new archive. Will you want to review?"

"No, that won't be necessary. As soon as you have them en route to the hospital, install it the new."

Mamon left and I watched as they sliced near my eyebrow and upper cheek then stitched it up, caused a bruising and swelling to occur in the area where Suzy had stomped my face and smeared dirt on my body in a few locations. Time passed, and they took more readings before wiping my head down again. The archive ended with the delivery of my parents and me to a hospital.

"I had to tell you," Susan said. "When you had me watch your rape archive I decided I'd look here for you and I found this. I had no idea. I didn't know anything about it before. I couldn't just let you walk away and not share this. You never went to that house."

I sat there, stunned. I felt as if I'd phased into another world. Something far darker and less free overcame me an opposite feeling of when I was outside the Archive recording. Now it was as if I were trapped inside a second layer, smothering in a mental onion. All those months of anguish, of not knowing what to believe about myself, feeling betrayed by Sara then raped by Suzy. Suzy. I stared at Susan.

"Who are you?" I looked at her bony fingers reaching towards me. I saw the outline of her jawbone and noticed her thin eyebrows dipping with concern. Something looked unnatural about her now.

"No, Ben, it's not like that. I'm the person you've been writing for months. I'm here for you now, telling you the truth. I'm…in love with you, and that's why I've shown you this." She reached for me trying to put her arms around me.

"Love me? You're in love with me? I told you about all those nightmares. You knew of my regular meetings with Laurel. I needed help. You knew I needed help."

"I know. I'm sorry, Ben. I didn't know all of this. There was nothing I could do."

"What were they doing to me? What did they put in my head?" I started feeling around the back of my ears but felt little except maybe something like a bump on my left ear. Was that always there? I think I'd always had it but how could I be sure?

"I really didn't know about any of that," she said.

I stood up, harshly tapped to clear the clouded windows and looked down onto the city lights from below. Music suddenly came on in the room, a woman singing, "... you gotta look back, look back, you gotta look back on the books. Tell me baby, do you love me, or did you love me just for my looks..."

"Get out. I want to be alone," I said.

"Please... Let's talk, Mamon will contact— "

"I said get out. And you know what, don't contact me." I walked to the door and opened it. I could see my brusque action shocked her.

"I'm sorry. So sorry," she said, and tears welled up in her eyes as she stared with great concern and slunk out the door. I closed the door on her and sat down again. How could she have thought I'd be okay with her, with all of this?

Here I thought I'd been raped by Suzy, but in reality I was taken advantage of by Mamon. I glanced down at the gifts for the twins. I wanted to smash something. How could I have left them alone with him? I grabbed my goggles from the gear bag and navigated to the twins' currently recording archive and found them asleep in a large bed looking completely at ease and happy. I tried different angles to see if anything might jump out as incorrect, as something made up about what was being recorded, but nothing appeared out of order. Nothing found in the fast rewind I did through their activity during their visit either - no needles or odd blue gel rubbed onto their heads, nothing I could attribute to abuse. They spent a good deal of their time playing the video game and generally having what looked like fun, but how could I know it wasn't all fiction, doctored items made just for me to cover up? I switched to the live feed of them again. They were okay. You need time to fake the history, so they must be fine.

As I sat down again, I noticed Susan's laser instrument. She must've left it here earlier. A little pressure from my finger clicked the yellow beam on and it hit the wall. I clicked it off, but the yellow mark on the wall glowed, a short-term stain that quickly faded.

The song refrain played. "Tell me baby, do you love me, or did you love me just for my looks." It continued as I took a long sip, "... you gotta look back on the books," and I recalled the footage from Mamon's journals.

I felt an anger rise in me as I put on my goggles and adjusted them. He may be out to help as Susan had been suggesting, but she could've been fooled as easily as I. He certainly wasn't out to help me. At the controls, I changed my view to the beginning of what I captured in Mamon's office.

⚏THIRTY-TWO⚏

I slowly forwarded the pages to a freeze-framed image with a handwritten index.

I. Dream Monk History & Symbols
II. Saint Center
III. Faux Life Movement
IV: Light's Religious History
V. Botanical Energies
VI. History
VII. [Illegible writing that looked like PRSnL. Personal?]

The combination of a sun and vines logo of the Center decorated the middle of the page above, "Dr Luc Mamon." I fast-forwarded through the journals and found many weeks' worth of reading. The journals were a combination of Cy Twombly paintings and the illuminated Book of Kells: scribbled notes on every page, filled with scientific-looking formulas, graphs plotted in spectacular dotted detail, hand-drawn plant diagrams, and anatomy illustrations. I flipped forward to the beginning and found a list of religious quotations. A small note at the top read: Need matched control symbols from monks.

From Lao Tzu (Taoism): "Following the Light, the sage takes care of all."
From Mundaka Upanishad (Hinduism): "In the effulgent lotus of the heart dwells Brahman, the Light of lights."

From the Bible (Christianity): "I have come into the world as Light."

From Kurozumi Munetada (Shinto): "The light of Divine Amaterasu shines forever."

From Psalms (Judaism): "The Lord is my Light; whom shall I fear?"

From the Dhammapada (Buddhism): "The radiance of Buddha shines ceaselessly."

The twelve sons of Ra, the twelve sons of Jacob, and the twelve tribes of Israel = "twelve saviors of the treasure of light."

My eyes were twitching, trying to read as quickly as I could. Several more pages continued with lists of quotes, references to light in religious texts, or figures in mythological history that had light as their focus. I couldn't find any significant thread or reason for the list beyond justification for a belief that God and Light are synonymous. At the end of this first journal was a single quote in large bold letters.

Use your own light and return to the source of light. This is called practicing eternity. - Lao Tzu

In VI. History (of Life in the Universe), I found cutout images pasted onto the beginning pages. Mostly they were pictures of beautiful cellular structures or galaxies followed by pages and pages of grids in the shape of doughnuts.

On the adjoining page a chart titled Final Black Hole series: Culmination-Alignment and contained notes written along the edge of the chart: As I worked the calculations for destined paths of black holes in our torus [universe], I noticed an unusual alignment coming into play around the center. Galaxies must be aligning = each galaxy has at least one black hole inhabiting it. I will need to force energies collected and projected with mindlight as a magnifier...

Seemingly, out of place on the next page was a diagram of the eye and the path of its connected nerves through the brain. Scribbled at the bottom I found Stars are the parents of all life forms. Our mind is an amalgam of their offspring. Our bodies formed from their interaction with us. Our eyes reflective of their shape, made to handle their words. Look into the night sky, feel the photons entering your brain, coming from light years away, a journey that began for some of them billions of years ago. You are connected through space and time to it all.

I thought again of them sticking a needle into my eye. My scalp started itching. I kept flipping through pages, and when I got to the end, I found an illustrated history of the human skull and brain. The last branch of the timeline showed skulls as you'd see at the top of any classic Halloween decoration. The other branch showed pointed skulls with a slit down the middle. The brains in these skulls had points at the top that moved beyond the bone housing as if they were pushing out of the skull. Without its skin and muscle packaging, the images of the brain and spine suggested a bulb and roots system. I anxiously felt along the top of my head again.

VII. PRSnL Personal? was the last. The other journals were disorganized, but nothing like this final one. It looked more like a room after the twins had one of their spinning fits, more sketchbook than journal. Small diagrams and writings ran in zigzags about every page. The writing slanted and wiggled frantically as if he hadn't enough time to get out all he wanted to say. Symbols, strange iconography were crammed into every inch.

My eyes felt jumpy as I tried to find a decipherable passage. The symbols looked familiar, shoving their way in front of the words, almost embossing the page with their energy. I finally found something legible after about twenty pages of flipping.

Difficulty with the memory enhancement drugs: As yet they aren't permanent. Permanence of memory is a necessity for proper understanding of self, for self-awareness that is able to guide and keep one cohesive, or focused. Impossibility (?): To increase biophoton production to aid in the assembly of a cohesive society suffused in the Light awareness, which would generate and conduct light in a manipulable fashion. The failures of past Eugenic measures could be related to a misunderstanding of the importance of Self.

The aspiration to manipulate genes comes from some ancient desire of wanting to do the best for yourself and your children, this is nothing new, but the form we should aspire to is. Historically, eugenics was unsuccessful as a way to enhance the human race because its pursuit was influenced by fear and bias. Instead of trying to create one form, one skewed idea of perfection, each individual should be treasured, fostered so that they may add their special light in the best manner that their composition is able to give.

I recall years ago, first considering how the problems of Choice could be a catalyst for most modern mental distress. Being provided with an abundance of options is what has throttled many minds in the world. Waves of anxiety overcame me when I entered the general listings of the Archives earlier that evening, unable to think of an appropriate search term – instead, I started scanning the branches of options to navigate. I froze up, unable to choose. Which route would get me to my destination most efficiently? I started clicking away, selecting a path by chance. Time wasted. That's the simplest example of the choice humankind faces.

Years in the past if one wanted to communicate with a foreigner, people had to wait weeks maybe even months as information was walked door-to-door in paper letter form. Then with the introduction of the telephone information began jogging along electric lines, but it wasn't until the onset of the Internet that possibilities in communication really found momentum. Now, literally at light speed, we can talk with anyone anywhere at any time. It's as easy as thinking of a person or subject and generating a list with that thought. Those lists take on the Mandelbrot pattern in form. Astoundingly vast amounts of choice. Because of my discovery and development of Informed Light, information movers utilize light in the same way philosophers moved great thought through small words like truth and love. The ancient Greek philosopher Anaximander was not far off thinking our world is only one of the myriad that evolve and dissolve in the "boundless". One of many, one of the myriad universes, yes, but now all understood to be interconnected. The universes are bound and ours in a particular fashion. Bound by its limitations of intellect, bound by its limitations of language. We have the potential to be much more.

As our universe began to meet the center or complete its revolution around the torus, the Synchronistic Activity Waves started linking information, revealing connections between form and thought. A society trying to choose from a complex menu, and consequently choosing nothing will be disastrous. The next evolution of mind has begun and will heal the neurosis of Entropy/Choice.

On the next page, an image of Mamon's face looked out at me this time without his cone turban, his head malformed. He'd not surprisingly chosen to keep it wrapped. On the same page I read:

Revelation: The universe is a communicating conscious energy. It has been working to evolve life forms to facilitate manipulation of energy of our planet/galaxy... to create a black hole, an exit, and pull energy into its universe in a similar manner that a light god once did with ours. The chief remaining question: What is the struggle for light ultimately for?

He'd been using himself as a guinea pig. A large image of Mamon filled the lower half of the next page, again without his turban, but this time it showed the cone-shaped head flowering. It had a creepy fluorescence to it. I'd seen all kinds of body mutilation for fashion, but this was different. I couldn't take my eyes away. His split skull image sent a jolt of panic, hitting my feet before my head and had me out of my seat.

I pulled the goggles off, stuck them in my bag, and clicked my communicator to hail a taxi. It took me no time to gather my stuff and get to the waiting platform outside.

"Where to?" the car announced.

"The shuttle port."

It was close to 3 a.m. when I checked my watch. The city did not rest. 3 a.m. was as active as 3 p.m. People filled the by-ways of every surrounding tube. I kept scanning their faces as they passed, watching their oblivious expressions, imagining them with their heads like Mamon's, pointed and flowering. Everything took an eternity, but I arrived at the port and found my terminal.

Two women waited with me. They styled each other's hair, and chattered relentlessly, "Your hair, it's beautiful, just precious, really precious. Here, let me paint more."

I stretched a screen and tapped to call Lenny with an emergency signal attached to it. Lenny's face filled the square.

"What is it?" He'd been asleep.

"Lenny, sorry to wake you."

"What's the emergency?"

"I need you to pick me up."

"Up there?"

"Wake up, Lenny. I need you to meet me at the port, the one on the ground. I should be there in an hour. If you leave now I won't have to wait long."

"Hold on. It'll take me an hour to get there."

"Just put on some clothes and the car on accelerated till you get to the port."

"Okay, hey, you sound upset. I'm awake now. I'll be there, don't worry."

"Thanks." The screen disappeared. I closed my eyes briefly and experienced quick flashes of glowing trees as odd immediate dreams while I slipped in and out of consciousness. The laughter of the hair ladies kept me awake, and I watched them as they poured drinks for each other. The twinkling lights of Chicago tilted into view from their window.

The shuttle door couldn't open quickly enough. I ran to the waiting area for arriving transportation. A couple of buses rolled past, and I wondered if it wouldn't have been better to take a taxi rather than relying on Lenny. I gave his car a call to make sure he didn't fall back asleep.

"Lenny, good, you're on your way," I said, recognizing the interior lights of his car.

"The dash says I have thirty-four minutes until arrival. You okay?"

"I'm fine. I'll fill you in when I see you." I clicked off abruptly feeling like everything was bearing down on me as if Mamon knew and tracked each action.

I bought a coffee and watched some ads on the screens. 'Do your houseplants look like this?' Two flowering orchids wilted on the screen as a woman with a towel wrapped around her wet hair frowns. 'Let Spring-to-Life work for you.' The flowers bounced back, and so did the woman's smile.

I pulled my goggles out and forwarded through the pages, seeking something more. The pages flipped by with images of cells and plants and skulls. I navigated to the 'V. Plant energies & their Use' volume and carefully turned the pages this time finding a systematic process for animal and plant integration. I found smaller animals, an odd rat looking creature with a flat leaf-shaped face, but my head began to throb when I came upon dog transformation pictures and worse when I saw guidelines for work on humans. The human transformation illustrations looked less plant-like than the dogbush. One man had a head shaped more like a pineapple the way its leaves pushed out at the top. But on the next page, my worries were confirmed. I found my father's name in all caps beneath a silhouette of a flowering head. Beneath it read, "Secondary Processor/16th year of preparation/Equivalent DNA" but underneath was my name written in as well as "Accelerated treatments" with the date of the accident beside it. My head was being prepared for this, whatever this was. On the following pages I found a mirrored version of the silhouette, two heads labeled E/F and written underneath was, "Vestigs processing unit"

Under that, a line of symbols and then "Conjoined twin = ideal design for necessary temporal lobe transference element. Truncating and sealing of the fontanel is enhanced during early germination." A nauseous dread took over my body. A side dissection showed how the back left half of Ed's brain and the back right half of Francis's would be grafted to the rear of Mamon's head. The grafting progression of all three skulls continued on the next page. In the final illustration, Mamon's exposed brain emanated light. The light beam widened and climbed toward the top of the page and joined Lenny's headlights as he drove toward me and parked.

⚏THIRTY-THREE⚏

"As Dad used to say, you look like a three-legged dog that's been tied to a speeding bus," Lenny said when I closed the door.

"Just take the fastest route to the Saint Center," I said humorlessly.

We drove with striped highways pecking into our eyes. The oncoming headlights kept me awake as I relayed the events of the past 24 hours, showing him the journals with me, Dad and the boys, about Susan and the FLM.

"If what you say is true seems like you were an afterthought. Do you think your father knew about any of this and just let you raise them for Mamon?" Lenny said.

"I have no idea… I doubt it. I know Dad wasn't faking all those years of being angry at Mamon."

"They must've been keeping a close eye on your Dad to get to the accident before any of the other emergency services."

"All I can think is if they did that to me, there has to be some truth to what he wants to do to Ed and Francis." I pulled up their real-time archive, and now instead of sleeping, I found the boys already playing the game in the same room I found them last time. They looked happy, laughing at the game.

"They seem okay. I think they're probably fine. You can just ask Mamon what's going on, force him to explain but, right, best to after you get the boys out," Lenny said.

We continued to go over possible options, and by the time we arrived at the Center, a halo of dawn's gray-yellow light signaled the end of night. Lenny pulled to the side of the complex near a few fir trees. I started playing the possible conversation in my head. I'd be calm and say very little, explain I'd finished early and wanted to get them out of his hair.

I turned to Lenny as I stepped out into the cold morning, visible breath streaming like a bleating goat. "Tell me I'm not being stupid."

"Can't all be fiction. Even if nothing's happening now, it could," Lenny said.

"Okay, you know the plan," I said as my teeth began to tap lightly together from nerves more than cold.

"You get em and I wait. No message from you in thirty and I call in the guns of Brixton."

"Right," I said.

I turned from Lenny after he gave a final reassuring nod and ran across the frost-covered lawn. I glanced back once I reached the entrance just barely making out my scuffle tracks through the frost on the grass. The sky looked like a neon bruise, an intensely bright rainbow sunrise as I'd never seen. I averted my eyes to stop the pain the light was causing them.

The greeter barely looked up from his screen when I passed. I didn't recognize him but waved hello and kept going, feigning confidence. The only employee I'd had regular contact with besides Mamon was Martina, and it was unlikely I'd run into her this early. I owned this place. I kept talking to myself knowing I was out of my league as I glanced about at the beetles in the walls and the patterns on the floor, at the complication of it all.

I hiked to the room taking the routes I'd been before, down a few hallways, passing gas-masked scientists twiddling with plants in rooms. None noticed me. It felt like forever until I reached the lab where the twins had played the game. I found it closed and dark but tried to open it anyway to see if I could find an adjoining room, something that might lead to where they were. The door made a loud squeak as I pulled it. The only other door in the room was for a closet. I went back out and down the hallway to the passage where I'd found the dog bush. Two men came out of a door and advanced toward me. They looked like they recognized me.

"Dr Mamon is expecting you, come with us please."

Expecting me? Since there was no anger in them, no obvious malice I thought it could still all be okay.

We passed the jungle area on our way to Mamon's office. Lack of sleep wore on me, but enervated nerves itched at muscle and tendons. The office doors were shut with bright light spilling through the cracks. I peered into the room through squinting eyes as they opened the door for me and found the desk and floor split wide. A wall of dry sauna-like heat greeted me. Light beamed up towards the ceiling now with mammoth tendrils of long colored glass poked down through the roof like some kind of octopus-chandelier. Light reflected off of it and saturated color spots glimmered on the pictures all about the room. Entering, I quickly went to the edge where the floor lay open. I felt like one might when standing in a spotlight as you walked into a surprise party.

As I looked down, Mamon looked up. His eyes focused on the tendrils of glass above, but they shifted towards me. Each of our faces must've mirrored the other's expression, shocked at the sudden sight. His, at my presence, mine at the view of the twins strapped into elaborate operating chairs, heads shaven, and clear tubes with blue-green fluid plugged into their spines.

"I wasn't sure if you'd want to join us after her call, but here you are," shouted Mamon up at me.

He signaled to the two who stood next to me. They led me down to the lab below. A ring of brightly glowing towers encircled the room. The tubes emerged from them and stretched out in curving rows along the floor towards the center where Ed and Francis were plugged into what could only be called chairs, but with all their tubing and instruments they were obviously much more. More men moved to stand guard between me and the boys.

"I'm glad Susan was able to convince you," Mamon said, not looking up from his screen as we approached.

"Convince me of what?" I said tensely. I tried to shield my eyes from the light flashing off the machinery. The twins looked like strange baby birds with their heads shaven and eyes wide-open. They stared mesmerized at a screen flashing with symbols - the game. Their heads now were slightly elongated at the top with incisions, flowering splits that looked ugly and painful

"Susan explained you have been informed and would like to join the FLM. I assume she convinced you that what we are working on is worthwhile. However, I am sorry, Ben, at this time you are not needed," he said casually, staying focused, not turning toward me, and continued with some adjustments.

Light shifted and grew brighter on the boys.

"Ed! Francis!" They didn't move when I called to them. More men entered the room and spread out focusing on me, obviously as a means to prevent my harming any of the operations. There were two carrying black batons who stood beside Mamon. I noticed the tray of syringes on one of the carts. "If I'm not needed, then why'd you stick a needle in my eye?"

This caused him to look up at me from his work. "She shared more than instructed. Fine. That will have to wait." He returned to focusing on the screen.

I stood there trying to figure out what to do until I finally just angrily said, "We're leaving. I'm taking them with me now. You still don't own them, right? My father owned them, right?"

"It is interesting how much you sound like your father when you show anger," Mamon said and spoke sternly in a foreign language to the two that stood next to him. I started walking towards the twins and was grabbed by the man closest to me. I punched at him but missed his head entirely, landing my punch on his collarbone. He was shorter than me and struggled to keep himself from falling. My hand throbbed with a jarring pain as I moved closer to the boys.

The two with the batons split up and advanced. One swung at my leg, knocking me toward the second. I twisted my body, trying to avoid the second, but his baton sliced through the air at my head. I felt a sharp pain in my mouth, one to the other side of my head, and then nothing. When I came to, I found myself tied to a chair with blood dripping from my chin into my lap. A gap now existed where most of my front teeth used to be. It took me a short time to regain focus. Several men adjusted instruments at the splits in the twins' heads. They poked at Francis and Ed more, and I started yelling stop, causing intense pain in my mouth.

"I've read your journals," I said, spraying blood. Mamon looked over at me. "I know about your plans. You can't cover up killing my brothers."

He paused for a moment before responding, "Where in my journals did I write about killing them?" His voice had a wounded tone. "I love your brothers. I always have. This is what they were made for." Mamon waved his hand at a few of the men, and they approached with a gag.

"Look at them. They don't have a choice," I said.

The twins sat still, frozen and staring. I struggled as Mamon strode over to me. His eyes conveyed a kind of patronizing warmth. He placed his hand on my shoulder and handled my face examining my mouth. I tried to shove his hand away.

"I wanted them to threaten, to calm you, not inflict this kind of damage. I am sorry for that." He looked at the ceiling and thought for a moment. "It is about a returning home, getting beyond our mental walls. Your father never recognized their great potential when the accident occurred, when your brothers were created… Miracles. They are a treasure. Without their coming into being I am not sure I would have had the idea at all. I have been watching people all my life… one soul being tortured is too many, but millions have suffered horribly under the ignorance we have lived with." Mamon looked at Ed and Francis. "He owned them, your father owned them, so there was no stopping it, but before he left with Ed and Francis, we argued at great length about the suffering we could prevent. They all argued with me until I unleashed the light, and then they began to understand. They started to see what I had seen; that it needs to end. All those who gave their lives for the Cohoba development, for this moment in time ... I am justified."

He squinted at the ceiling as if searching for an answer and then back at me with great intensity. "Have you ever had a family pet suddenly crushed by a car and die?" He turned away hunting for something else, but then back to me and started again with greater anger in his voice, "Have you studied the overwhelming plight of humanity? Its oppressive beauty?"

He pointed to the pictures on the wall above. "The Archives - a great documentary triumph - filled with...so much... so many examples... Have you spent time watching the slow process of an old man getting out of a chair? Ever seen a poverty-stricken woman lose pocket change?" He looked down from the pictures and into my eyes again. "Is there anyone you find yourself feeling superior to? A janitor maybe, a refuse plant employee, the woman who sells you a drink? For you, is there an artist whose work is not worthy of your attention? Those people you look down upon, have you spent an hour with any of them, ever? Spent time coming to understand the complexity of their lives? I know you can understand. You've worked with the saints reading their journals... Don't you feel the thick lump of suffering building in your chest when you think of their lives? Our whole edifice is founded on their unavenged tears. The architecture of their lives, of our lives, it is unfathomably powerful."

Mamon looked up into the colored tendrils of light with sincere grief in his eyes. "I can bring an end to their sufferings, to yours. We must recognize that evolution favors those creatures best adapted to their environment.

That is what I decided many years ago: to end the ignorance, end the misunderstanding, and bring forth the evolution. I will do this," he said and backed away from me a little, "only I have been shown. This is how we set the code working." He swept his arm around the room and ended at the boys. "Their song and the Lexicon have revealed the key, and now I'll be here to gather and set it free, set us free. The final contraction is occurring now."

He looked up at the tendrils again and back at me. "The monks have given me the path to redemption, the gods have told me this is the right time, and I will not fail you. Sit and watch Ben, you can be one of the first. One of few lucky figures in history to witness the inauguration, the shedding of our limitations."

He went back to the panel as the scientists continued poking at my brothers' heads, holding brightly shining objects close to the sides of their faces and adjusting small connections on the surrounding equipment. The points of their heads were manipulated into position. Mamon, with a tray of operating instruments and long tubes, joined the others at the back of the twins. He dipped his hands in a substance coating them white, then emptied electric-blue gel into the palm of his hand from one of the tubes and spread it around the surface of the twin's heads where they'd already been cut. The back of their heads expanded with the enlarging brain petals, pushing against their skulls with tiny cracking noises. I struggled hard against my restraints but couldn't free myself.

The petals grew and bent against each other. One of the scientists took a long scalpel and removed half of each of their blossoms causing a good deal of blood to spill to the floor. They spread more of the blue gel onto the cuts, which slowed the bleeding immediately. My mouth throbbed with pain, and the tender spots had me hoping they could not feel any of what was occurring.

Mamon gave a signal to men monitoring it all through a window from an adjoining room. A split chair emerged from the floor behind the twins. Mamon, removed his clothes and head wrap as the attendants plugged some of the tubes from the tower into sockets that had been embedded into his upper spine and neck and arranged them so that they would fit through the split in his chair. His head extended twice regular length with well-defined petals wrapped in a tight bud. Looking resolute, he sat down as the chair continued to rise and recline, positioning his head just above their blossom. As he rose with the chair, the light from above coalesced from many smaller scattered beams into single larger versions hitting each of the towers around the room. The tubes of liquid glowed brighter.

Several assistants brought out an expansive cape of small mirrored leaves and wrapped it about his body - a mountain of flickering light. Plastic stretching sounds screeched into the room as the petals of Ed and Francis's head grew further into one massive bluish-veiny peach-hued blossom. The twins were working up their baritone song, and that woozy feeling began. The screens repeatedly flashed a series of symbols that I began to recognize as the ones shown by the tree-men in my dream. The ones that were supposed to signal my stopping all of this. They never said how.

Sleep pulled at me, but I could see Ed's face. It began looking like he was aware, something in the way he held his head, in the way his eyes stretched wider. I managed to click the laser on. A yellow beam cut a crackling path through the air towards the twins. Mamon looked over at me from his central operating chair beneath the glimmering blanket when the yellow beam caught his attention. He shook his head to stop, but I moved the laser to shine on the twins. I thought maybe that's it, maybe I've stopped it as I waved the laser on their blossom and watched the petals hold the yellow glow, but they still stared at the screen, singing, and I began to lose consciousness. My eyes began to shut as the laser moved from the twin's blossom on to their screens. The yellow glow covered the transmission of the symbols completely. I blacked out again.

I woke to the pain-drenched screams of my brothers. They'd managed to free themselves but looked terrified by the tubes coming from their spines and new shared connection of their heads. The screens previously flashing symbols glowed dull yellow and blank. I could do nothing except watch as the twins ripped their heads back and apart, screaming in agony, tearing their blossom in two. Watery blood sprayed onto everyone within reach as they rocked out of the chair and to their feet. Round and round, their flower-petal heads whipped as anger manifested into one of their chaotic tornadoes. Bodies of scientists flew, smashing against tables and equipment, landing on the floor.

The chairs the twins were connected to became a fountain. Tubes of blue-green liquid waved like unattached summer hoses on high, whipping about in all directions. Leaves sprouted from the faces and hands of men trying to manage the pandemonium. Mamon climbed out of the chair with his tubes still connected, tossing his cape over some of the flailing tubes. He tried to calm the boys' anger, but in their confusion and fury they knocked him into a panel. A chain reaction sent the rest of the towers in the room dominoing, one against the next until all but one lay gasping electric jolts. Sparks showered from the ceiling, and a great shifting multi-colored light undulated down in two wide beams. The single pillar seemed to be trying to contain one, holding it in place. The second much larger fell on the center of the room. Everything quaked with their energy.

Ed and Francis caught sight of me. They ran over, "Ben, Ben. My head hurts. Make it stop!" Ed pulled on my still bound arms, his face streaked with horrific maroon lines. "I'm bleeding!" Francis showed me the blood he'd gotten on his fingers. Ed pulled at the bindings on my wrists, slicing my hands but freeing me. I untied my feet and tried to use consoling words, but I could only manage "You'll be okay. You'll be okay," as I watched as tiny leaves sprouting from the holes along their backs. A few remaining scientists helped Mamon to his feet. He walked through the spectrum of light dragging the tubes from his spine behind him.

"What have you done?" He shouted, looking at the destruction. His tattered brain-petals swatting about.

"There is still time." He grabbed onto Ed's arm. "We can still save it. Look, look at the light." He yanked Ed trying to force him to look. Ed shoved, but Mamon held on moving them closer to the beam. The twins or Mamon must've let go, and the twins went flying towards the covered chairs. They pulled the cape and freed the hoses beneath. Blue fluid washed over Ed's body. He scratched his head as his blossom swiftly extended and leaves overwhelmed his neck and face. Francis roared. He scratched at the mounding leaves on Ed's body until Ed accidentally pulled Francis into the blue stream and leaves multiplied on his body also. The fluid continued to spew down on them as the foliage muffled their voices.

"No!" Mamon yelled with arms outstretched just beyond the reach of the spray. "Stop it, turn it off."

I looked around the room helplessly trying to find a way to cut off the flow.

Mamon turned to me, his face a ball of squinting crinkled anger, "This is your fault."

"Get something. They're going to choke on those leaves," I said.

"It is too late." He walked towards me, and I backed away towards the fallen towers. He looked around, dazed and manic, but still encroaching. Mamon stuck his arm into the path of the light beam. I lost sight of his hand, and it rippled as if underwater up to his elbow.

"See this, Ben. This is beyond you and me. Now we have no way of knowing… no way to control it."

He stared at me, but kept his arm swimming in the light, then stuck his head beneath it and gazed up at the ceiling as if taking a shower. I heard something like singing coming from him, but it warped and became stifled. Then from behind the chair emerged the walking forest that was now my brothers. They grabbed hold of Mamon's arm and pushed him hard into the remaining tower. The light above started sending out waves that I could physically feel as they hit me. The tower started tilting and fell, crushing Mamon beneath. When it hit the floor, the building quaked.

I backed away from the intensifying shower of sparks and saw the twins fall backward as some of the ceiling slid to the floor on top of them. I ran through blinding light to the staircase shelter. It seemed the most secure, but as I turned to look back for the boys, I found myself in the spectrum beam reflecting off the operating chairs. My body felt drugged. For a few seconds, I experienced a blissful warmth course through me. A waterfall of glass shards began pouring down into the center of the room.

Everything darkened as the beam's transmission finally ended and paper littered the air, flipping over and over - pictures of the people once lining Mamon's office walls. The vibrations in the room increased, and I started quickly up the stairs feeling more anxiety with each step I took that led me further away from where the boys' bodies lay — nothing to do but run. I just escaped as an enormous section avalanched down.

The spiral stairs felt near impossible to climb as the complex quaked. At a landing I stopped to get my bearings and leaned on a door, holding onto the bar for balance, but the building's motion opened it, and I tumbled into a room with long glass cocoons that had slid together towards the door. Inside were men whose heads were malformed and in early stages of blossoming. The room tilted more and knocked me into one. The icy green eyes of the man inside blinked opened. He looked familiar, and I could see he was alive. I searched for a way to open the glass container, but couldn't figure out how. I had no choice but to abandon him too.

I sprinted out and continued up the stairs to the first landing. The saints' sleeping area was in turmoil, petals of the great stained-glass flower ceiling fell in large shards. The walkway offered shelter, and I stopped for a second while more of the ceiling dislodged in an oddly uniform fashion as if designed to wilt under such circumstances.

The massive glass column at the center of the room had collapsed into the operation below. Shimmering dust sifted through the bright, otherworldly light. As the rest of the ceiling fell, I darted towards the exit. Among a row of spilled saints, I found Amelia. Her head pulled from its cover, revealing tiny petals. I scooped her up, and as she rested on my shoulder, I worried this wasn't sleep. She had only the one arm, but her caroca cube dangled and banged against my legs as I tried running towards the reception area. I passed others I'd helped, feeling guilty but rushing through the maze of rubble around me. The exit came into view only a few yards ahead as the building shifted, the ground I ran along buckled, and I tripped toward the door with Amelia.

⚏THIRTY-FOUR⚏

Through lash bars of cracked eyelids, light flashed as I watched multi-colored clouds drift into view, interrupting the solid cerulean blue in the transparent ceiling above me.

"I know you're awake, come on, open them lips up. You can stare at the sky another day ... talk, dog breath." A blurred Laurel face came into focus between continued light flashes as my mind stuttered back to clarity. "This better be the last accident you get in. I'm not playing Nurse Nelly for your catatonic body ever again."

I blinked my eyes. Laurel's hand gripped mine. The bright light from above caused her forehead to glow and harsh shadows to darken her eyes. I turned my head working my stiff neck, experiencing the peculiar sensation of movement with hazy vision. The bedside table had been decorated with some cut daffodils in a vase.

"He moved his head," Laurel called out in the room.

"Nurse Nelly, Who's that?" I managed to mumble through semi-dysfunctional lips.

"Oh, shut up ... but keep talking." Laurel had a little moisture at the corners of her eyes. She squeezed my arm.

"Dead, they're dead, Laurel!" I said remembering the ceiling collapsing on the Ed and Francis.

"Who's dead?"

"The boys!"

"The slugs from the government have them, said they wanted to cut them up for cat food, and I agreed—" she sucked in air. "Those two belong in the grinder," she said straight-faced and melted into one of her wrinkle-eyed grins. "They're safe." She patted my arm then rushed out of the room unexpectedly.

My knees crackled as my legs stretched under the covers. Everything felt foreign; my body didn't quite feel connected to my mind. I heard the crackling, but the flesh logs belonged to someone else. I managed to push off the heavy down comforter and look around. I hadn't been in this room since I lived with Laurel during my recuperation before. The steel bell clanged outside, and with each clang, another flash appeared in my vision.

Laurel returned a minute later and sat on the bedside; somewhat out of breath with her eyes a little red and puffy. "Sorry for leaving like that. I had to ring the bell to alert them." Laurel touched my cheek, "I'm forgetting myself, can I get you anything?"

"Yeah, you got any salve for sore asses, feels like mine's been getting kicked for days."

"Try four months." She smiled.

"Four months?" I sat up and my right ass cheek felt bruised. "What'd you do with it while I was out?"

"More than any good friend should ever have to. You won't believe what we've tried to bring you around, but you're awake now," she said this with great relief trying to hold herself together and forcing a smile on her face. "I'm sick of washing that flesh box of yours. Hate those things." She looked uneasy. "I'm going to fix you a lunch plate so don't go anywhere," she said and left quickly again.

Go anywhere? I felt tethered. There was a cord growing out of my navel connected to a caroca. They're even more disgusting when attached to your own body. My lips were dried out and my teeth felt too big for my mouth. Nothing found on my bedside table except the daffodils and a small yellow pulsing lamp.

She'd dressed me in one of those tight monitoring shirts, reporting all my stats to the equipment that hung on the headboard beside me. The dinner bell rang outside again, and a few minutes later, Laurel returned with a cup of broth and a glass of ice water.

"I figured this is what your stomach could handle and wasn't sure how well those false teeth would work for you since you haven't used them yet."

"I wondered why they felt weird. They knocked mine out."

"We were going to replace with new ones, but I wanted to give you the option to choose specifics. These are just temporary. There's bots in the water to perk you up."

"Thanks. Where's Ed and Francis?" I asked as I raised the glass to sip. Laurel pulled the curtains more to the side so I could look out. The light was incredibly bright. At first, it looked like vivid glowing blobs coated the tree limbs outside the window until my eyes adjusted some and I could see it was snow.

"Like I said, I rang to bring them in. They've been working in the barn. Crazy April snowstorm we had last night. Those poor little flowers are having a horrible time."

"And they're fine?"

"I just said a horrible time!"

"I meant the twins."

Laurel smiled. "I tell you, I always thought they must've carried bad karma from a past life. Any god wanting to make reincarnation difficult might split you into twins to create a trickier climb up the rebirth ladder, but with their luck, you have to wonder. I was really happy to have had them for the holidays. Sorry, you sort of missed out." She started to adjust my pillows.

"That's right, I missed the holidays," I said gesturing towards the decorative yellow lights along the wall. The whole room flashed disconcertingly again as if prompted by my gesture.

"They're festive, aren't they? We dressed you up with ribbons and stuck candy canes everywhere, so you looked festive too."

"I bet you did," I said.

She looked at me as if trying to hold something back.

"I wanted so badly to help. I've wanted to talk to you about my doubts about your accident. Many times I've wanted to tell you the truth." She started tearing up again.

From downstairs came the Twin's baritones yelling, "Laurel!"

"Up here, boys!" Laurel called back squeezing my hand.

A bull stampede worked its way from the hallway downstairs to my room. Ed and Francis entered wearing winter hats. They grew excited and strangely shy, almost afraid, and didn't come to the bed. Lenny came in after them but strode right up to me.

"Welcome back, Dorothy." Lenny tugged on my foot that stuck out of the bedsheets.

That was all the twins needed to release their pent-up happiness. They followed Lenny's action and almost pulled me off the bed by my ankles.

"Yeah, Dorothy Ozzy," Ed shouted, swinging my leg back and forth.

"Hup Hup Doooorthy," Francis yelled, swinging the other one.

Except for a little pock-marking on their faces, they looked as they always did.

"Watch out now. You'll send him back to the land of vegetables pulling on him like that," Laurel chided.

"He's not vegetables, you can stop washing him with your sponge now," Francis said.

"She hated washing you with a sponge," Ed said, "but I washed under your pits."

"I did the other one," Francis said as he dropped my leg back onto the bed.

"Aw, thanks guys, I bet you were a big help. Come over here." I put my arms out, embracing them with relief to find them alive.

"Yeah, you know 'specially since we're all dead, we gotta stick together," Francis said into my ear.

"You forgot to take off your boots before you came in! Look at this mess! Go remove them right now," Laurel said a little harshly.

"I'm already sticking together," Ed said still hugging me and ignoring Laurel.

"That's enough, I better not find any tracks on the floor when I get down there." Laurel swept the twins from the room. They protested and didn't take their eyes from me until they were out the door.

"What's that dead business about?" I asked Lenny.

"Accordin' to the world history books you're a doornail."

"What's that mean?"

"It means you're outside of the public eyes. We all are. No longer being recorded in the main Archives," Laurel said, returning to my bedside to adjust my legs and the covers.

Lenny looked at Laurel. "Do we explain everything already? He just woke up."

"Sooner is best for this buttsore. Look at him." Laurel swished her hand at my face.

"Sure you don't want to rest up a little first?" Lenny said as he picked up my glass and took a sip.

"That's bot water. You'll be feeling better in no time," I said. Lenny smirked and stood a little straighter. "I want you both to imagine the last thing you remember is running from a collapsing building after seeing your brothers die. That was a long day of bad revelations, and I'd like to know how it ended, so get on with it." I waved at them to continue.

"Luckily, Lenny contacted me," Laurel said with her nose tweaked in the tissue.

"Sorry I didn't follow the plan. I went sort of bugnuts when I watched the sky pouring psychedelic colors, and then when the roof started collapsing... She's the first I thought of."

"Not all the gray matter in this boy's head must be bird droppings," Laurel said.

"How'd they get us? Digging the twins out of that'd be tough."

"According to the Archives, everyone died in the collapse. Rescue teams thoroughly explored the ruins. Some were saved, but sadly, many of the saints that weren't killed immediately died when their life support system failed. All those saints' lives... just horrible." Laurel stopped to compose herself. She took a quick breath and continued. "You and the boys and a few others were found alive. Mamon wasn't so lucky." Laurel stopped to wipe her eyes and blow her nose.

"I was there when they pulled you out. You were all bloody and screwed up like a horror movie. Thought you were a goner. As fershnickered as you looked, you had nothing on the bushboys. That leaf junk saved 'em from all the glass," Lenny said.

I started thinking of what it must've taken to dig anyone out of the rubble. It seemed like an impossibility. "How could rescue teams help us without everyone in the world finding out?"

"Lizard's friends," Laurel said.

"Lizard had friends who could move thousands of pounds of rubble and somehow cover it up?"

"Mamon already had the Center hidden with what he was up to, but yes, I learned recently that Lizard's friends are part of a large organization which you sort of know as the FLM," Laurel said.

"Did you tell her about Mamon and the FLM?" I asked, looking at Lenny.

"She already knew about 'em. The old midget married a dream spy and was in bed with Mamon all along."

Laurel pinched Lenny's leg and he wiggled away from her.

"I was not. Truthfully, I wasn't sure if he was alive or dead for most of the time they had him. If I'd said anything it would've meant never seeing my Leonard again," she rested her hand on my arm. "Len...Lizard, worked with the FLM for years. He couldn't pass up the opportunity to work on the Lexicon. When the group split Lizard took a side and it wasn't with Mamon."

"Susan told me about a criminal faction," I said.

"None of Lizard's group were criminals," Laurel's eyes welled up. She looked at the bed. "I should've warned you, but I had no proof without archive evidence. Mamon threatened me." She smoothed the blanket a little. "They had Lizard when Mamon called about your accident. Mamon told me what hospital you were at and that I was to arrange your recuperation here. I still didn't have proof Lizard was alive but I'd have done anything. I would've gladly taken care of you even if he hadn't threatened me. You know that, right? The story he told me about your accident stank as soon as I heard it. But your face matched what the archives showed. I tried to nudge you towards reviewing your archives so possibly something would become clear, but when nothing changed after a year ... and all those nightmares I might have prevented ... I'm sincerely sorry."

Lenny walked to the window. "Bunch of fat rat nests, who knows how many they manipulated to make this all happen. Plus, you know, without being able to call for help Laurel was stuck."

"I understand, Laurel. I don't blame you at all. I know how much you have suffered about Lizard. Makes more sense why you hated Mamon," I said.

She took a tissue and blew her nose. "I'll be back. I need a minute," Laurel said and left.

"She's done everything in her power to take care of us," Lenny said once we were alone.

"I know. I wish she wouldn't blame herself. It must've been hard on her with Mamon directing what she had to do and not being about to tune into Lizard whenever she wanted. Not knowing if he was okay or not."

"It's great now that they can't track us. You can do anything you want," Lenny said. "We've been loving life on the farm. Fifty acres of woods, fields, streams, basically

Turkish delight. Hey, and we've almost completed construction on a new house out by the orchard."

"That's right, what about the MAc? There's a lot to consider here. What about Mom? Is she here?" The light from my window had a pulse to it. I looked from Lenny's face to the window and experienced another bout of flashing. The similar startling lightning quality blinded me with its intensity. After the last flash, Laurel was suddenly standing next to me with a man that wasn't Lenny.

"Ben, are you okay? You were staring pretty hard there," Laurel said.

"Where's Lenny? How'd you get here?" I asked.

Laurel put her hand on my forehead and looked at the health panel next to my bed.

"Seems normal doesn't it, Leonard?" She said.

I turned to look at the man standing next to her. He wasn't much taller than Laurel. "I'd like you to meet my husband, Lizard."

"You were there," I said and recognized him as the person I'd seen in the glass cocoon when I was trying to escape at the center.

"Hey Ben," Lizard extended his hand to shake. "Awake finally. Good. Just take it slow. I remember feeling similarly out of it when they first revived me." His eyebrows rested high on his forehead. He pulled off his hat, no blossom now but weird hair growing back in patches.

I looked at Laurel as she sat on the bed next to me and back at Lizard's scalp. He noticed and ran his hand over it.

"I think this is where I get to thank you for saving me and getting me back to work on the Lexicon," Lizard said.

"We're working on – and I need to—" His voice wavered away into incomprehensible nonsense.

Light blinked, and I found myself saying, "I watched my real accident archive…" I paused, wondering how I'd gotten to that statement. They stared at me with concern, and I looked again at Lizard's hair patches. "I saw where Mamon messed with my head after the accident, but I guess it's not exactly the same as what happened to you," I said continuing but briefly forced my eyes closed to see if I could stop the flashing that persisted. Laurel and Lizard turned to my health panel again. Laurel flipped to a different screen, but Lizard spoke up.

"This is just his brain adjusting." He turned to me again, "You should be fine. I went through the same treatments, and the scans on my brains haven't triggered concerns. From what we can tell, Mamon had many people in process. The ones we've examined don't exhibit anything unique in their brain activity. Even the Twins seem fine. I'm sure a little more rest and you'll—"

Lenny walked in wearing a short redhead wig and a bushy mustache of the same color, like some bizarre Irishman. He was walking next to Amelia. "Thairs sum one ah'd like ye ta meet," Lenny said using an Irish accent.

Amelia, walking with the aid of prosthetic legs, strode over to me.

"Who's coming through that door next? Do you have Mom out there?" I asked, trying to appear nonchalant.

"Hello," she said. "No. Me and this large leprechaun are the last."

"I'll be calling your mother in a minute to let her know you've come around. You should know that Amelia did about half of the work taking care of you," Laurel said.

Lenny moved in closer to the bed. "Or occasionally me and tha boys would, yur loyal servants." Lenny pumped his pelvis at Laurel bringing attention to extra stuffing he'd added beneath his pants.

"Enough of that," she gave him a swat on the stuffing. "Ben needs more rest. I'm going to get started with dinner. Lenny, go check on the twins."

Lenny waved as he marched out of the room. Laurel touched Amelia's arm before she walked out with Lizard.

With just us, I felt self-conscious lying back still and shifted to sit up more. "I think I need new legs instead of teeth. I'm really sore."

"I'm sure we could get you some." Amelia smiled back, displaying her prosthetic legs for me to admire.

"You look great standing up," I said, feeling stupid but happy to be alone with her.

Amelia laughed a little, "You look great out of a coma, but we'll catch up later. I should probably go help fix dinner." She backed away to the door.

"Okay. See you later then," I said, wishing she didn't leave so quickly.

I lay back again and must've fallen quickly asleep. The low sunlight in the room surprised me when I woke. A set of clothes had been placed on the chair next to me. I struggled but managed to get into the pants, wondering what to do with my caroca and sat back down. The sky was darkening and the spotlight from the chicken coop shone yellow on the chickens not gone to roost yet. Wind blew against the windows, giving that calm and protected indoors feeling.

The delicious smell of onions frying in butter and roasting meat reached my room. I turned from the window and looked down at the pattern of the rug. When I lived with Laurel before, I'd spent a lot of time staring at it. It soothed me, but as I looked now, I felt a slippage in the center of my head, a shifting, and my head started to hurt as the light faded unnaturally. The dark spaces between the rug's dense pattern widened until the black spread leaving but a few of the same type of symbols the trees shared with me before. They glimmered and spun for a moment, something opened inside of me, and a sped-up song filled my head, but I couldn't make out the lyrics. The shadows behind the symbols worked like bubbles in boiling water. Heat packed my chest in waves echoing out until it reached my brain as if something was trying to jumpstart. The glowing from below the symbols increased rapidly and the room flashed entirely white and then quickly faded back to normal.

A heavy crash came from downstairs, and I heard the twins laughing. My caroca started swinging as I got to my feet. I needed out of the room, away from the anxiety the light and rug generated.

"Hey, I'm living outside of recorded history," I said as I walked into the kitchen to find them at the table passing food. I made a pig face at the boys, pushing the tip of my nose in the air, and started snorting loudly.

"You're a pig," Francis said snorting at Ed.

"No, you're a pig," Ed said and snorted repeatedly.

The caroca swung and knocked into the twins when I went closer to them. Laurel came quickly over from the stove, cut the cord of the caroca with scissors, and dumped the cube in the trash as if it was an old piece of fruit.

"Good riddance," she said, dropping the lid of the can. "You shouldn't be out of bed."

"I guess I don't need that?" I said.

"Guuuh-ross," Ed said.

"That plug will fall off in a few days," Lizard said.

I sat at the table and Laurel fixed me some more broth, but anyone who's smelled her food and had the willpower not to eat it was stronger than I. After dinner, the night filled with pleasant talk and laughter. We avoided serious conversation and just took pleasure in each other's company. I tried to ignore the continuing flashes but shortly after we'd moved from the kitchen into the back room, they started to tire me out. I didn't say anything because I didn't want to ruin the fun, but the strobing increased to an intensity that caused me to feel faint. Lenny noticed.

"Hey, maybe better get you under covers again," Lenny said and came over to help me to my feet.

"I don't know ... I'm probably ..." I said and almost fell onto him before he grabbed my arm to hold me up.

"What were we thinking?" Laurel said, and they all led me in a parade up the stairs. I fell asleep immediately.

⩵THIRTY-FIVE⩵

I awakened like the day before, staring out of the glass ceiling at a blue sky with rainbow-tinged clouds, but today my head ached, and my gums felt sore where my teeth had been. It could have been the false teeth needed replacing or didn't quite fit. I started to tap on the communication console when I found a note resting on the side table.

Dear Horseteeth,

Don't get out of bed! Just buzz me when ready. Yes, now ... go ahead. I'll bring you breakfast or send Amelia.
~ L

I clicked the console and sent an alert. A few minutes later, Laurel arrived.

She plopped down a tray with buttered toast, a banana, and juice. "You gave us all a stupid scare last night."

The scent of buttered toast was comforting. I took a big bite, said "Thanks," and adjusted the tray. "I bet I did. My head hurts." I took a sip of the juice. "Is something different? This is possibly the best juice I've ever had." I wasn't exaggerating

"Oh, that's nice of you to say. It's the same orange juice I always make. I added a larger dose to it for your achy parts," She said. "Lizard has one of his friends coming in a few days. He's an expert on brain trauma, but it's tough to get him out here quickly so you'll have to make do with the juice until then."

She grabbed my head and started to massage. These comforts she provided were something I felt I could never repay. I've made a few paintings for her over the years, but they didn't feel equivalent. She tilted my head back and forth, stretching out my neck muscles and adjusting my spine.

"Breathe for me please," She said before cracking my spine twice and letting go.

I began the deep breathing exercises until she took hold of my head again and stared into my eyes. Her wrinkles wavered like lake ripples, and something shifted in the lower part of my skull. I saw the bright light again and started to sing. I sang like the twins did when we last visited Laurel, the song forced its way out of my body as if I wasn't in control. It was like releasing air from a balloon. Glazed green I sang with oxygen and fevered light undulating out from me into Laurel. Then she slapped me.

"Don't!" she said.

"What?" My cheek stung painfully.

"I'm sorry, honey, oh, your head," she touched my cheek. "but you started making me drowsy."

"I what?"

"You were singing, and I started to feel like I might fall asleep." Laurel looked shaken. Her face filled with concern, "You'll all be fine, just fine." She massaged my scalp and temples. "Crazy weather we're having. It's so warm. That snow will be gone before the sun sets."

"The weather?" I could tell she was holding back. Her avoidance worried me more. "Not something strange just happened and we should explore it? Not the answer lies within?" Laurel looked away, upset and not responding. "Okay... I'd love to get out of this bed and touch some snow while it's still around." I said, trying to smooth things over.

"Amelia said something about trying to get into her old wheelchair today and taking it more slowly than you just jumping out of bed."

"I'm ready to ride," I said with a grin.

"Just finish eating and spend some time cleaning yourself. You never got that shower last night. I'll send Amelia up in a little while." Laurel patted the banana and left. Avoiding the conversation might only be her protecting me, worried I wasn't ready to deal with whatever state my brain was in. The light from the window pulsed. Everything outside looked more vivid – hues turned on high. Spring appeared to be fighting back. Soft greens and pinks decorated the tips of the trees in the distance. The road on the edge of the field shimmered with melting patches of snow and rows of stalks from spring bulbs poked up along her walkway to the barn.

I cleaned up quickly in the bathroom, then returned to Laurel's breakfast tray. When was the last time I had a banana? I finished it, wishing she'd brought two, and opened my message center. Susan's name stood out from two that must've been written within hours after kicking her out of my hotel room. Hard to believe it was four months ago that I'd visited her. The first email was full of apologies but also anger and accusations. The second, with her saying she was moving on. Before I finished, I was interrupted.

"Ben."

I turned to find Lizard next to me.

"Hey, you startled me," I said.

"I snuck in. Sorry. I saw Laurel leave and I'm sure she wouldn't approve of my idea," he said. He stood too close to me, and his wild patches of hair made him look a little crazed.

"It's fine—" we said together and then smiled at the coincidence.

"Laurel not approving, sounds like the opening to something interesting," I said continuing.

"It's fine if you don't feel up to this and please forgive me, but I was listening in on your conversation. I'm part of the team in charge of monitoring activity on the farm ... and I keep an especially close eye on her."

"I don't think we were talking about anything private."

"I'd like you to take a look at something." Lizard tapped the wall and a blue grid surfaced. He navigated until he'd found what he sought. He put two videos side by side, "This is your singing just now with Laurel. This is Ed and Francis singing with you and Laurel in the kitchen months ago. I'll crank the volume way up when you're singing." He played both again. "See? No sound, no song only the ambient noises from the room and that slight static-y white noise."

"I remember that, but they definitely had the song coming from them," I said.

Lizard started pacing excitedly, looking up and down until he seemed to remember something else. "Yes, yes right, Laurel said the same thing but, on the archive, it comes up like the static. I'd been trying to locate anything that might show what Mamon did with the boys, and

Laurel mentioned the singing. I also found one of them after they went riding. You found them that time too. I showed the boys the archives but couldn't get them to repeat it. They said they needed the game, which we don't have. But just now, you did the same thing. If you could sing like that again, and I could run tests…" His face had a manic quality similar to how I'd seen Mamon talk in some of his lectures.

I sat there searching for the tune. I tried to match what I felt before, figuring that maybe something would click.

"Ooouuuhhh. Gggrrrggghhh. Uuuuhhhhmmm—"

"Sounds like a bear trying to work something out of his ass." Lizard laughed. "And Laurel will think this all too soon so hold off until later." He tapped the wall and marked some archives for my future access. "Look, even translated, many passages of the Lexicon are difficult to grasp but maybe not to you since you've had the song. Don't rush this stuff but I'd love it if you started looking at the code in the beginning, so we can compare anything you see to what the boys have shared about the symbols. I've got to get out to meet up with Lenny at the house now. Plus, we've all been given our orders to keep quiet. I'd better let you rest," He saluted and closed his mouth tightly.

"If I figure anything out I'll let you know," I said.

He saluted again and crept out of the room and down the hall.

I turned to the wall, read a little of the reference information, and found where the code began. The body contained a long list of symbols with no breaks or sentence demarcations. Some of the symbols looked familiar like ones you'd see in coding textbooks, but most just resembled scribbles or, I don't know, fake language kids might make up. None of it looked like what the trees had shared with me. I paged down to get a feel for how long it was. As the symbols scrolled, I felt increasingly warm. I kept going and noticed a definite rise in body temperature. My face flushed as my pulse quickened. I kept scrolling and watching. The symbols went on and on. I couldn't stop and didn't until Amelia arrived pushing her chair, breaking me from the sweaty trance.

As she entered, another flash occurred but this time from outside as if a thunderstorm with shocks of lightning were happening, happening somehow without a storm. Amelia and I both looked out the window stunned until the flashing ceased and she turned to me.

"This weather! Very strange. You look like you have a fever. Should you be sitting up?" She rushed over and sat beside me.

"I think I'm okay. You came at a weird moment." She helped me sit back against the pillows.

"Tell me about it," she said. "Those flashes have been happening for weeks. It's felt unreal since I left the center as if I'm awake in a dream every time I walk outside." We looked out the window again. "With any of the reporting and conversation I've heard no one seems worried about them." She turned to me and put her hand on my forehead. "You are warm."

"I think I'm alright. I was feeling a little dizzy before you came, but I'm fine now." My body settled back to normal.

She felt my cheeks and neck. "No, you feel a little feverish."

I wished her hand would've spent a little more time on my neck. Her skin was soft, and touching me brought her face closer to mine.

"Laurel was telling me the snow won't last. I'm sure I'm fine, and I'd really like to go out and feel it before it's gone."

"Alright, but just a quick trip. Do you need help getting dressed?"

"No, I'll be okay."

"Be right back then." She took the breakfast tray and left.

***

It felt lovely outside. The air was crisp and chilly. Amelia stopped when we reached the front stone patio leading to the walkway.

"Is it too cold for you?" she asked.

"Actually, I'm a little warm." I took my jacket off. The light sweater I'd found in the dresser was enough. Amelia cautiously strolled me down the path. I put my hand down to touch the snow. Bright light reflected off of it, momentarily blinding me until we rolled to the front of the barn.

The scent of Laurel's herbs rose up to greet me at the barn entrance. Amelia swung the lower half of the door open. The upper already leaned against the wall covering part of the giant penis portrait. We moved past the cow stalls, and I could hear the hum of generators in the back.

"Hello?" Amelia called out.

"Helloooo!" The twins shouted in return, "We're back here."

Laurel came to greet us. She had some straw in each hand. Amelia wheeled me into the area where Ed and Francis sat working on one of the biggest pots I'd ever seen.

"Look at the pile Amelia scooped up," Laurel said to the twins, dumping straw into my lap. "Here cover that before someone steps in it." She smiled and put her hand on my shoulder.

"Ew, don't somebody step in that," Ed said.

"Yeah, throw some more stuff on it," Francis added and flung some of the wet clay from his hand onto my shoes.

"Hey, look what you guys have been doing. Wow, that's incredible," I said. "How do you fire them when they're that big?"

"Lizard built a special kiln. We'll be selling these all over the planet in a couple of years," Laurel said.

The twins' screens hovered about their heads. They were taking turns watching the pot and watching their screens, their heads automatically switching at the same time.

"You're right on time, this one's just finished. Don't you think so boys?" Laurel asked.

"Yeah, it's done," Ed said, not bothering to check out the pot and continuing to look at his screen.

"Oh yeah, it's done right now," Francis said.

"Another masterpiece," Amelia said after Laurel shut down the power and their giant slowed to a halt.

The twins got up and walked over to me. Ed put his arms around my head and Francis around my neck. A great ease filled me, a certain sense of being home.

"Hey! Hey, go wash up first," I said.

"You should come with us," Ed and Francis said together.

"We got a whole new house that we're gonna live in by the trees," Francis said.

"I'm eatin' the apples next Fall which is what Laurel says," Ed said looking very serious.

"No apples messin' on the new house she said, right Laurel. No apple crapola!" Francis said, his voice getting louder with excitement.

"Can the chair make it?" I asked Amelia.

"I could push you most of the way, but you'd have to walk some. I don't know though, we said a short trip out remember."

"I feel stupid sitting in this chair. I'm fine and these legs could use a little exercise anyway."

"Get those bodies showered up first," Laurel commanded the twins.

"No way," Ed and Francis said.

"This junk's just junk," Ed said, pointing to each arm. "Let's see the house and then wash up sometime."

"Fine, just keep your hands out of your mouths." Laurel turned out the lights but left the news radio on.

I never understood why she kept that old radio. It mostly played static. Laurel's birthday wasn't far off if I remembered correctly. Maybe I'd get her a new one.

"Hey, it's Laurel's birthday party next week!" Ed suddenly shouted.

"I was just thinking her birthday was soon. You must be reading my mind," I said laughing.

"We're making surprise presents for her with Lizard tomorrow," Francis said as we went out into the driveway.

We entered the path through the snow-covered fields. The sun grew even more intense and we all began squinting until we adjusted.

"Oooooh! Haaappy birthday to you! Happy birthday to you! Happy birthday dear Laurel, happy birthday to you!" They sang together and started again. And then again. On the fourth time, we all started laughing at their non-stop enthusiasm. We continued rolling along the muddy path that led down to the fields and the orchard. The snow had melted in patches leaving the fields spotted with greens and browns. A warm breeze grew and tousled our hair as we came to the end of the drive. The wheelchair couldn't go beyond this point, so I stood to walk.

The house by the orchard came into view when we turned the corner. The sun still shone brightly on the fields ahead. In the distance, a mammoth rainbow filled the sky, the fattest rainbow I'd ever seen.

"You know that rainbow is for me!" Ed said staking claim when it appeared.

"No, it's for me too," Francis said.

"It's for all of us," Amelia said which made the twins smile at her.

In the few minutes, we spent watching it expanded even further, taking up a good portion of the horizon. Lenny's loud wolf whistle caught our attention as he and Lizard joined us wearing tool belts and hard hats. The twins' screens bounced next to their heads, and I noticed they had them in preview mode. One channel had a soccer game for about five seconds, the next displayed an elephant eating an apple from the hand of a woman. I looked up to see the boxy gray wooden house with the flowering apple trees around it. The snow felt cold on my feet, but the view of the house in the field with the rainbow backdrop made me forget the chill for a moment. My head began to pound with a mild headache.

"She's looking good, right?" Lenny said as they joined us.

"Right! Look at that house," the twins and I said at the same time.

"Hey!" The whole group of us said recognizing that the twins and I had said it together.

"Hey!" All of us said in happy union again.

"Weird," we continued speaking together, losing the smiles.

We performed a synchronized head ballet, looking around at the intense brightening of the sky as our faces contorted with confusion.

Ed started gurgling in the back of his throat. Francis joined him, but with a thick choking sound and at once they started humming. Their heads noticeably vibrated from it. I felt the symbols busy at the tip of my mind, and my vision started blurring a little as my tonsils hummed along with them. Then the song erupted from me, and light reflecting off the snow began to increase even more. It joined with the rainbow in the sky and consumed all dark forms: tree, land, and house until there was just the seven of us enveloped in light. Lizard protectively wrapped his arm around Laurel.

I reached towards the twins, but I couldn't move my legs. The song erupted from them, harmonizing with me and I gripped my skull to try to stop the throbbing. Heat increased, but as I pressed the painful spot - analgesia, comfort, ease set in. Press the spot to stop the hurting. Press the spot to stop the hurting. The song continued uncontrollably. I watched Lenny sink to his knees on the muddy ground gazing at the sky. Amelia looked bent, but her legs kept her upright. I kept pressing the expanding locations to ease the pain, singing, unable to stop. Fragrant musky fluid ran down between my fingers as the skin at the tip of my head split. The skin curled, and I looked at Ed and Francis. They continued singing also, but their heads weren't changing. A final pop and my petals unfolded with so much pleasure I fell back, landing on my ass, laughing through the song as I settled into the mud. The surrounding light lowered so you could make out the horizon of a brightened landscape, enormous volumes of little red particles moved around us like murmurations of starlings. The twins breathed in puffs of the particles through the song, and their heads began to burst forth the same way I'd witnessed at the Center. The seams where they'd healed split first. They stretched multiple small petals before exposing four large bright pink stamens that rolled out with mottled gray lumps attached to the ends. A light red pollen disgorged high into the air from their blossoms. A huge gushing fountain stretched beyond the treetops. The wind carried it quickly, far out over the house, moving with determination, with a destination. A few minutes later a hardhat fell to the ground as Lizard and Laurel's heads simultaneously bloomed launching new shades of red and pink. The plumes of pollen were beautiful, monstrously beautiful as the color of the sky shifted to match their pollen colors. Hours passed, the pollen clouds dissipated, and I began to hear a serenade in my head.

Eventually, the twins' screens hovered down, alighting at my knees. Broadcasts flipped by showing crowds of people doubled over in fields and forests, in stadiums and concert halls — from the doddering to newborns each head expelling red flecks as the pollination continued around the planet and all of us listened to the same internal ineffable song. Over time, my eyelids lowered, reducing the day's light. Even blossoms in their twilight are drawn toward the sun as was I - feeling no pain, untroubled and joyful.

At last, all eyes could feel the consolation from color. At last, no fear of solitude, a rapture in unity - all attained. The droning bloom song of now, so abrupt, but here, at last:

And that full moon hole in the wall of night is where we peered at everyone's bright tomorrow, but all that is boundless, all that has promise is Now. Here on this side of the whole are flickering rays through the stream, not a barrier of shadow and void.

AFTERWORD:

The following is nonfiction, all true, and happened in 2002 after I completed the first draft of BULB. All these years later, I'm still trying to wrap my brain around it.

At about 1:45 a.m. I left a party at my friend Mary and Bob's house. A summer storm hit hard earlier in the evening and the trees darkening the road plus the storm forced me to concentrate. I'd had a few drinks earlier but not enough to not inhibit me. I was heading south on route 611 and just after Curley Hill Road, I noticed an accordioned car had scattered its bumper, glass, and other parts across the yellow lines.

"Keep Going" briefly raced through my head, but no one was around, someone might be inside the crushed vehicle and other cars could wreck if they ran into the debris. I backed up my car to the middle of the road and put my caution blinkers and high beams on. Plumsteadville Police was written on the trunk, black letters on white. I yelled hello, feeling as if I were in some dream or movie scene, as I walked closer. I was not prepared for the vision I found on the driver's side lit by the interior light nor was I ready for the alien smell of opened human head and engine oil.

Others stopped and after a cellphone call, the area swarmed with red and blue flashing hazard lights. I stood in the rain avoiding the glaring car beams for about fifteen minutes, finally gave my name and went home to nightmares.

Joseph was a few years younger than me. He had a wife, a family and a station of other officers that respected him. I wanted to attend his funeral, feeling a strange obligation since I'd found him. I'd read the interment was to be at five and I left work a little early to attend but when I arrived, only a few minutes after five, I found heaps of flowers over his grave but no people. Could've been the papers misreported the time, or possibly, I had read it wrong. I thought it fitting though. I never knew Joseph in life, but in death, I'd met him twice, alone.

There'd been moments in the past where I'd found myself thinking what are the odds of this happening. Obviously, since I've read a good deal of Jung and wrote my first novel with coincidence as a main theme, synchronicity is an interest of mine. I know everybody experiences synchronicity, but I don't believe in fate, no controlling supernatural force has my life mapped out. Not everything happens for a reason. I can't subscribe to the religious pathology that offers people hope through ambiguous belief and faith. However, standing at the grave, I couldn't help but think of a character in my book whom I'd named Joseph and wonder how or if there was anything similar about the two. I knew it to be an insane stretch, trying to connect officer Joseph and my character Joseph in some baroque fashion, but I was looking for anything that might make sense of it all. Later, I considered how Joseph was the first Plumsteadville police officer to die in the line of duty, and how he'd died in a car accident on a rain-slicked road. I thought of the deer on the highway in BULB's rainy car accident and how Plumsteadville is in Bucks County. Also, how I'd been drinking, and Joseph had been on his way to assist with a drunk driver. All those connections seemed absurd, but they were likely the product of a without-exaggeration pattern of coincidence that was even more extraordinary though not as emotionally difficult as finding Joseph.

These events that followed writing BULB were of such questionable odds that it left me wondering if I'd unearthed some sign. I'm seriously no kooky new-agey, believes-in-magic type, or a self-proclaimed mystic ready with The Answers, but the following incidents, like the story of my finding the officer Joseph, are true: I started writing BULB in 1998 after a failed internet relationship with a Susan from Chicago. The book was going to be an epistolary novel, something like a direct use of the saved email correspondence, but when I started reading it, it felt far too personal and cringe-inducing. Better ideas, using only a portion of the letters, arose and eventually became what the book is today. After a brief month and half of editing and far too early, I started licking stamps and hitting send on emails to agents. While waiting for responses, I went back to editing. One night I was trying to develop a sense of déjà vu in the novel by renaming minor characters with variations of Susan. I'd already renamed a waitress and a hotel patron, Sue, and Suzanne respectively when I started receiving instant message popups asking me if I was Marco. While editing, I was using a well-known music software at the time called Napster. Napster had a poorly designed messaging aspect. Messages would just pop up from anyone that wanted to say something to you. I ignored all the popups from thirteen-year-olds saying "Your music sucks" and also ignored the first couple I received asking me if I was Marco. Finally, after the user wouldn't stop, I responded that I was busy, thinking they'd leave me alone.

"Okay fine, but are you my friend, Marco?"

Having lost my focus, and needing a break anyway, I began a basic chat session. Age-Sex-Location talk. She asked what I was doing, and I told her about trying to develop a déjà vu feeling by renaming characters, Susan.

She asked if she could read it, and I said no. She asked could she read it if she could freak me out. I doubted someone from Melbourne could over the Net until she sent me her name: Suzan.

She'd done it. Especially as I hadn't answered any of the other messages that popped up and couldn't recall when I'd ever discussed anything other than music on Napster messaging.

I sent her the book.

The following morning, I woke early and drove to the airport, the oddity of the Napster Susan coincidence still occupying my thought. I was visiting my sister in North Carolina and while waiting for the plane to take off, I cracked open Douglas Coupland's latest book, Miss Wyoming. At the beginning of the book, you're introduced to the main character whose name just happens to be Susan. She was also on a plane, but unlike mine, her plane crashes and she's the only survivor. Feeling ridiculous, getting a little nervous, I wrote everything down - obviously so when they recovered my body and found it I'd be known as the one who was forewarned. I landed with no problem in Raleigh.

A couple of days later, I felt incredibly excited to receive an email with my first partial manuscript request. It was from The Susan Herner Agency. Still in shock, I hit respond to send the chapters and saw the return email address: twosues@worldnet.net. As it turned out, there were two Susan's that worked at the agency.

All this might not seem as insanely strange as it did to me, but now having read my book, and knowing how much of it is about synchronicity, synchronistic activity waves increasing -- and the fact that the only person whom I'd based a character on from my life that I'd kept their real name intact in the book was Susan, you might be with me on the spectacle of it all. It could have been that I was some powerful conductor of the Higgs Boson particle, that I had God physics on my side, or yeah yeah, Susan is just a common name. Right. I tried to convince myself of it. How many Susan's do you run into during a regular month and never even notice?

I'd left my ATM card in the machine a few days later. I received two messages on my answering machine that day saying they'd found my card and would try calling again later so we could arrange for me to get it back. How did they get my number? Possibly in the yellow pages that were still somewhat commonly used then. I checked the caller ID and there were the last name and the telephone number. When I called, I got their answering machine "Hi, you've reached Susan's machine..." I almost dropped the phone. We met up, she gave me the card and looked completely normal, but I didn't pursue conversation because what was I going to talk to her about? "By the way, your name Susan has been playing a peculiar role in my life for the past week." It would've appeared too strange, even for me.

For at least the next month, I waited for more Susans to come into my life, one that would show me the full view. I wish there was some great final revelation, but there wasn't. I got over it. No more coincidences of Susan after the ATM card call. Since that time, I'd say I've confronted an average amount of Susan, but in that brief timeframe…to have come across that many - in the ways that I did - I'm not surprised I was standing at the grave thinking about how finding Joseph might have some secret meaning waiting for discovery. I suppose, if I am honest, I'm still on the lookout.

Thanks for reading BULB. If you have time to spare, a short review left on Amazon would be much appreciated.

Please if you wouldn't mind, email me a story of synchronicity that you've experienced.
bwind3@gmail.com

ABOUT THE AUTHOR:

Bradley Wind was born and raised in Pennsylvania. He is a prolific visual artist whose work has exhibited in the 20th century wing of the Philadelphia Museum of Art.

He worked as a toy designer for K'nex Industries, a manager of IT for Pearl S. Buck International and is currently a director of IT for a child-focused non-profit. He keeps bees, raises chickens and two lovely girls with his wife in Chester County, Pennsylvania.

A Whole Lot was his debut novel.
Available Now on Amazon.com